A...

When **Virginia Heath** ...
fall asleep, so she made ...
time while she was stari... ... ...got older,
the stories became more ... ...ed, sometimes taking
weeks to get to the happy ending. Then one day, she
decided to embrace the insomnia and start writing them
down. Over thirty books and three Romantic Novel of the
Year Award nominations later, it still takes her forever to
fall asleep.

Regency Rebels

Regency Rebels:

The Lavish Lords

VIRGINIA HEATH

MILLS & BOON

First Published in Great Britain 2024
By Mills & Boon, an imprint of HarperCollins*Publishers* Ltd,
1 London Bridge Street, London, SE1 9GF

www.harpercollins.co.uk

HarperCollins*Publishers*
Macken House, 39/40 Mayor Street Upper,
Dublin 1, D01 C9W8, Ireland

ISBN: 978-0-263-32335-1

MIX
Paper | Supporting
responsible forestry
FSC™ C007454

This book contains FSC™ certified paper and other controlled sources to ensure responsible forest management.

For more information visit: www.harpercollins.co.uk/green

Printed and Bound in the UK using 100% Renewable Electricity at CPI Group (UK) Ltd, Croydon, CR0 4YY

THE DISGRACEFUL
LORD GRAY

For Claire Sayers, who gave Gray his name, and for Trevor, my adorable, naughty Labrador, who made the perfect hero's sidekick.

Chapter One

July 1820

There was no doubt about it. Lord Fennimore was going to have his guts for garters. Especially after the unfortunate shredded underwear incident of last night. The commander of the King's Elite had no discernible sense of humour which didn't bode well for Gray's newly discovered, but no less coveted ambition.

'Trefor! Give it back. *Now!*'

There was no point in chasing him. The blasted dog saw everything as a game and had been in a state of playful overexcitement ever since they arrived in Suffolk yesterday—and who could blame him, really? Aside from a few brief weeks after his birth, Trefor had always been a city dog. If one ignored Hyde Park and St James's, vast open spaces of green were completely alien to him. But the green here was never ending, filled with flat fields to dash across, abundant trees to relieve himself against and sticks aplenty to chase with impunity. Doggy paradise. And Gray's mischievous mutt seemed determined to reach this strange, alluring new horizon at lightning speed with curmudgeonly old Fennimore's slipper clamped firmly between his jaws.

To tease Gray, the dog dropped the stolen booty at the boundary to their rented property and eyed him mischievously, his powerful tail wagging nineteen to the dozen, his floppy ears pricked and his enormous pink tongue lolling out of one side of his mouth like a juicy slice of ham.

Gray examined his cuffs, looked at the sky, some trees, anything but his dratted hound while he slowly edged his way forward, hoping to convince the animal he wasn't fixated on his superior's now slobbery shoe at all. Mere inches away he lunged like a panther, only to growl as the dog snatched up the blasted slipper again before he could reach it and raced towards the tree-lined horizon once more.

'*Trefor!*'

This time Gray did give chase, not only because of his dour superior's footwear, or because the animal had disappeared into a small wooded copse, but because a couple of sheep had also appeared in the distance and his dog had even less experience of sheep than he did wide open spaces. He needed to make a good first impression on the Viscount Gislingham. He needed to befriend him. Ingratiate himself. Be the perfect neighbour and work his way into his small, intimate social circle. More than anything, he needed to impress Lord Fennimore if he was ever going to stand a cat in hell's chance of getting that coveted promotion. Something unlikely to happen if his out-of-control canine injured one of the flock and the Viscount banned him from entering the grounds; the mission shot in the paddock before it had even started.

Not that Trefor was violent; he was a licker, not a biter. He adored everyone and everything and loved them enthusiastically. Something the dim-witted sheep would not know as he came bounding towards them intent on saying hello. Why had he insisted on bringing his dog along? All his lofty claims that a proper country gentleman would have at least one loyal hound at his side seemed to be doomed to be ruined by the said hound from the outset because, while Trefor was exceedingly loyal, he was also completely untrainable.

The dog failed to materialise out of the clump of trees, their trunks so densely packed Gray had to skirt around them before he encountered the unexpected steep bank of a deep yet narrow stretch of water which cut through the flat pasture.

Marvellous.

There had to be water.

Trefor's absolute favourite thing in the world bar footwear, sticks, balls and sausages. There was no point hoping he hadn't found it or wasn't fully immersed in it. Some things were as inevitable as day following night or another carpeting from his furious superior about his unruly, destructive pet mere hours since the last. This morning, more than Lord Fennimore's slipper would be going home soggy—not that Gray blamed Trefor for that either. The summer sun was already blazing in the sky and it was only eight o'clock.

Last night, thanks to the sticky heat, the huge weight of the new responsibility on his shoulders, his overwhelming desire to show old Fennimore that he was exactly the right man for the job and the strange bed, he had slept so fitfully he would have dunked himself in this convenient stream in the small hours had he known of its existence. Because of his unexpected morning sprint, the cold wash he had revelled in a scant few minutes ago in his new bedchamber was now wasted and his meticulously ironed shirt was clinging to his hot skin in a manner no gentleman would allow to be seen in public.

Not that he was much of a gentleman. Not any more

at any rate, although that was all of his own making so there was no point being angry about it. He was over it now. Nearly a decade after his life had imploded, he was actually rather philosophical about the experience. Life was too short for regrets, especially when he had racked up so many.

Gray had come a long way since those dark days of his youth. He shared little in common with the reckless, needy adolescent he had been that fateful summer. Or the aristocratic brother he hadn't seen since his heart had been ripped in two by betrayal. Betrayal that had come courtesy of the cold, unfeeling father who had instigated it behind Gray's back and the woman who hadn't truly loved him at all. Nor did he have any regrets about what might have been. The wife and immature, romantic and ultimately futile dreams of the future he had once believed should have been his now rarely crossed his mind. It was what it was. Done and dusted. And fate had sent him hurtling down a very different path, one he was pleasantly surprised had led to adventure instead of matrimony.

He was now older, much wiser and was clearly what he had been born to be. A spy tasked with bringing the enemies of the Crown to justice. A man who had seen and done more than most. Experiences that had made him hardy, resourceful and tenacious. Aside from having his childish heart shredded and creating the mother of all scandals, he'd had an interesting life since. Travelled the world. Seen and done some amazing things, met a variety of fascinating people, both eminently good and outrageously bad. Temporarily dallied with considerably more women than the single one he had originally pledged to spend eternity with, and he now worked for His Majesty's government instead. How many of his former peers could say that?

If he, or his incorrigible mutt, didn't make a total hash of this mission, soon Gray would also command the Invisibles—the highly trained, most covert and most important branch of the King's Elite—answerable only to Lord Fennimore, the Home Secretary and the King in that order. Not bad going for a man disowned by his family for losing his entire fortune in the gaming hells at the tender age of twenty-one. He had craved adventure and entertainment far more than he wanted to conform.

Still did, truth be told. Ten hard years and a brutal betrayal still hadn't managed to dampen his mischievous zest for life or his tendency to live entirely in the moment. Life was too short to ponder what might have been. If it was meant to be, it would have happened. It was as simple as that. There was no point lamenting the fickle finger of fate or wasting time being angry or crippled by remorse. Better to live his life much like Trefor did. Enjoy the here and now, forget the past which couldn't be changed and let tomorrow sort itself out.

Gray craned his ears until he heard joyous splashing and the dog's trademark swimming grunt. A cross between a cough and snort, muffled slightly no doubt by the obstruction of the stolen slipper betwixt his teeth. Gray tracked it several yards along the bank, then stood and glared at the animal deliriously paddling in a happy circle below.

'Well, I'm in for another blistering lecture thanks to you. Were the old man's drawers not enough? I thought he would have an apoplexy when you shredded them, but at least he brought spares. I'm fairly certain he only brought one pair of slippers.' He put his hands on his hips and channelled the disappointed expression his father had always worn when addressing him. It felt odd on his face. 'I hope you are proud of yourself, young man?'

Judging by the joyful wag of Trefor's fierce whip of a tail in the water, he was. Happy and proud and gloriously cool. It took around five seconds to decide not to attempt to drag the dog out. The slipper was ruined. Beyond hope. Lord Fennimore's lecture was now unavoidable, yet the day was young, the spot secluded and the water enticing. A nice, refreshing swim would certainly take the sting out of the tongue lashing and it would be a terrible shame to waste the opportunity. Especially when the hopelessly wayward part of his character still couldn't resist the seductive lure of the moment even now.

His dog saw the indecision and swiftly dropped the slipper as he climbed up the bank. It took approximately three seconds of foraging in the undergrowth before Trefor found a suitable stick, then he sat like a good boy and gazed at his master winsomely, the invitation to play clear in those manipulative, soulful dark brown eyes. As resistance was futile, and before he did anything remotely sensible like reconsider, Gray tugged off his shiny new boots, stripped off his newly tailored aristocratic clothes and waded happily into the water.

'We should probably find a little shade to set up your easel.' Thea gazed up at the clear blue sky and the unobstructed sun and frowned. Much as she loved the sunshine, it didn't love her. Pale, sensitive skin was the redhead's curse. Any more than twenty minutes' exposure and she was guaranteed to look like a beetroot for days.

Harriet rolled her eyes dramatically, greatly put upon despite dragging Thea out of bed at the crack of dawn to chat to her while she attempted to paint. Watercolours were Harriet's new hobby and, like all her hobbies, destined to be abandoned because nothing truly held her wandering interest for long. 'You wouldn't burn if you'd wear a bonnet.' Not that she was wearing one either, or a lace cap—when everyone expected mature widows of good breeding to wear one of those at all times.

'You know a hat in this heat will only make my head hot and then my dratted hair will turn into a big ball of frizz.' Thea began to stride towards the trees, knowing her companion wouldn't really begrudge her some shade as long as she kept her company. They were an odd partnership, separated by thirty years in age yet the very best of friends as well as neighbours. Probably because Harriet was basically naughty and devil-may-care by nature and didn't give two figs about it, while Thea feared she was exactly the same, but worked hard to control it. A classic case of opposites attracting. Or birds of a feather flocking together. Living within spitting distance, and in the absence of any other local ladies who held either of their interests long, they had formed an unlikely bond shortly after her friend had been widowed.

'Aunt Caro has invited half the county for tea this afternoon and for once I'd like to look a little less of a disaster than usual.' Although the humidity was already playing havoc with her coiffure. Despite all the pins and plaits her maid had used to tame it this morning, Thea could still feel a great many of the unruly strands making a determined break for freedom from their tight shackles and twisting themselves into their preferred upright corkscrew shape.

She castigated the Almighty daily for saddling her with vertical, twirling, wayward hair. While she rather liked the colour—the red was unique and gave her a touch of dash as well as giving her the excuse not to wear the insipid pastels other unmarried girls had to wear—the unpredictable curls were a menace. When all the other young ladies had artful, bouncing ringlets framing their face, Thea wore a veritable halo of fluff.

'Will a certain Mr Hargreaves be there?'

'Lord, I hope not! The man is such a dreadful bore.' And an obvious fortune hunter who Thea suspected was one of her aunt's cast-offs, not that she would ever admit such a thing even to Harriet. Her suspicions about her aunt's infidelities were hers alone and, no matter how many times her friend pumped her for gossip, she kept her counsel. While she loved her uncle to distraction, he wasn't a particularly good husband and had neglected his fragile second wife abominably over the years. At times his tone towards Aunt Caro was overly antagonistic and bitter, and if he was in the mood to be ornery with her then it was uncomfortable to watch. Poor Caro, in turn, had sought comfort elsewhere over the years and, although Thea didn't condone it, she tried not to judge. Theirs was the unhappiest of marriages and a stark warning of what could happen if you settled for the wrong person.

Mr Hargreaves was one of several who might have warmed her aunt's bed on her frequent forays out. The pair shared far too many knowing looks when they assumed nobody was watching them. 'All he talks about are his superior connections—as if the fact he knows Lord and Lady So-and-So should impress me.'

'He's handsome though. If one has to be bound to a man for all eternity, it's best he is easy on the eye. I insisted upon that when I had to marry. Crudge, God rest him, was exceptionally easy on the eye and liked to ride. Such pursuits do wonders for a gentleman's buttocks. In my humble opinion, there is nothing better than a pert pair of cheeks encased in tight buckskin.' Her incorrigible older friend had a wicked glint in her eye. 'Did I ever tell you I seduced him first?'

'Repeatedly.' And in intriguing detail. Practically all

of Thea's knowledge of procreation came from Harriet's detailed confessions.

'I was already falling in love with him, was certainly in *lust* with him, and saw no point in beating around the bush with a long and protracted courtship. Obviously, it all turned out for the best. We married in haste and got to enjoy seeing each other naked a great many more times than we would have done had we adhered to the fashion for protracted courtships.' She sighed again. 'And, by Jove, did that man look good naked... Mr Hargreaves has a pleasant posterior. Or at least I think he has. I haven't managed a thorough scrutiny yet to be completely sure, but I did catch a *hint* of a glimpse at last month's hunting party. Decent thighs—which usually are a good sign. They suggest a certain robustness. Although, in truth, I want more for you than him. I want you to have some adventure and excitement first. Your life is far too predictable and regimented for one so young. It's a crying shame... wait... Is that a dog barking?'

They both paused and listened. After a beat of total silence broken only by the chirping sounds of the morning chorus, a succession of rapid, high-pitched woofs could be heard coming from the trees.

'That doesn't sound good.'

'No, it doesn't.' The bushes beyond rustled violently and the dog barked again, setting her vivid imagination whirring with possibilities. 'Do you suppose the poor thing is in distress?'

Thea adored animals. The thought of one in pain was too awful to bear. More barking set her heart racing, but answered her question. With images of a poacher's trap and a grisly death in her mind, Thea picked up her skirts and broke into a run. Twice this last month her uncle's gamekeeper had found snares on the estate and evidence that someone was helping themselves to his pheasants. If the poor dog's paw was caught, it would panic and injure itself in its quest to free it.

Thea plunged into the trees, following the sound, then skidded to a halt at the top of the bank at the unexpected sight of an exceedingly pert pair of male buttocks.

Very nice and very naked male buttocks.

A pathetic squeak of shock popped out of her mouth before she covered it with her hands and the buttocks disappeared beneath the water a second before the owner of them turned around, his own hands covering the most important part of his modesty. Which was now quite submerged, but leaving little else to her imagination. Her eyes travelled upwards from those hands to the flat abdomen bisected by an arrow of intriguing dark hair which widened over a broad chest. Muscled shoulders. A gloriously strong set of biceps. Twinkling blue-grey eyes stared cockily right back at her, clearly amused and set in one of the most outrageously ruggedly handsome faces she had ever seen.

'Good morning, ladies.'

'Er...' For the first time in her life, Thea had no words at all. Her cheeks were glowing scarlet and it took all her strength to stop her eyes wandering back to where they had just feasted, making her blink and gape like a hooked fish. Because it was the right and proper thing to do, she immediately averted her badly behaved eyes and stared off into space, mortified.

'Good morning, sir,' said Harriet's voice over her shoulder, then she unsubtly nudged Thea with her elbow. 'I take back everything I said about buckskin, Thea. It is *vastly* overrated.' Shamelessly, her friend barged past—no doubt to get a closer look. Harriet would never avert her eyes. 'And who might you be?'

'Lord Graham Chadwick.' In her peripheral vision, the

naked man executed a courtly bow with one hand still clutching his unmentionables, apparently completely comfortable and unrepentant in his nudity. 'But do call me Gray. I am new to the parish.'

'Ah, yes! You have recently rented Kirton House, have you not? Why—we are practically neighbours, my lord.' Typically, Harriet was not lost for words. Evidently, she felt the situation warranted small talk, no doubt to prolong the encounter for her own outrageous reasons. 'I am Lady Crudgington of Exley House and this is Miss Theodora Cranford, your new landlord's ward.'

'His *ward*?'

Hearing herself mentioned by the naked man himself, Thea guiltily looked up, heartily ashamed that her eyes had scandalously manoeuvred to his impressive chest again when she had been trying so hard to keep them properly latched elsewhere. After a valiant battle with the wayward, impetuous inner Thea, her eyeballs reluctantly flicked to his. The cocky smile was gone, replaced with an expression she couldn't quite fathom.

'The very one, although Thea has long passed the milestone of her majority, so is technically just his niece now.' Harriet shot her a loaded glance. 'Content to wither in her uncle's house until Cupid sends her a worthy knight in shining armour to finally whisk her away.'

Before her interfering friend began matchmaking in earnest, something she was prone to do at every available opportunity, Thea had to interrupt despite having no earthly clue what she should say. 'Mr Gray... I mean, Lord Graham... Er...'

Could this be any more mortifying?

'We heard a dog... I came to rescue it... I didn't mean to interrupt your... Um...' Gracious, now she was waffling like a ninny and her silly eyes were darting every which way possible. It probably looked as though she suffered from an uncontrollable facial tick. One which explained why no knight had thus far bothered saving her. Her face was so warm and doubtless so very red with guilt that one could toast crumpets on it if there happened to be some handy.

To save herself from further embarrassment and to give her naughty eyes something suitable to do, Thea rapidly turned her back and stared resolutely at the trees. 'Put some clothes on, sir! You are a disgrace. What do you think you are about, cavorting naked in my uncle's stream?'

Hopefully that let him know in no uncertain terms that she did not consider him shining-knight material and was horrified by his total lack of propriety rather than itching to stare unabashedly at his wet body. His shirt and breeches lay in a heap near her feet, so she snatched them up and without turning around wafted them in the general direction of her friend. 'Give him these! Immediately!'

She could hear him wading towards the bank and, if she turned her eyes slightly to the right, could see Harriet holding his shamelessly discarded garments in such a way that Lord Whatever-His-Name-Was would have to rise out of the water to reach them. She shot her friend a pointed look which was, of course, completely ignored.

'Tell me, my lord, how exactly did you come to be naked in Gislingham's brook? Are there no bath tubs in Kirton House?'

'I apologise wholeheartedly for shocking you, ladies.' She saw his big hand grab the proffered clothes, then heard the water move as he sunk back into it. 'But I blame my dog. He led me astray. Trefor is a *very* bad influence. It is entirely his fault you caught me cavorting.'

At that, something fast and as black as pitch emerged

out of the foliage with an enormous stick in its mouth. He took one look at Thea and simultaneously dropped the stick and shook himself, sending a spray of muddy water all over her favourite green-sprigged muslin, before wagging his tail cheerfully.

Then he lunged.

Two big, wet paws hit her squarely on her belly and she lost her balance. Arms waving like a windmill in a gale, she struggled to stay upright. Instinctively she threw one foot behind to steady herself, only to realise too late that she was stood on an incline. Thea tumbled clumsily backwards, her feet lifting from the bank as gravity took over. To her utter horror, she landed with a huge splash in the water mere inches from the irritating naked man's groin.

Chapter Two

Judging from her furious expression after she emerged coughing and spluttering from the water, Gray shouldn't have laughed. Especially as she was, unbelievably, Gislingham's ward and he needed to make a good impression. But with Trefor already swimming in excited circles around her, her vibrant hair plastered over her face and her blush so ferocious she practically glowed, he couldn't help it. It had been a spectacular fall.

'Here… Let me help you up.'

She slapped away his proffered free hand. 'No, thank you! I know where *that* has been!' Outraged and delightfully flustered, she dragged herself to her feet, shooting daggers at her companion who was also snorting with barely contained laughter, as she tried and failed to climb up the slippery bank. 'Don't just stand there, Harriet! Do something!'

Keeping his *filthy* hands to himself and wondering exactly how he was supposed to fix this mess before Lord Fennimore had him lynched for his carelessness, Gray watched the older woman brace her legs and heave the fuming redhead out of the water. Despite his now-subdued mood, it was a wholly pleasant sight. Miss Cranford's soaked, thin summer dress was stuck to her shapely body like a second skin, moulding wonderfully to reveal a gorgeous peach of a bottom, and because she had to hoist her dripping skirts up to scramble up the incline, he saw a great deal of a very fine pair of legs from ankle to mid-thigh. He had always had a thing for bottoms and legs. Hers weren't covered in stockings, giving him a splendid view of her pale alabaster skin, which nicely filled in some of the blanks in his suddenly rampant imagination.

She would be wonderfully pale from top to bottom, and, like a Titian, that paleness would perfectly set off all her riotous hair. Although darker now that it was soaked, Gray remembered how it had popped and crackled in the sunlight when he first saw her, like the dying embers of a warm winter fire. Evidently, he now had a penchant for redheads as well as bottoms and legs. Who knew? It was these surprising, unforeseen revelations which made his meandering life interesting. That and the enormous potholes it consistently threw in his path.

He did a quick flick through his many happy memories, disappointingly sparse these last two years since ambition had come unexpectedly knocking, and came to the unfortunate conclusion he had never bedded a redhead before. Something he needed to remedy—but not yet. It was a crying shame he couldn't bed this one, because she was a tasty morsel if ever there was one, but Gislingham's ward wasn't his mission.

Gislingham was.

For the foreseeable future, Gray had to be on his very best behaviour. But he would store it in his mind for future reference and try to repair whatever damage he had done, making a mental note to seek out a suitably willing redhead as soon as he was able as a reward *if* he miraculously managed to save things.

While the ladies were occupied on the opposite bank, he swiftly pulled on his shirt then sank down in the water to wrestle on his breeches. Something much easier said than done. Only once he was semi-decent did he risk scaling the bank.

Miss Cranford was striding across the parkland by the time he had grabbed his boots, her fists clenched tightly at her sides and her lovely legs tearing up the ground, oblivious of the already besotted Trefor trotting along beside her. Gray didn't bother calling his hound back, instead he sprinted bare foot to catch up with Lady Crudgington, who was still grinning, intent on eating an enormous slice of humble pie.

'My sincerest and humblest apologies, ladies. My lack of propriety was unforgivable.' Yet another thing for Lord Fennimore to justifiably rant about and one he couldn't blame on his dog. 'I feel dreadful.' Which was true, but for entirely different reasons. He blamed the spectre of ambition which had unwelcomely crept up on him and simply refused to go away no matter how much he tried to tell it that he was a wandering gypsy at heart. With every passing moment, that coveted promotion was slipping away, as all things he coveted tended to do if he wanted them too badly. And as per usual, it was all his fault. He really did need to work harder at being a better spy. Especially as his tendency to live in the moment had created this moment— one he would much prefer not to have happened at all.

'A bit of water never hurt anyone, my lord, and it was *very* funny.'

'Traitor!' Miss Cranford's head whipped around and she positively glared at her companion.

'Well, it *was* funny, Thea. You'd think so, too, if you weren't in a snit about your hair.' The older woman dropped her voice conspiratorially, while clearly intending for her delicious friend to hear. 'It takes for ever to tame the natural curl, poor thing, and she wants to look her best for Mr Hargreaves this afternoon.'

'I most certainly do not want to look my best for Mr Hargreaves!' Miss Cranford stopped so abruptly, Gray almost walked into the back of her. The flecks of copper in her dark eyes matched her hair. They narrowed in accusation. 'Look at the state of me!' Noticing the two muddy paw prints on the front of her dress for the first time, she rubbed at the stain ineffectually. 'This will take hours to repair!'

'It would be my honour to buy you a new gown, Miss Cranford, to replace the one my dog has ruined.' On cue, Trefor nuzzled her thigh with his head and began to wag his tail so fast the whole of his gangly body shook, gazing up at her in canine adoration. Gray watched her eyes drop to the animal and soften and in that second found himself liking her a great deal. And his dog. She clearly had a weakness for the mutt, which might be the only hope he had. 'Trefor is very sorry, too, if it's any consolation. Look at his eyes.' Only the most hardened of individuals—or Lord Fennimore—could not be seduced by those sorrowful eyes.

Her hand dipped down to tickle the dog's ear. 'You're a good boy really—aren't you, Trefor? Just boisterous is all. I don't blame *you* for what happened in the slightest.' He heard the intended dig as she glared somewhat half-heartedly at him, and he did his best to look contrite. She was calming down and seemed in no hurry to stop petting the dog.

'Miss Cranford, I really do feel wretched. I should have behaved with more decorum. In my defence— although I am well aware what you witnessed was wholly indefensible—the parkland was quite deserted when I ventured into the stream. Trefor loves water, you see, and he especially loves it with me in it. Had I had any inkling that somebody would stumble across me so early I would never have sullied your delicate sensibilities with the sight of me *cavorting* in my birthday suit.' He felt his lips twitching again and bit down tightly on the bottom one to stop it. Good spies didn't ruin contrition with laughter. 'I can assure you it will never happen again.'

'Well, I for one enjoyed it immensely, my lord,' said Lady Crudgington with a wicked grin. 'Do feel free to cavort in my presence whenever you see fit.'

'Harriet is incorrigible.' A vibrantly blushing Miss Cranford was crouching down to tickle Trefor's suddenly skyward-facing tummy, rather than looking directly at him. He silently willed his dog to remain prostrate and adorable for as long as it took to earn her forgiveness.

'That I am, young man, and proudly so. I behaved myself for thirty years and *that* was quite long enough. I keep hoping a little of me will brush off on Thea, but alas, she is too buttoned up nowadays for her own good. She has become one for rules, Lord Gray, whereas I am one to break them. Which are you?'

Most definitely the second. Obeying rules for his first twenty years had ultimately left his life in tatters. 'I shall allow you to work that out for yourself, my lady. I couldn't possibly comment.'

'A kindred spirit! How marvellous, Lord Gray.' She whacked him with her elbow.

'His name is Lord Graham.'

'Which doesn't suit him at all. Gray is his preferred name and it matches his eyes, so he shall be Lord Gray to me now for evermore. It sounds so much more romantic than Graham. Do you have any objections to your new name?'

'Not at all. You may call me what you wish. I've never

been particularly fond of it.' It reminded him too much of his unfortunate links to his father and brother.

'Splendid! Then it is decided. An exciting new name for an exciting new gentleman! It is just as well, for the society hereabouts is very staid, my lord. With the notable exception of my lovely young friend here and her charming uncle, I can barely tolerate most of them. However, I think I shall enjoy having you as a neighbour. I even approve of your dog.'

So did Miss Cranford, who had happily turned into Trefor's willing slave as she petted him, all the previous fraught tension in her delectable, damp body beginning to disappear in the thrall of his dog's spell. 'Is Trefor a mongrel? Only I've never seen a dog that looks anything like him.'

Gray stared in mock affront. 'Cover his ears! Don't let him hear that, Miss Cranford! He will feel inferior.' He bent over to scratch the shameless mutt's belly, enjoying the way her eyes shyly locked with his for a second before she hastily returned them to the dog. 'In actual fact, he is the result of two centuries' worth of careful breeding. He is a St John's. Rather aptly, bred to be a water dog to help the fishermen of that smelly port haul in their nets. They are excellent swimmers with the most amiable of temperaments. He's come all the way from Newfoundland.'

'Really?' It was obvious she was a dog-lover. She had barely taken her eyes off Trefor since he had cosied up against her.

'Indeed. Many moons ago, I was in the merchant navy.' Gray had run away to sea within days of the momentous scandal exploding and had happily stayed at sea while it blew over, the dust settled and society quite forgot about him. 'My ship was docked in that very harbour and one of the fishermen was offloading a litter of puppies, intent on drowning any he could not rehome that day. As Trefor was the runt of the litter, none of the other fishermen wanted him.'

'And you took him?' Her lovely eyes left his dog's belly and locked with his, impressed. It had the strangest effect, almost as if he was suddenly bathed in sunshine that he never wanted to leave.

'I couldn't let the poor fellow die.' The truth. Seeing Trefor's tiny puppy face buried in a wrinkly bundle of black, fluffy fur, Gray had been smitten from the outset. He'd been the runt and empathised.

'That is very noble of you, my lord.' The softness in her eyes which had been wholly and exclusively for his dog a few seconds before was now directed at him. Bizarrely, it made him feel taller. 'Why did you name him Trefor?'

'Because it reminded me of home.' Good grief—more truth and one he had never shared. Gray blamed the hypnotic copper flecks in her eyes. Eyes that were coincidentally exactly the same shade as his dog's—minus the alluring copper, of course. 'I grew up in Wales. As a child I played on Trefor Beach.' With Cecily. Always with Cecily. The girl who had lived next door. The deceitful, conniving love of his life who had brought about his youthful downfall. 'I adored it.' As he had adored her until she had shredded his heart and stomped all over the remains.

Cecily's treachery aside, life had certainly been simpler then. Back when he was able to avoid his father because his mother kept Gray out of sight. The beach had been his mama's favourite place and she had been his absolute favourite person. Certainly the only member of his immediate family who hadn't found him wanting. 'I haven't been back there for years.' Not since his mother had passed, in fact, and had left him feeling like a cuckoo in a nest with only his overbearing father and equally staid and pompous elder brother for company, regularly disappointing the both of them simply by breathing.

That was when everything in his life had started going downhill—but at least he'd still had Cecily. Still clung to her and all they would have one day, biting his tongue and trying to please his father. An endeavour which had been ultimately pointless in the grand scheme of things, when Gray had never wanted to join the army or the church as good second sons were supposed to do. From his earliest memories, all he had ever wanted to do was raise horses. As a child he had lived in the stables. He'd loved animals. Had a way with them.

He found himself frowning at the buried memory, wondering why it had chosen today of all days to pop into his mind. Routinely, he avoided the past as a point of principle. It couldn't be changed, so why ponder it? Especially when the moment always held more promise. Or disaster. That wish for a farm filled with the finest horses he could breed was nothing more than all those carefully laid plans had been. A disappointing mirage of a future fate had never intended for him. One he would have loved if things had been different and a fine example of why he preferred now never to look too far ahead or too far behind. He had mourned the loss of that dream almost as much as he had Cecily.

Yet there was something about Suffolk which reminded him of home. Ridiculous, really, when home was more than two hundred miles away and nothing in the universe could ever tempt him to return there. He ruthlessly pushed the memories away, knowing the unwelcome spectre of his past would not help salvage this mission. 'Please allow me to compensate you for the dress. It is the very least I can do.'

'It's only a bit of mud. Nothing that won't come out in the wash. I have plenty of other dresses to wear this afternoon.'

'For Mr Hargreaves?' A faceless man Gray suddenly, and irrationally, disliked.

She smiled and his breath caught. She was pretty beforehand, in a classic English rose sort of way, but that smile did something miraculous to her features. It turned pretty into beautiful. Achingly, uniquely beautiful. 'For my aunt's tea party this afternoon.'

'She has invited half the county,' said Lady Crudgington with mock solemnity, 'which in Thea's world means less than twenty. Aside from being staid, the local society is also distressingly small. The tea will be nought but a hot, claustrophobic room full of dullards. Unbelievably tiresome.' Lady Crudgington wound her arm through his, her eyes twinkling with mischief. 'You should come, too, young man. Introduce yourself. Meet your other neighbours and see first-hand how dire they all are, while keeping me entertained with your scandalous maritime stories. Shouldn't he, Thea? I shall happily vouch for his *credentials.*'

Her hair was an unmitigated disaster. So horrendous it had made its way on to her unwritten list of her Worst Hairstyles of All Time. Not quite as bad as the epically awful Fuzzy Chignon of Eighteen Nineteen, when the combination of cold winter rain and Colonel Purbeck's stuffy drawing room had created a gargantuan tangle of fleece-like spirals that had soared towards the ceiling— but dangerously close. Thea had caught Mr Hargreaves staring, perplexed, at the top of her head three times in quick succession as he sipped his tea, as if he couldn't quite believe what he was seeing either. Hair shouldn't be vertical. Especially when it had enough pins in it to secure an elephant to the ground.

She resisted the urge to excuse herself to circulate among the other guests, knowing at best it was a flimsy excuse to wander past the mantel mirror and witness the mounting disaster for herself, as she had several times already. With every passing minute her wayward hair became even more wayward and the sight of it would only depress her. If she couldn't fully tame her hair, how was she ever going to tame the streak of wayward selfishness that ran straight through her? The older she got, the harder it was becoming to behave when the urge hit and Impetuous Thea bubbled back to the surface.

She glanced at the door for the umpteenth time instead and tried to tell herself she was relieved that their new neighbour was not going to make an appearance. Another flimsy lie when she had spent most of the morning, all of luncheon and the entirety of Mr Hargreaves' conversation thus far thinking about the way Lord Gray's bronzed skin and intriguing muscles had looked, slicked with water.

Thea had never seen anything quite like it. Even as he had insisted on accompanying them to the boundary of the garden, the thin, wet shirt had been practically and gloriously translucent as he had chatted amiably about his dog and the navy and his utter wretchedness at what he had inadvertently done. When her eyes had begun guiltily wandering to his chest again, she had hung back to play with Trefor and been subjected to the equally enthralling sight of the damp linen clinging to his broad shoulders and back. Like her wayward hair, the wayward part of her character then refused to catch up, so it could feast on the sight for the rest of the way home—and feast it had. Thea was heartily ashamed of herself. Proper young ladies shouldn't be ogling disgraceful scoundrels. Or worrying about the state of their hair for them either.

It would almost be a relief to see the man fully clothed. But then again, another part of her—the prim, proper, sensible part—never wanted to see him again, in the hope the memory of his body would quickly fade and her silly, flustered pulse would beat again at normal speed. Merely thinking about it all made her cheeks hot.

'Can I fetch you some more tea, Mr Hargreaves?' Which she would collect by way of the retiring room and dab mercilessly at those same cheeks with a cold flannel until they became decent.

'You are most kind, Miss Cranford.'

As she took the saucer from him, she felt his fingers purposely brush against the back of her hand in an obviously flirtatious manner and immediately gritted her teeth. There was something about Mr Hargreaves and his blatant, ardent pursuit of her when her aunt wasn't looking that raised her hackles, but ingrained politeness made it difficult to call him out on it in a room full of guests. Instead, Impetuous Thea broke free for a moment and she pretended to catch her slipper on her skirt. With more force than was necessary, she sent the cup flying, spilling the last dregs of the tea deliberately in his lap. 'Oh, I am so sorry!' She grabbed his napkin and passed it to him, enjoying the way the lukewarm stain quickly seeped into the pale kerseymere fabric. 'Will you have to go home to change?' She certainly hoped so.

'Not at all, Miss Cranford. It is just a drip.'

As was he.

No matter how many times he pressed the match, Thea could not imagine an eternity shackled to him. A lifetime of spinsterhood would be more appealing—not that she was resigned to the shelf just yet. At three and twenty, she wouldn't make a fresh-faced bride, but neither would she be a matron. As Aunt Caro frequently reassured her, there was still plenty of time to find the right sort of husband. Preferably one who regarded *her* with a heated look in his eyes, rather than her aunt, and wasn't solely after her money.

He would be respectable and trustworthy, not a scoundrel. Noble in both thought and deed, and—and this part was not negotiable—in possession of enough of his own fortune that hers merely complemented it rather than supplemented it entirely. He didn't need to be handsome and wear his breeches well. Both would be nice, of course, but they were in no way essential. Thea wasn't Harriet, after all. No indeed. She enjoyed stability and discipline nowadays far more than the pleasing aesthetics of a broad pair of shoulders. Once bitten, twice shy, and all that. Since the soldier, she had vowed to be sensible and suppress the impetuous, wayward part of her nature that acted on impulse and got her into trouble. Because that same day, while being taken for a fool, she had also learned the hardest of lessons. Her selfish pursuit of forbidden fruit had consequences.

Dire ones.

After she had self-righteously stomped out of the house to dally with that soldier, the worst had happened and her poor uncle had paid the price. Just as her father had all those years previously when he had slammed out of the house, justifiably at his wits' end with his precocious daughter, and had failed to come home alive. Common sense told her it was an unfortunate coincidence. That fate wasn't punishing her for two isolated and immature outbursts, done in the heat of the moment many years apart, but she secretly carried the burden of guilt regardless. And while her rational, sensible brain often dismissed her fear as silly, superstitious nonsense, the similarities were too eerie to be coincidence. Two momentous temper tantrums brought about by her own selfish desire to do something quite contrary to the will of others and the two people closest to her heart had unfairly paid the price.

Since then, Impetuous Thea had been locked in a box just in case she was tempted by forbidden fruit again and was only rarely, and cautiously, given an airing when the situation warranted—and never to satisfy one of her own selfish whims.

It had proved to be a constant battle between her rebellious character and her stubborn will, but for the most part she kept a tight lid on the destructive elements of her personality. Since then, her world had been calmer. A trifle repetitive and safe, perhaps, but she was content. She had Harriet and her uncle. Aunt Caro and Bertie. She rode Archimedes. She visited the village and her neighbours. Occasionally allowed Harriet to drag her out to shop. Her world might be small, but she read voraciously, losing herself in exciting romances and adventures in the absence of any of her own. All worthwhile and proper pursuits for a gently bred young lady.

Heavens, even to her own ears she sounded dull. Three and twenty wasn't old yet, although frequently she felt positively middle-aged. An older, staider, duller version of Harriet who had half as much fun. Nothing dreadful had happened for years despite Impetuous Thea's constant escapes. She had argued with her uncle at least three times since that night and he was still as robust and full of life as he always was. Of course, without proper supervision, Impetuous Thea would have probably argued with him a thousand times in the last three years if she hadn't practically chewed through her lip to stop the words coming and then silently seethed in her bedchamber for hours until she was calm again. Maybe it was all that suppressed emotion that was making her feel so unfulfilled?

Or maybe it was her increasing habit of dissatisfied introspection because there were simply too many hours in the day to fill with the proper pursuits she allowed herself. No wonder the disgraceful Lord Gray's buttocks were taking up so much space in her thoughts. The sight of them had been the highlight of her year!

With an irritated sigh she wandered to the sideboard, conveniently located next to the door and blissful escape, and picked up the teapot. A maid could deliver the beverage back to Mr Hargreaves while Thea avoided him and his wandering hands for the rest of the afternoon.

Horrid man! While she was not averse to a suitor some day, and Lord only knew decent men were thin on the ground in this sleepy corner of Suffolk, she didn't want one who fitted none of her sensible criteria or who made alarm bells clang in her mind.

Mr Hargreaves had a paltry annual allowance and a decidedly dubious past. He also shared heated looks with her aunt. Three very sound reasons to cross him off her list. The flesh-crawling bit made four, although that was more of a feeling than fact so hadn't thus far made the list at all. Henceforth, it would be added. There had to be some attraction, or at least the potential for some eventually. As Harriet said, if one had to be bound to a man for all eternity, it was best he be easy on the eye.

Perhaps Harriet was right and she did need more excitement in her life before she settled down with the sensible, independently wealthy husband she would spend eternity with. Then perhaps her life wouldn't feel so dull even if her choice of husband did. Each day did tend to feel exactly like the previous, blurring and merging into one homogenous infinity of sameness.

Infinity of sameness! Now she was in danger of becoming pretentious to counteract the dullness. Could one be a pretentious dullard? Mr Hargreaves certainly was…

'Hello again, Miss Cranford.'

At the sound of his deep voice so close to her neck, Thea jumped and poured half of Mr Hargreaves's tea over the sideboard. 'Mr Gray… Er…my lord. I'm so sorry, you startled me.' And despite the fine suit of clothes he wore with impressive aplomb, her errant mind had immediately stripped him of them. She knew exactly how impressive those shoulders were beneath that jacket, and she had seen his bottom. Valiantly, she willed her cheeks not to combust, yet they heated regardless just to spite her.

'I'm an informal fellow—as you have unfortunately seen. Gray will do just fine.' He was smiling. Amused. Little crinkles fanned out around his silvery blue eyes. Eyes which were almost wolf-like in their colour.

'Gray suits you.' Heavens—she had said that out loud. How frightfully impulsive and bold. Clearly, after her perfectly acceptable run-in with Mr Hargreaves, Impetuous Thea was not safely locked back in her box. She forced her gaze to shift from his hypnotic stare and came face to face with another man. Significantly older. Salt-and-pepper hair and a scowl that could curdle milk.

'Allow me to introduce you to my second cousin Cedric.' Gray grinned as the older man bristled. 'He *is* a very formal man and prefers to be called Lord Fennimore at all times. Even by family.'

Chapter Three

The rampant disapproval at the use of his Christian name was coming off Lord Fennimore in waves, but Gray was unrepentant. The old man had insisted on accompanying him on this mission because Gray was apparently new to his precious King's Elite. Two loyal and highly eventful, successful years chasing criminals wasn't new in Gray's book, but his commanding officer was a stick-in-the-mud who took for ever to impress. With Flint guarding his new bride and their key informant in their investigation in the wilds of Scotland somewhere, Warriner and Hadleigh minding the fort in London and Lord and Lady Millcroft on a similar mission in Norfolk, Lord Fennimore had reluctantly drafted Gray into front-line duty to prove his mettle, dangling the carrot of the yet undiscussed promotion temptingly in front of his face.

'Let's see how you do, young man, and then perhaps we shall talk.'

Hardly a blood-sworn promise, but the best anyone could hope for from the wily, manipulating, tenacious commander of the King's Elite.

But it was that tenacity which had served them well. Espionage was a long and patient game. After two years of covert, dangerous investigations and far too many deaths, the King's Elite had severely weakened the dangerous smuggling ring. Thanks to the new Baroness of Penmor, the French ringleader was dead, and his co-conspirators scattered in chaos. There was no longer a chance of them restoring Napoleon to power any time soon. However, despite having the names of the high-ranking British traitors who had sold the contraband on the black market, they still had no clue about the identity of The Boss—the elusive, faceless mastermind who had run the English side of the vast operation. So vast it had threatened the British economy as well as its security. The government wanted the traitors rounded up and tried as soon as possible, but without tangible proof of their guilt, all the evidence they had hinged on the testimony of one woman.

Or, in legal terms, and without further proof, hearsay.

They quickly realised they needed more than the word of just one witness if they were to make the charges stick. The Boss had no interest in Napoleon, or laws, or lives. He only cared about profit. Under Lord Fennimore's guidance the King's Elite had allowed the dust to settle, watched and waited. A man like The Boss would be ruthless in repairing all they had destroyed and they didn't have to wait very long for the smugglers, suppliers and greedy distributors to begin to piece together some of the tattered remnants of the operation.

Already, more illegal brandy was trickling back on to British shores and, because they had been allowed to do so unhindered, the smugglers were becoming bolder.

The Boss didn't know they knew. Nor did he know the net was closing in and they intended to catch him redhanded. The Boss also did not know they had narrowed down his true identity to one of two men. He was either the Earl of Winterton in Norfolk or Gray's target—and the delicious redhead's guardian—Viscount Gislingham. Whoever he was, he would soon be rotting in the Tower, awaiting his execution. And Gray knew he spoke for all his comrades—both living and recently dead—that that day couldn't come soon enough. Too much blood had been spilled already.

'I hope you don't mind, Miss Cranford, but I thought it made sense to use your invitation to introduce the both of us to our new neighbours. Hopefully I shall make a better first impression on them than I did on you.' Fennimore had practically spat feathers when Gray had confessed to being caught in the altogether by Gislingham's niece. He had yet to appraise him of Trefor's hand in practically drowning her. 'Once again, allow me to offer my sincerest apologies.'

There were two pretty, pink circles on her cheeks at the reminder, but she held his gaze politely. 'None are needed. Let us draw a veil over it.'

She blinked rapidly, luring his eyes to her ridiculously long, brown-tipped lashes before her hand fleetingly went to her riotous copper curls. She had beautiful hair. Unusual, but invitingly tactile. The obviously natural ringlets were not uniform. Tight spirals and loose curls wove together, begging to be touched and properly examined. If he pulled one, for instance, how much longer would it be? Double? Triple? Perhaps quadruple the length? In sunlight it crackled like fire. Wet, it deepened to auburn. Here in this bright drawing room it was vibrant, but the lack of direct light brought out the other tones. Bronze. Gold. The merest hint of chestnut. What would the pale moonlight do to it? He was staring at her head and she saw it. A little wrinkle of annoyance appeared between her russet brows, no doubt at his impertinence, before she quashed it.

'Would you like me to introduce you to my uncle and

aunt?' Of their own accord, his eyes had now dropped to her lips. They were very kissable indeed. Soft, plump, a deeper shade of pink than the blush that stained her porcelain cheeks. Why couldn't he stop gazing at her when he knew he needed to focus on being a better spy?

'We would like that very much indeed, Miss Cranford.' Lord Fennimore shot him a withering glance and inclined his head, giving away no indication as to exactly how much the pair of them were looking forward to meeting their potential nemesis. 'You are most generous in forgiving my *idiot* cousin. Rest assured we have had words about the incident.' His superior had said all the words, mostly in a very loud, agitated voice which had sent poor Trefor into hiding for hours. Unfortunately, they were all justified.

Lord Fennimore held out his arm and Miss Cranford took it, and for some inexplicable reason Gray felt a pang of jealousy. 'Please lead the way.'

He suppressed the errant emotion and focused on the job in hand. At his best guess, there were twenty or so people in the room, all regarding them with interest. The fact they did nothing to disguise it was refreshing. In town, showing interest was one of the Seven Deadly Sins and everybody schooled their features to look bored. Provincial society was very different and one Gray was surprised to find himself comfortable within. Once upon a time he had loathed it, couldn't wait to leave it and headed to the capital as soon as he was able. But it was actually rather nice to see what people were thinking for once. It made him oddly homesick.

Holding court on the striped damask sofa was an attractive woman of middle years wearing a fashionable day gown which must have cost more than a month's worth of his salary. French lace and silk. You couldn't spend your days catching smugglers and not recognise some of the spoils. She turned her head towards him, then smiled, her gaze flicking briefly to his reluctant new distant cousin, then sliding back to his. 'Strangers? How exciting, Thea.'

'Lord Fennimore. Lord Gray. This is my Aunt Caroline, Viscountess Gislingham. Aunt—these are our new neighbours, who have recently taken residence at Kirton House.'

As introductions went, it was very proper, yet he was convinced he detected some censure in her tone beneath all the politeness one would expect from a well brought-up young lady. A quick glance to his right and Miss Cranford's features were quite bland as Lord Fennimore stepped forward to take the Viscountess's hand.

'It is a pleasure to make your acquaintance, my lady. I hope you do not mind our unannounced arrival. We were keen to meet you all.' He was almost as keen to meet the wife of The Boss as the man himself. Wives were rarely innocent, in his experience.

'It is always a delight to make new friends, my lord.' The Viscountess's eyes slowly panned to Gray's again and held, making him wonder if she was saying more than hello.

As the old man stepped back, Gray stepped forward and bowed. 'You have a beautiful home, my lady.'

Her gloveless fingers grasped his. Squeezed softly. 'Thank you. One you are *always* welcome in.' A definite invitation. Unexpected, but interesting. Something which might come in useful for the mission. He felt the back of his neck prickle and was instantly suffused with guilt—even more unexpected, but there regardless. As he stepped back he tilted his head to investigate the source, despite already knowing in his bones it was she. Miss Cranford's face was still bland, but her eyes were not. They were disappointed. Was she disappointed in her aunt or him? Ridiculously, he hoped it was the former.

'I shall let Thea take you on the rounds to meet everyone and then you must come directly back to me.' The Viscountess smiled at Lord Fennimore. That smile morphed into something entirely different by the time it reached Gray. She glanced up at him through her lashes, then the tone of her voice dipped ever so slightly as she lingered over the vowels. 'I *absolutely* insist.'

It was a subtle invitation, purposefully ambiguous, yet to him—a man of the world who knew how the game was played—he was now left in no doubt. The Viscountess wanted to play. Something which should have excited him, because it gave the King's Elite a way into the Viscount's circle, but instead he found it distasteful because Lady Caroline was not her niece. More evidence of his lack of focus, no doubt, and time to be that better spy.

For the next few minutes, while his nostrils twitched at the alluring perfume Miss Cranford wore, they were introduced to the gentleman who seemed to hang on their hostess's every word. The local solicitor, Mr Partridge. The second son of the Marquess of Allerton. A local landowner who dabbled in stocks. They were soon joined by the very Mr Hargreaves that Miss Cranford had apparently worried about her hair for earlier, although it took all of three seconds for Gray to work out the cut of his jib. All were much the same age as he was. Good-looking and knew it. All were cloyingly sycophantic and clearly all had enjoyed the Viscountess Gislingham's exclusive *company* at least once, if he was any judge.

'Follow me, gentlemen.' Miss Cranford's voice held a hint of snippiness as she brusquely turned, that sultry perfume wafting like a siren's call to tempt him, and glided in the direction of a particular group of ladies, three of whom happened to be the wives of the men he suspected were the other woman's lovers. Was that deliberate? If it was, was the point directed at him or her aunt? And why did he have the overwhelming urge to tell her she didn't need to worry about him because he wasn't attracted to her aunt in the slightest? Gray had to bite down on his lip to stop the words coming out, knowing they would be a lie. If he had to seduce the Viscountess for King and country, then he would. Regardless of the beautiful redhead's disapproval and his peculiar, misplaced guilt.

What the blazes was the matter with him? He had waited two years for the chance to head up an important mission—he wouldn't let his uncharacteristic reaction to a hitherto unknown woman stand in the way. It was probably the responsibility and the heat. Despite the lighter coat, he could still feel the back of his shirt sticking to him. Nerves and the hot July sun would do that to a man.

Thea found Harriet on the terrace soaking up the sun. Because the whole world believed a woman's skin should be pale to be beautiful, her friend was determined to fly in the face of convention and was lounging with her head tilted back to capture every ray. Typically, like her rebellious streak, the healthy tan suited her. Thea wandered to the bench and plopped her bottom on to it, irritated. 'You left me with Colonel Purbeck.'

'Of course I did. The man spits when he talks.'

'A true friend would have promptly rescued me.'

'Ah...but I could see that Mr Hargreaves was eager to talk to you, so I knew you would be all right.' Harriet cracked open one eye and then shuffled to sit upright when she saw Thea's miserable expression. 'I was only teasing about Mr Hargreaves. Aside from the breeches and his face, he has little else to recommend him.'

'I know.'

'What's wrong?'

'Nothing.' She huffed out a sigh. Watching Lord Gray flirt with her aunt had left a sour taste in her mouth. Not that she was interested in him. If one ignored the fine face and impressive body, the man had too much of a mischievous glint in his unusual eyes for her to consider him as anything more than a pleasant conversation partner. Not that they had had a pleasant conversation. Thea had introduced him to everyone bar her uncle, who had slipped away for a nap, and then had delivered him eagerly back to Caro all in the space of ten minutes. Without all those tiresome introductions and her irritation at her aunt's blatant interest in their new visitor, the errant yet persistent memory of him *sans* clothes made it difficult to think of anything remotely interesting or even banal to say and he seemed to have no desire to fill the void.

He had immediately come to life in front of her vivacious aunt, though, as soon as she had delivered him back. He had practically bent over backwards to charm her. Not that Thea coveted that sort of charming or approved of anyone who fell for the flirty façade her uncle's slightly self-absorbed and highly strung wife presented to the world.

Still, being so blatantly overlooked rankled when she was obviously younger and single. And deep down she was thoroughly disappointed that the handsome new stranger no longer passed muster.

'Do you think I've become dull?'

'I despise dull people. We couldn't be friends if you were the least bit dull.' Harriet's eyes dipped to where her hands fiddled idly with the fabric of her skirt. A sure sign she was tempering her response.

'I sense a but...'

'But you *are* a little too buttoned up nowadays, truth

It seemed horribly ungrateful to loathe the generous gift he had saddled her with.

'Very noble—but exactly how many more years are you prepared to wait for the worst to happen? It has already been three.' Which coincidentally was the last time she and her uncle had really argued, when Thea had defied him to sneak out of the house past midnight to kiss the handsome officer who she had met at the assembly rooms the week before. With hindsight her uncle had been entirely correct in his censure. The man had been too old, too worldly and wholly focused on her fortune. He was taking flagrant advantage of her youth, her rebellious nature and her inexperience to further his own ends.

Unfortunately, at the time she had been too outraged at being forbidden to see him and too wilful to accept the edict. While Impetuous Thea was out, the worst had happened. If Bertie hadn't been there to save him, her uncle would now be as dead as her father.

'Edward's condition has neither deteriorated nor improved. You need to face facts, Thea. While you sit around waiting, being the overly dutiful niece and the devoted daughter Edward never had, your own life is passing you by. Mr Hargreaves notwithstanding, you could be married already, living close by and still being the dutiful niece who visits daily, yet you have thwarted every potential suitor who has shown an interest.'

'None of them was suitable. They all just wanted my money.' She didn't want to end up shackled to a vulture. 'With great wealth comes great responsibility. I have to be sure I entrust it to someone worthy.'

'Or perhaps your exacting standards are too high on purpose? You are the most suspicious person I know.'

That stung. 'I'm an heiress! I have to be suspicious! Every fortune hunter, ne'er-do-well and chancer who ventures into Suffolk automatically seeks me out and plights his troth, keen to get his greedy hands on all that money. I have to be cautious.'

'Cautious, yes. Not overcautious and determined to denounce them all as villains. Lord Selwyn, for instance, didn't turn out to be a swindler as you suspected.'

'But he *was* a fortune hunter.'

'And Mr Taylor, the young widower, was in fact a widower and not a bigamist either.'

Thea threw her hands up in the air in exasperation. 'Yet he was in debt up to his eyeballs and hopelessly in love with my fortune, too.'

'Yes, granted, both saw the money before you, but Captain Fairway had his own fortune.'

'And three illegitimate children by two separate mistresses. I knew he was a philanderer!'

'There is always something wrong with them—fortune hunter, philanderer, scoundrel…what was the name of the chap you thought was a highwayman?'

'Chisholm Hunter? I'm still not entirely convinced that he wasn't. There was something very shifty about that man.'

Harriet glanced heavenwards and briefly closed her eyes before continuing in an uncharacteristically measured tone. 'Your overly suspicious nature has given you an imagination as vivid as your hair, darling. In the absence of any real reasons to discount them you now have a tendency to make things up.'

'You think I should have settled? For a man I have no faith in nor any true affection for? Leap first into marriage without any forethought or rigorous contemplation? Like my uncle did with Aunt Caro? Look how miserable that hasty decision has made them! Might I remind you, you also found fault with all those gentlemen, too, as I recall.'

Harriet rolled her eyes again. 'Only because you continually hammered home their faults and I am a good friend and want to please you. However, while you continue to repel each and every gentleman who glances your way, the clock is ticking. In two more years you'll be well on the way to being considered an old maid. And I don't want you to leap into marriage. I want you to risk the leap of faith. It's the most splendid feeling in the world, darling. You stand on the precipice, not ever truly knowing what is the right course of action, but you take that chance. You abandon your fears and leap.' She sighed romantically. 'I adore leaping. It's the ultimate *grand gesture*. The test of true love is the grand gesture.'

'So I should abandon all hope of finding a decent, upstanding, *genuine* man to love, and simply settle?'

'Leaping isn't settling, darling. It's throwing caution to the wind and trusting your instincts and laying yourself bare in front of another in the hope they feel the same. But if you are seeking absolute perfection inside and out before you dare to jump, which I am coming to suspect you are, then you are doomed. It doesn't exist. Nor should you use your aunt and uncle's marriage as the benchmark to justify your exacting standards—or your fortune as a barricade to hide behind. Your uncle would never have given it to you if he'd had any inkling you would use it to shut yourself off. He despairs of your stand-offishness as much as I do.

'Every human has flaws, but unless you allow yourself to properly get to know a gentleman, warts and all…and he, you…and cease being instantly suspicious or stand-offish, you will never come to know if they are minor flaws you can live with or major ones which will make you want to grind their face under your heel when they dare to say good morning. If you want to fall in love and be loved in return, then you have to give it a fighting chance to blossom. Nothing blooms in the desert. You have to take that gloriously abandoned leap of faith. Your greatest flaw is that you dismiss people out of hand instantly.'

'I do not.' Surely she wasn't that pernickety? 'I judge every man on his merit and give them all adequate time to show it. A little cautious suspicion gives them the opportunity to prove their mettle.'

'Adequate time to prove their mettle? Really? Then I assume you are prepared to give our new neighbour a proper chance? Youngish. Handsome. Solicitous and *local*. His appearance is very fortuitous, seeing as you have given up all hope of any of the other bachelors in the county meeting your high expectations. Perhaps he is the *one*? He seems...' Harriet grinned '...quite lovely.'

It was Thea's turn to roll her eyes. 'And typically, you judge a book solely by its cover.'

'Not at all! While I'll grant you he has a splendid cover, he was most pleasant after we caught him so magnificently naked—and his dog clearly adores him. We humans could learn a lot from dogs. Animals are rarely wrong.'

'He's a shameless flirt.'

'I didn't see him flirt.'

'Well, I can assure you, he was certainly shamelessly flirting with Aunt Caro a few moments ago.' Something which bothered her, despite her infinitely better judgement and professed lack of interest.

'He's here?'

'Indeed he is. With his frowning cousin in tow.'

Harriet was up like a shot. 'How positively splendid! Let's hunt him down and monopolise him. I'll dutifully extol your virtues like a good friend and you can probe with pertinent questions which matter to you. Start to get to know him… Why, we don't even know if he is married or betrothed! And a young man who voluntarily lives with an older relative would naturally be more sympathetic to your dutiful attachment to *your* uncle. How serendipitous is that? The fates appear to be miraculously aligned for once.'

This needed to be nipped in the bud. Especially as Harriet was beginning to sound reasonable. 'No, thank you. He doesn't interest me in the slightest. Nor I him. He made no effort to impress me, yet every effort to charm my aunt.' A lie; he had tried then lapsed into silence after she had been stand-offish because Impetuous Thea *had* been interested. 'I'm afraid I have his measure already—and he comes up woefully short. If I'm being brutally frank, I'm not even sure I like him.' Although she had, before she reminded herself of all the reasons why she couldn't entertain it. She still had a penchant for parts of him.

'Are you sure?'

'Until you mentioned him, I had forgotten he existed.' She held Harriet's gaze, determinedly ignoring the image of Lord Gray's pert, bare buttocks and broad, bare back which had apparently seared itself on to her mind.

'Hmm…' Harriet looked sceptical, then shrugged. 'Only I cannot recall a time when I have ever heard you sound so waspish over a mere man after such a *short* acquaintance.'

'That's because it's his fault my hair looks like this!' Thea petulantly pointed at her head, but she was already talking to her friend's retreating back. 'It might have been a short acquaintance, but it was certainly eventful. Cavorting in the brook in his birthday suit *was* disgraceful!' And thrilling. It *had* been quite the highlight of her dull year. Drat it all to hell.

'All I ask is that you give the fellow a fighting chance,

Thea! This might be exactly what the doctor ordered!'
Harriet stopped, spun and inhaled deeply. 'I can positively
smell the romance in the air.' Then she was off again,
striding with such purpose there was no point attempting
to reason with her. There was nothing Harriet loved more
than meddling. Especially in what she considered was for
a person's own good. As a mark of protest, sensible Restrained Thea remained exactly where she was and would
remain so for the foreseeable future despite the baking sun.

Chapter Four

Gray spent the better part of an hour with the Viscountess, being a very good spy, and learned nothing new whatsoever. She was amiable, if a little self-absorbed, her conversation mostly a ploy to receive a compliment. It was obvious she lived a small and inconsequential life. There was a brittleness about her, a need to be adored, which was quite sad for a woman her age and said a great deal about the state of her marriage. Gislingham himself had yet to make an appearance and his wife didn't seem to know or care if he was likely to. Clearly, they lived completely separate lives, which meant she was unlikely to know anything significant about her husband's nefarious business dealings. With Lord Fennimore the unwilling captive of the droning Colonel Purbeck and the deliciously smelling Miss Cranford mysteriously missing from the gathering, he found himself eager to move on as he extricated himself from the sofa.

If nothing else, he could have a little snoop around. This rose-covered mansion in the heart of the countryside, a good forty miles from the coast, didn't appear to be the likely lair of England's most wanted smuggler. Nor did the aged servants seem to be his criminal accomplices—

but appearances could be deceptive. Look at Lord Fennimore. To all intents and purposes the world thought him a crusty old peer. One who turned up diligently at Parliament to vote and was a reliably reluctant guest at society events—yet for over twenty years had managed to hide the fact he ran the King's Elite. Not that anyone in society circles or outside of it would know about that organisation either. Therefore, where better to hide than here? Who would suspect a respected country squire of high treason? In another life, he certainly wouldn't.

Of course, in that other life he had no ambition either, other than to embrace whatever whims or pathways he took a fancy to and that had crept up on him unannounced. One minute he had been at a loose end on the cusp of leaving the merchant navy, the next he had accidentally fallen into working for the King's Elite. Up until then, he had had no concept of possessing either the valuable skills necessary for covert espionage or the burning desire to see justice done. Yet because of things he had seen and his nagging conscience, he had approached the Excise Men with suspicions about the particular shipping company he happened to be working for at the time and inadvertently soon found himself spying on them.

After the resounding success of that first mission, Lord Fennimore simply assumed he would continue and Gray hadn't corrected his assumption. For the last two years he had been working beneath Seb Leatham in the Invisibles, blending into the background, pretending to be someone else. Learning the trade and loving it. With Seb now working in a wholly different way alongside his new wife, Gray wanted more than anything to step into his friend's shoes, knowing they would be the perfect fit. After an aimless life of searching for nothing in particular beyond what was happening in the moment, he had finally found his place.

If only he could convince old Fennimore.

For the umpteenth time he huffed out an irritated breath at this morning's incident. His thoughtless lack of propriety had not helped his cause, but at least it had got him here, thanks largely to Lady Crudgington. Miss Cranford had seemed horrified to see him and had introduced him around the room most begrudgingly. He had made a much better impression on the Viscountess, although prudence dictated he be cautious with her. She liked male company. More than liked it, if his suspicions were correct, which made aligning himself too closely problematic. If Gislingham was the jealous type, Gray risked alienating him. The first priority had to be getting closer to their chief suspect. Only once all hope of that was dead could he risk a dalliance with the wife to get what he wanted. Or the ward.

Miss Cranford was entirely off limits until he understood the lay of the land. For the sake of the mission, she had to be his last resort even though she was the family member he was most drawn to. As much as he was tempted to shamelessly flirt with her and was wildly curious to know whether her vibrant blushes ended just below her demure neckline or travelled all the way down those shapely legs to her toes, seducing a gently bred young woman tended not to go down well with protective male relatives with a cruel streak a mile wide. Doing so would not only alienate Gislingham, it would probably result in getting Gray killed.

He could pretend to properly court her, he supposed.

The errant thought caught him unawares. Not because he wasn't supremely confident in his abilities to thoroughly charm her, more because it terrified him to have even thought of it. He had willingly come within a hair's breadth of marriage once before and had ended up broken-hearted and deceived. From the tender age of ten he'd had his future with Cecily mapped out. They were going to wed as soon as he turned twenty-one when he finally gained his financial independence; they would buy a nice house near their favourite beach in Wales and raise fine horses and the best Welsh lamb alongside their bushel of children.

Then his father and hers had brokered a different deal, one Cecily had been given a choice in, and to Gray's horror the love of his life decided she would much rather be a wealthier marchioness wedded to his elder brother than live on that farm with him. It had been that same week that the walls of Jericho had come tumbling down. Blind with grief and convinced she would change her mind if only he could quickly enlarge his fortune to supersede his pompous brother's, Gray had taken every penny of the money his grandfather had left him in his will to London and the hells where the savvy owners, gamblers and card sharps had quickly relieved him of it. It had been the harshest way to learn his lesson—daring to dream was as pointless as regret, and risking your heart was for tougher men than him.

He now avoided all serious overtures of intent, even if the serious overtures would be just a ruse to infiltrate Gislingham's confidence. He couldn't bring himself to toy with another person's feelings as Cecily had done his. Heartbreak, it turned out, took for ever to get over. He avoided touching hearts with the same diligence that he avoided commitment and he wouldn't trifle with Miss Cranford's no matter how much his body wanted her.

Assuming she would be interested, of course. Which she didn't appear to be in the slightest. She had barely said three words to him between all those polite introductions, so he had given up trying. Probably because he didn't have Trefor with him. She had *adored* Trefor...

Good grief! Another pointless train of thought in the grand scheme of things. He needed to be a better spy, not jealous of his dog.

He rounded the shrubbery and stopped dead. The object of his musings was lying flat on her back on a stone bench, a gauzy shawl draped over her face like a shroud leaving her fiery copper hair to crackle in the sunshine. One hand rested gently on her belly while the other was thrown over her head. The artful pose, reminiscent of one of the epic tableaux of the Renaissance where some ancient Greek heroine had been cut down tragically in her prime, was doing wonders for her bosom. Her covered face allowed him to gaze longingly at it for a few moments as her chest gently rose and fell with her breathing in her splendid, fitted coral gown. Bizarrely, despite that unexpected bonus, he missed seeing her smile. That stunning smile combined with her current alluring position would be quite something to witness.

A sensible, dedicated spy would silently retrace his steps and take another route to continue his unhindered reconnoitre. But for some reason, his feet had already decided to head towards her as if pulled by some invisible cord. He was halfway across the lawn when he realised she wasn't asleep, in fact, and much to his amusement, she was talking to herself.

'Give *him* a fighting chance, darling.' If he was not mistaken, she was snippily mimicking Lady Crudgington. 'You are a little *too* buttoned up.' The hand that had been on her belly wafted in the air. 'I cannot recall a time when I have ever heard you sound so *waspish* over a mere man, Thea.' Gray suppressed the spontaneous snort which threatened to erupt as she blew a raspberry so fat the floaty shawl quivered. 'Settle for a *wholly* unsuitable man before you become so *decrepit* and wizened no one will ever fancy you and to hell with the consequences. Your exacting standards are *far* too high and your imagination is as *vivid* as your wayward, vertical hair. And while you're about it, become a total scandal, why don't you? Throw yourself at the fellow. Stand on the precipice and *leap*! The clock is ticking after all. Tick-tock, Thea. Tick-tock.'

He did laugh at the second raspberry, making her sit bolt upright, the delicate shawl slipping to puddle at her feet and her lush mouth a delightful *O* of embarrassed outrage. 'How long have you been there!'

'Long enough to know that Lady Crudgington thinks you should give Mr Hargreaves a fighting chance, but that you are not so enthused by the idea.'

She was simultaneously blinking and blushing furiously. 'Yes... Mr Hargreaves...indeed...and you are correct. I am not at all enthused by the idea.' Primly, she straightened and adjusted her clothing. 'If anything, I am thoroughly unenthused.'

'I'm exceedingly glad to hear it. Having had to listen to him for the last half an hour, I found his conversation quite...'

'Sycophantic? Insincere? Grinding?'

He smiled at her accurate assessment. It was refreshing she didn't mince her words. 'Yes. To all. You can do much better than him.'

She beamed again as she had this morning and the sight of it did odd things to his heart. 'Thank you, Lord Gray! That is *exactly* what I keep telling Harriet, but she is determined to meddle.'

'Well, I dare say the meddling is necessary. You are on the cusp of decrepit.'

'You heard everything, didn't you?' The blush on her cheeks mirrored the deeper one staining her collarbone and disappearing beneath the lace edging her close-cut bodice. 'It's very rude to eavesdrop.'

'Surely eavesdropping involves listening to an obviously private conversation between two or more people. As you were loudly talking to yourself, out in broad daylight, I didn't think it counted. It gave me a very interesting insight into the young lady you are beneath that impenetrable exterior.' She looked attractively flummoxed and guilty at his assessment, which was very intriguing. 'Besides, like you, I sensibly came out here to hide and get some fresh air, so the eavesdropping was merely an unanticipated bonus. How could I resist it?'

'For a big man, you move with impressive stealth. Was it your intention to sneak up on me?'

'You credit me with too much talent, Miss Cranford. All I did was walk across the grass. If you hadn't been talking so much, you would have heard me. Do you mind if I sit—or is that grossly improper? If it is, I can hide somewhere else.'

She hesitated, then wrapped the filmy shawl around her shoulders, her jaw set and her eyes riveted on a distant spot across the lawn, feigning complete indifference politely. 'We are in view of the house and Harriet will be back presently.' Gray decided to take that as acceptance and sat on the opposite end of the seat to her.

'Why are you hiding? When I left you, you seemed to be having a high old time. My aunt appeared *most* enamoured of your charm.' He detected the hint of disapproval and decided to pry. These little rifts and obvious censures, leaked in confidence, proved time and time again to be fertile hunting grounds for spies.

'Your aunt obviously enjoys socialising.' A very delicate way of saying the woman basked in the glory of being the centre of attention, particularly when surrounded by a bevy of eager, much younger gentlemen.

'She does. More so than my uncle, so he indulges her.'

'I was hoping to meet your uncle before I outstayed my welcome. Will he be rejoining the party later?'

Her dark eyes clouded as they stared straight ahead. 'My uncle's health is not good, my lord, and hasn't been for several years. He managed much of the first hour, but prolonged socialising does take its toll on him. He needs his rest and sleeps like the dead most afternoons. I do not expect Uncle Edward will make another appearance today, I'm afraid. You shall have to meet him another time.'

He could tell by the worried look in her eyes she believed this to be the case and felt a rush of anger towards the man for his duplicity. Poor health was a convenient and ready excuse to disappear to do his dirty work. He'd wager every hard-earned coin in his purse that Gislingham was currently up to no good somewhere on this estate— or elsewhere—while his niece worried over him unnecessarily. 'That is a shame. Perhaps my cousin and I would do better to call upon him in the morning?' Before he left today, he needed to do a thorough reconnaissance of the grounds and as much of the bottom floor as he dare. His gut told him Gislingham ran his operation from this house and Gray needed to know exactly where.

'He is at his best in the mornings and enjoys small, intimate company. I know he is keen to meet you—especially as Harriet has already apprised him of this morning's unfortunate events.'

That didn't sound good. 'Should I expect a thorough telling off when I come calling?'

'Not at all. Uncle Edward has a very warped sense of humour and found the state of me upon my arrival home hilarious. I fear Harriet brings out the worst in him.' Gray

sincerely doubted that. He had lost many comrades thanks
to The Boss at his worst.

'Lady Crudgington is indeed a force of nature.'

'And very curious. She left me determined to give you
a thorough grilling.'

'I suspected as much. But she was distracted by a fruit
scone and clotted cream on the sideboard, so I managed
to escape her clutches before I crept out. I can only cope
with so much heat from the drawing room...and Mr Hargreaves.' Gray might as well take advantage of her dislike
for the man. 'He brays when he laughs.'

The ghost of a smile played at the corners of her mouth.
'Colonel Purbeck spits when he talks.'

'Hence I stumbled across you shrouded like a widow.'

'I'm sorry about that. It was most improper.'

'Propriety is hardly a field it would be fair for me to
judge you on and, anyway, it is vastly overrated. Don't
you think?'

Her fingers played with the dangling edges of the shawl
as she glanced up at the cloudless sky and, inadvertently
giving him more clues as to her character, she avoided answering his question. 'Alas, I adore the sun, but it doesn't
adore me. With my fair skin, I burn easily, so I have to
ration it. Hence the shroud.'

'Then perhaps I should escort you back inside. The afternoon sun is always the worst.'

Prudence dictated that she should grasp the opportunity to escape inside seeing as he had offered it. It wasn't
proper for an unmarried lady to be in such a secluded
place in the presence of a gentleman without a chaperon
and she knew Harriet had no intention of coming back
outside and wouldn't be caught dead anywhere near the
garden if she suspected Thea was alone in it with Lord

Gray. But her friend's criticisms rankled and as much as Thea wanted to discount everything she had said, there was a great deal of truth in her words. She was becoming unacceptably jaded and had an ever-increasing suspicion of the motives of others. Since the smooth-talking soldier that dreadful night, she did make snap decisions about men and she did push them away. The fear of Impetuous Thea falling for a money-grabbing bounder, the huge responsibility of the unwieldy fortune her uncle had amassed on her behalf and the sense of responsibility and love she had for him had made her reluctant to consider anyone seriously.

To her shame, that reluctance had made her unacceptably stand-offish to the point where she risked never finding a decent man, and that simply wouldn't do. Because one day when the time was right and the gentleman perfect, she did want to live happily ever after. She wanted to be loved and adored. Wanted to love and adore back. Wanted to fill her home with the happy sound of children laughing, the closeness of family and the promise of a future she could look forward to. Uncle Edward had insisted she have financial independence so that she could marry the man of her dreams without having to compromise as he had done. True love, he often waxed after a bit too much brandy, was the greatest joy in the world and worth all the hideous turmoil in the long run.

Somehow, while waiting patiently for true love to come, she had allowed those alarm bells to start clanging well before she got to know a gentleman, which made a lifetime of spinsterhood a foregone conclusion. If she had created the vicious circle, she could jolly well unmake it.

'I suppose I can tolerate a little more sun.' In a concerted effort not to be stand-offish and judgemental, she would be cordial and properly get to know this handsome new gentleman beyond his compelling, wolf-like eyes and splendid physique. Harriet was right. Aside from the fact he was local, he did live with an older relative as well, so might understand her situation. He was the first gentleman she had met in for ever who had not actively sought her out to begin with. They had met wholly by chance without the allure of her impressive bank balance, so perhaps she should give fate a fair crack at the whip before she wielded the repelling Shield of Suspicion. 'Tell me something about yourself, Lord Gray.'

She could tell she had surprised him because his dark brows momentarily drew together. 'What would you like to know?'

'I suppose it makes sense to start at the beginning. Where did you grow up? Who are your family?'

'Very close to the mountains of Snowdonia. My father was the Marquess of Talysarn.'

'Was?'

'He died a few years ago while I was at sea. My elder brother now holds the title.'

'How sad. You missed the funeral?'

His face clouded and he paused before he answered. 'Yes.'

'Is your mother still alive?'

'Alas, my mother died many years before. She was a lovely woman. I miss her greatly. You lost your parents young also, I believe?'

'I have no memories of my mother. She died when I was a babe.' Although Thea still missed her, wondering what her life and her character might have been like if she had grown up with a woman's guidance. Probably less wilful and impetuous.

'My father was a don at Cambridge. He taught mathematics and is still widely regarded in that field.' Which was probably why he never quite understood his daughter. Thea had no head for figures and the only thing they had had in common was a boisterous sense of humour and their twin fiery tempers. 'Did you go to Cambridge or Oxford?'

'No… I went abroad.'

'To study?'

'After a fashion. I'm not much of a scholar, I'm afraid. I certainly have no head for numbers.'

'Me either.' They had something in common. Something deathly dull and inconsequential in common. 'Aside from swimming scandalously naked with your dog, what do you enjoy?' Why had she said that? Instantly her cheeks heated while she wrestled Impetuous Thea back into her box.

He shot her a sideways glance and chuckled, the deep sound warming her in places that had no right being warmed. 'I thought we had drawn a veil over that. Or is the memory too awful for your tender sensibilities to forgive and forget?' He was flirting. Despite refusing to meet his eye she could hear it in his voice, but she was already blushing and doubtless he could see it. What had made her bring it up again? He would think she couldn't stop thinking about it, which was, of course, mortifyingly true. Aside from the memory of him naked, the wayward, wilful part of her nature was seriously considering swimming naked in the brook, too. It was ridiculously hot— even for July…

As if he could read her mind, he stared knowingly at her, the wretch. Better to acknowledge the discomfort head on and then brush it blithely aside. She was almost twenty-four, for goodness' sake. Ladies of that age were expected to be a bit more worldly, no matter how well bred and proper they were.

'I have forgotten it.' *Liar.* 'As much as one can forget

such an outrageous anomaly so early in the day, especially as the day is nowhere near over yet and here you are again—being exactly where you shouldn't be and encroaching on my privacy. Thankfully, it was a brief encounter, so therefore unlikely to make a lasting impression on my *tender* sensibilities. I am hopeful it will be nought but a distant memory by tomorrow.' Gracious! Her true tartness had materialised out of nowhere when she had intended to be nothing but polite. Clearly she needed a much stronger padlock on the box around Lord Gray.

'That is good to know. Nothing makes a man happier than knowing he is quickly forgettable. Especially when all his *credentials* have been laid bare for scrutiny. I shall sleep soundly tonight, secure in the knowledge the spectre of my bottom will not be encroaching on your dreams.'

It was funny that she could hear his smile. Funnier still that her own mouth was curving upwards, too, when this entire conversation was outrageous. Gloriously so. Not being immediately suspicious was liberating. 'So shall I. For they would hardly be dreams, Lord Gray. I fear if your bottom scandalously encroached, surely, they would be nightmares at the very least. When one is as decrepit as I, one needs one's beauty sleep.' She was flirting! When she never flirted any more in case it gave untrustworthy men the wrong impression. This man clearly brought out the worst in her and she hardly knew him.

'If you got any more sleep, you'd be dangerous.'

'Although I should warn you, I doubt Harriet and my uncle will allow me to forget the incident completely until they have fully had their fun at my expense...' Had he just paid her a compliment? Thea gave up staring off into the distance and risked flicking him a glance. He was sat staring cockily right back at her. Utterly gorgeous, the seams of his coat straining slightly against the muscles of his folded arms, those unusual blue-grey eyes twinkling with mischief. Her heart did a little stutter at the sight. That and his scandalously pretty comment, which the sensible part of her cautioned was probably best ignored. Reacting would only encourage him, making him think she was interested, and she certainly didn't want that. Just in case he was a bounder in wolf's clothing. 'Kindly repeat what you just said.' So much for ignorance and disinterest. Impetuous, easily seduced Thea was loose and running roughshod all over the terrace.

'I *said*, if you got any more sleep, you'd be dangerous. Obvious decrepitude aside, you are quite beautiful enough already, Miss Cranford. I'm not entirely sure I could cope with any more. I find myself already totally smitten with you.'

Internally she was sighing and was in grave danger of melting into a puddle at the man's feet. He thought her beautiful. Was already smitten... How lovely. Of course, outwardly, she hoped she looked unimpressed because she was far too sensible to be waylaid by flowery words any more—no matter how lovely Impetuous Thea thought they were to hear. 'Oh, my!' She fluttered her hand in front of her face and batted her eyelashes. 'What a swoon-worthy compliment! If only I hadn't seen you similarly flirting with my aunt a short while ago, I'd be tempted to be flattered.'

'There is a distinct difference. Your aunt flirted with me first and it would have been rude not to respond in kind. That was merely social flirting, Miss Cranford, and therefore innocuous. My flirting with you was wholly unsolicited and wholly spontaneous. It was *genuine* flirting.' The arrogant grin suited him and Thea found herself enjoying it.

'Ah—I see.' She tapped her lip and attempted to look

thoughtful, enjoying this unexpected sparring match with a man who met none of her strict criteria, but seemed to be able to pick the locks that bound the chains around the inner Thea's locked box. 'So if social flirting is innocuous, does that make *genuine* flirting noxious?'

'It makes it dangerous. Especially when both of us engage in it as we are now. It hints at intent.' He raised his dark eyebrow. 'At promise...'

Instinctively, she folded her own arms, mirroring his casual pose. 'I hardly think I am flirting, Lord Gray.'

'Gray will do just fine. And you are most definitely flirting, Miss Cranford. I'm afraid I recognise all of the signs.'

'Really? Pray enlighten me, for I confess I am at a loss.'

He shuffled closer on the bench and leaned in conspiratorially, smelling sinfully of sunshine and spicy cologne. 'To the unobservant, it would be difficult to tell, but there are subtle clues. Your insistence on reminding me of this morning, for example. Unconsciously, despite all my very proper clothes, your mind is scandalously picturing me naked.'

She scoffed, bristling, wondering if he really *could* read her mind. 'I most certainly am not! Ewwwgh!' She shuddered for effect. 'I can assure you my brain has far better things to think about than the unsavoury picture of you in the altogether, although even if I was, which I most definitely am *not*, a person's private thoughts hardly constitute flirting.'

'The coquettish side glances and pretty pink blushes which accompany them does.'

Thea turned her head and stared him dead in the eye. 'I'm a redhead and if I am a bit pink, then I have clearly been in the sun a tad too long, my lord.'

'A plausible denial, to be sure—but it doesn't fool me. And I thought we agreed you could call me Gray going forward, seeing as you've seen me in the altogether? But...your preoccupations with my impressive, manly nude body aside, there are other damning clues which only a true connoisseur in the subtle art of flirting would pick up. A moment ago, for instance, when you brought your finger to your lips... Why, it was obvious you were doing so to purposely draw my eyes there and set me wondering if they are as soft and inviting as they look.'

She had touched her lips quite innocently, or so she had thought, but now they tingled. 'You are delusional.'

'Right now, we both know the position of your arms has only one true purpose.'

She didn't unfold them. 'To show you I am not a fool, nor suffer fools gladly?'

'To display your figure to its best effect.' She hastily uncrossed her arms and gathered the shawl tighter, irritated at the missish response when he reacted with a knowing chuckle. 'And...' The word came out in a sultry whisper as his head leaned closer still before he paused and failed to finish his sentence.

'And?'

'That was a test and, I'm sorry to tell you, you failed.'

'I did?'

'Indeed. Because *you* leaned closer, too, obviously eager to hear what I had to say despite my intimate, wholly inappropriate conversation and my close proximity to your unchaperoned person being most impertinent.'

'You *are* impertinent.'

'I am—but you'd like to kiss me regardless.'

She would—which came as a huge, unwelcome shock—but she most certainly wouldn't.

Ever.

On principle.

'Oh, Lord Gray, you are labouring under the most fanciful of misapprehensions.' With purposeful, indifferent, possibly flirtatious slowness, Thea stood and shook her head pityingly. 'Perhaps it is you who needs to be mindful of the sun's rays and ration them going forward, for today they have clearly addled your mind.'

Chapter Five

'Did you have to bring that dog?' Lord Fennimore glared at Trefor's rapidly wagging tail and grimaced.

'Miss Cranford was very taken with him. I reasoned his presence would only help our cause.'

'They won't let him in the house.'

'He will be perfectly content tied up outside for the duration of our visit. He loves to sleep in the sun.' Unbidden, images of Miss Cranford lying in the garden instantly sprung to mind and he found himself smiling. Granted, flirting with her yesterday might well have been foolhardy and counterproductive to their mission—undeniably his superior would castigate him for the misdemeanour if he knew and a truly sensible spy would have avoided it— but Gray had enjoyed it immensely. She was tart, sharp and tasty. A glorious, intelligent and feisty armful and he would not regret the overwhelming, yet too-brief indulgence in the slightest. In that moment, it had felt right and life was too short for regrets. 'Besides, as we are posing as country gentlemen, he gives us an air of the authentic. What says Suffolk more than two robust fellows striding across the fields with their faithful hound in tow?'

'We could have ridden instead. It would have been a

darn sight quicker than constantly stopping and waiting for that dog to continually sniff the air.'

'Trefor is rusticating. Which is what *we* are supposed to be doing.'

They turned on to the Viscount's short drive, both lapsing into silence as they mentally prepared themselves for the task in hand. Again last night they had meticulously gone over their backstory. Lord Fennimore was still convinced the closer Gray stuck to the truth of his past, the more chance he had of manoeuvring himself into Gislingham's inner circle. With the Viscount's extensive web of criminal contacts, it would be simple to make enquiries and the truth would be swiftly and categorically confirmed. Lord Graham Chadwick was a ne'er-do-well of the first order and had been since birth. He had lost his twenty thousand-pound inheritance at the gaming tables in just three short months. He had been understandably disowned by his only brother and his father, the upright and blemish-free Marquess of Talysarn, and then disappeared off to sea when he had worn out his welcome and his line of credit in the capital. After that, nobody really knew what had happened to the lad...

Before the men had left for Suffolk, the necessary lies had been sprinkled among a few reliable government allies and in the browned pages of certain parish records. The errant Lord Gray had returned after a scandalous decade of adventuring and been taken under the wing of Lord Fennimore—a distant cousin of Gray's dead mother—in the hope of encouraging him to tread the path of the respectable going forward. To that end, and to keep him away from the seductive mischief of town, Lord Fennimore had rented a property deep in the countryside.

Until yesterday, Gray had been entirely satisfied with the story. Now, despite knowing the filtered, censored truth was perfect for their purpose, he wasn't so keen. Yesterday, Miss Cranford had asked about his past and, oddly ashamed, he had brushed over it. While no longer a wastrel, he had been. Once he had given up all hope of winning back Cecily, he had lived an aimless life doing whatever had pleased him. There had been no master plan, no commitments nor any responsibility. Once the pleasure in the place, the woman or the entertainment waned, he had moved on to seek diversion elsewhere. Whatever it took to make him forget the pain in his heart, he actively pursued it until the pain became an ache and eventually that ache became a scar. Bitter truths he had never admitted to anyone and never would. Better the world chastise him for being a wastrel than pity him for being a love-addled fool who hadn't quite passed muster.

But such a past would make him more appealing to the crooked Viscount. As old Fennimore had rightly pointed out when he had suggested, over the soup, that they tweak the truth a little to mask the fact he had been home and almost respectable for two whole years: birds of a feather always flock together. A confirmed reprobate stood a greater chance of becoming a friend than an upstanding, reformed character. However, the same foibles which would make him more appealing to Gislingham would make him significantly less appealing to Gislingham's lovely niece.

As much as it irrationally pained him, that couldn't be helped.

King, country and his promotion depended on it.

Gray secured his dog to a low fence near the dappled shade of a horse chestnut and the pair approached the front door, both supremely aware that this first meeting with the man would be crucial. His superior handed over their calling cards to an ancient butler who had made no effort to remove the buff apron he wore or to discard the polishing rag he held in his hand. Such a conscientiously informal greeting was a nice touch, suggesting there was nothing to hide behind this heavy oak door but an unpretentious country squire.

'Lord Cedric Fennimore and Lord Graham Chadwick— we have come to pay our respects to his lordship and Miss Cranford if they are at home.'

The butler did not attempt to suggest they might not be and cheerfully welcomed them to sit in a bright parlour while he informed his lordship of their presence. They waited less than five minutes before the old retainer reappeared and asked them to follow him. He led them up a flight of sweeping, creaking wooden stairs to a small sitting room stuffed with furniture unashamedly built for comfort over style and not at all what one would expect from a man who earned hundreds of thousands of pounds from illegal free trading.

Before they sat, Miss Cranford hurried in, smiling, looking stunning in turquoise and with her riotous Titian hair already escaping its pins. The sight was quite the highlight of his morning and, without thinking, Gray turned his gaze and unwaveringly drank her in. Her eyes flicked to his, dipped briefly, then focused solely on Lord Fennimore.

'My lords, how lovely of you to come. My uncle will be with you presently. He is just finishing off something in his study.' Unconsciously, her head gestured to the door opposite the one they had entered.

'His study is up here? On the first floor?' An interesting titbit Gray tucked away for future reference. At some point, he needed to go through Gislingham's desk and private papers; most probably in the dead of night after breaking in.

'He prefers these apartments to the larger rooms downstairs. They are more self-contained and easier to navigate now that his mobility is not what it was. Please... Sit.' She gestured to the furniture nearest the enormous bay window where the lace panels billowed softly in the breeze. 'Bertie is fetching tea.'

'Bertie?'

'My uncle's manservant. He sees to all his needs. We would all be quite lost without him.'

Lord Fennimore took one of the two large wing-backs while Miss Cranford perched on the sofa, the picture of a proper hostess who never blew raspberries or allowed her eyes to wander freely down his naked body. This was the Miss Theodora Cranford she wanted the world to see. He rather liked knowing that, with the right encouragement, she was a completely different Miss Cranford underneath. Because he simply needed to, Gray sat next to her. 'You look particularly lovely this morning, Miss Cranford.' And she smelled divine. Whatever perfume it was that she wore, it had now become his absolute favourite scent in the whole world. Reminiscent of the heady evening jasmine he had encountered in the Orient.

She ignored the compliment, but smiled politely as she refocused on his companion. 'We did not expect you this early, although the hour is a good one for Uncle Edward. He's an early bird by nature, as am I.'

As she was intent on ignoring him and his ridiculous need to flirt with her, he decided to resort to basic good manners to see if she would respond to that instead. 'Something we have in common—although I confess I would sleep longer if it were not for Trefor. He needs to get out early...to do dog things.'

That worked. 'You should have brought him. I adore dogs.'

He couldn't resist an I-told-you-so look at Lord Fennimore. 'Despite *Cedric's* forceful objections, I did. He's currently sat on the drive.'

'Then you must bring him in! Uncle Edward is a dog person, too. Left to us, we would have a house full, but my aunt loathes them. They make her sneeze.'

'Perhaps he is best left where he is, then? I should hate to cause her ladyship any discomfort.'

'And the dog is a menace,' added Lord Fennimore with barely disguised irritation. 'My young relative has been most neglectful of the animal's training.'

'Her ladyship has gone shopping in Ipswich and we do not expect her back until much later, so Trefor is welcome to visit. Besides, a little wildness is perfectly acceptable in a dog. It gives it character.'

Gray didn't argue. If his poorly behaved mutt would aid the transition from new acquaintances to friends quicker, he would shamelessly use him. He fetched the dog and did his best to wrangle him back towards the Viscount's private apartments without Trefor's blurred tail knocking anything over in its exuberance. By the time they reached the sitting room, the tea had arrived, along with a large bowl of water for the hound. A middle-aged servant stood pouring, but paused with the cup and pot held aloft as the dog barrelled towards him. He needn't have worried. The dog only had eyes for the deliciously smelling redhead. Like Gray, Trefor was irresistibly drawn to her.

'My uncle is finishing up his business for the morning. Something he insists on doing himself rather than employ a secretary.' Another interesting insight and not at all the norm. Most estate owners employed a legion of staff, from bookkeepers to estate managers, but then most had nothing to hide. 'Bertie, this is Lord Gray.' Miss Cranford's eyes did not lift from the animal as he ran in giddy circles about her feet being thoroughly petted, almost as if she was purposefully avoiding his gaze at all cost. 'And this handsome rascal is Trefor.'

'*The* Trefor?' The servant was soft-spoken, but clearly amused. 'The one that almost drowned you?'

'The very same.'

'What do you mean he almost drowned you?' His superior's eyes darted between Gray and their hostess before skewering him alone.

'Trefor knocked her into the brook.'

'It was an accident,' said Miss Cranford graciously, oblivious of the way old Fennimore's eyes had begun to bulge at the revelation. 'And hardly poor Trefor's fault. My maid got all the mud out of my dress, so no real harm was done. Apart from to my hair, which was a disaster all yesterday.' Her eyes wandered to Gray's briefly and she unconsciously blinked rapidly, a sure sign she was not quite as composed in his presence as she wanted him to believe. 'I blame Lord Gray entirely for that shambles.' Was she rattled by the flirting? He certainly hoped so.

'I thought your hair looked lovely.'

'I thought it looked an absolute fright.' A deep, chuckling, slightly slurred voice came from the doorway. 'Had me laughing for hours.'

Viscount Gislingham was not at all what Gray had imagined. He was tall and broad, a full head of thick sandy hair, greying at the temples, and a face that was undoubtedly considered handsome in its prime—before the stroke which had apparently now frozen half of it. That aside, he was smartly turned out. The well-cut green coat covered a jaunty striped-silk waistcoat that was all the colours of the rainbow. He was also much older than his wife. A good twenty years older. He walked into the room, leaning heavily on a cane, his left leg dragging slightly.

'Don't get up, gentlemen, for then I shall feel the need to shake your hands immediately and as only one of them works properly, and I have a wonky leg which is little more than useless, I will doubtless fall over and embarrass us all. Let's save the hearty handshakes for the end of our visit. Besides, I've worked out which of you is which already. Harriet was very fulsome in her descriptions.' His head nodded to each of them in turn. 'Welcome, Lord Fennimore, and welcome, Lord Gray. I am glad Kirton House is peopled again. It has been empty and miserable far too long. The grounds have been neglected, I'm afraid—so feel free to do with them as you will. Anything would be an improvement on those acres of grass and daisies.'

The manservant took his weaker arm and manoeuvred his master to the vacant wing-back while his niece hovered nearby. 'Tea, Uncle?'

'Indeed. Two sugars, if you please.'

'Half a teaspoon and not a speck more. The physician has him under strict instructions to keep his weight down.' Gislingham rolled his eyes at his servant's determined admonishment, then huffed in a good-natured way at his guests.

'Once upon a time I was master of this house, now I'm scolded like a child. Between Thea and Bertie's conspiratorial nagging, I now have no vices left.' The Viscount settled himself before making a fuss of the bouncing Trefor at his knee. 'If that were not enough, my pride is further dented by my inability to climb down stairs. I can go up them well enough, but I have to suffer the indignity of having the footmen carry me down.'

'You could always move your bedchamber and study downstairs,' Lord Fennimore said reasonably, earning him a stunning smile from their intoxicatingly jasmine-smelling hostess.

'Exactly! I have said as much a thousand times, for there is plenty of space, but my uncle is stubborn. He absolutely refuses.'

Gray saw the Viscount exchange an odd look with his servant before his expression became shuttered. Hardened. 'We are not discussing that again, Thea. I like my privacy, always have and always will. I picked footmen with strong backs for the express purpose of transporting my knackered carcase down and reward them handsomely for the inconvenience.' As if the Viscount sensed Gray was watching, his serious expression swiftly evaporated and he was all easy charm again.

'I take it this is the handsome fellow responsible for sending you flying, Thea?' Clearly not a good judge of character, the dog lapped up the attention, his eyes half closing in ecstasy as Gislingham rubbed one of his floppy ears. 'And the other equally handsome fellow is responsible for rendering you speechless with his unabashed nudity?' He glanced up at Gray and grinned. 'I'd have paid good money to see my niece mute for once. I had thought such a miracle impossible. I'd shamelessly imitate you and stroll about buck naked, too, if I thought it would get me any peace, but the sight would likely send all the servants running for the hills before it silenced her and then who would carry me downstairs?'

'I was hardly mute, Uncle.'

'Harriet said your jaw dropped to the floor and you were stuttering and spluttering while glowing crimson like a beetroot.'

'Harriet exaggerates.' She carefully placed the cup within his reach, but out of the radius of Trefor's ferociously wagging tail, the apples of her cheeks a little pink again as she resolutely avoided glancing anywhere near Gray's side of the sofa. 'Once I had recovered from the shock of Lord Gray's abysmal lack of propriety, I gave him a thorough telling off. I would have said much more—but I ended up in the brook.'

The Viscount laughed and shared an amused look with his manservant before grinning lopsidedly at Gray. 'She told you off? I am impressed. Thea is usually painfully, politely aloof at all times to everyone bar me and Harriet— and even then she tempers her words. It is most irritating because she used to be such an entertaining, stubborn and delightfully troublesome child. Blissfully cursed with a true redhead's quick temper. Age has softened the shrew in her and I miss it. You must provoke it, Lord Gray. I wonder why?'

'She professes to have forgiven me, has promised to draw a veil over it, yet continues to reprimand me regardless. I *have* apologised for the misdemeanour, my lord. Repeatedly.' Gray smiled at the older man, attempting to appear contrite despite the overwhelming temptation to spar and flirt with his niece again rather than doing the job he had come here to do.

'My Thea is a hard nut to crack. Far too picky. And shrewish. It's why she's still unmarried despite her lovely face and figure. I live in hope that someone will break through that tough outer shell and take her off my hands. But the young gentlemen hereabouts have proved themselves to be very lily-livered in the face of her icy indifference. It will take a great deal of perseverance on your part, Lord Gray, to chisel through it. I hope you are up to the challenge.'

'I'm sure Lord Gray has worked out already it's not worth his effort.' Her eyes met his properly for the first time since he had arrived and there was definite challenge in them, warning him not to play along with her uncle's jesting. 'When it comes to *unworthy* gentleman, no matter how handsome or penitent, I have skin as thick as an elephant's. In fact, I am positively pachydermatous.'

'She thinks herself clever, too. Worst thing I ever did, paying for her governesses. Some of those lacked perseverance, too, but it was fun to watch her run rings around them. She's a troublesome handful. It's what I've always enjoyed most about her. Never could predict quite what she was going to do.' He smiled indulgently at his niece, who quickly focused blandly on her teacup. Was it the reminder of her childhood wilfulness, her uncle's teasing or Gray's attempts at flirting which made her uncomfortable?

'I'm an irritatingly persistent fellow, my lord. Dogged, even. For the sake of your continued sanity I shall do my best to mine through to that soft kernel.'

The mobile half of the Viscount's face curved into a smile, one too friendly for a murdering cut-throat. 'I cannot tell you how relieved I am to hear it. Harriet said you showed promise.'

Gray's eyes wandered boldly to hers, then lingered. Despite the very long list of good reasons why he couldn't, there was a tantalising, fiery woman beneath her icy aloofness. One he irresponsibly wanted to know better.

'I wouldn't allow him anywhere near my niece if I had one.' Lord Fennimore must have seen the heated look and decided now was the optimum time to drip in their story for maximum effect. Something they had agreed on, although it now suddenly left a bitter taste in Gray's mouth. 'Miss Cranford's assessment is quite correct. He is unworthy…although I am hopeful I can turn him into the gentleman he was born to be. Gray has always been very wild.' Once she learned exactly how wild, all his chances of pursuing the attraction for King, country or himself would be bludgeoned to death with the unpalatable truth.

'He was? Do tell.' Miss Cranford picked up her teacup and settled back, all ears.

'I'll spare you all the gory details, although it would be very easy for you to find them out...' Drip, drip. Fennimore was teasing his prey with bait. 'Suffice it to say that he had to leave these shores in disgrace a decade ago and has only recently dared to return. As the only family member who deigns to speak to him and out of the affection and respect I had for his dear mother—my cousin—I have taken it upon myself to rehabilitate him. To his credit, he has trod the path of respectability for over a month now...'

Chapter Six

'The light here is very poor.'

As it was blazing sunshine everywhere, Thea bit her tongue. Harriet had already dragged her to three locations, and made them set up her easel in the blistering heat twice before declaring the site unsuitable. The reflections on the brook were not shimmery enough, the vista from the highest point duller than usual and now it was the fault of the light. 'I doubt you will find a spot with more light.' Thea pointed up at the scorching yellow ball in the sky for emphasis.

'Which is exactly the problem. There is far too much light and it is washing out all the colours. We need some dappled shade. Perhaps we should head over there to those trees?' Trees which sat dangerously close to Kirton House and a certain handsome scoundrel Restrained Thea would be quite delighted never to see again. Not now that she knew her initial assessment of the man was quite correct and she never should have allowed herself the luxury of flirting with him.

That foolhardy bit of flirting had given Lord Gray ideas he had no right having. Not when he possessed none of the necessary attributes on her list, despite what anyone else had to say on the subject, including Impetuous Thea. Lord Gray was neither trustworthy nor respectable. He certainly wasn't the least bit proper. A complete rascal. A thrill-seeker. A man who made poor choices and lived for nought but fun. A man exiled from his family and shunned by society. Not that she held much stock in society, but their universal condemnation couldn't be wrong. You could only fool some of the people some of the time after all. Lord Gray was the sort of man who led people astray. Thea did not want or need the temptation of such a wholly unsuitable fellow, no matter how much her wilful side was drawn to him.

His poor cousin had his work cut out trying to turn him into something vaguely resembling respectable and, being a realist, Thea was highly sceptical of his chances in view of the overwhelming evidence to the contrary. His wildly outrageous flirting after such a short acquaintance said a great deal about his commitment to becoming respectable. The only attribute on her list the outrageously flirtatious Lord Gray happened to possess was being easy on the eye. Too easy on the eye.

'You paint. I'm going home.' Where she could avoid any contact with the wastrel, Harriet's unsubtle meddling and her own embarrassing preoccupation with the image of the man's bare buttocks.

'The walk back to the house is significantly longer than to those trees and you are already beginning to resemble a lobster. Are you certain you want to risk it?' Instinctively Thea's hands went to her cheeks and probed. The sensitive skin just under her eyes did feel warm. Harriet smiled with mock sympathy. 'Think of your complexion, darling, and don't be a spoilsport. I promise we shall bury ourselves into a secluded, shady nook where I can paint to my heart's content and you can read whatever nonsense you are currently reading without burning to a crisp. I shan't traipse you anywhere else. Promise.' Thea hesitated, and her friend spotted it. 'Unless it's a little too close to the abode of a certain handsome nude bather, in which case I completely…understand.'

'What is there to understand?'

'That his close proximity unnerves you and your inappropriate attraction to the man frightens you because he is not at all what you *think* you want.'

'I most certainly am neither unnerved nor frightened nor attracted! I couldn't give two figs whether I see the fellow or not.' And like a sap, she was already striding purposefully towards the dratted trees to prove it, despite that being the exact opposite thing to the one she wanted to do. 'I'm simply fed up trailing after you in the heat.'

'If you're sure, Thea, darling. I'd hate to think my choice of spot was the cause of any distress… Although I am intrigued to meet his cousin properly. All I managed was a brief how do you do.'

'Are you talking about Lord Fennimore?'

'Indeed I am. I thought he was very distinguished, with an attractive, confident manner about him. I like a confident man. *And* he's apparently a bachelor to boot. He definitely requires further scrutiny.' She gazed wistfully towards Kirton House, then shrugged at Thea's bemused expression. 'Don't look so surprised. If you think decent gentlemen the right side of forty are thin on the ground here in Suffolk, you should try being my age. They are either married or so dreadful nobody can bear their company. Like Colonel Purbeck, who completely dominated Lord Fennimore at the tea and I couldn't muster the enthusiasm to suffer his droning company—even for a handsome stranger. Not when it is inevitable I will collide with him naturally in the grounds one day. Not today, of course, seeing as we are avoiding his gorgeous younger relative at all costs.'

Because Harriet was speaking loudly, Thea slowed her pace. 'Keep your voice down or he'll hear us and then my day will be well and truly spoiled!' The last thing she wanted was that shameless flirt coming to his door to investigate. Not when she now knew she should have trusted those alarm bells and not been goaded by Harriet into getting to know him better—then outrageously goaded by him into flirting.

Although the flirting on the terrace had been fun at the time despite the fact her subsequent reaction to it was unnerving. His boldness and confidence had tempted her to be bolder herself and for once she forgot to be polite and instead, for a short while, had been her true self in front of him. The old, unburdened Thea who always did as she pleased and acted before thinking. The one who had exceedingly poor taste in men.

Yet she had still found herself looking forward to his potential visit the following day, despite there being no firm plans, and had spent far too long at her *toilette* in preparation, wondering if she should allow a little bit of Impetuous Thea out of her box again just for the thrill of it. Until she realised that was exactly the problem. Like the seductive soldier who had been the last man to thoroughly lead her astray with no thought to the consequences, Lord Gray was too tempting.

Yesterday she had initially kept her guard up each time he tried to flirt because there were witnesses—that had been hard because the parrying, teasing comments had been on the tip of her tongue the entire time, but she had promised herself she would resist. A resolve which had hardened to granite once she had found out about his dreadful past. Her impeccable instincts had been correct all along and she should have heeded their warning rather than listen to her flighty inner self. He was as bad as Mr Hargreaves—if not worse.

However, despite his blatant unsuitability and her obvious lack of interest during tea, Uncle Edward had continued to make unsubtle hints that Lord Gray should court her right up until the second he had left. Because he was a thoroughly disgraceful scoundrel all the way through to his perfectly proportioned bones, Lord Gray had intimated that he fully intended to do so. A prospect as disagreeable as it was appealing—and that simply wouldn't do. Henceforth, he and his dangerously silver tongue would be avoided unless it was under the strict confines of a proper social occasion filled with a room full of people to act as chaperons. Aside from the fact she didn't trust him, Thea also did not trust the buried part of her which his face, body and mischievous, bold manner inappropriately responded to.

The part that kept whispering that she and Lord Gray were well matched.

Harriet paused, shielded her eyes from the sun and rather unsubtly stared at Kirton House. 'I don't think anyone is home. Look—the windows are all shut. Nobody shuts their windows here unless they are out. We should be perfectly safe walking past—not that I see what the problem is. I found Lord Gray positively charming and am quite happy to further the acquaintance with him, too.'

'It's far too hot to socialise. This afternoon all I want to do is read.' She waved her book for emphasis. 'Something I have been denied this last hour because of your dithering.' Thea ploughed on, somewhat relieved that Kirton House did indeed look deserted. The dust needed to settle, more internal locks and safeguards needed to be applied, before she was brave enough to weather another minute with him.

I'm an irritatingly persistent fellow.

Indeed he was—irritating in the extreme and so confident and cocky. His outrageous flirting on the terrace and her peculiar reaction to it were still too fresh in her mind. What sort of man mentioned kissing within a scant few hours of meeting a lady? Now she couldn't think about him without thinking about kissing him, which played havoc with her pulse. Clearly her body was as outraged as her sensibilities were. His utter cheek and overall lack of propriety were astounding, as was the way everyone dear to her seemed intent on matchmaking.

Matchmaking! With a man who had been so wicked he'd had to leave England in disgrace! They could matchmake all they wanted; nothing would convince her to be tempted by that smooth-talking scoundrel ever again.

I shall do my best to mine through to that soft kernel.

Where he would find she didn't have the feeble shell of the common or garden nut at all, but the tough, granite exterior of a castle. A castle whose battlements were protected by a hundred archers and fearsome-looking knights with vats of boiling oil which they would enjoy pouring on his annoying dark head the moment he had the audacity to attempt to breach the defences and find the real Thea locked in the dungeon beneath...

Dungeon? Since when had she thought about her life as a prison? Now there was an unsettling thought to add to the new and unnerving list of them.

'You're doing it again, you know. Talking to yourself.'

'I never said a word.'

'Maybe not out loud, but by the scrunched-up sourpuss expression and your nodding and shaking head, you were ranting inwardly to yourself. You really need to stop doing that, you know. It's very odd. If I stumbled across you and didn't know you to be a perfectly sane person by and large, I'd think you were a recently escaped inmate from Bedlam.'

Thea did not dignify the accusation with a response, lest it condemn her further, and instead plunged into the trees, ruminating on the idea that she felt trapped by the life she had created for herself. Dismissing it from her mind as humbug brought about by her own foolish lack of propriety with *him* on the terrace, she found the ideal spot—a small clearing around an enormous, ancient fallen trunk that was completely bathed in sunshine one end and sheltered by an umbrella of filigree leaves the other. It was also reassuringly surrounded by so many trees, nobody would see them if they happened to be striding arrogantly by. Not feeling particularly generous after being virtually forced into compliance, she left Harriet to wrestle with the easel and took herself to a patch of soft grass in the shade and dropped her bottom down. Resting her back against the gnarly old trunk, she opened her book decisively and decided to revel in one of life's simple and uncomplicated pleasures—a good, reassuring book.

It had taken months to track down a copy of *Pride and Prejudice* by the unnamed author of *Sense and Sensibility*. Having found none existed in Suffolk, she'd had to send to London for a copy. Already, just a few chapters in, she was backing the dashing Mr Wickham and saw a lot of herself in the feisty heroine Lizzie. A sensible young woman who didn't suffer fools or idle flattery gladly. Like Lizzie with the arrogant Mr Darcy, Thea would not waste another second thinking about *him*.

After five minutes of silence where she tried and failed to focus on the words, she sensed her friend watching her.

She looked up to find Harriet holding up her paintbrush like a proper artist and measuring her. 'I hope you don't mind, Thea dear, but I'm going to paint you. The muse has struck and I simply must listen.'

'The *muse*?' Her eccentric companion always thoroughly embraced each new hobby with over-the-top enthusiasm before discarding it like an old newspaper. 'You have a muse now?'

'A most insistent one.' Harriet waved her arms about her expansively, undeterred by Thea's dubious expression. 'This charming little clearing, the aged wood, the emerald grass...the butterflies dancing on the hazy pollen-filled air combined with your vivid, Celtic hair... Don't you see it?'

'See what?'

'The charming whimsy, of course! Why, it is reminiscent of the mythical Scottish faerie stories I adored as a child. The tableau is perfect...simply divine... Take your shoes off, darling. Faeries don't wear shoes.'

'Will it give me some peace if I do?'

'Most assuredly. I'm itching to get started. The light is magnificent.'

'Hallelujah.'

Harriet grinned and began rooting around in the undergrowth, returning with a handful of cheerful dandelions, white Queen Anne's Lace and some tangled ivy. 'For your crown,' she explained with mock solemnity. 'Every faerie has to have a floral coronet.' Thea suffered having the foliage poked into her hair, but scowled when she felt a pin removed, causing a fat corkscrew to fall over her eyes, reminding her she was fundamentally just as wayward as her hard-to-tame hair. She reached up to stop Harriet's interfering hands and withdrew as hers was impatiently swatted away. 'Allow me a few curls to feed the muse. I can hardly paint a Celtic riot of hair without something riotous to go on.'

'One pin.'

'Three.' As they were already sailing through the air into the bushes, it was pointless arguing, so she glared so fiercely that her friend stepped back with her palms raised before she dared pull out one more. 'I have enough hair… Lounge against the trunk again, Thea. Try to look wistful and magical as you read.'

Harriet scurried back behind her easel and the peace for Thea to enjoy Mr Wickham in his smart regimentals descended at last—although for some unknown and worrying reason, now Lord Gray's mischievous, disgraceful dark head was sat on top of the broad shoulders of her fictional hero. And his shoulders were broader, much broader, and his buff breeches tighter. Despite the unwelcome encroachment on her reading pleasure, she stubbornly persevered until Wickham and Lord Gray were interchangeable, one and the same. Distracting and enticing. And thoroughly naked once more.

It was most disconcerting.

Lord Fennimore shook his head and tucked his pocket watch back in his waistcoat while he watched Gray lead their mounts to the stable. 'Five hours on horseback! We must be missing something.' But it was highly unlikely they had. Shortly after dawn the King's Elite had set off en masse in search of water deep enough for smugglers to utilise that conveniently also ran directly to the sea. Every waterway which had seemed initially promising had tapered off inland, until eventually each group of agents had arrived at the prearranged meeting point in Leiston—the closest point on the Suffolk coast—with the same conclusion. Leiston *was* the closest significant body of water to Gislingham Hall. And it was two hours away.

Hardly the ideal distance between a committed, ruthless, prolific smuggler and the hundreds of barrels of illegal French brandy delivered daily on to English shores. 'Unless Gislingham is not our man at all. Which doesn't make sense, when we know he's involved.'

Their intelligence had been faultless thanks to the new Baroness of Penmor; so faultless that the French side of the operation was in tatters and several English traitors had already been charged before being ruthlessly murdered in gaol by The Boss's henchmen to ensure their silence.

If Gislingham was the mastermind of the whole operation, the geographic isolation of the Viscount's house combined with his obvious poor health had thrown a huge spoke in the wheels. The Boss relied on water and communication and ran a tight ship. While the Viscount clearly had all his marbles and only seemed to suffer from some physical disability, the set-up at the hall did not lend itself to the task.

Or perhaps it did. So well that nobody would ever suspect foul play. The odd and inconvenient location of his study, the loyal and constantly hovering manservant, that pointed, cold response to his niece when she reasonably suggested he would find life easier downstairs. *'I like my privacy, Thea.'* Fiercely liked it despite the obvious inconvenience it caused. The jovial, easy fellow had disappeared for a few seconds then, replaced by a calculated, stubborn man whose tone had brooked no argument. The odd look which passed between him and the manservant. There was something there. A dark secret. Gray was sure of it.

Another agent, posing as their groom, took the reins and led the horses away, leaving the pair of them to wander back to the house, stretching out their aching limbs.

'We were never going to find what we needed straight away.' Not when The Boss had run rings around them for two years. As much as Gray wanted a quick resolution, he knew it was also highly unlikely. Suffolk could well be their home for many months. A daunting prospect indeed when just a few days of Lord Fennimore was significantly trying his patience. 'This was always going to be a waiting game. Now that we have made the acquaintance we can build on it. Once his guard comes down we'll discover more. We've been here three days. I'll wager in three weeks Gislingham Hall will have given up more of its secrets. In three months...'

'Field work is so frustrating!'

'Which is why you don't usually do it, sir.' Although Gray didn't hold out any hope of the old man disappearing back to his desk in Mayfair any time soon. He wanted The Boss brought to justice more than any of them. Lord Fennimore had built the King's Elite from scratch and, despite his gruff exterior, felt every agent's death keenly. They had lost nineteen men in the last two years, nine of whom were slaughtered when they were ambushed at Penmor castle just seven weeks ago. Those losses were still raw. Many more had been injured, including Gray, the cracked bone and damaged muscles in his arm barely healed. This mission was intensely personal for both of them. 'If it's any consolation, I think Gislingham likes us.'

'He likes you well enough and seemed to like you all the more once I apprised him of some of your dubious past. That is a good sign.' The Viscount had found the younger Gray's exploits entertaining. Unlike his niece, who hadn't bothered trying to disguise her wholehearted disapproval.

'Not if you want me to seduce Miss Cranford at some point in the future.' Where had that come from? At no point had a seduction even been tabled, let alone sanctioned.

Old Fennimore's bushy eyebrows disappeared into his hair as he glared. 'I categorically forbid you to seduce Miss Cranford! Or his obviously willing wife for that matter. Both ladies must be our last resort. Especially now that we have made such a good impression on Gislingham. The man might find you amusing and might well see you as some sort of kindred spirit, which is excellent, but I can assure you that will soon stop the moment you make a play for one of his womenfolk.'

'I wasn't going to seduce Miss Cranford.' Which was a crying shame because he sincerely wanted to. He couldn't get her and her tart mouth out of his mind. 'I was merely pointing out that if you over-egg my scandalous past then it will put her off me for the future—should a seduction be required.' And Gray was an optimist at heart. If the need arose, he would happily seduce her, for King, country and himself. It might get his unusual, tenacious fascination with the woman out of his system where she had apparently taken root. 'Besides, it would be foolhardy to completely alienate a potentially fertile source of information.' Or have her hate him. That would be awful after their splendid flirting and after he had spent all last night and the one before dreaming about her. 'I can be very charming and very persuasive. Who knows more about the Viscount's comings and goings, save his wife, than his only niece? They are obviously devoted to one another.'

'That is a good point.' By the look on his face, one his superior had not considered. 'You are correct. The seeds are sown. Gislingham can make his own enquiries henceforth if he's a mind to, but I shall cease scaring off Miss Cranford. Just in case. We run the risk of over-gilding the lily and we can't afford to burn all our bridges so early in the game. Befriend the girl. Earn her confidence—but do not touch.'

Gray opened his mouth to speak, then promptly shut it. There was no point questioning why his curmudgeonly superior had agreed with him, as he would only take it back and spoil the victory. The important thing was he *had* agreed with him. A momentous occurrence in itself. He would take it as a step in the right direction and keep his sarcastic, disbelieving but incredibly witty retort to himself.

'It makes sense for you to be cordial to Miss Cranford and try to pick her brains, although after seeing her reaction to you, her uncle is right. You will have your work cut out. She was heartily unimpressed with you.'

That stung. Lord Fennimore's laughter stung more. 'No, she wasn't. I thought she enjoyed my flirting.'

'She loathed it, dear boy. Her face was an absolute picture of disgust.' He was still chuckling, totally unaware how much his words bothered Gray. 'But while it is vastly entertaining to watch, such things have a tendency to grate after a while. Avoid any and all flirting until you have improved her low opinion of you. From this point, until further notice, you are to be a complete gentleman around her and save the scoundrel for her uncle.'

Any and all flirting! That blow stung the most of all, despite him seeing the sense in it. For the sake of the mission, the promotion and his constant endeavour to be a better spy, Gray would reluctantly comply. Even if it royally spoiled his mood.

As they turned on to the path towards the house, he spotted a black head appearing and disappearing in the window. Trefor was bouncing up and down to get a better view of his master's arrival, pink tongue lolling, big ears flapping with excitement. Gray might well be a constant source of disappointment to his superior most of the time, his family all of the time, but at least Trefor was always pleased to see him.

'That dog is quite mad.'

'The poor thing has been cooped up inside for hours. I'm going to take him for a walk. I could do with one myself.' The truth. His neck was aching and his spine and leg muscles were constricted. 'Five hours sat on the back of a horse has made me as stiff as a board.' And five hours of listening to Lord Fennimore was grinding on his nerves. There was only so much bluster a man could take before he bit back.

As soon as they opened the door, Trefor shot out like a bullet, his brown eyes pleading and expectant, the tantalising message in them clear. It was a beautiful summer's day. Too beautiful to waste it all on work, and Gray needed some space. Something that was blessedly plentiful here in the middle of nowhere. Living cheek by jowl with a staid perfectionist reminded him too much of living with his humourless father. It was a lot like wearing a collar too tight. Initially bearable, but so damned constricting soon after that you wanted to ruthlessly tug it off. They had done all the spying they could for one day and the balmy evening of freedom beckoned. Like his former home, this beautiful countryside was perfect to disappear in and roam around. 'Come on, boy!' He and his hound could explore the endless horizon for hours. Throw and catch sticks. Sniff the air. Enjoy. Breathe. Live in the moment...

'I'll come with you.' In one fell swoop, his lovely walk and dream of a pleasant evening was spoiled, too. Capital.

Chapter Seven

'Must he chase butterflies?'

Gray's fist tightened around the stick he was carrying, snapping it in two. 'He's a dog. They chase things.'

'Not if you trained him properly he wouldn't. A good hunting dog walks obediently next to his master, awaiting his command; he doesn't run off and chase insects or bark at sheep or spend an eternity sniffing one patch of grass.'

Oblivious to the litany of criticism, Trefor's black nose was now glued to the ground as he found the scent of something which took his fancy and followed it intently. He did that a lot and it was something Gray had often wondered if humans could exploit. In the same way packs of hunting dogs chased a fox or located whichever unfortunate bird their owner happened to shoot for fun rather than food, perhaps good sniffers like Trefor could be used to hunt down other things which the less sensitive human nose could not. Like barrels of illegal brandy, perhaps? Or gunpowder or criminals? The heady, intoxicating perfume favoured by beautiful redheads...

'Now what is he doing?'

'He's tracking something.' At speed, apparently. His wagging black tail disappeared into some bushes before popping out again as the dog found a better route to whatever it was he was seeking with great urgency. Because Gray couldn't be bothered to listen to Lord Fennimore any longer, or trust himself not to bark at the man for being such a moaning old windbag, he picked up his pace and jogged after the dog into the trees, then smiled when he saw what it was Trefor was clearly hunting.

Jasmine.

Miss Cranford, hair down and feet bare, was draped across the top of the trunk of an enormous felled oak, propped on one pale elbow reading while Lady Crudgington painted. They turned simultaneously at Trefor's delighted bark.

'Good day to you, ladies.'

In her scramble to get off the log quickly, her skirts caught momentarily on the stray nub of a branch, giving him a tantalising glimpse of knee before she pulled them back in place, looking mortified at being caught being less than proper once again.

'Lord Gray! How delightful!' Lady Crudgington was the only woman present who appeared happy to see him. Miss Cranford's smile was polite. Forced. But she was blushing again as she stuffed one foot in the slipper Trefor had not picked up in his mouth. She made a half-hearted attempt to salvage the other one from his jaws, then quickly stopped herself, attempting to stand with all the decorum of a genteel young lady regardless of the lack of one shoe and a head full of weeds. That, combined with the wild tendrils of hair which she was desperately trying to stuff back into her chignon, made her lack of an exuberant welcome understandable—and ripe for some sport. Correct appearances were important to her. Just as Lady Crudgington had said, Miss Cranford was a little too buttoned up.

'We have a habit of meeting when you least want us to, Miss Cranford. Fear not, I only saw half of one scandalously pretty bare leg—but I shan't tell a soul about your impropriety.' Because he knew it would vex her, he winked as he tapped the side of his nose and laughed as she tried to think of a suitable way to put him in his place in front of her friend. Already, he knew she was more polite in front of others and more her tart self when alone with him. He rather liked that.

'A true gentleman wouldn't have mentioned it.' Despite her snooty expression, one hand had already found its way to Trefor's ear as he danced at her feet in adoring circles, that slipper still tightly clenched in his mouth.

'But a true gentleman would have looked his fill, too, Miss Cranford. Be in no doubt of that. I am simply more honest than most and, in my defence, it was a very fine example of a leg.' At the sound of a twig cracking beneath Lord Fennimore's obstinate boot behind him in the trees, and mindful that he was under strict orders not to be flirting with her at all, he rapidly changed the subject to avoid the obligatory lecture. 'We were walking across the meadow, minding our own business, when Trefor scented you. After that there was no stopping him. The mutt seems to be irresistibly drawn to you, Miss Cranford.' Exactly like his master. He wouldn't mind being caressed by those elegant, pale hands either. 'I think he likes your perfume.'

To prove his love, Trefor threw himself on the ground and flipped over, his eyes rolling back in his head as she bent down to tickle his tummy. Gravity allowed the loose tendrils to escape again and they crackled copper in the sun's waning rays to torment him. He enjoyed the sight for a scant few seconds before his superior found them all in the clearing and he had to behave himself. 'And here is

Cedric now.' Fortunately, too late to hear Gray's teasing banter with the young woman he had been expressly forbidden from wooing—the one frantically tugging wildflowers from her hair. 'I'm sure I speak for both of us when I say we apologise for interrupting whatever it was we interrupted.'

'You are not interrupting at all.' Lady Crudgington beamed at the old man, who blinked a little awkwardly, then miraculously smiled back. At least Gray assumed it was a smile. As he had never seen one and they had been bouncing around on horseback all day, it could just as easily be a spot of wind. 'We were just finishing up. I've been painting Thea as a faerie. Come and look, gentlemen—and give me your honest opinion.'

Dutifully they both stepped forward and gazed at the picture. The garish daub was barely comprehensible. He assumed the brown splodge was the tree trunk and the orange explosion in the middle to be Miss Cranford's hair, but aside from that it had neither shape nor form. 'What a rare talent you have, Lady Crudgington.' Gray's eyes sought and found Miss Cranford's, which had lifted. Hers were suddenly filled with mirth at his diplomatic choice of words. 'This work positively screams summer. Doesn't it, *Cedric*?'

'Er…yes. Summer and faeries.'

'Painting is Harriet's newest hobby,' said Miss Cranford, uncharacteristically deadpan. 'Would you believe that a sennight ago she had never before picked up a brush?'

'No! *Really?*' That she had used one at all came as a surprise when the paint appeared to be slapped on with the leafy end of a carrot. 'Then I am doubly impressed.' To stop the laugh escaping, Gray tapped his fingers to his lips, making sure his thumb wedged up his jawbone to prevent it bursting open, while imagining all sorts of sad things to conquer the urge.

'As…am…I.' Lord Fennimore's staccato response was almost his undoing, but he rallied manfully before Lady Crudgington put him out of his misery.

'You lie more convincingly than your cousin, Lord Gray, and heaven only knows I appreciate the sentiment, but we both know it's a travesty. Before you arrived, I attempted to soften the harshness of the lines with a wash, but applied too much and now it is ruined.'

'Not that it was much better before she applied the water.' Miss Cranford was giggling. It was a luscious, earthy, naughty sound that immediately conjured images of rumpled sheets and lazy, cosy mornings. Not at all the subdued and tempered laughter of a prim and proper miss—the sound travelled straight to his groin.

'True. Another shocking disaster in my quest to become a grand master. But it was worth all the wasted effort to watch you two handsome gentlemen attempt to spare my feelings so inarticulately. That was priceless.' Her hands went to her hips and she smiled. 'Now that you are here, you might as well make yourselves useful and help me carry my equipment back to the house. We have dallied long enough on our quest not to be bored senseless by Suffolk, but I promised Thea I would keep her company at one of Edward's dreadfully dull business dinners and we must head back to change.'

Lord Fennimore stepped forward and was soon press-ganged into putting away cakes of paint and folding the easel, leaving Gray with nothing better to do than retrieve Miss Cranford's slightly soggy shoe from his dog's mouth. He passed it to her and she sat on the trunk again to put it on. When she had finished, he held out his hand to help her up and she took it, and the impact that tiny, innocent touch had on his body was as unexpected as it was pleasant. He felt her everywhere, head to toe, the tips of his fingers tingling and itching to tug her into his arms and tangle in her hair.

If she felt it, too, she did a very good job of hiding it and showed no desire to continue holding it once she was upright again. If she had tugged her hand away quickly, he might have thought she was bothered, but she didn't. If anything, she disentangled herself absently while brushing the dust from her dress, then, retrieving her book from the tree trunk where she had discarded it, she hugged it to her body. 'Isn't the weather lovely?'

'Oh, dear. I have been relegated to small talk. That is not a very good sign.'

'I am trying to be polite, my lord.'

'No you're not. You are trying to minimise our connection to one of indifferent acquaintances when you are fully aware I am not the least bit indifferent to you and I suspect you are not the least bit indifferent to me.' Gray had dropped his voice to prevent his superior catching him doing exactly what he knew he shouldn't be—but being a good spy when she was so close and so beautiful it made his heart ache was practically impossible.

She glanced down at the book in her hands and made a great show of reading the gold-embossed lettering on the spine. 'I am not the slightest bit interested in flirting with you, my lord, so please desist.'

'Dear me… Icy politeness, too.' He stepped forward and looked around her. Lord Fennimore was distracted and going pink as he fought with the easel. 'What happened to the fiery, tart redhead I met on the terrace? The one who blows raspberries and gives as good as she gets.'

'You caught me at a bad moment, my lord, and I temporarily forgot myself.'

'I liked her. I should like to get to know *her* better.'

'If you are going to continue to flirt, I shall have to terminate this conversation, my lord.'

Aloofness. She did that very well when she had a mind to—but he had always enjoyed a challenge. 'All right, no flirting. But, I beg you, no small talk either.' Gray smiled and rapidly changed tack. 'A business dinner? That does sound dull.' It threw her and she blinked, but quickly rallied, clearly relieved the uncomfortable subject had been sidestepped.

'My uncle finds it difficult travelling into town to manage his affairs, so once a month his banker and solicitor travel down. They arrived this afternoon, so should be long done with most of the dull stuff, but sometimes the conversations continue over dinner.'

'Very dull, then?'

She smiled, her shoulders and spine relaxing a little. 'Yes, very. Unless you find talk of investments riveting.'

He yawned. 'Does your uncle have extensive investments?'

'Not extensive. He prefers to invest in what he knows.' She blinked as she regarded him, as if that was explanation enough. Or she was mindful that she had already said too much.

'Are you purposefully being cryptic or is it a secret? Something dark and mysterious, perhaps?' Was she involved? Complicit in her uncle's crimes? As soon as the thought popped into his head he dismissed it. His gut told him no and he trusted his instincts.

'Nothing so exciting, I'm afraid, else I wouldn't need Harriet to save me. Uncle Edward invests in imports and exports. Years ago, he lent money to a friend starting such a business and discovered he had a talent for it, too. Since then he has always dabbled.'

Imports and exports. Smuggled brandy in exchange

for English guns? Too coincidental to ignore. 'I should imagine Lady Crudgington is a godsend at such events.'

'Indeed she is. Men of business are prone to be serious and, as Harriet rarely is, she is an excellent diversion.'

'Much like me. I pride myself on being an excellent diversion. As your new and most neighbourly neighbour, I'd be happy to come, too—to help alleviate some of your boredom. My dour cousin and I have no dinner plans for this evening.'

'You are very bold, sir, to invite yourself to dinner.'

'I am that, Miss Cranford. Bold and diverting and very, very hungry.'

'Is there no food at Kirton House?' That sparring twinkle in her eye was returning, telling him she was not as politely indifferent as she would have him believe, nor as buttoned-up as she wanted to be. It cheered him immensely despite the fact that a dedicated spy would stalwartly resist the overwhelming urge to flirt with her when the advancement of his career hung in the balance and they had one very dangerous criminal to catch. Perhaps he wasn't that dedicated? Or more likely, promotion or no promotion, the wild streak in him that always took advantage of the moment ran too deep to be tamed so easily.

He leaned closer, far closer than was necessary, and treated his nostrils to her unique, inviting scent. 'There is. But the company leaves a lot to be desired.' Her gaze followed his to where Lord Fennimore was glaring at his dog. 'Pity a poor neighbour and give him something lovely to stare at across the dinner table just this once. I'm sure your uncle won't mind extra guests and you would be bestowing an act of gratefully received charity on a very worthy recipient. Aside from Lord Grump Weasel over there, I don't know another soul in Suffolk. I get lonely...'

'Ah—I see. Because of absolutely nothing to do with me, I should pity you *and* suffer you again at dinner to-night?'

At that, Lady Crudgington turned around and beamed. It was too well timed, so very innocent, he would bet good money she had been shamelessly eavesdropping the whole time. 'Are Lord Gray and Lord Fennimore also joining us, Thea?' She seemed delighted at the prospect and he was quietly confident Gislingham's niece would be too polite to rescind the invitation in front of Lord Fennimore, who was also smiling, clearly impressed with his subordinate's canny opportunism while oblivious to the shameless flirting that had led to it. 'How positively splendid! And there I was trying to figure out a way to get to know our new neighbours better.' Lady Crudgington rammed the easel into Gray's chest unceremoniously and wound her arm possessively through his superior's arm. 'You must sit next to me tonight, Lord Fennimore. I have a million burning questions...'

Chapter Eight

Against her better judgement, the emerald silk she had been too reticent to wear had beckoned and, before she could think better of it, Impetuous Thea had put it on. Now, waiting for the arrival of their unwelcome dinner guests after a mind-shattering report of the current state of her ever-increasing finances with the solicitor, she was supremely conscious of the bold gown's low neckline and tightly fitting bodice. It was a gown which displayed her figure to the very best effect without the need for folding her arms at all. A gown that had sat in her wardrobe for almost a year for that very reason. She should have sent the dratted thing back and insisted the modiste attach some shielding trim the moment it had arrived last summer, because now she was purposefully wearing it. For him!

If the abundant display of cleavage wasn't enough, she also had butterflies in her stomach which simply refused to fly away no matter how much she tried to distract herself from thinking about them. 'Would you like more wine, Mr Rendell?' Being the perfect hostess gave her something to do.

'I'll have some.' Harriet held out her glass. 'And if you don't mind me saying, Thea darling, you look like you could do with some, too.' Her friend shared a conspiratorial look with her uncle before dropping her voice to a whisper. 'Might help calm those nerves.'

She didn't dignify such an outrageous—and entirely correct—assumption with a response and snatched the proffered glasses away to refill them. Despite thoroughly enjoying the odd tipple, Thea had purposely eschewed all alcohol thus far this evening because of him, too. The last thing she wanted was the heady wine lowering her inhibitions and releasing Impetuous Thea into the wild, when she clearly was in dire need of all of them if this inappropriate dress was any indication. With a little wine in her system, she was prone to be more vocal with her opinions and the suppressed rebellious and wilful aspects of her character came to the fore. Aspects which were only too ready to jump to the fore with him when no alcohol whatsoever was involved.

She was pouring when she heard him arrive in the hallway and found her hand quiver a little at the prospect. Good gracious, she *was* nervous. Nervous and excited and decidedly off-kilter. To give it something to do other than flutter, she poured a third glass, gripped it with both hands and feigned nonchalance, her back to the door while she awaited the butler to announce him.

'Lord Fennimore and Lord Graham Chadwick, my lord.'

Despite the instant awareness, Thea turned slowly, the politest of indifferent smiles pasted on her face, just in time to watch him stride into the room looking quite something in his evening clothes. The deep red silk waistcoat and its matching fat ruby stickpin might have been a garish choice on someone else, someone less cocky and confident and intrinsically disgraceful, but he effortlessly carried it off.

'My Lord Gislingham.' He inclined his head towards her uncle, then turned his gaze to hers. She watched his eyes widen slightly, then heat, making absolutely no attempt to hide his pleasure at what he was seeing. She felt the warmth of it all the way through her shockingly inappropriate dress, straight through the gauzy linen shift she also never usually dared to wear, to the scandalously cut corset Harriet had bought for her last birthday—the one which maximised her décolleté in the most inappropriate way.

'Miss Cranford. I am delighted to see you.' Because of course, he could see rather a lot of her. Her tightly trussed bosoms were positively heaving beneath her chin now that he was here and those wolf-like eyes were gazing at her so intently. 'You look beautiful tonight.' He meant it. She could see it as plain as the perfectly straight nose on his handsome face and that knowledge did odd things to her pulse.

Her uncle inadvertently saved her from stuttering something inane and nonsensical in reply by immediately introducing him to Mr Rendell, the solicitor, and Mr Squires, his private banker. As Thea went to war to control her rampant nerves and flighty body, she took a big gulp of the wine in her glass before she became aware of Harriet grinning at her. Bravado had her feigning a yawn of boredom and sipping even more wine, before she sailed across the room to greet Lord Fennimore as if his cousin had ceased to exist.

It was then that Aunt Caro decided to grace them with her presence, making a beeline for the wickedly rugged and irritatingly confident Lord Gray and attaching herself to him for the rest of the pre-dinner drinks like a limpet. As she had previously excused herself from the dinner pleading disinterest, as she did nearly every social occasion which didn't involve her cronies, Thea could only assume that her aunt had had a rapid about-face the second she learned their flirtatious new neighbour had arrived. Husband and wife usually avoided each other like the plague and Aunt Caro had her own dining room down the hall. One that was never short of an irritating sycophant or three which she hoped might make her husband jealous.

However, Thea couldn't really judge her. Uncle Edward was no better a husband than Caro was a wife. Half the time he treated her with barely contained hostility, the rest of the time he pretended she didn't exist—as he clearly was determined to do tonight. Rudely, he did not even cast her a withering glance as she sailed into the room. They were an odd partnership, one Thea had long ago given up trying to understand but was determined never to replicate. Marry for love, Uncle Edward often cautioned. Settle for nothing but the deepest and all-encompassing kind. Hard to do when every man she knew came with a desire for a veritable mountain of coin.

The next two hours were painful. Not because the conversation was stilted, because it wasn't. Her uncle had always been a lively dinner companion, Harriet was her customary entertaining self and Lord Gray certainly held up his end. He was quite the raconteur, it turned out, delighting everyone with his outrageous stories of faraway places and exotic, colourful people. Even her aunt was on good form, no doubt because of their scintillating new guest, and the formal room was filled with lively debate and much laughter.

It was Thea's own conversation that was stilted to the point of non-existence. No matter how much she racked her brains for a witty retort or an interesting sentence to contribute to the proceedings, nothing came, and to cover the lack of things coming out of her mouth she put far too much in it. Wine mostly, but there had been a second helping of trifle which her tight corset was now bitterly regretting. She was so stuffed it was a wonder the laces had not popped under the strain caused by her unladylike gluttony and her scandalously upward-thrusting bosoms.

Lord Gray did not seem similarly afflicted despite his second helpings and seemed vastly amused by her rigidly upright posture and pained expression. She had just spotted the wretch smiling behind his napkin when he caught her subtly trying to adjust a particularly jabbing stay when she had assumed nobody was looking. Except he was. Drat him.

Constantly.

To his credit, and no doubt just to vex her, he skilfully avoided Aunt Caro's blatant flirting without appearing the slightest bit rude or uncomfortable with it, which might have earned him points in his favour had he not persisted in locking eyes with Thea repeatedly and allowing her to see the mischievous passion for her dancing in them unabashed. He flirted with her, too. More than once, but so subtly and swiftly that if you blinked you'd miss it. None of the other guests appeared to notice, but she didn't miss it. How could she when he had positioned himself in the seat directly opposite hers? Her own fault for not sticking to the correct rules of etiquette and failing to label the place settings.

Twice, thanks to his excessively long legs, his booted foot had found her slipper. The first time she had withdrawn her foot like a frightened deer. The second, and she was going to blame the wine entirely for unleashing the wanton within, she had allowed it to linger next to hers until common sense returned and she kicked him hard in the shin. He covered the pain well, but he'd almost choked on a boiled potato in the process. It was Thea's lone successful moment in a meal devoid of any and she blamed his presence entirely for that, too.

'Shall we enjoy our port over a game of billiards?' Her uncle seemed buoyed by the excellent company. 'I'm rather good if I sit in a chair to pot and you'll forgive me certain liberties.'

'A splendid idea!' Lord Fennimore had already started to rise.

'Surely all the gentleman aren't going to abandon us for a silly game?' Aunt Caro's eyes were fixed on Lord Gray as she said this, but he didn't appear to notice.

'I'm only playing if there is money involved.' He stood, his big body unfolding from the chair and suddenly looming in front of Thea. Goodness, he was tall. She had noticed it before, of course, just as she had noticed practically every minute detail about his impressive physique, but never from this angle. He noticed her looking and, to hide it, she glugged more wine, hoping the glass would prevent her from seeing his cocksure look—but the glass magnified it and that, and the additional wine, made her head spin.

'Oh, there is always money involved, young man,' said her uncle with a heartening twinkle in his eye, 'and although I like you a great deal, do not think for a second I shan't enjoy relieving you of some of it. Once I've trounced you at billiards I shall give you a thorough drubbing at cards. I like to win, Lord Gray.'

That he did. Always had and, since his stroke, tiny victories in parlour games or on the stock market made him feel less redundant and more like his old self. She tried not to judge him for it, realising it must be a massive blow to one's self-esteem to not be as robust as before—

but sometimes he went too far and outright cheated. He was a charming cheat, but shameless. Winning was now everything, by whatever means he deemed necessary. His poor sportsmanship the previous Christmas over a spirited game of Speculation had been so blatant and outrageous, Thea had almost allowed herself to lose her temper with him again before Bertie interceded and poured oil on very troubled waters. But she now actively avoided playing any sort of game with him just in case she succumbed and did lose it. That said, it wouldn't hurt for Lord Gray to be thoroughly drubbed. He was far too sure of himself.

'Challenge accepted, my lord. I hope you don't expect any leniency from me.'

'Leniency! By Jove, you'll be begging for mercy by midnight, dear boy. Mark my words.'

'Well, if you gentlemen are intent on making a night of it, I shall bid you a good one,' said Harriet, rising. 'I want to get up early to paint the sunrise.' The Judas wasn't fond of Aunt Caro's penchant for superficial gossip and her constant need for reassurance. Her aunt feared ageing above all else and discussed it at great length, while Harriet totally embraced it. She was sensibly abandoning ship while she still could. She caught the butler in a vice-like grip. 'Have my carriage brought around immediately.'

In a flurry of activity, the gentlemen and her friend left, leaving Thea sat with just her aunt at the big formal table. 'Shall I order some tea?' It was a half-hearted invitation. Her aunt was well meaning, but hard work. More so than usual with every passing year, although Thea had no idea why. Caro's maid had told Thea's maid it was because she was on the change and her courses were about to stop. This, apparently, made her more fragile.

Something Harriet dismissed as pure self-indulgence, but then Harriet was made of sterner stuff than her poor aunt and she had had children. Both her sons were now grown and had flown the nest while poor Caro's womb had remained barren, largely because Uncle Edward had not set foot in his wife's bedchamber in years. Callous, self-serving, unfeeling witches, he was often prone to say when the port flowed freely, were not at all his type.

'Yes, dear, it has been ages since it's been just the two of us without your uncle dominating your time. I've missed our little chats. Let's take it in my sitting room.'

Splendid. Another hour of interminable torture beckoned. The idle gossip of a very bored woman who filled her days with visits and luncheons held minimal appeal, not when Thea's silly pulse would undoubtedly quicken at the prospect of *him* a few feet away down the hall. Stripped of his coat as gentlemen playing billiards were prone to do, those muscles in his arms and back would bunch as he gripped the cue, the fabric of his breeches pulled taut over his equally taut buttocks as he leaned over the table to take the shot...

Good gracious! Would she ever get the image of his naked body out of her mind?

With heavy feet and a slightly spinning head, Thea followed her aunt. Then the pair sat like bookends at either end of the uncomfortable damask sofa. Aunt Caro always favoured this room to receive her visitors, although heaven only knew why. Probably because her husband avoided it. It was west facing, which meant it caught the full heat of the sun from mid-afternoon through to evening, making it stuffy by the end of the day. The opulent Venetian chandelier was burning brightly, adding to the oppressive temperature, and all the windows were firmly shut because of Caro's hay fever. Like dogs, flowers made her sneeze so all the arrangements in the rooms she preferred to use were silk and needed constant dusting. Their bright, fake petals always depressed Thea because they reminded her too much of her poor aunt. Desperate to be as adored as all the other flowers, but lacking in something elusive and special as each day passed. Ground down by Uncle Edward's determined indifference.

'Lord Gray seems taken with you.'

'Is he? I hadn't noticed.' Now even her aunt was matchmaking! Inevitable, she supposed, but irritating. The one thing her aunt never did was attempt to foist her off on a man. Until today, it seemed.

'You would have to be blind not to notice, Thea, dear. He barely took his eyes off you all night.'

'I have no interest in Lord Gray.' But her skin warmed regardless, simply by thinking of him.

'I am pleased to hear it.' Thea had not been expecting that.

'Why?'

Her aunt frowned as she sipped her tea. 'While he is a charming dinner companion, exceedingly handsome and a delightful gentleman for any woman to play the flirt with, I have to confess I made some discreet enquiries into his background and was shocked by what I found.' Not shocked enough not to want to flirt with him herself, though, Thea thought ungraciously before she chided herself for the reaction. It was petty to criticise her aunt when she herself had severe doubts about Lord Gray and had still happily succumbed to flirting with the charming wretch.

'Lord Fennimore has already apprised us of his long tenure in the merchant navy after his family disowned him.' For some reason, she didn't want her aunt to have the satisfaction of putting her off the man. 'I had already decided he was a thoroughly bad sort within a few hours of meeting him, but Uncle Edward seems to like him.'

'Edward has always been attracted to naughty boys. He is too easily led astray.'

Pots and kettles. Both as bad as one another while Thea tried to navigate the murky chasm called their marriage. 'Uncle likes interesting company and, despite his dubious background, one cannot deny Lord Gray is interesting.' Thanks to the wine, perhaps more interesting presently than he had any rights being. Images of him in the brook *sans* his shirt kept dropping into her mind willy-nilly, as they had done all night. After her fourth glass of wine, and in the absence of any suitable conversation to delight their guests with, Thea had given up trying to ignore the errant thoughts and had decided to enjoy them for the duration of the meal, but made a mental note to limit herself to one glass at dinner going forward until her obsession waned.

'But under the circumstances, he shouldn't be *gambling* with the man.'

'I don't see any harm in it. Bertie will step in if Uncle Edward overtaxes himself.' They paused while the tea was brought in and Aunt Caro poured.

'I wasn't talking about your uncle's health, dearest, more our new neighbour's penchant for reckless wagers. When I said I had made discreet enquiries, I was thoroughly shocked by what I discovered over luncheon with Lady Horndon yesterday.' She picked up her cup and stared over it, quite pained. 'Lord Gray was disowned by his family *after* he lost his entire fortune at the gaming tables! And it was a sizeable fortune, be in no doubt. He remains, to this day, both shunned *and*, to the best of everyone's knowledge, penniless. I doubt the merchant navy is *that* lucrative. While I am reassured that you seem immune to his charms—and we both know heiresses do attract shameless fortune hunters—I hope he doesn't see your uncle as a means to an end either. Will Bertie have the wherewithal to step in if Lord Gray takes advantage of *him*, I wonder?'

Thea felt sick. So sick the trifle threatened to make a reappearance. Up until that moment, she had not considered Lord Gray as a fortune hunter when she normally considered every man in possession of a pulse as one as a matter of course. A shameless flirt, yes. A bad influence, definitely. But he didn't outwardly seem like a man who only saw her money. Not when those unusual silvery eyes darkened with blatant desire every single time their gazes locked...

What on earth was the matter with her? He had to be a vulture, too. It certainly explained his single-minded preoccupation with her instead of her attractive, flighty and easily seduced aunt. The unpalatable truth jarred, but couldn't be denied. She knew only too well that a fortune hunter could feign whatever emotion he so desired to part an unsuspecting heiress from her money. But attempting to seduce an heiress aside, was he truly such a man to stoop so low as to take advantage of an invalid? 'He wouldn't? Surely?'

'We barely know the man.' The truth. 'Yet he now has a seat at the table after a scandalously short acquaintance. And the gossip was bad enough to have made its way here to Suffolk where it had remained fixed in people's minds for a decade and could easily recall it when I happened to mention his name. All I know is he has lost a fortune, yet dresses like a man in possession of one.' Another good point. That beautifully tailored red silk waistcoat positively oozed class. 'Where does he get his money from?'

'Perhaps Lord Fennimore is subsidising him?' Thea

wasn't entirely sure how she felt about that either. A man of Lord Gray's age should be supporting himself, not living off an elderly relative. Or anyone else for that matter.

'Perhaps...but did you see his ruby stickpin? Jewels of that size do not come cheap.' Something a dedicated shopper like Aunt Caro would know. Aside from idle gossip and a diary filled with luncheons, the only other thing that woman did was shop.

Chapter Nine

To say the Viscount swindled him out of ten pounds would be unfair because it hadn't been a swindling in the strictest sense. However, Gislingham's unlikely victory at billiards had certainly come about with the use of some foul means peppered among the fair, which he made no attempt to hide. The weaker arm and leg caused him to lean extensively on the table, where the sleeve of his shirt, his wrist and on one occasion his elbow nudged the balls in directions which favoured him, but hampered Gray. At worst, it had been a good-natured, unsubtle, comical and vastly entertaining bit of knavery. All done with a charming smile and a wink. He was either an out-and-out cheat or the cheating was a test to see if Gray was brave enough to call him on it. He hadn't, but despite being ten pounds lighter in the pocket, he'd left the table liking the man. A great deal more than he should.

Now Lord Fennimore was being treated to a dose of the same warped rules and the same boisterous camaraderie. If Gislingham hadn't been one of England's most wanted criminals, he was exactly the sort of fellow you would want for a friend. Funny. Loud. The sort of man who drags you into his outrageous antics and makes you very glad to be there. No wonder he was so good at what he did. The charmer and the murderer. He was a dangerous contradiction indeed. Not that Gray had learned anything remotely useful over dinner. Despite his niece's claims to the contrary, the Viscount and his cronies had let nothing slip over the dining table or the billiard table, despite old Fennimore's subtle questions.

To see his superior in the field was also interesting. He must have been a canny spy in his day, for already he and the cheating Viscount were as thick as thieves, backslapping and laughing like old friends. While Lord Fennimore was keeping him occupied, Gray decided it was probably a good time to visit the retiring room via a meandering poke around the ground floor.

Fortunately, this late, much of the house was quiet and dark. One lone footman sat snoozing near the front door and somebody was in the kitchen in case they were summoned to feed or water the guests. Everyone else appeared to have turned in for the night aside from Gislingham's quiet manservant, who had been downstairs several times to check on his master and encourage him, unsuccessfully, to get some sleep before reluctantly leaving with a reminder that he would be back soon. That made venturing up to their host's private apartments nigh on impossible.

Instead, he methodically worked his way around the downstairs rooms, consigning their position and layout to memory as he went. Like the dining room, each room he entered was formal and dressed to impress. Persian rugs, ormolu clocks, bold damask sofas which looked pretty but were not really made for men to sit on, huge urns stuffed full of silk flowers and peacock feathers. This was very much the public face of country aristocracy who were conscious of their place in the social pecking order and keen to make the right sort of impression. Form and fashion over function, like his father's house in Wales. Nothing at all like the informality of the Viscount's private sitting room. Another contradiction.

There was a neat, feminine study with a dainty mahogany escritoire near the window. It was unlocked so, like a good spy, he carefully rifled through it, but found nothing but notepaper, quills and inks. On the opposite wall, illuminated by the moonlight, was a flattering portrait of the Viscountess from her youth, hair down and smiling winsomely in a garden. As there were no other family pictures anywhere to be seen, he came to the conclusion this room was hers, although it had the air of a space rarely used.

The next room seemed to have no purpose other than to be a place to house a harp. By the looks of it, it had never been played. Another small parlour looked to be a receiving room of some sort. A third room served as a second library, although why they needed another when the one down the hall was twice the size he had no idea. Perhaps they were big on reading here at Gislingham House? As Miss Cranford had said, there were plenty of places downstairs to accommodate the Viscount's lack of mobility, all more convenient than the rooms he favoured out of the way.

Curious. Although significantly less private.

Across from the dining room was the drawing room they had gathered in before dinner. He already knew that room well. The door was ajar and one lamp glowed softly on the mantel. He would have walked straight past it had the lace at the French windows not been billowing slightly. Either a servant had forgotten to lock them, or someone was in the garden. He had a very clear idea of which someone he hoped it would be. Like a man lured to the rocks by the sirens, he soon found himself peeking out of the French doors and he wasn't disappointed.

Miss Cranford was stood at the stone balustrade on the terrace, staring out at the stars, the moon casting her in an ethereal silhouette. A few tendrils of her heavy hair had, typically, broken free and caught on the breeze. The same breeze moulded the fabric of her gown to one side of her body. The exact same gown which had haunted his thoughts since he had first seen her in it earlier and which had fair taken his breath away for most of the evening. More than once he had allowed himself to imagine what it would be like to peel her slowly out of it. Unpin her heavy hair and let it fall over the pert breasts that had taunted him as he had tried to be a good guest and failed to be a better spy.

In no hurry to stop staring, he lounged against the frame and looked his fill. She sensed him. Her head whipped around, her lush mouth momentarily slack. 'Lord Gray!'

'We've been over this. It's just Gray… Thea.'

'It is Miss Cranford, my lord, as well you know. And I shall remain Miss Cranford to you till the end of time.'

'As you wish.' Although he fully intended to always call her Thea from this moment on. It felt right on his tongue. 'I thought you had long gone to bed.'

'I wasn't tired.' Without thinking, Thea put her hands to her hair and began to tuck the errant strands back in their proper place. She did that a lot, he realised, as if she was embarrassed by her hair. Although why a woman with such exquisite tresses would be embarrassed by them was a mystery to him. 'After the stuffiness of the drawing room and the big meal, I needed some fresh air.'

'Too much trifle does that to a person. How many bowls did you have? Three?'

'Two. And a gentleman wouldn't mention such a thing.'

'I suppose a gentleman wouldn't mention all the wine

you drank either, so I won't. But we both know you drank far more than you usually do because my presence opposite rattled you and now you cannot sleep for exactly that same reason.'

Her lovely eyes widened and blinked twice. 'I was not the least bit rattled.'

'Liar. Of course you were. You scarcely said boo to a goose all evening. It was most unlike you. You are still rattled. Admit it.'

Stop flirting with her, you fool. Think of the mission. Your promotion. Lord Fennimore's specific instruction! Your heart...

'I believe I would know if I was rattled or not, my lord, and can assure you I wasn't then nor am I now. Let me say it plainly, seeing as you seem to be having some trouble understanding—disgraceful scoundrels are not my cup of tea.'

'That's a shame. Because tart and fiery redheads are exactly mine—and, for the record, I *was* rattled. Every time I see you I'm rattled. I'm rattled now. Can't you tell?'

This was madness.

He was going out of his way to seduce her—willingly and for his own selfish reasons rather than all the lofty, patriotic reasons he was supposed to be upholding. This was not the time to live wholly in the moment! What the blazes was wrong with him? What was it about this woman that drew him? Lust, yes, but he desired more than a single night of passion. He wanted to know her. Talk to her. Understand her. Knowing full well she was the sort of woman it would take more than one night of passion to tire of.

'Are you a chancer, Lord Gray?'

'I suppose that depends on your definition. Do I take

chances—yes. If opportunity knocks, who am I to turn it away?'

'But what if the opportunity presented encouraged dishonesty?'

Her suddenly fierce expression bothered him. 'I am not a criminal, Thea, if that is what you are suggesting.'

'But would you take advantage, sir?'

'I would hope not...'

'Hardly a reassuring answer when I know about your dubious past.' Oh, dear. Bad news certainly did travel fast. In this case, in less than twenty-four hours. Which meant the family had been digging. That was good for the mission, even if it felt depressingly bad right now. 'I know you squandered an entire fortune at the gaming tables and ran up huge debts all over London!'

He folded his arms, instantly defensive, but didn't deny it. There was no point denying the sorry truth. 'My dubious past is exactly that. The past. It has no bearing on who I am now. People can change.' And in the main he had, and for some peculiar reason he wanted her to know it. With age had come some wisdom to see his desperate, immature quest for more riches all those years ago would not have made a single jot of difference even if he had miraculously won more than he had ultimately lost. Cecily hadn't only wanted his brother's larger fortune—she had wanted his title as well. Now she was a viscountess and the mother of Gray's two nephews and niece. Children he had never seen, that were never meant to be his, borne of a woman who had loved his brother's superior prospects far more than she had ever claimed to have loved Gray. It had taken losing everything—his heart, his fortune and all his self-esteem—to finally grow up and see life through a crystal-clear lens.

Now, he had the ability to err on the side of caution

if he felt the situation warranted it. Granted, he still had some of the same tendencies of the young man he had been. The love of spontaneity. Adventure. The zestful, joyful, reckless lure of the dream. The heady, reckless heat of the moment.

'A leopard doesn't change its spots.'

'Well, actually, having had the good fortune to witness some leopards in India first hand, I can tell you categorically that they can. New-born leopards have big black patches that slowly develop into smaller spots.'

'You are being pedantic.'

'Hardly, I'm merely...'

'Are you still in debt?'

'No.' More truth, but money meant nothing to him any longer. It had been the root of his downfall and his heartbreak. Money turned goodness into bad. Twisted, manipulated and destroyed things. He had enough to get by, but was considerably richer in other ways. Ways an uppity young lady who had grown up in cossetted luxury in this quiet corner of England couldn't possibly understand.

'Not even to your cousin Lord Fennimore?'

'I owe him a debt of gratitude for seeing past the reckless youth I was and giving me a second chance.' Another completely honest answer. Despite everything, his superior had believed him capable of more else he never would have enlisted Gray into the King's Elite. Lord Fennimore hand-picked every agent and hadn't picked a duff one yet in all his twenty years in charge.

'And you owe him nothing else? The clothes on your back, perchance? That expensive ruby sat in your cravat.' Her finger flicked it and he caught her hand, annoyed that she thought so little of him despite knowing her opinion was probably justified based on what he allowed the world to know.

'This ruby is all I have left of my mother. Left to me in her will, if you must know, and more precious to me than anything else I own. She wore it as a pendant. Never took it off. It is the one thing I never gambled away. Even when those creditors were banging on my door, baying for my blood, I refused to part with it—knowing it would likely clear a huge chunk of my debt if I did. And as for the clothes on my back, I earned them in the same way I earned everything since that reckless summer when I lost it all. Through hard work.'

'Do you consider thrashing my sick uncle at the gaming tables hard work?'

Gray felt instantly queasy at the accusation. As low as he had fallen all those years ago, he had never stooped that low. Ever. He had trod a solitary path of destruction till the bitter end. 'I am insulted that you would think I would take advantage of your uncle—especially as he just relieved me of ten pounds and did so through flagrant cheating. What made you think such a thing?'

She tugged her hand away and folded her arms. 'Because it's all a little too convenient, don't you think? Your supposed interest in me—an unmarried heiress—combined with your sudden desire to socialise with my wealthy invalid uncle.'

It was a little too convenient, that was the problem, and while he knew he had to brazen it out, lying to her didn't sit right. Under different circumstances, with a different sort of man from him, her suspicions would be wholly justified. 'Until this moment I didn't know you were an heiress.' The honest truth. 'And frankly, neither do I care. We met by chance. I was in the brook. Throwing a stick at my dog, if you recall, and while I will admit to intentionally furthering our acquaintance since, I did not do so because of your dowry and nor did I do it to ingratiate myself with your invalid uncle.' King and country aside, this persistent need to seek her out and flirt with her was not something a good spy would do. He was selfishly jeopardising everything because he couldn't seem to control himself around her. A very worrying prospect indeed when he had promised himself he would never be that drawn to a woman again.

Say goodnight and go back inside! Thea is off limits.
'Then why did you do it?'

He raked a hand through his hair and, in the absence of the desire to do his job properly and leave her well alone, decided to continue to stick to as much of the truth as he dare. 'Because we are neighbours. Because I felt awful that you stumbled across me naked in the brook and wished to make amends.' *Stop there!* 'Because I am irresistibly drawn to you and, despite your obviously poor opinion of me, I would like to get to know you better. I have no expectations beyond that Thea. None.' Good grief, what was he doing? Why was he actively pursuing her, almost courting her, when that wasn't who he was at all?

'I certainly have no interest in your uncle's money, your money or—Heaven forbid—marrying for money. I am quite content being a solitary scoundrel and make no apology for that. Nor have I attempted to cover that up. A true chancer would have covered his tracks well, not displayed all his shortcomings to the world. I haven't lied, Thea. I took the twenty thousand pounds, left to me in good faith by my grandfather, the day I turned twenty-one and lost the lot in the hells in a matter of months. Then I went to sea and travelled the world, during which time I like to think I grew up a great deal. Being the worst gambler ever born doesn't make me a confidence trickster, nor the sort of scum who preys on the vulnerable. Although your uncle is hardly vulnerable. He has a mind as sharp as a tack and you insult us both by insinuating otherwise.'

She stared deeply into his eyes, searching for the truth, then dipped her head, her hands disappearing behind her back. 'Uncle Edward is nobody's fool... I jump to conclusions. I apologise for suggesting you might take advantage.' Her eyes flicked to his again defiantly. 'Although you might have just said that when I asked directly.'

'You didn't ask me that directly. As *I* recall, you asked me if I was the sort of fellow who would take advantage and I said that depends...'

'On what?'

'On the situation.' He wanted to kiss her. Badly. Kiss away all her nagging doubts about him and make them both feel better.

Don't do it!

He couldn't kiss her. Wouldn't kiss her. She already had her suspicions and he was under strict instructions to befriend her.

Avoid any and all flirting!

And deep down he knew that kissing her would be dangerous to him personally. Something about Thea tempted his dormant, embittered heart to stir. He had to protect it at all costs. 'Some situations demand I take advantage...' Some devil inside of him had apparently taken control of his body, his voice and his mind. He had lost the ability to think straight, simply because she was there.

Against his woefully absent better judgement, he reached behind her and took her hand. She stared at her palm wrapped in his larger one, a little bemused—but didn't pull it away. 'Would I take advantage of an invalid— even one who just crowed like a cockerel for relieving me of my money after he shamelessly cheated at billiards? No. Of course I wouldn't.'

'Uncle Edward is a shameless cheat.' Her voice wavered slightly as she blinked at where they were joined. 'I hope you called him on it. Nobody ever does because he can be so charming...' He was still holding her hand, his thumb moving in lazy circles over the sensitive centre of her palm. As she tried to change the subject, she also tried to gently disentangle it. He wasn't going to let her get away with that again either. Not when this foolhardy discussion was nowhere near done and he felt as if invisible cords were wrapping themselves around them, pulling them closer together. From nowhere, the self-destructive, needy part of his soul that had led him headlong into heartbreak with Cecily had apparently fully possessed him.

'Would I take advantage of the darkness and the pale moonlight? This empty, quiet garden? The close proximity of a beautiful woman who likes me far more than she wants to, who is as rattled as I am and is desperately fighting the attraction?' He could feel his jaded, stitched-together heart beating faster in his chest, urging him on, controlling him in the heat of this all-consuming moment against all his head's sensible objections. *'Absolutely.'* Gray leaned closer, the air crackling expectantly between them, his fingers finally giving in to the temptation to touch one of the loose tendrils framing her lovely face as he slowly inhaled her intoxicating perfume. 'I would be a fool not to.'

'I don't like you.' But her voice was breathy and she made no attempt to step away, her eyes dropping to his mouth before attempting to fix indifferently on his face— but failing. She was being lured into the fire, too, attempting resistance as he was, but failing. Whatever strange, magnetic force existed between them, it was too strong to fight. Worse, he didn't want to.

'Liar.' It came out as a whisper a second before his lips touched hers and she proved his point by sighing against them and kissing him back.

What should have been a simple kiss wasn't. He'd kissed many women since Cecily, yet none, including the woman who had so mercilessly bludgeoned his young heart to a pulp, had ever felt like this one.

All the usual sensations were there—the quickening pulse, the building lust and need, the delicious sensation of skin touching skin, the understandable and natural urge to deepen the kiss and taste the woman beneath—yet woven among those familiar sensations were new ones. A sense of rightness and belonging. The strange feeling in his chest, dangerously in the exact vicinity of his hardened heart, which should have terrified him but didn't. The peculiar sense of relief that he had found her and she had found him. Because out of nowhere, this unplanned and unexpected kiss was significant. Monumental. Meant to be.

Meant to be!

Not again...

Never again!

Shaken, it was Gray who pulled away first and removed his hand from where it had embedded itself in her curls. Most of the pins were now gone—he must have removed them, but had no memory of it—and all that molten copper shot with silver in the moonlight hung to her waist, where his other hand had made itself at home in the perfect curve at the base of her spine above her hip. Her arms had snaked beneath his coat and looped around his back. He could feel the heat of her palms on his shoulder blades and the soft press of her breasts flattened against his chest.

They were both breathing heavily. Both a little stunned at the intensity and power of just that one once-in-a-lifetime kiss to pull them out of the conscious world and send them into another, sensual plane where time and place no longer mattered.

Where the past apparently no longer mattered either.

'That was…enlightening.' He sucked in a calming breath and blew it out slowly. Although enlightening was entirely the word, he was more confused than enlightened. Torn between the half of him that was now immune to anything beyond the carnal and the old Gray who romanticised physical displays of affection and had willingly given all of his heart unconditionally once before. That long-forgotten need had inexplicably re-awoken. Almost as if his shattered heart was suddenly now miraculously whole and ready to give itself completely again.

That didn't make any sense.

She was staring up at him, swollen lips parted, arms still clamping him to her. Of its own accord his head bent again and her eyes fluttered closed, until he remembered his heart knew he couldn't kiss her again tonight—or ever. For his own sanity. Last time he had allowed himself to feel, it had taken years for the wretched pain of loss to lessen. He had been an empty, broken husk cast adrift in the world. Only recently he had found himself again. Found purpose. Dared to look a little towards the future rather than living entirely in the moment. He couldn't—wouldn't—lose sight of that again. Gray was all done with being lost and he had finally found his place.

Reluctantly, he let go of her and stepped back. 'Apparently, there is still enough of the gentleman in me to remember the number of glasses of wine you drank over dinner. More's the pity.'

The sensual spell broken, she blinked and her eyes dropped to the floor. 'Yes...that was a mistake. Brought about by too much...' Her fingers gently touched her lips and she sighed, then stiffened. 'If you will excuse me, my lord... I am not myself. The wine has...er...never mind... Goodnight.' Then she picked up her skirts and practically sprinted inside.

Needing the distance, Gray made no attempt to go after her. It *had* been a mistake. A big one—for both himself and the mission. What had he been thinking? He took himself to the bench and sat heavily, trying to analyse exactly why he felt peculiar and why he had kissed her when every sensible thought in his head had screamed at him not to. Yet all he could listen to was his heart. An organ he had believed was now immune to those sort of feelings.

What was it about Thea that drew him? Why, when he had staunchly avoided thinking about it for almost a decade, was this place and that woman churning up all the things in his past he would prefer never to revisit? Was it another strange symptom of turning thirty? Like his new-found ambition, was he suddenly looking for more in his life? Had his broken, wary heart really finally mended and now sought someone else to adore as it had Cecily, or was all this uncharacteristic introspection and behaviour symptomatic of the new weight on his normally weightless shoulders? Dredging up his past to sabotage his future?

Yes!

That had to be it. With his record of failing, and his legendary ability to disappoint, he was subconsciously destroying this new dream before Lord Fennimore callously did it for him. It was always much easier to orchestrate your own downfall, on your terms, than have another tell you, yet again, that you didn't quite measure up—despite all your best attempts to convince them otherwise. The countryside, the comfortable, gentrified house, the gentleman's clothes, the rules and restrictions of this provincial society reminded him too much of the home of his youth. Fond memories of bygone days with his mother, with his childhood sweetheart before his world caved in and he lost himself in grief. He was obviously transferring his father's, his brother's and then Cecily's disappointment of the younger Gray on to the man he was now, muddying the water with nonsense from that miserable, wretched, god-awful time and making it real once again.

But he wasn't that green, unworldly, naïve boy any longer. He was a grown man hardened by life and enriched by its many experiences. He no longer needed to keep sabotaging his own destiny and he certainly did not have any desire to tread life's future path with his hand holding another's when for ten carefree years he had competently walked it all alone. He could do this. He'd earned that promotion and, by Jove, he wanted it! The ghosts of his past could go to hell. He would not do them the courtesy of failing, nor allow them anywhere near his foolish heart.

Decisively he stood and stalked back into the house. As it was when he had left it, it was as silent as a tomb aside from the boisterous male laughter still coming from the billiards room down the hall. That was where his mission and his future lay. The awful past and the boy who wore his heart on his sleeve were dead and buried. He had mourned them both enough before he had set his gaze staunchly forward.

He walked purposefully until he saw the staircase. The single lamp that had been burning on the landing had died. Because he was a man who knew exactly when to take advantage and needed to be a much better, more focused spy, Gray turned and gripped the banister, then hastily withdrew when he saw a shadow grow on the panelling.

'Lord Gray? Are you lost?' Bertie appeared above him, his face bland while his eyes narrowed slightly with suspicion as he came down the stairs to meet him.

'Not at all, my dear fellow. I've been out on the terrace, lamenting the new hole in my purse. I am still not entirely sure how I lost to his lordship... But enough melancholy for things past.' Truer words were never spoken. 'It's time I fetched my cousin and headed home to my bed.'

'Yes, my lord. It is rather late. And contrary to whatever he says, his lordship does need his sleep, too. I shall accompany you, if you don't mind, and shamelessly use you to force him to listen to reason.' Like a sentry, the manservant walked next to him through the hallway. 'I suppose he cheated?'

'Very subtly.'

'Then that *is* a first.' The servant smiled. 'My lord and master has the most competitive nature. Always has had, but it's worse now—since his stroke. He takes shocking advantage nowadays. He can be quite ruthless at times.'

Chapter Ten

Like the biggest of cowards, she avoided him for a week.
He and Lord Fennimore had certainly been keeping her
uncle entertained during that time. They had gone shooting, played cards twice and dined with him once again.
She had obviously been invited to the latter, but had foisted
herself on Aunt Caro and suffered Mr Hargreaves for the
evening instead. The closest they had got was when she
had spotted him twice walking his dog in the distance and
she had hidden. It was pathetic. She was pathetic! All because Gray had kissed her senseless and, in so doing, had
forced her to dream about the dratted, splendid kiss every
single night since.

And it had been splendid. Nothing at all like the
kisses of the army officer who had led her astray all
those years ago, which were perfectly pleasant but nowhere near as thrilling. Or the one lamentable slip under
the mistletoe the Christmas before last, when the was-
sail was clearly off and she had stupidly allowed Colonel
Purbeck's ambitious nephew liberties she had instantly
regretted. Like his uncle, the younger Purbeck, although
significantly more handsome and interesting, made far
too much spit. That unfortunate but blessedly brief in-

terlude had been a moist affair which had quite put her off kissing for ever.

Until Gray… Heavens, that man knew how to do it! Thea still hadn't forgiven him for her outrageous and wanton reaction or herself for actively allowing it to happen while doing absolutely nothing to stop it. Blaming the wine was cowardly. Not when the worst of it had left her system by the time he had happened upon her on the terrace and when Sensible Thea hadn't been bothered to make any effort to talk Impetuous Thea out of the folly. In fact, quietly and only to herself, she was prepared to admit in that one moment she wouldn't have listened anyway regardless of which Thea was in charge of her mind. In that moment, she had wanted him to kiss her. If she wasn't very careful in the future, the shameful truth was she probably would let him kiss her again. In a heartbeat.

Obviously, and despite all her concerted efforts in the last few years to the contrary, the scary truth was she still had appalling taste in men. Chancers, ne'er-do-wells and fortune hunters still held far too much appeal, although she was still not certain quite which category Gray fell into. Definitely the first two, but the jury was still out on the latter.

'Order me three cakes of the Prussian green, one Dutch pink, an Ackermann's yellow and four of the Azure blues.' The poor shop assistant was struggling to write down all the things on Harriet's order because she was rattling them off so fast. 'And get me one of every kind of brush they do.' As this was the second time in a month they had made the pilgrimage to Ipswich to buy more paint, he probably thought her friend was in the process of painting an entire battleship. She did go through it at an alarming rate.

'I'm hungry. You promised me luncheon.'

'Patience, Thea. I haven't even started looking at paper and charcoal yet.' Which would effectively kill another hour.

'I'm putting my foot down.' To prove her point, she did. The loud thud on the shop floor raised a few eyebrows and made Restrained Thea wince. 'I need to eat and the charcoal and paper you really don't need can wait. I've suffered the milliner's, the haberdasher's and now the never-ending paint purchasing, when lord only knows you have enough art supplies at home to last a lifetime. Frankly, I'm rapidly losing patience.'

'She's always crotchety when she's hungry,' said Harriet in an aside to the shop assistant, 'and she is hungry most of the time. Who knows where she puts all the food she devours. By rights, she should be as fat as a house. I'll be two minutes, darling. Promise.'

Which meant twenty at least. 'I'll wait by the door.' Where Thea had every intention of tapping her foot and generally looking impatient in the hope it chivvied her friend along. She didn't hold out much hope.

She had been stood there belligerently for a full five minutes when she saw him through the window. Or at least she assumed it was him. The same dark head, the same ridiculously broad shoulders. The same stupid, instantaneous effect on her silly pulse. Only his clothes weren't right. The Gray who had just ridden past the shop was dressed nothing like a gentleman.

She took herself to the corner of the window and peered through the piles of fancy goods displayed there and scanned the busy street. She picked him out almost immediately, sat hatless atop his enormous horse, deep in what looked to be a very serious conversation. That in itself was off, when her irritating new neighbour was always mischievous and didn't appear to have a serious bone in his irritatingly perfect and manly body.

Next to him, similarly dressed in dusty commoner's clothes, were Lord Fennimore and three other men who she had never seen before in her life. Two more dusty strangers rode up and pulled alongside. One passed a note to Lord Fennimore, who read it quickly, then passed it along. Gray frowned and, if she wasn't mistaken, it seemed whatever grave news was in that missive prompted her naked bather to begin issuing terse instructions to his companions. Instructions for what?

Intrigued and desperately trying to convince herself it was more his suspect behaviour than her overwhelming desire to see him better, Thea checked Harriet was fully engrossed in her purchase. If her friend caught wind of their presence, she would insist on saying hello and the thought of that after her scandalous reaction to his kiss was horrifying. If she never had to say hello to him again, it would be too soon. But that natural reluctance did not mean she wasn't curious to see if her instincts were correct.

He was up to no good.

Because he was a chancer and a ne'er-do-well—and very probably a fortune hunter, too. Tangible proof would stop those silly butterflies flapping whenever he was around and perhaps she would also stop picturing his bare buttocks and tasting his lips while she slept.

Satisfied the shop assistant would keep Harriet busy for a little while longer, she ventured silently out of the door and surreptitiously picked her way along the street, keeping her back close to the shop fronts in case she needed to escape. Feeling like a government spy on a secret mission, she darted behind a flower stall opposite the very inn they were due to dine in, to watch and attempt to listen to him incognito.

The random snippets of conversation which floated her way over the hubbub of the busy street made no sense. 'Another shipment arrived last night...Excise Men have turned a blind eye...We need more...six thousand pounds.'

Six thousand pounds! Excise Men and shipments! Suddenly the dusty, unobtrusive clothes and the five strangers made her feel uneasy. What was he involved in? She had accused him of being a chancer and now that appeared to be the tip of the iceberg. Either that or her rampant imagination was running away with her again.

But she had heard it with her own ears. Damning things. Why would the Excise Men need to turn a blind eye to shipments if everything was above board and legal? She hadn't imagined those words, but hadn't heard the whole sentence. She was about to risk edging a little closer to hear more when Harriet's hand appeared out of nowhere, grabbed her arm with more force than was required and tugged her into plain view as she waved, oblivious of her complete lack of decorum or Thea's reluctance.

'Yoo-hoo! Lord Fennimore! Lord Gray! Fancy seeing you here?'

Both men turned, obviously startled, but both covered it quickly and smiled. The man she was avoiding quickly leaned to speak to one of the other men and within seconds their five strange companions rode off while their new neighbours dismounted.

Practically dragged at speed towards them by her purposeful friend, Thea pasted on her best I-have-no-recollection-whatsoever-of-spying-or-of-an-illicit-midnight-kiss expression and stubbornly refused to blush. He would not see that his presence bothered her, nor would she ever let on the annoyingly invigorating effect he had on her heart.

'Ladies, what a pleasure!' It was Lord Fennimore who attempted a smile while his usually bold, flirtatious companion merely nodded. There was no mischief in his silver-blue eyes today either and inexplicably she missed that. 'I see you have been shopping.' Solicitously he took the package Harriet was carrying. 'Can we escort you back to your carriage?'

'You may escort us to the inn where we are having luncheon—and, if you've a mind to, why not join us?' Harriet had already woven her arm possessively through Lord Fennimore's, blithely ignoring his slightly bewildered expression, and was determinedly leading the way. It left Thea to trail behind with the only person in the world she'd wished never to see again. Silently she willed them to turn down her friend's off-the-cuff invitation.

'I am afraid business precludes us from enjoying the pleasure of your invitation, Lady Crudgington.' It was the first time Gray had spoken and, despite saying what she had vehemently willed him to, she experienced the deflated sense of disappointment at his polite refusal. 'We have already eaten and have an appointment.'

'Really? What sort?' It was none of her business, but Thea wanted to know. To let him see she had noticed his peculiar apparel, she allowed her eyes to fix on the scruffy coat. 'If you will forgive me for being blunt, my lord, you are not dressed for *serious* business.'

His eyes held hers unwaveringly. There was none of his usual warmth in them and she found she missed that, too. This was a very different Gray from the man who had kissed her so thoroughly on the terrace. 'My cousin and I have been thinking about breeding horses. We both have a nose for good horse flesh and have been looking for suitable animals since we arrived in Suffolk. It is quite staggering how much more expensive a decent stud is if you are wearing a fine coat.'

'Indeed it is,' said Lord Fennimore, turning around.

'And while we are still relatively unknown here so far away from London, we thought it best to capitalise on that anonymity. Two middling, hard-working farmers can negotiate significantly better deals than two lords in polished Hessians.'

'Very prudent,' said Harriet, staring up at him adoringly. 'What a clever man you are, Cedric... I can call you Cedric, can't I?'

The older man blushed and stammered. 'Why...yes. Of course.'

'Splendid. And you must call me Harriet.' Her friend brazenly squeezed his arm again, running her other hand over his bicep. 'How strong you are, Cedric. It is such a pleasure to meet a gentleman who hasn't allowed the years to soften him. So many gentlemen of *our* age allow themselves to run to fat. Tell me, do you enjoy a good ride?'

'I do.'

'So do I! We must ride together one morning. An invigorating gallop across the dewy, dawn-kissed fields to get the juices pumping. Wouldn't that be lovely?'

'Er...yes...'

Thea allowed her gaze to flick to her silent companion's at the same moment his turned to her and there it was, that glorious, warm, amused, dancing light of mischief. Fleeting because he quickly snuffed it and stared at the inn.

'Saturday, perhaps? I shall call on you at, say...seven?' Harriet was shameless in her pursuit and poor Lord Fennimore could do nothing but nod while his expression suggested he wanted to run. Very fast down the high street. As if his breeches were on fire. 'Thea and Gray can come, if they've a mind to.'

'I am helping my uncle then as you well know.' The truth, but she'd have lied shamelessly to get herself out of any prolonged and enforced contact with *him*. 'Dear Ber-

tie is going away for a week at least and therefore I shall
be needed constantly.' A big, fat lie. Uncle Edward would
rather die than have her attend to his personal needs while
Bertie enjoyed his annual visit with his family, but at some
point during the mornings she would help him with his
correspondence. As usual. Thea's days were all depressingly much the same.

'Then it'll be just us, then, Cedric,' said Harriet coquett-
ishly. 'How exciting.' The older man simply blinked and
offered a peculiar cross between a grimace and a smile
before he was practically dragged onwards.

They reached the door to the inn and the blessed escape from the awkward cloud that hung between Thea and
Gray. The package exchanged hands again and while Lord
Fennimore bowed politely, his cousin simply inclined his
head and refused to meet her eye. If she had to use an ad-
jective to describe his behaviour, then only one sprung to
mind: shifty. Thea had caught him up to no good and he
knew it. 'Good day, gentlemen.'

'Good day, ladies. Enjoy your luncheon.'

Harriet couldn't resist one last attempt. 'Cedric—can
I trouble you to assist me in getting these packages to the
carriage?' They all knew full well that the servants would
do that, but Lord Fennimore smiled, then hesitated, then
to Thea's utter horror, and his disgraceful cousin's if the
sudden hard set of his jaw was any indication, he grabbed
every package. 'It would be my pleasure. Gray and Miss
Cranford can wait here and mind the horses.'

Before Harriet disappeared, she looked back, her traitorous lips silently mouthing one word. *Leap.*

Gray found himself reluctantly stood all alone opposite
the siren who had haunted his thoughts and his dreams for
the past week. The very woman who tempted him heart

and soul as no woman had since Cecily and whose magnetic draw frankly terrified him. He could feel the pull
of it now despite vehemently trying to suppress it. After
the ill-advised, earth-shattering kiss that had apparently
confused the hell out of him, he had promised himself he'd
keep a safe distance from the vixen. Something he had
managed with a great deal of difficulty when her uncle
was his mission. But thanks to his now encyclopaedic
knowledge of her schedule, manage it he had.

Thus far. Although he knew such avoidance was un-
sustainable. He needed a better line of defence long term.
Women who tugged at his heartstrings were strictly off
limits.

For ever.

That was the mantra he silently repeated in his head
over and over as he tried and failed not to be sucked in
by her toxic allure, with her dangerously less than a foot
away, blatantly staring, those dark eyes slightly narrowed
with either hostility or suspicion. Or outright indignation
after he had passionately kissed her, stalwartly avoided
her and was now doing his damnedest to forget about it.
Like a coward, he stared at the ground, hoping she was in
no mood to converse with him either, only to watch her
foot tapping impatiently.

'Horses, you say?' So much for that ploy. What had
possessed him to resurrect his old dream as an excuse?
Granted, he had more than enough knowledge to be able
to blag his way around the lie, but that dream churned up
the past again and reminded him of the blindly hopeful
young man he was. The foolish one who had paid an awful
price for daring to dream.

'Yes. We want to purchase one stud and at least four
mares.' The blasted sultry jasmine scent was like opium.
He wanted to lose himself in the smell. Bury his nose in

the perfect alabaster spot just behind her ear that he had tasted all too briefly and now desperately wished that he hadn't. 'Cedric hopes that breeding horses will keep me out of mischief.' Now he was grateful for his scandalous past and would ruthlessly use it to hammer a huge wedge between them—for his own safety. 'It might work.'

'Might?'

'A leopard doesn't change its spots.'

'Yet only last week you said a leopard could.' Damn her excellent recall.

'Technically it does, yes. But it is still a wild animal and, as such, must be approached with caution.' Or not at all. Preferably not at all. Inexplicably, he could feel the heat of her body this close to his, the gentle tug of the invisible cords which pulled them together, and immediately took a step backwards in the hope it would make his own body less aware of her. It didn't work. Already his heart was pumping, his cravat too tight and his eyes kept drifting to her lips. The vixen had bewitched him and whatever spell she had cast was too strong to completely ignore.

'I thought you didn't know a single soul in Suffolk?' One of her hands found its way to her hip and forced him to recall in exact detail how perfectly his own hands had fitted in the cradle of that curve. Fortunately, her hostile glare went some way to taking his thoughts away from the carnal. 'In which case, who were your companions?'

'Staff. Grooms. His stable master. Cedric brought them from his house in Mayfair.' Gray was thinking on his feet and hoping he would have the opportunity to brief his superior on his mounting tower of lies before it all came tumbling around his ears. 'We need people we trust to see to the horses once we purchase them.'

'Interesting.'

'How so?' It was apparent she was studying his reactions carefully, something as disconcerting as it was worrying. It was obvious she was suddenly suspicious, more so than when she had accused him of being a chancer, which meant something had caused her hackles to rise. Had she heard him talking to his men? Because he had learned from one of his Invisibles that she had no fixed plans for the day, it hadn't occurred to him they would collide with her an hour's ride away in Ipswich. A foolish assumption when this was the largest town anywhere near in the vast ocean of unspoiled countryside and probably the only place ladies like her could shop. He and Lord Fennimore needed to be more careful because Gislingham's sceptical niece was nobody's fool.

Damn and blast, she was as sharp as a tack, which was part of the problem. Since Cecily, he had avoided dalliances with exceedingly clever women despite having a penchant for them. Clever women fired his blood as well as his loins. Clever women were dangerous. Losing them hurt. He would never risk that pain again.

'It doesn't suit you—the horse-breeding. It seems too sedate a pastime to hold your interest. A man who once blithely took root at the gaming tables and then sailed the seven seas strikes me as one who would seek something more adventurous to occupy his time. Something more thrilling and dangerous?'

'Is that how you see me? Thrilling and dangerous? I *like* that.' The flirting had leaked out of its own accord before good sense could stop it. Worryingly, she kept having that effect on him. The timely arrival of the afternoon post gave him a moment to steel himself, but as the noise created an excellent diversion she took the opportunity to lean close and hiss in hushed tones, her warm breath torturing his ear and giving his primed body all manner of wholly inappropriate ideas he really could not afford to indulge.

'I have found no reason to reappraise my initial assessment of you, my lord. *You* are a chancer and a ne'er-do-well. A man with scant regard for the proper rules of society. I suspect you are a scoundrel to boot. A deceitful, lying, self-serving scoundrel of the first order! Am I correct?'

He found himself leaning closer, too, so that his mouth was scant inches from her crackling hair. Those invisible strings pulling again and he was apparently powerless to fight them.

'Are you still miffed about that kiss? I knew it rattled you.' Hell—it had rattled him. Petrified him, truth be told. Because it had meant something. Something he had never expected to be seduced by again. Her lush mouth opened to speak, then promptly closed. The delicate, outraged blush which stained her cheeks made him smile as his eyes shamelessly feasted on her lips. 'I knew it.' And against his better judgement he needed to touch her again. One last time. To test the waters and see if what he suspected was true. His hand had made its way to her arm, the backs of his fingers grazing the filmy fabric of her sleeve. He couldn't seem to stop himself, any more than he could stop wanting to kiss her again or revel in the heady feelings of excitement and rightness welling in his chest.

He needed to, though.

Ruthlessly crush this moment in his fist because she was dangerous. Both to his mission and his heart.

Yet his index finger had finally found her wrist and softly traced along the outer edge of her hand, down her little finger. Her own hand tangled and closed around his.

Did she feel it, too? That inexplicable connection, that need to be close.

She ruthlessly snatched it away, stared at her palm before her fingers closed tightly around it in front of her heart. 'Why, you insufferable—'

'What are you two whispering about?' Lady Crudgington appeared from nowhere, arm cosily wrapped in
his scowling superior's, her expression intrigued. 'Are
you two *flirting*?'

'We most certainly are not!' Thea gripped her reticule tightly with both hands and poked her pretty nose
in the air. 'Well—*I* am categorically not! Lord Gray is
a law unto himself. Normal rules of decorum do not appear to apply to him.' A comment which earned him a
blood-curdling glare from Fennimore, but also saved him
from himself and those lethal, invisible cords. For the first
time in his tenure in the King's Elite, Gray was supremely
grateful for the comforting, familiar protection of the old
man's hearty disapproval. It made secret, whispered, un-
sanctioned, highly dangerous conversation impossible
henceforth. Or at least he hoped it would—seeing as he
apparently couldn't control it all himself.

Chapter Eleven

There was something not quite right about Lord Gray. Thea felt it in her bones. Granted, she always felt her ludicrous suspicions in her bones, but this time it was different. She had decided that after hours of tossing and turning as sleep eluded her and her mind circled around the words she had heard.

Shipments.

Excise Men.

Turning blind eyes.

It all pointed to something illegal—like smuggling. A topic which was particularly pertinent at the moment. The London papers were rife with terrifying stories of bloodthirsty cut-throats and traitors, all lured by the easy riches of free trading, and had been for months. Even in this quiet corner of rural Suffolk, the news had caused a stir. It was all anyone could talk about yesterday at the inn as Thea had choked down her luncheon, and it was a little too coincidental that she had overheard Gray talking about shipments on exactly the same day as a veritable battalion of Excise Men were crawling over the port of Ipswich, searching every boat with a fine-toothed comb.

His behaviour had been decidedly odd, too. He had

looked uncomfortable. Guarded. The charming flirt had been missing for nearly all of their brief interaction, until he used it ruthlessly to prevent her from asking questions. It galled that, like a dolt, she had fallen for it. His touch had made her momentarily forget about his shady-looking companions and his unbelievable assertions that he was going to breed horses. That gentle, possessive brush of his fingers down her arm and bare hand had made her silly body want and her lips hungry for his kiss again. She had felt that touch everywhere, in places that shocked her, and the illicit memory could still conjure those same feelings of desire instantaneously even now.

Why was that, when she knew in her bones he was not at all who he pretended to be and not at all trustworthy? He was a gambler. A fortune hunter. Very probably a smuggler if his reference to the Excise Men was anything to go on and he had the charming, practised air of a skilled philanderer, too. She didn't want to be drawn to him or feel how he made her body hum with excitement. And she certainly didn't want to like him, spar or spend time with him. Or pathetically hope that all her suspicions about him were wrong so that they could continue from precisely where they had left off on the terrace after he had kissed her—and she had wantonly and greedily kissed him right back. Clearly Impetuous Thea was predisposed to be hopelessly attracted to scoundrels no matter how hard she tried not to be.

Horses!

There had been no sign of such an endeavour at Kirton House thus far. Of that she was in no doubt. She might well have been avoiding the scoundrel for the last week—but she had found her feet taking her within viewing distance of the house on more than one occasion and had, to her great shame, watched it quite intently for several minutes as she slowly strolled or rode past on the off-chance she might catch a glimpse of him.

At least today she was watching the house for quite different reasons. Today, Thea was on a mission. A dawn mission to ascertain exactly what was what and decide if her suspicions about the man were well founded. Thea knew horses. One couldn't grow up in the countryside without a rudimentary knowledge of what such an endeavour would entail and she had significantly more than a rudimentary knowledge. Uncle Edward's stable was the envy of the county. If her new neighbour was intent on breeding them, there would be signs. An exercise area. The stables would need to be readied for the stud and the brood mares. There would be hay. Lots and lots of hay. And those *grooms* would be busy. Although perhaps not this early in the morning. After a night of never-ending insomnia, she had flung herself out of bed as the sun had begun to rise and left the house as the clock struck five. By her calculations, she had a good half an hour to spy before the servants rose at six.

After checking the coast was clear, she risked leaving the dense bank of trees that shrouded the brook from the house and attempted to look nonchalant as she walked, clutching the basket she had brought by way of a disguise for all she was worth. If spotted, she reasoned she needed a good excuse to be out and as one of the local farmer's wives was on the cusp of giving birth, the hastily wrapped bread, cheese and fruit cake she had grabbed from the pantry would look like the perfect, helpful gift from a thoughtful neighbour. All perfectly plausible.

She heard a bark and froze. Then in a panic dropped to the floor, hoping the patchy carpet of wild flowers would be enough to hide her. The dog barked again and didn't stop, causing Thea to scramble on her hands and knees back to the cover of the trees, her eyes never leaving the house.

Thea had barely made it when to her horror the front door opened and the man himself, complete with bouncing hound, emerged into daylight. Dressed in just his shirt and breeches, he didn't appear ready to be seen outside, but her eyes drank in the sight regardless as he stretched and flexed his arms. Magnificent arms aside, he wore those breeches well, too. Even from this distance, how well couldn't be denied. Drat him.

He grinned down at his dog and ruffled Trefor's black ears, then he appeared to prise something out of his mouth. She watched, fascinated, as he threw it, marvelling at how far those strong, muscled arms beneath that gloriously flimsy white linen could send it. The dog bounded after it, tail wagging, picked it up and began to run back to his master. But then he stopped, sat and pointed his nose skywards, sniffing the air.

What had possessed her to throw herself guiltily on the ground rather than shoot him a withering glare as she marched past? When she had every right to be striding across her uncle's land no matter what time of day it happened to be! Now there was every chance he would find her if his dog was this curious.

Suddenly feeling very exposed and stupid crouched among the leaves, she held her breath for a full ten seconds, but it was too late. As if he sensed her, Trefor's eyes locked with hers and he began to race towards the trees at speed. He barrelled through the undergrowth with what appeared to be a leather cricket ball in his mouth. He took one look at Thea and then deliriously nuzzled his head against her shoulder while his tail whizzed from side to side.

'Trefor!' At Gray's shout from behind the screen of

trees, the animal froze momentarily before continuing his worship of Thea. 'Come on, boy! How can we play catch if you've run off with the ball?' There was a pause, as if he had stopped walking and was listening, then he spoke again. 'Fetch the ball, Trefor! Fetch the ball!'

Realising he had no idea she was here and was probably content to walk on by, she felt no compunction to apprise him of her presence—or allow his dog to. With minimal movement, she prised the soggy ball out of Trefor's jaws and tossed it in the direction of both the trees and his master. Immediately, the animal bounded after it, rummaged and then proudly held it aloft in his mouth as Gray called him again.

'Come on, Trefor! Do you want me to throw it again or not? Fetch the damn ball!'

Bizarrely, Thea got the distinct impression the dog knew exactly what his master was saying, because he dithered for a moment as if torn. Then he decided to bring the dratted thing back to her, dropping it in her lap and then eyeing it expectantly as if it was the only thing in the world that truly mattered. She tossed the surprisingly heavy ball again as if it were something offensive and whispered to the dog, 'Go! Shoo!' Her arms gesticulated wildly, but silently, in the direction of the man she very definitely did not want to see while she mimicked his instructions in a whisper. 'Fetch the ball, Trefor. Fetch it for *Gray*!'

Fetch was clearly the magic word because the dog was off like a shot, another thing Thea was determined to mimic. She scrabbled to stand, simultaneously snatching up her basket, before darting to the bank of trees in the opposite direction and escape. She hadn't moved two yards before the dog followed. He did a quick circle of her legs before dropping the dreaded ball at her feet again. It clipped her toe and made her wince, but self-preservation made her bite back the instinctual cry of pain.

Fearing imminent discovery, she grabbed it and threw it again, though this time she put all her weight behind it. The ball flew beyond the canopy to the meadow beyond. There was a dull thud, then a yelp, and Thea realised she had managed to hit *him* in her panic.

Good heavens, what disaster!

To compound her misery and despite her spirited throw, the dog had stubbornly chosen to stay put at her feet and helpfully decided to bark in case his master was left in any doubt of her location. 'Shh!' A command which apparently made him bark louder as he proceeded to follow, then hamper her hasty dash for freedom. Inevitably, and to her complete mortification, the shambles continued.

'Were you attempting to kill me or simply knock me out?' He emerged through the branches, rubbing his temple, typically handsome and windswept—the wretch.

'If I had been attempting either I would have succeeded, believe me. I dare say it's no less than you deserve.'

'For kissing you?'

And just like that she felt the power of that kiss all over again. 'For being a scoundrel! I am on to you, Lord Gray.'

'On to me?' While his face was expressionless, his wolf-like eyes were amused. 'I see you are still obsessed with my being a chancer and...' He snapped his fingers as if searching for the right word. 'What was it again? A ne'er-do-well?' He stopped dead and stood on the bank a few feet away from her, his hands on his hips as he glanced around, taking in the basket, her dishevelled appearance and then smiling knowingly as his eyes finally rested on the brook. 'In view of your apparent vehement dislike of me, this is in an interesting venue to choose this morning. The original scene of the crime...'

Foolishly, she allowed her gaze to follow his to the water and immediately pictured him in it. Naked. Shameless. Then the splendid kissing sprang to mind and, to her mortification, a ferocious blush began to creep up her neck. 'Crime is an *interesting* choice of word!' Before he mentioned how naked he had been that fateful morning, Thea decided to vent her suspicions openly to detract him from the blush. People went red with anger, too, although perhaps not in quite the same way. 'Especially when one is a criminal, Lord Gray!'

'It's just Gray—and what the blazes are you talking about?'

'Horse-breeding indeed? Do I strike you as daft, *Lord* Gray? Kirton House is not ready for horses and I heard you yesterday! Excise Men turning a blind eye to shipments! Six thousand pounds of ill-gotten gains! You are worse than a ne'er-do-well. It wouldn't surprise me if you were a smuggler!'

He was silent for the longest time before he threw his dark head back and roared with laughter. 'A smuggler! That is priceless. I believe Lady Crudgington's assessment of you is spot on. Your imagination is as vivid as your hair, Thea!'

'I know what I heard. I have excellent ears.'

'I know. I nibbled one of them. Sensitive, too. You moaned, if I recall, the second my lips found it.'

'Stop it!'

'You're the one who brought up your ears.' Those unusual silvery eyes were dancing as he slowly edged towards her. 'Now I can't stop thinking about them.' Nor could she stop her stupid ears tingling with the memory. She had moaned when his lips had found them. Moaned loudly and writhed shamelessly against him. That was mortifying.

'And stop right there!' Thea held her hand outstretched, palm out in warning. 'I will not allow your incessant flirting to succeed in scaring me off or distracting me from saying what you do not want to hear this time! I heard you. Clear as crystal. Discussing an illegal shipment with Lord Fennimore and all those strange men—illegal shipments worth six thousand pounds.'

'That's right. I was.' He folded his arms across his chest and stared at her levelly. 'It was all anyone could talk about at that inn in Ipswich. Although surely you must have seen the Excise Men yourself swarming along the river that day, too? They were very hard to miss and the subject of much speculation from the locals. By all accounts, the free traders sailed it all into the city as bold as brass only that morning. Although I dare say you can read a better summary in the newspaper if you've a mind to? Even in the wilds of Suffolk smuggling is big news. Especially nowadays. After that big trial in the capital a few weeks ago...'

Chapter Twelve

Gray watched her mouth open as if to speak, hesitate, then clamp shut as his convincing lie marinated. Thank the lord he had had the wherewithal to link her accusation to the smuggling trial. A trial which had been all over the London scandal sheets since they had first arrested Viscount Penhurst two short months before. His arrest on charges of high treason, subsequent conviction and sentence of execution had been all anyone could talk about—as only a story about English peers complicit in a plot to restore the hated Napoleon to power could. Penhurst's brutal murder in Newgate alongside another convicted and titled traitor just a few weeks later by the very criminal gang they had diligently smuggled for had created widespread fear and panic.

As it should have. If those smugglers had been able to get into Newgate, there was no telling what they were capable of. The whole country was obsessed with unmasking The Boss—not just the King's Elite. For good measure, and to compound her indecision, he decided to drip in a little bit more.

'Rumour has it, it is the exact same gang of cut-throats that lynched that fellow in Newgate! Who'd have thought they would turn up here—unless here is where the criminal mastermind of it all lives?' He watched her carefully, looking for clues, and saw only shock at the suggestion. 'Perhaps this particular corner of Suffolk is not so sleepy after all?'

A delightful crease appeared between her eyes. 'Perhaps...' Then she shook her head and refused to meet his eyes. Several seconds ticked by during which she chewed on her lush bottom lip to torture him. 'I suppose I owe you an apology for jumping to conclusions?' Although she didn't look convinced. Gray had introduced doubt, but not conviction. He made a mental note to set the Invisibles the task of making the house look like a suitable place to breed horses as soon as possible, mindful the suspicious minx might well check.

'Well, if you are going to jump to conclusions, the very least you can do is make them outrageous. I have little time for lily-livered conclusions. Choose a course and commit to it wholeheartedly. That's always been my motto. Besides, no harm was done. Part of me is supremely flattered you think me that exciting—another part feels duty-bound to respond to your gracious apology with one of my own.' Best to get it over with. Old Fennimore would only nag him incessantly until he'd fixed things and it wasn't her fault Gray couldn't control his emotions around her.

He'd made a hash of things yesterday. First with his stand-offish belligerence brought about by sheer panic and then with his uncontrollable flirting, brought about by lord only knew what. His emotions around her were uncontrollable, when he prided himself on his control, and his normally reliable ability to rise above panic had saved the day on several occasions—particularly now that he was a government spy. Yesterday both attributes had deserted him and he had behaved exactly how he'd felt—terrified of the strange spell she held him under and yet a slave to it at the same time.

Neither would help the mission and, as his superior had vociferously pointed out in loud, clipped tones after the incident at the inn, he was supposed to be befriending Thea and ingratiating himself into her family circle, not making her want to kill him or insulting her with his inappropriate urges. Hiding and avoiding her was a pathetic way of dealing with the situation and after only a week already proving problematic, seeing as they had now collided twice in quick succession despite his best efforts not to.

He was now under strict orders to smooth things over, pour oil on troubled waters and behave like a gentleman going forward. Something he had promised to do at his earliest convenience. That promotion hung in the balance, dangling like a carrot again. If he didn't make things right, that carrot would soon turn into a hard stick for his permanently disappointed superior to beat him with. For once, he needed to seriously consider the consequences before he allowed temptation to lure him to live in the moment. A depressing thought when every moment with her crackled with promise as well as danger.

After the unexpected and hostile exchange with the woman who seemed destined to be an itch he couldn't and wouldn't dare scratch, the King's Elite hadn't left Ipswich till after dark last night and had discovered nothing new. A slap in the face when they had learned too late from the Excise Men that The Boss had had the audacity to dock not one, but three ships just outside of Leiston the night before. Hundreds of barrels of brandy had then been offloaded into carts and smaller boats and at least a quarter of those had sailed brazenly up the River Orwell into Ipswich to be sold at almost the exact hour they had arrived in the place. To know that his associates were there, bold as brass right under their noses while they had been oblivious, galled him. Constantly thinking about her, and that kiss, when he was determined to be a better spy had galled him more.

'I'm sorry about my flirting yesterday...and for stealing that kiss last week. It's hardly a surprise you think me a scoundrel when I keep behaving like one. I really have no excuse other than to say you seem to bring out the worst in me and I've always had a tendency to act on impulse rather than think things through—as my indelibly stained reputation will undoubtedly attest.'

'I bring out the worst in you!' She didn't appear convinced of his sincerity either. 'That rather shifts the blame for your behaviour on to me, when I have done nothing to encourage it and repeatedly tried, and failed, to discourage it.' She hadn't always discouraged him. She had gazed at him with desire in her lovely eyes, held his hand, wound her arms around him and thoroughly kissed him back. Things a gentleman wouldn't mention.

'You are absolutely correct and once more all I can do is apologise and strive to do better in the future.'

'Again, another lacklustre statement. *Striving* to do better is nowhere as reassuring as a definitive promise to do better. It gives you a certain amount of leeway.'

He sighed and smiled. 'All right—no leeway, I will behave myself henceforth.'

'Thank you.'

'And I shall limit my flirting to only the social kind rather than the real.'

Her auburn brows came together in a frown. 'Now you are being pedantic and changing the parameters of your apology.'

'I'm a shameless flirt by nature and know for a fact I cannot swear I will *never* flirt with you again. I am only human, Thea, and you are the single most beautiful woman I have ever laid eyes on. You are a huge temptation, make no bones about it, but I shall alleviate a great many of your concerns by being upfront about my intentions—something which I know bothers you. What with you being an heiress and all.' And him in fear of what remained of his heart. 'I should like to state, for the record, that any social flirting I send in your direction is harmless because I have too much respect for you to shamelessly seduce you for sport and can't trust myself not to attempt to seduce you if I risk kissing you again. But as I have no desire to court you under any circumstances, stolen kisses are now strictly out of bounds.' He drew a cross on his heart with his finger. 'I am still a gentleman underneath it all and know that courting a proper young lady like yourself should only be done if the gentleman has designs on marriage, which I certainly don't.'

His completely honest response obviously surprised her as much as it did him, because the previously furrowed eyebrows raised, one disappearing under a heavy spiral of shimmering copper which refused to remain behind the ear she repeatedly attempted to curl it behind. That curl appeared shockingly lonely all on its own and his fingers itched to release every spiral from her coiffure and then arrange them artfully over her naked shoulders and breasts like Titian would undoubtedly do if he had the great fortune to have her as his model. More unchecked, unwise, unwelcome thoughts to cloud his judgement and bring about his downfall. Those invisible cords threatening to control his every movement like a marionette if he allowed them.

'I'm not altogether sure what you want me to say to that.'

'Nothing at all.' Definitely nothing at all. If she confessed to having a similar attraction to him, then no amount of sensible reasoning would be able to stop him from kissing her again until they were both a tangled, breathless heap on the secluded river bank. 'I am simply laying all my cards flat on the table and proposing a cautious truce.'

'A cautious truce?' She had given up trying to tame the curl and stood completely baffled instead. 'And I suppose I am expected to believe that on the back of it a leopard *can* change its spots? This sounds like a cunning ploy.'

'Nothing so devious or so premeditated. I am being honest. Frank. Expressing my limitations and desires plainly, for both our sakes. Because we both know you thoroughly kissed me back and that horrifies you as much as my partiality to you frightens me.' She blushed prettily, but he carried on before she could deny it. 'I can't say I blame you. I am a shameless flirt. A scandal. A tiny bit of a rogue. I am certainly not marriage material nor the sort of suitor a woman like you deserves, so we both have a vested interest in nipping this unwelcome attraction firmly in the bud. Hence the cautious truce. From this moment on I propose we give each other as much space as possible to prevent unwanted temptation. If social engagements throw us together—which they inevitably will— we can indulge in a bit of harmless flirting and nothing more. We must be casual, platonic acquaintances. Polite neighbours. We'll pass the time and chat if we meet, but never purposefully seek each other out or dally too long in each other's presence. A clear line has been drawn.' He swiped the air with his hand decisively and watched her blink in either affront or disbelief.

'Don't get me wrong. If I was in a mind to court a woman, you would be exactly the type I would choose. I have always admired intelligent, quick-witted females, especially those that come wrapped in such enticing packages, and something inexplicable about you calls to me and perhaps on a far deeper level than I care to admit. But, alas, my courting days are done and as I have no desire to dabble with the institution of matrimony again—even for a woman as tempting as you—I need to keep you at arm's length. For my own sake. And you have a reputation to preserve, so cannot go around kissing disgraceful gentlemen senseless. We cannot trust ourselves to be alone together. Well, I certainly cannot trust myself to be alone with you, so shan't be. Gracious—who knew complete transparency would be so cathartic?'

Aside from following Lord Fennimore's orders, verbalising his frustrations made him feel oddly relieved. Telling the truth was like lancing a boil and doubtless would result in them feeling better now that they both knew exactly the lay of the land.

'You have been married?' Why had he let that slip?

'No. Almost. Once.' More honesty which his mouth felt compelled to share in the spirit of the moment and against the express wishes of the cautionary voice in his head. Gray never discussed that part of his past. Not even with his friends. 'Poor Trefor is patiently waiting for some exercise and I did promise him some vigorous ball throws. Why don't I escort you back to Gislingham Hall, in a politely platonic and casually neighbourly way, and while on route we can both speculate as to what is happening between your friend Harriet and my grumpy cousin Cedric. Local gossip is perfectly acceptable between neighbours.'

He didn't dare attempt to offer her his arm, knowing that if she took it he'd want more. She nodded slowly after a moment of thought and they began to walk side by side.

'What happened between you and the lady?'

'It wasn't meant to be.'

'Ah, she broke your heart, Lord Gray.' It was a statement, not a question, which meant his expression must have given him away at some point. He hoped he hadn't appeared completely devastated and, in case he had, became flippant.

'Into smithereens, *Miss Cranford*.' He put emphasis on the formality, hoping it would remind her of their new boundaries.

She was silent for an age, staring down at Trefor as he danced backwards and forwards between them, waiting for the forthcoming doses of affection he always believed were his due. Eventually, she succumbed and leaned down to pet him as they walked. 'Then you have my sympathy, Gray. I know a little of what it feels like to be disappointed by another.'

'You do?' The idea that some blaggard had misused her or broken her heart immediately raised his ire. He wanted to punch the faceless man for having the audacity to hurt her and had to stop his fist clenching at his side. 'Are you nursing a broken heart, too?'

'No.' She stared off into the distance wistfully before flicking her gaze back to his. 'My heart has remained blessedly untrampled, but experiences have made me jaded. When one is an heiress...'

'One becomes the target of every fortune hunter in England?' Aspects of her character suddenly fell into place and he felt for her. He had never considered how difficult it must be if the shoe was on the other foot. Fate had cursed him with an inadequate fortune which had led to his love not being enough for Cecily. Thea had been cursed with the opposite. 'Then you also have my sympathy in return. It must be hard to not know whether a gentleman's interest in you is nought but financial. Money always brings out the worst in people.' As it had in Cecily. Money and a title. 'With the clarity which only comes with hindsight, I am strangely glad I lost all mine. I've found life much simpler without the burden of it.'

She paused in tickling his shameless dog's belly to look at him, although this time with openness rather than her customary guardedness or suspicion. 'It *is* a burden. One that seems to get heavier with each passing year. Nobody else seems to appreciate that irony. Especially my uncle. He has made it his mission to reinvest the enormous sum he gifted me, believing it gives me independence and freedom, when the opposite is in fact the case.'

An interesting confession that gave him an insight into her situation. 'I should imagine it makes you very suspicious of people. Men in particular.'

'Every would-be suitor has fallen foul of those suspicions. Sadly, all justifiably, although perhaps not quite to the outrageous extent my vivid imagination suggests.' She smiled then, the beautiful smile that took his breath away and made him question his solemn pledge to keep her at arm's length until he could leave her and those invisible cords behind. 'Hence you were immediately found to be guilty of smuggling when there are a thousand other more likely explanations for yesterday.'

As that was uncomfortably too close to the truth, Gray decided it was prudent to subtly change the subject. 'There is no need to apologise. I did behave like a buffoon.' He waved it all away as if it was of no matter and decided it was time to be that better spy he kept promising himself he would be. But it wasn't the mission that brought on the change, it was his wavering resolve. Having her companionably next to him, talking about personal things, was making him like her all the more. 'You gave your uncle control over your fortune?'

'Not at all. I abdicated all responsibility for it, and

gladly, the same day I celebrated my majority, yet he still persists in educating me on the topic in the hope I will take over. That banker and solicitor you met are also my banker and solicitor. Their report this time took over an hour to deliver and I was forced to listen to it. My uncle then asked my opinion as to whether I wanted to speculate in coal mining or keep persevering with the shipping in light of the excellent return on my investment.'

'You invest in shipping?' Surely that was a damning titbit, one he needed to thoroughly investigate, but Gislingham Hall already loomed in front of them. 'What sort of shipping?'

She hesitated at the edge of the gardens, her eyes gazing towards the house rather than him. 'I am apparently the proud partner in a fleet of merchant ships which sail backwards and forwards to the Orient. Transporting silks, spices and other luxury items which are in high demand... See, I do listen, I just can't bring myself to want to care. Although there are benefits.' She gestured to the bold printed fabric of her frock. Then frowned at the twin dusty patches marring the fabric at her knees.

As he was determined to be a gentleman, Gray politely did not ask how they came to be there. 'That also explains the jasmine. Whenever I encounter you, the unique scent of your perfume sends me right back to that distant continent.' A lie. It drove him mad with lust. 'Perhaps I crewed one of your ships? Wouldn't that be a coincidence?' Not quite as coincidental as one of those ships taking a detour to France to pick up illegal brandy before it sailed back home. 'Name some of them.'

'I have no idea, although probably should. The written reports I get are very detailed. My uncle insists upon that, but my eyes glaze over before I've read a full page and I find it all so daunting I take them away from every meeting and then pretend I've read them.'

'If you don't read them, what do you do with them?' Because he now urgently needed to read those reports. 'I assume your uncle would become suspicious if you burned them.'

'They are shoved in a trunk in my dressing room. A travesty I suspect my uncle knows, because he has an uncanny knack of knowing everything that goes on under his roof, but he is an eternal optimist and believes one day I will miraculously take an interest in those ever-increasing figures. I cannot see that day coming any time soon, although I suppose one day I will have to. When...' Her face clouded briefly. 'When he is no longer around to take care of things.' Gray wanted to pull her into his arms and simply hold her, more so when she smiled bravely and bent to pet his dog rather than let him see that sadness. Another unsettling insight into her character he did not need. He clasped his hands behind his back to stop from acting on the impulse. 'Thank you for escorting me home, Trefor.' Her dark eyes shyly lifted to meet his. 'To my great surprise, it has been a pleasure. Although I do think the lines between casual acquaintances and friends have become blurred. We have certainly shared far more with each other than polite neighbours normally do.'

'Our cautious truce is in its infancy, so we will forgive it a little leeway. Once we've both learned the parameters, no doubt it will become easier, especially as we have vowed never to be alone together again.' Even as he said it, Gray didn't believe it. He had enjoyed talking to her openly and the cosy intimacy that created perhaps even more than he had enjoyed kissing her. He bowed politely, resetting the boundaries. 'Good day, *Miss Cranford*.' But his feet felt lighter and the day seemed much brighter all the way home regardless.

Chapter Thirteen

'Don't you look ravishing?' Mr Hargreaves used the fact that Thea's hands were occupied to run his fingers over her sleeve. The brief, bold touch did not make her skin tingle as Gray's had done, nor did it elicit any of the peculiar, needy feeling his had either. As usual, the unsolicited flirtations of her unwelcome and determined would-be suitor made her cringe. 'Once this game is done, I would be delighted to take you on a turn around the garden.' He had glued himself to her side at the start of the croquet match, intent on charming her—or so he claimed—and had succeeded in being a thorough pest for the duration.

'I am quite familiar with my own garden, Mr Hargreaves. And if you don't mind me saying, you are becoming quite over-familiar with my person.' She glared at the spot just below her elbow where his hand remained. 'Kindly keep your hands to yourself.'

'How long are you going to play the coquette, Thea? I've made my intentions quite clear. I hold you in the highest affection. Real, genuine, heartfelt affection.' He gave her a heated look which was nowhere near as incendiary as the ones he frequently gave her aunt when he thought nobody was watching. 'I am desirous of a proper courtship, not this flirtatious toing and froing, and while I enjoy the chase—' his hand had found its way to the small of her back '—I am ready to offer you my heart.'

Heart! As if he had one! Insufferable man! He had a very warped view of things if he assumed her increasing hostility was flirting. She shrugged off his distasteful touch and stomped forward, letting her disgusted expression convey how abhorrent she found him. And he had the bare-faced nerve to call her a *coquette*. Unbelievable. 'I have a mallet, Mr Hargreaves, one I am not averse to using.' To prove that, she lined it up in front of the ball, imagined it was his thick head and gave it a spirited whack. It rolled through the hoop, knocking his ball sideways in the process. 'Oh, dear! It will take you a few turns to recover, I'm afraid.'

By which time Thea fully intended to be done with the silly game and striding purposefully back towards the house. She had had about as much of her aunt's friends today as she could tolerate. Thanks to Aunt Caro, the lawn was currently stuffed with the dullest and most sycophantic individuals in Suffolk. Her uncle had pleaded fatigue long before the interminable, impromptu garden party had started and Harriet had miraculously disappeared to the retiring room a few minutes after Colonel Purbeck and his surfeit of flying spit had arrived and was yet to reappear. Knowing Harriet, she was likely to already be in her own parlour, sipping tea and congratulating herself on her hasty exit.

If Thea whipped around this course speedily, she could escape for a full hour before the next round of afternoon tea was served. Aside from the fact that the heat was making her rebellious hair twirl vertical and her pale skin glow beetroot in places, an illicit, quiet, hour reading was suddenly very appealing. Although, in truth, an hour watching paint dry would be more appealing than spending another minute in the company of Mr Hargreaves. The vulture was making a great show of examining his stray ball from every angle as he lined up his shot. Then he hit it with such precision, it rolled softly next to hers.

'You cannot get rid of me that easily, dearest Thea. I came here today with the express intention of talking to you about our future and I will not be deterred from that.'

'It's Miss Cranford to you. I never have and never will give you leave to call me by my first name, *Mr* Hargreaves.' Sudden awareness of another vexing male cut through her irritation and, of its own accord, her head turned in time to see *him* stride on to the lawn looking his usual rugged, confident and handsome self. As if realising she was watching him, Gray turned and their eyes locked. He paused mid-step, seemed to take a deep breath, then inclined his head politely in accordance with their declared truce, before striding on towards the hostess with his cousin.

It had been a brief and altogether mundane exchange, exactly as he had promised, yet just that had the most unnerving effect on her body. Her pulse had quickened. Her nerve-endings had suddenly jumped to attention and her skin heated further, although this new warmth had nothing whatsoever to do with the glorious weather and everything to do with the disgraceful scoundrel who had kissed her senseless in this same garden only a week ago and thoroughly charmed her yesterday with his confession. Where she should be relieved he had no intentions of either seducing her or wooing her, Thea couldn't seem to feel anything other than intense disappointment at the prospect.

And more curious about the wretch than she had ever been. Who was the woman who had broken his heart? He must have loved her very deeply for the rejection to have such a lasting effect. Strangely, that made her envious. To have such a handsome, entertaining and exciting man head over heels for you must be the most wonderful feeling. One she hoped she would experience, but sincerely doubted she ever would. The burden of her fortune had made the plight of true love nigh on impossible, when most men desired great wealth far more than they desired true love.

Apart from Gray. He seemed to be genuinely sympathetic to her situation, almost as if he had first-hand knowledge of exactly how money brought out the worst in people. Another thing she had pondered over incessantly since yesterday. What had happened in his past to shape him? How irreparably had his heart been broken? Did he really mean never to attempt to kiss her again when, by his own admission, he thought her the single most beautiful woman he had ever seen? Her heart had done a little sigh at that heady compliment, because she had seen the truth of it swirling in his unusual, expressive eyes. Instead of wanting to adhere to the terms of the truce, she now had so many burning questions and desperately wanted to learn more. He had become a conundrum. An intriguing, alluring, attractive conundrum...

'It is your turn.' Mr Hargreaves's grating voice dragged her guiltily back to the present.

'I concede. I have a headache.' Thea tossed her mallet aside and rudely headed in the direction of the kitchen, purely because the kitchen was situated at the opposite end of the lawn to Lord Gray. Perhaps he would stop occupying so much of her brain if she couldn't see him.

'Then allow me to escort you back.'

'No, thank you.'

'I insist.' His fingers touched her elbow and she tugged it away as if burned. 'For I suspect this sudden headache has more to do with your reluctance to discuss the next steps of our relationship...' Thea had had enough.

'Are you quite stupid, Mr Hargreaves? Or is your desire to acquire my fortune so strong you will stop at nothing to get it?' Gray was right. Who knew complete honesty would feel so cathartic? 'Let me say it plainly, for the record and to avoid any more misunderstanding henceforth, I claimed a headache because I have no desire to entertain you—as a potential suitor or even a croquet partner, Mr Hargreaves. Kindly leave me alone. Preferably indefinitely.'

Thea marched across the lawn feeling pleased with herself. For once, she had allowed Impetuous Thea to take over because she had known Impetuous Thea wouldn't mince her words. She sincerely hoped the thick-skinned cretin would finally get the message, but no sooner had she rounded the tall, clipped topiary hedge that hid the kitchen and outbuildings from the house than her unwanted companion grabbed her elbow again and spun her towards him. 'I am in love with you, Thea!'

'Really? Does my aunt know? For I am quite certain she will not be impressed to learn that her lover's heart is engaged elsewhere.' Clearly, Impetuous Thea was not done.

'I don't know what you mean!' The outrage was constructed. Too constructed and for once she wanted to call a spade a spade and let the rebellious part of her do what the sensible, polite side of her never had.

'I *know*, Mr Hargreaves. I have *known* from the outset. Is it not bad enough that you have made my uncle a cuckold, but that now you intend to hurt my poor aunt as well?' Caro was a broken, barren bird trapped in a loveless marriage to a man who loathed her. A woman whose entire sense of self-worth was inextricably attached to her own waning attractiveness. With every new wrinkle,

Thea watched a little piece of her aunt die. 'Your rejection will devastate her.'

She watched, fascinated, as he digested this. For a moment, she was convinced he was going to attempt to perpetuate the lie and deny the affair. But he surprised her.

'The heart wants what the heart wants. I do not love her. If you give me a single grain of hope, Thea, then I shall end things with her today.' His fingers closed painfully around her upper arm and refused to budge as she tugged. 'This very moment... It's you I want. It is you I have always wanted!'

'It looks as if I've arrived just in time.' Seeing as the nauseating Mr Hargreaves appeared about to thrust his unwanted attentions on to her and Thea was poised to knee the fellow hard in the unmentionables, Gray thought it was prudent to emerge from the shrubbery. Not because the fellow didn't deserve a swift kick in the jewels, because he did, and not because he didn't think Thea could stand up for herself either. She was more than capable if the acid-tongued stream of comments coming out of her tart mouth were anything to go by, but Gray had stepped in simply because he couldn't bear the thought of her being manhandled by that scoundrel—or any other— under *any* circumstances.

He was going to determinedly think of his rescue as merely the noble act of a gentleman and steadfastly ignore the surging possessive anger which had made him follow the pair of them in the first place, despite promising himself, and her, he would maintain a polite distance and ration all contact with her going forward. Regardless of their wholly necessary truce, those powerful strings had pulled him once again and now here he was. And he was glad of it.

The jealous anger was still churning inside his gut, now combined with vengeful fury that she had been accosted. He hid both behind a bland, cold expression. Inside, he wanted to kill Hargreaves. Tear the blighter limb from limb. Pummel his deceitful, conniving, vile face with his fist until it was nought but a bloody smudge at the end of his arm.

'Lord Gray!' It was obvious she was relieved to see him, although in view of what he had just witnessed, she would doubtless have been equally as thrilled to see anyone, truce or not. 'Yes—timely, indeed. I am exceedingly glad to see you.'

'I am sure you are. Allow me to escort you back to the *safety* of the lawn.' He held out his arm as he glared at the brute and felt a fresh surge of possessiveness as she gratefully took it. He'd deal with Hargreaves later. That snake would never dare bother her again.

'Thea has a headache. I was merely escorting her back to lie down.'

As Gray locked his free palm securely over hers in the crook of his elbow, his eyes narrowed at the liar menacingly. 'I'm certain the only pain she was suffering was you, Hargreaves.' The idiot had the cheek to look affronted, which gave Gray the perfect excuse to indulge his roiling temper. 'Touch her again and I'll break your nose.' Along with both arms and legs.

'How dare you threaten—' Hargreaves didn't get to finish the sentence. Like a cobra, Gray's fist grabbed him by the cravat.

'How dare you manhandle a lady!' He lifted the other man so that he had to stagger backwards on tiptoe as he pushed him against the wall. 'How dare you ignore her rebuttals! When a lady *says* no, that means *no*! She is entirely correct in her assessment of you. You are a fortune-hunting weasel. A deceitful, conniving, self-serving vulture.' He twisted the frothy knot tighter, enjoying the way the toad's eyes bulged beneath the pressure. 'Apologise… Apologise for being…!'

'I'm sorry, Thea…'

'You do not deserve to call her by her first name!'

'I'm sorry, M-M-Miss Cranford!'

'Swear you will never come within ten feet of her again!'

'I s-s-swear it! Please let me go!'

'Are you satisfied with his apology, Thea?' He turned to her and felt some of his anger dissipate, almost as if he could hear her thoughts telling him that the idiot wasn't worth the effort.

'It will do.'

Hargreaves coughed and spluttered as Gray dropped him—'Get out of my sight!'—then ran like the pathetic excuse for a man he was towards the gardens.

'Thank you.' He felt her hand against his arm. That single, gentle touch shouldn't have felt so significant, yet it did. Slowly, he turned to face her and she was smiling. 'Although a part of me is annoyed I didn't get to finish what I started. I was going to kick him.'

'I know. I saw. Perhaps I saved him, too?'

'Would you really have broken his nose?'

'Into a million pieces. Then I'd have put all those pieces in a pestle and mortar and ground them to paste.' He had meant to be ironic, but to his own ears the reply was too forceful. 'The man is a menace.'

'The man is a pest. Calling him a menace gives him far more credit than he deserves and I am used to rebuffing unwanted advances from men of his ilk. Although granted, he is perhaps the most nauseating one so far.'

'You shouldn't have to put up with nonsense like that.'

'What? Men shamelessly flirting with me? At least he didn't kiss me.' The dig stung and she saw it, then smiled kindly. 'A poorly timed and unfair joke, Gray. I realise I had a significant hand in that kiss, too, and likening you to the irksome Mr Hargreaves is unfair. The man makes my flesh crawl.' Did that mean he didn't? Probably best not to pursue that line of conversation, especially as he could still feel the warmth of her hand on his arm through several layers of clothing and all over his body.

'You should tell your uncle what he did. He'll put a stop to him ever setting foot here again—regardless of what your aunt wants.'

'You heard everything again, didn't you?' Her expression was pained.

'Yes. But I had worked it out for myself well beforehand. It doesn't take a genius to see what is plainer than the annoyingly intact nose on Hargreaves's face.'

Her hand slipped from his sleeve and she sighed. 'I had hoped it wasn't common knowledge.'

'It isn't. Perhaps I am a little more perceptive than most guests.'

'Or more likely, they are all far too polite to gossip about us within earshot.'

'You can trust me to keep your counsel. I'm good at keeping secrets.' Never a truer word was spoken and once again his mission and his conscience were misaligned. 'Does your uncle know of his wife's infidelities?'

Her gaze flicked to his briefly and she shook her head, bemused. 'Indeed, you are perceptive. For I am sure there has been more than Mr Hargreaves. He is just one of a line spanning many years. But to answer your question, who knows? Like our guests, I have always been too polite to ask my uncle or confront my aunt. My uncle never utters her name in my presence unless he has imbibed too much after dinner. Then he calls her a cold, callous, self-serving and unfeeling witch. He hates her, when he never hates anyone, and I have no idea why. But it is deep-rooted and heartfelt. And if my aunt mentions him, it is also to criticise. Theirs is an odd relationship. One I am not entirely sure I understand, but alas there is fault on both sides so I try not to judge. He despises her and treats her with disdain; she disrespects her vows and fills her life with people who treat her better than he does. Yet neither seems inclined to separate as so many other unhappy couples do all the time. Uncle Edward cannot bear the sight of Caro and has more than enough money to set her up in her own household—but doesn't. Nor, to my knowledge, has she ever asked him to. I have never understood what exactly it is that holds them together— but I've never really thought it's my place to say.'

'Marriage can be a fraught institution.' His close brush with it had been—well, before it had even started. 'Whether the couple marry for love or for other reasons.'

'Is this another of our casual, platonic conversations, Gray?' The wry smile was mischievous. 'Only it feels a tad too personal for two people who are actively avoiding each other. At least I was avoiding you—as per the terms of our agreement, of course.'

'I was avoiding you, too, until that buffoon followed you across the lawn. Then my ingrained, long-forgotten gentlemanly manners kicked in and I came to rescue you. Now that I am assured you are safe from further inconvenience, as per the terms of our agreement, I shall bid you good day, Miss Cranford.'

Chapter Fourteen

'It's Thea. And I am curious. Seeing as you know so much about my situation, surely it's only fair you tell me a little bit about yours?' She watched him pause mid-step before warily turning around. At the last moment, he pasted his customary cocky expression on his face and that made her more intrigued. Whatever was in his past was something he was reluctant to talk about. She felt that in her bones.

'Further questions surely fall outside the parameters of our truce, as we dally longer than necessary.'

He was right, but suddenly the truce was as restricting as the silly corset Harriet had bought her. She wanted to know more. Oddly wanted to spend more time with him. 'Yet you have asked more than your fair share, nonetheless. You have already teased out the shocking state of my aunt and uncle's marriage, my fear of my finances and my abhorrence of unworthy, greedy men like Mr Hargreaves. I am merely seeking reciprocal knowledge in kind. For the sake of balance. It strikes me, we might have something fundamental in common. I am jaded and wary of romantic attachments to men because too many than I care to count have grievously disappointed me by being fortune hunters. You are jaded and wary of romantic attachments with women because one of them has grievously disappointed you because...? *It wasn't meant to be* really tells me nothing at all.'

Beneath the seemingly relaxed posture, those impressive shoulders stiffened and his spine became straighter, yet despite his obvious reluctance to talk, he stared her straight in the eye. 'I was young, foolish and caught up in the romance of it all. The sickness passed.'

'She broke your heart. To smithereens. Your own words, Gray, not mine. Who was she and what happened?'

The hand on his left side closed into a fist as he gazed heavenwards, then he raked that same hand impatiently through his hair and gazed at her levelly as if he had made an unpleasant decision to take vile medicine and was determined to get it over with. 'Her name was Cecily. Her father's estate bordered ours. We grew up together.' The staccato sentences were matter of fact. Almost clinical in their delivery. 'Her mother and mine were great friends. Cecily and I were inseparable.'

His childhood sweetheart then. 'You loved her.'

He sidestepped her comment. 'We made plans and promises. Far too many of them with hindsight and, like a fool, I believed them to be as real for her as they were for me. But, alas, I was mistaken. When my father brokered the suggestion behind my back that she marry my older brother, Cecily was given the choice by her father. Me or him. She chose him.'

'Because of the title?'

'No doubt. And the promise of the greater fortune, although I wasn't destined to be poor. My maternal grandfather had left me a generous bequest that had been held in trust until I became of age, but that paled into insignificance against the stately grounds of Talysarn and all the riches which would come with it.' His fingers went to play with his cuffs. A tiny, nervous gesture for a man who usually exuded confidence. 'My father told me the news in his customary cold and dictatorial way, expecting me to stand aside and accept the decision made by two peers based on what suited them, not me. As I'm sure you would expect, I exploded and immediately rode like a man possessed directly to her house to rescue her, assuming she would be as distraught by the outrage as I was, but she wasn't. She wasn't even particularly apologetic either. Circumstances change, she said, and she would be a fool to turn down such an advantageous offer. Needless to say, her life then went one way and mine quite another.' He shrugged as if it was of no matter, when Thea knew it was and her heart wept for him. He had suffered a triple betrayal. His father, brother and sweetheart had all simultaneously stabbed him in the back. 'At the time, I thought myself devastated. Now I am merely philosophical about the experience.' He was lying. She knew it because his unwavering silver gaze faltered and for a moment he refused to meet her eye.

'How old were you?'

'Two weeks shy of twenty-one. So you see, it really was a very long time ago.' Coincidentally, around the same time as he would have taken control of all those funds left in trust. Without thinking, Thea found her palm smoothing down his arm in sympathy as several pieces of the puzzle fell firmly into place. 'And, with hindsight, much too young to have been seriously considering marriage.'

'Oh, Gray—that must have been quite a year.' Aspects of his character now made sense. Of course he would prefer to live in the moment when all those longed-for plans of his youth had been crushed in the worst possible way.

'To lose your love, all those hopes and dreams and your fortune in one fell swoop.'

She felt the muscles bunch under his coat. Then heard him exhale slowly before they relaxed. 'Clearly I am not the only one of us who is perceptive. Yes, like a fool I thought Cecily would reconsider if my riches superseded my brother's, when I should have thanked her for her shallowness and moved on without a backward glance. Any woman who puts money and social status above love isn't really the sort any man should give his heart to.' Or vice versa. Another thing they had in common.

'And then they banished you.' It beggared belief. To be left reeling and floundering at such a young age. So vulnerable and alone. Thea instantly hated his awful family and the loathsome Cecily. If she ever met the witch, she would receive the full extent of Impetuous Thea's acid tongue and worse. Much worse.

'I was never banished. Disowned—yes. My father could not stand the scandal. But I left. Ran as far away from them all as I could get. I didn't want or need the reminders. Of all the skewed decisions I made that fateful year, it is the one that turned out to be for the best. Bizarrely, it made me. I grew up. Learned things about myself I never would have learned any other way and it allowed me to get the perspective I couldn't find here in England.' His eyes flicked to her before wandering to fix on something in the distance. 'But despite what you are obviously thinking in that overly suspicious brain of yours, I *am* over it. I would never have come back otherwise. Now, can we dispense with all this heartfelt honesty? By my reckoning we are now even and thus never need to discuss anything beyond the superficial and polite ever again. We really do need to work harder on this truce of ours, else it will collapse before it has had a fighting chance to get going.'

Thea didn't call him on it, suspecting he was partially over what happened yet intrinsically scarred by it at the same time. It was the easy, confident, charming Gray smiling at her now, although he was different and always would be. She understood there was a deeper, more sensitive human being under all that swagger. A complicated man of many layers who had lived a much harder life than she could possibly imagine. A man who had been a scandal, weathered it and emerged as someone she could respect. A man she was coming to like a great deal. Yet another thing which surprised her, when it had been an age since any man had piqued her interest enough for her to care about them on any level. 'Now I see we have a great deal in common. One way or another, money has changed us both and not necessarily for the better.'

His warm palm softly captured her hand where it still rested on his arm—it was a friendly gesture, not the least bit flirtatious, but to her surprise she wanted it to be. She certainly felt his touch everywhere. 'Things happen for a reason, Miss Cranford. Every trial and tribulation leads us to the path we were meant to take.' He was coincidentally leading her back up the path to the lawn and the rest of the guests. Back to the safe haven where their cosy intimacy had no place and temptation was well out of reach. However gentlemanly he was attempting to be, she knew it was himself he was ultimately protecting. She bothered him. Their fledgling relationship bothered him. His feelings towards her scared him. Feelings he would rather deny than articulate; run from rather than pursue.

'It's Thea. And I suspect our truce has unexpectedly made our path veer in a very different direction from the one for which it was intended, for I am convinced we were never destined to be polite, indifferent acquaintances, Gray. I am coming to believe we were meant to be friends.' Or more. Not only Impetuous Thea hoped they would be more.

His step faltered again and he glared in mock affront. 'Fate can be such a cruel mistress.'

'There you are!' Gray dropped the leather satchel on the kitchen table at the exact moment Lord Fennimore burst through the door, tugging ineffectually at the thoroughly ruined cloth at his neck with one hand while clutching a fresh cravat in the other. 'Where the hell have you been? And what the hell have you been doing at such an ungodly hour?'

'My job, sir.' Without being asked, Gray briskly removed the hopelessly knotted disaster from his superior's collar and then set about tying the new one. Not one of the King's Elite could tie a damn cravat to save their lives and whenever they were on a mission they had to forgo servants. Spare beds were always better occupied by agents, so Gray often found himself acting as a valet. 'I took advantage of the prolonged absence of Gislingham's constantly hovering manservant and broke into his private apartments before *dear Bertie* comes back.' An idea which had come to him after hours of staring at the ceiling thanks to a certain redhead he couldn't seem to forget or avoid.

Were they friends now? If they were, he was supremely uncomfortable with the concept. As much as he found her surprisingly easy to talk to, the level of honesty he confided in her bothered him. She had made him talk about Cecily, for goodness' sake, for the first time in almost a decade and without that much pushing. The words had come, jagged and dry like rocks in his throat, then once they had, more tumbled out. It was unnerving. More unnerving was how much lighter he felt as a result of it all. Lighter and worryingly hopeful, and unfortunately, those niggling hopes all seemed to involve her in some way. He didn't want to be Thea's casual acquaintance. Friend. He wanted to kiss her again. Take her to bed. Make plans. Blasted plans, for pity's sake! No wonder he couldn't sleep!

'Good God, man! You might have told me! Were you seen?'

'Of course I wasn't seen. But with eagle-eyed Bertie away all week, it was too good an opportunity to miss. I found Gislingham's study, picked the lock on his desk and borrowed a few of the papers concealed in a strong box within it. I was careful to take only a tiny, random sample and hopefully I'll be able to return them before his sentry returns and our dastardly Viscount will be none the wiser.'

'What did you find?'

'Hard to say. It was too dark to read them properly and I didn't dare risk a light. Stocks and bonds mostly. Some accounts, I believe, and some private correspondence.' Most particularly, a thick stash of letters tied with ribbon had sat in that dusty strong box, kept quite separate and secure from the plethora of everyday correspondence in the unlocked drawers. 'I'm hoping there is enough to give us a flavour of what he's up to and perhaps throw up a name or two to investigate. Something tangible which will stop the blighter continually running rings around us.'

So Gray had hauled himself out of bed, determined to do something practical with the insomnia, even if that something took him within feet of the siren tucked up in her own bed asleep. Not that he had ventured up to her floor at all, despite knowing there was potential evidence about nefarious shipping investments stuffed at the bottom of her trunk. There was foolhardy and then there was madness. A sturdy plaster ceiling, wood and bricks had served as a necessary barrier. One that blocked out any hint of alluring jasmine in the air. But still he had felt her and the pull of those damned invisible cords, and that alone had tortured him.

He stepped back to assess his work and tweaked the folds of the cravat. 'Where are you off to at this ungodly hour?'

'Riding. With Harriet...' Lord Fennimore's suddenly jerky movements and sheepish tone were not like him. He looked hilariously awkward. Gray bit his lip to stop the bark of laughter escaping. 'You should come, too.'

'You want me to come riding with you and Lady Crudgington? I doubt the lady in question will be pleased to see me—not when she seems very taken with you, sir.'

'She's bound to bring a chaperon of her own and a thoughtful gentleman brings another to show that he would expect the proper proprieties to be adhered to!'

'You want *me* to chaperon *you*?' The laughter escaped then and earned him a glare. 'How...quaint.'

'That is the correct way of doing things, young man, and therefore that is exactly the way this shall be done! I shall use the opportunity to pick her ladyship's brains about Gislingham and you will ride at a respectful distance behind!' He marched out, slamming the door behind him.

Wearily, Gray set about fixing himself some coffee to prepare himself for the ordeal and sat drinking it while watching his dog eat breakfast, trying not to hope that Thea would be the other chaperon. Because he couldn't afford to indulge that whim. Not when the blasted woman had already crawled under his skin and made a home there. Friends! Not while he still had the remaining shrivelled, battered remnants of his heart. Those bludgeoned pieces had taken many years to heal and wouldn't survive another pummelling. Thea was just too tempting. Tempting enough to make him want to dismiss his painful past out of hand and plunge headlong into...what? Nowhere he was in a hurry to go to again. To take his mind off the unthinkable and frankly irrational thoughts it kept dwelling on, he decided to do something practical.

By the time Lord Fennimore was back, snapping orders and generally complaining about Trefor, Gray had relaid the fire, hauled in a day's worth of logs and made two rounds of toast and slathered them in butter. The pair of them ate in silence, as was the old curmudgeon's way, but he could see the man was also nervous and found himself intrigued at the idea. The unflappable head of the King's Elite, a man who loathed pointless socialising, most people as a matter of course and had always been content with his crusty old bachelor ways, was in a total flap over a woman. Life certainly liked to throw up surprises.

If nothing else, following the pair of them would be hugely entertaining and, while Gray had never been a letter writer, because he didn't really have a soul to write one to any more, he fully intended to fire off a brace of letters to his friends and comrades Warriner, Leatham, Flint and even Hadleigh, regaling them with the unheard-of, miraculous phenomenon as soon as it was over. Lord Fennimore was nervous because he was courting! He couldn't resist a little dig to test the theory.

'You are not wearing *that* coat, are you?'

'What's wrong with it?'

'Black? Perhaps a little staid for a vivacious woman like Lady Crudgington? If you're intent on wooing her—*only* for King and country, of course—it sends out the wrong message. Black is for funerals and formal dinners, not invigorating gallops across the dewy, dawn-kissed fields...' Biting the inside of his cheek, he enjoyed watching the old man stare down at his attire and dither.

'Yes...you might be right. What should I wear? The green?'

'Green will complement your eyes.' Eyes that instantly narrowed at the sight of his uncontrollably twitching lips.

'Get your fun elsewhere, Gray! This is business. Pure and simple. If the lady has an interest in me, I'd be a fool not to take advantage! She is detached enough from Gislingham not to offend him and close enough to be useful. That is exactly what being a good spy is all about, rather than alienating the villain's closest living relative with your crass and improper and unwelcome seductions. Choose your opportunities wisely! Something I despair of you ever learning. Go sort out the horses! She will be here promptly at seven!' He stomped off indignantly, but came back to the stable with a face like thunder, wearing the green coat and smelling uncharacteristically of expensive cologne.

To say the next twenty minutes were tense would be an understatement. Lady Crudgington was late and his superior began to behave like a man jilted at the altar until she appeared on her pony, unrepentant, much closer to half past the hour, with the woman who had haunted his dreams smilingly trotting alongside on one of the biggest horses he had ever seen.

His heart gave a tiny stutter at the sight of her. The fitted blue riding habit perfectly both highlighted her alluring, womanly curves and made her glorious hair pop in the hazy, early morning sunshine. On top of those untameable curls was a ridiculous little hat set at a jaunty angle, designed more for fashion than to cover the head. She looked delightful. Frivolous, saucy and dangerously confident. Damn her!

Like Thea, Gray kept a polite distance as old Fennimore greeted Harriet and had to turn his back when he heard him mutter something cringing about propriety and being glad they both had had the foresight to bring chaperons.

'You are *so* thoughtful, Cedric.' Although as he'd suspected, the lady seemed vastly amused at the prospect. 'But such nonsense is entirely unnecessary. One of the benefits of both age and widowhood is that propriety can be ignored. Something I try to do at every opportunity. Don't you? Thea is here out of coincidence and nothing more. She's off to the village to collect the post and called upon me as she had forgotten about *our* engagement. We shall be heading in a quite different direction, Cedric, I can assure you. I have a much more exciting route planned for us—but as Lord Gray is now set to ride, too, he might as well accompany Thea and leave us in peace, don't you think?'

By the stunned look on his face and the lack of words coming out of his mouth, Lord Fennimore had not expected that, but there was nothing he could do about it without appearing foolish, prudish and curmudgeonly. Harriet pointed a finger at Gray and winked, clearly enjoying leaving both men floundering on the back foot with her outrageous suggestion. 'Don't do anything I wouldn't do, young man. Which, granted, gives you quite a bit of scope.' She nudged her pony forward with a grin as wide as it was naughty. 'Come along, Cedric! Let's see if you're man enough to keep up with me!'

Gray watched them leave while he considered his options. Riding all alone with the minx who continued to cause him insomnia was the last thing he should be considering. He could plead something more pressing to do and excuse himself, which in view of the current speed of his pulse was tempting, or he could accompany her. Something the devil-may-care, adventurous part of his nature was egging him on to do, but which scared the hell out of the rest of him. That route was unchartered and unpredictable territory, as well as a whole heap of temptation, yet there was no denying it was also the most prudent as far as his mission was concerned. If Lord Fennimore really did intend to use his morning gallop to probe Lady Crudgington for information, he should probably use this unexpected opportunity to do the same. Surely he could fight his urges on horseback? As long as he didn't allow his eyes to linger on that very tight riding habit.

'I can read your expression, Gray. If you'd rather not ride to the village with me, then I really do not mind.'

'Up until thirty minutes ago, I was fast asleep and had no idea I was riding anywhere, but, seeing as I was dragged up and am dressed for it now, I might as well.' Her huge horse was dancing around on the spot although she controlled it effortlessly. The smattering of white hairs on his chestnut muzzle were testament to his advanced age. 'He's skittish for a hunter.'

'He always has been. Uncle Edward has a stable full of younger and more temperate horses, but Archimedes was my father's and I am the only person who ever rides him. He would be miffed if I chose another.' She smoothed a hand down his mane to calm him, then stared quizzically at the three Invisibles clearing and levelling the pasture close by. Because they had the appropriate audience, his men were working up quite a sweat.

'My new exercise yard. The sand will be delivered later this week, so the ground needs to be prepared, then the posts for the fences dug. The stables are already in reasonable shape, so they'll do well enough in the short term.' Especially as his men had much better things to be doing with their day than prepping for horses that would never come. They were irked enough at the charade he was having them act out now. But it was better to be safe than sorry—although if he said so himself, it was the perfect place for an exercise yard. It caught enough of the early morning sun to be bright and airy, but was shaded by the house and the parallel copse of trees in the afternoon when the sun was at its hottest. And it was close enough to the brook to ensure a ready supply of cool, fresh water.

Why had he put that much thought into giving credence to a lie? And why did the fact it was just a lie suddenly depress him when he looked at her? Gray grabbed his reins and heaved himself on to his own saddle. He was barely seated when his poorly behaved mutt flew like a cannonball into the yard, barking.

Archimedes reared slightly, but again she controlled him as Trefor panted and wagged his tail far too close to the animal's busy hooves, his devoted brown eyes locked on Thea adoringly. 'I'm so sorry. I shut him in the house, but he has a talent for escaping.' He called to one of his men, 'Take the dog indoors!'

'Oh, let him come with us.' Thea bent down to pat Trefor's bouncing head. The contact made him jealous. Of his blasted dog, for pity's sake! 'Archimedes was merely a little surprised. He's fine now and I'm sure your delightful dog would enjoy a run to the village with us.' True to her word, the old horse indeed seemed to have settled and was now simply glaring down at the dog in warning as they slowly ambled forward. As she was a few feet ahead, that meant he got to stare at the delectable peach that was her bottom. Capital!

Gray set his jaw and prayed for strength, channelling all his lusty frustration into hating the talented seamstress who had created that seductive confection, reminding himself yet again that he really did need to work harder at being a better spy in the hope that would make his errant thoughts purer. Unsurprisingly, none of those things worked.

Chapter Fifteen

Coming here had been a mistake. Too forthright. A little bit needy. Impulsive, and probably made her shallow, selfish motives totally obvious. It was also completely out of character when she usually actively avoided all men. The wariness had given way to curiosity. He intrigued her. More than any man ever had before. The shameful truth was Thea had only offered to collect the post as a pathetic excuse to see him again—knowing full well he wanted to maintain a respectable distance. But after yesterday, and after thinking about him for most of the night, it had seemed a plausible enough reason to happen to be riding past at the time. She certainly hadn't expected to do more than say a passing hello, exchange a few pleasantries, then be on her merry way, content that she had at least seen him. Then quietly sigh and swoon in private all the way home, just as she had all night. She hoped all that swooning was borne out of knowing him better and liking what she learned and not solely because he had declared himself off limits. But in her head alongside all the new regard she had for him, Gray had become forbidden fruit. Something she had a proven penchant for.

Casually meeting him was hardly throwing herself at

him, but she had not factored in Harriet's matchmaking, nor Gray's ingrained sense of decency, and now the poor man felt beholden to accompany her and clearly did not want to. *'Something inexplicable about you calls to me and perhaps on a far deeper level than I care to admit.'* Words which still sang to her soul. That made her increasingly believe he was exactly what he claimed to be. Neither a fortune hunter nor a true scoundrel, but a man who saw past her fortune to the woman beneath. Gray was drawn to Thea. It was that simple and that glorious.

'Was it me, or was your cousin a tad nervous this morning?' She purposefully kept her conversation bright and friendly, hoping he wouldn't realise she had only come here for him when he had made it plain he would prefer to have little to do with her. But he had called her beautiful. Beautiful and tempting and exactly the sort of woman he would choose to court if he had a mind to. Those were not the words of a man who disliked you. In fact, if anything they said quite the opposite. He was avoiding her *because* he liked her. To protect himself. Because he couldn't trust himself to resist her. And to spare his heart. Yet instead of respecting his wishes, she was flagrantly going against them, claiming they were now friends when her body and mind clearly yearned for so much more. Was she here because she wanted to tempt him? To her shame and bubbling excitement, the answer was a definitive yes. She certainly wanted to tempt him to reconsider.

'Nervous? I've never seen him in such a state. He changed his coat twice, ruined goodness knows how many neckcloths and doused himself in cologne. It was one of the funniest things I've seen in a long time. Lady Crudgington has a most peculiar effect on him.'

'They were flirting yesterday on the lawn. Didn't you see? I was surprised Harriet had returned until I saw Lord

Fennimore. She loathes Aunt Caro's friends and finds most of our neighbours boring, but she is very taken with him so she went against the grain and came back.' She was babbling. A sure sign of her guilty conscience. 'Decent gentlemen of a certain age are thin on the ground, or so she says, and she approves of the way he wears his breeches.'

Images of Gray *sans* breeches suddenly swamped her mind and she felt a fraud for pretending to be his friend again, although he felt like a friend. A charming, handsome, intriguing, wholly male friend whose kisses were lethal. Was she wrong to indulge in a bit of harmless selfishness? When there was clearly a mutual attraction and regard between them? It wasn't as if she intended to stomp all over him and force her will. Not even Impetuous Thea was capable of that! No—merely a little gentle prodding. Perhaps if they spent a little more time together, both of them would lower their defences and nature would take its course. That sounded much better. She would leave it to fate and hope that this time it would look upon her kindly.

'His breeches? Good Lord.' His shocked expression was comical. 'Although I suppose he is in excellent shape for a man his age.' He was riding so close to her that she could reach out and touch him if she had a mind to. She did, but neither Thea was brave enough. 'I am convinced he is taken with her, too. I have seen him smile now on two separate occasions in her presence. It should also be noted, those are the only *two* occasions I have ever witnessed him smile.'

They speculated on the unlikely romance between Lord Fennimore and Lady Crudgington for the first half a mile of the short ride to the village, almost as if both of them knew it was a much safer topic than anything else, when their last conversations had been so intensely personal and significant. Once that was exhausted, an odd tension settled between them. Of things unsaid, or maybe that was just her take on the silence or her own guilt for orchestrating the entire meeting in the first place. Rather than let it hang, it was Gray who blessedly broke it. 'Why are you collecting the post rather than leaving it to a servant?'

'My uncle is expecting a letter, one he has been quietly fretting about, so I offered to collect it and, knowing Harriet would leave your poor cousin waiting longer than necessary for her to turn up, I decided to kill two birds with one stone and chivvy her along.' That did sound a more plausible excuse than forgetting Harriet and Lord Fennimore had a prior engagement, when it had been mentioned repeatedly in his presence yesterday at her aunt's interminable garden party. 'She has a dismissive relationship with clocks by and large and time keeping has never been her forte. As it was, even with my interference, she was significantly past fashionably late. Making the poor man suffer too long from Harriet's tenuous grasp of time seemed unnecessarily cruel.'

'Cruel—but entertaining. It made me glad he had woken me. That, and his request for me to be the chaperon. I've never been asked to be a chaperon before and never thought I would. It is those odd and wholly unexpected moments that make life so entertaining. I am the last person to ensure the correct proprieties are adhered to.' His eyes flicked to hers, the flirtatious challenge in them instantly reminding her of exactly how many odd and wholly unexpected times he alone had tempted Impetuous Thea to stray. Except, right this second, it wasn't exactly Impetuous Thea who controlled things, nor was it Sensible Thea. It was an odd amalgamation of the two which felt reassuringly like her old self. The Thea not jaded by fortune hunters, who never checked her temper or pithy comments in case they caused her poor uncle to keel over. The Thea who embraced life and enjoyed a little risk. Thrived on it. Hence her spur-of-the-moment decision to accompany Harriet and take a chance on a man she would never have considered anywhere near suitable only a few days ago.

Before she wrestled Impetuous Thea back in her box, she stopped at the end of the meadow as the village came in sight and decided to ignore all the guilt and simply enjoy the moment. She was tired of being too buttoned up and suspicious. She was young, the sun was shining and the day felt much brighter than any had in a long time. She might not be ready to leap off the precipice, but she was certainly prepared to edge a little towards it. 'This land is Colonel Purbeck's. If you don't mind, I'd prefer we skirt around the edges rather than cross it directly.' Crossing it directly would also take half the time, when she was inclined to linger. 'If he sees us, we'll have to call on him and…well…'

'The droning man spits when he talks.'

'Precisely.' She loved that he already knew her so well he could finish her sentences. She also loved the knowing smile she had only seen him use on her. The one that did odd things to her insides and made her forget all the reasons why she was supposed to be wary and suspicious. He didn't behave like a fortune hunter. Nor did his past indicate that he'd attempt to be one. He had a healthy disrespect for money. And a committed aversion to marriage. One he had been completely honest about lest she not know exactly where she stood, yet she was stood here despite it. 'Although he will be wounded when he learns Harriet prefers your cousin to him. Colonel Purbeck is also very taken with—' The gunshot came out of nowhere, startling them both. As Trefor barked repeatedly in warning,

Archimedes simultaneously reared, throwing Thea helplessly from his back.

She landed with a dull thud on the grass, winded but
otherwise intact, and managed to roll away a split second before one of his massive hooves hit her. Swiftly, she
scrambled backwards and well out of his way, blinking
and hearing only the sound of her rapidly beating heart.

Her old hunter was in a blind panic. One that needed to
be quickly controlled for all their sakes. Before she could
pull herself to her feet, Gray slid off his horse, patting his
horse's flank to send it out of the way before he stepped
bravely into the fray.

'Trefor! Back!' He pointed to where Thea now stood
and the animal listened, instantly pressing his body against
her legs as if protecting her for his master. After checking that she was all right, Gray motioned for her to stay
put while he dealt with the frightened horse, something
which worried her because Archimedes truly was skittish
to the point of being outright temperamental. Especially
around strange people.

'Easy, boy.' He kept his voice level and even, his palms
up as he edged forward. It was obvious, despite her accusation to the contrary only a few scant days ago, Gray
knew horses. 'Easy... Shh.' The erratic jumping was lopsided. Her big horse was hanging one leg at the rear. Not
only was he panicked, he was injured and it was all her
fault. She should have been paying closer attention. She
never should have been here in the first place. 'Good boy...
Easy.' He caught the trailing rein in his fist and wound
it quickly around his hand to steady him, his other hand
reaching out to stay the horse's head. 'Shh... It's all right.'
Gray rested his forehead against his muzzle and dropped
his voice to a whisper, breathing slowly to encourage the

animal to do the same, a soothing technique she had never seen anyone use before.

At first Archimedes fought him, then he slowly, miraculously, calmed. 'Thea—take the reins.' He waited for her to grab the slack before he risked unwinding his hand from the leather. 'He's hurt himself. The right fetlock. Hold him still while I check his leg.'

'He's lame!' Once again, she had been self-indulgent in her pursuit of the forbidden and fate was punishing her. Yet she had wilfully ignored the nagging voice of doubt in her head. 'Is it broken?' Thea couldn't hide the fear or the threatening tears from her voice as she stared on impotently. Archimedes was all she had left of her father. A broken leg would mean the old horse would need to be destroyed. She couldn't bear yet another thing she loved leaving her because of her own reckless selfishness. Gray gently probed the swollen muscle, then risked manipulating the joint. The horse flinched and so did she.

'I don't think so. But he's sprained it badly. He doesn't want to put any weight on it. Probably turned it as he reared.' He didn't need to mention that bad sprains could also be dangerous. Especially on a horse as old as hers. What had she done? This was all her fault. 'Let's get him back to the hall so I can check him over properly.'

Tentacles of panic wrapped around her organs that she tried to ignore. Panic was a selfish emotion and her innocent horse deserved better. 'Our stables has a big cart. Certainly big enough for Archimedes. Shall I fetch it?'

'Yes! And plenty of ropes and strong-backed grooms. The less he aggravates the injury now, the greater the chance is of it recovering.'

Grateful to have something to do rather than consider the bitter ramifications of her actions, she pulled up the skirts of the ridiculous riding habit she had worn solely for him and made no attempt to look ladylike as she heaved herself astride Gray's horse and then nudged the animal to a gallop.

The next two hours passed by in a blur, most of which was spent with Thea pacing and wringing her hands as Gray took charge. He coaxed Archimedes into the cart, secured him and rode in it with him for the entire painfully slow journey back to ensure her horse wasn't jolted. Then he took over her uncle's stables after the stable master suggested shooting the poor thing there and then, instead issuing rapid and succinct orders to the staff about the way he wanted the treatment to proceed.

Her horse's damaged leg was bathed in ice, then loosely wrapped in a poultice. Most ingeniously of all, he had lashed ropes over the ceiling beams tied to a hammock affair beneath Archimedes's stomach to support his weight and prevent him moving around. By the time it was all done, the sweet old boy was as comfortable and content in his stall as could be expected and well enough to munch on the carrots she had brought him by way of an apology—as if she could apologise for being so careless with his wellbeing. Now, alone in the garden, she sensed Gray come alongside her. One glance proved his expression was grave.

'Will he recover?'

'It's hard to say at this stage. The next few days will be crucial, but we'll have a better idea once the swelling starts to go down in a day or two. Then we can strap him up. Hopefully his lameness is temporary—as it so often is.'

'And what if the swelling doesn't...?' He silenced her by gently placing his index finger on her lips.

'Don't think like that, Thea. Don't think too far ahead. It serves no purpose. There are too many variables and all of them out of our control. He is calm and the fact that he is eating tells me that the pain is not unbearable. That is a huge positive and I find it's much more beneficial to focus on the positives than indulge in the what ifs. I will personally check on him daily and ensure that every possible thing can be done to see your horse back on all four of his feet again. Let's take this a day at a time.'

She nodded, too choked to say anything, and powerless to stop the tears she had been stalwartly holding back from falling. The guilt and shame was eating her from the inside and had been for hours. How many times did someone she loved have to get hurt because of her inability to control her own selfish desires? Thanks to her stubborn selfishness, her father was dead and her uncle nearly so. Because of her selfish desire to spend more illicit time with Gray, Archimedes was put in danger. Impetuous Thea was a menace.

'Don't cry, Thea.' He looked extremely ill at ease with her uncontrolled and noisy bout of emotion, but she couldn't seem to stop. 'Please don't cry.'

'Th-this is all my f-fault. I should never have taken him out this morning. It was a selfish thing to do.'

'Selfish? Of course it wasn't.' His thumb gently brushed one tear away. 'It was the fault of the blithering idiot who fired that gun.'

'You d-don't understand...' How could she explain it, when she knew to any rational person it would sound like nonsense? He wrapped his strong arms around her and she wept against his chest, grateful he was there and wishing he wasn't. 'I could have p-prevented this.'

She was apparently inconsolable, which affected him just as much as her horse's injury clearly affected her. In the absence of any clue as to how to make her stop crying, all Gray could do was hold her tight. A huge mistake. The second he took her in his arms, it played havoc with his emotions.

There was something unsettling about holding this indomitable woman when she was so distraught and he was powerless to stop it. For some reason she was intent on blaming herself for what happened and no amount of reasoning with her appeared to be able to change that. As in all things, there was nothing quiet and sedate about the way she expressed her grief. Each shuddering sob seemed to have the power to hurt his heart, while the front of his shirt was now completely soaked through.

A few minutes previously, Viscount Gislingham had appeared at the French doors, taken one horrified look at the dreadful state of Thea and retreated, stunned, back inside, shaking his head, leaving Gray to bear the brunt of his niece's breakdown all alone. The only weapons he had in his poorly stocked arsenal were the unwavering support of his arms as he held her and the odd platitude mumbled near her ear. The whole experience left him wrung out like an old dish rag and riddled with guilt that he couldn't do any more. But he wanted to. He'd move heaven and earth to ease her pain.

'It will be all right, Thea—I promise.' What was he saying? He was in no position to promise. Gray really had no idea if his common-sense treatments would work. His knowledge was rusty. He'd had no real cause to use it in the last decade and had long ago given up keeping up with the new ideas of the equine world. Although he was sure he'd read or heard mention of some fellow suspending a horse from the ceiling before and if a cooling poultice worked on a human sprain, it stood to reason it might work on other animals. The truth was, he might well have made no difference to poor Archimedes's situation whatsoever. He kissed the top of her head and buried his nose in her curls. She finally tilted her face up to look at him, her eyes so sad. 'I'll make this right, Thea. You can trust me.' He saw hope kindle then. Hope and belief in him that was both humbling and made him feel ten feet tall. Of its own accord, his head began to lower, intent on kissing away all her pain…

'Oh, my dear! Oh, my dear!' The Viscountess suddenly burst through the French doors, still wearing her bonnet and travelling clothes. 'I have just heard what happened. Poor Archimedes! And poor you!' The older woman rushed over and began to fuss around Thea, dragging her out of his arms and back towards the house, leaving Gray no choice but to impotently follow, ridiculously aggrieved to have been usurped in Thea's moment of need. 'I am sure he will recover, dearest. I know how much you love him.'

Back in the parlour, as a pale Thea quietly wept against her aunt's shoulder, Gislingham tapped Gray on the arm and gestured beyond the door, then limped out. Gray was glad to escape. Not because of Thea's tears—but because he wanted to be the only one who consoled her. Worrying and dangerous ground indeed. 'What happened?'

Gray told him every detail and watched the man bristle. 'Blasted Purbeck! The fool shoots off his gun at all hours with scant regard for his neighbours. We've had words about it before. A few years ago, back before this happened.' He pointed to his ravaged body. 'He came within a hair's breadth of killing me! He was shooting pheasants or grouse or something well out of season, and his bullet went clean through my hat. It took every ounce of my restraint not to punch the blighter on the nose. Now poor Thea's horse is injured! And for what? All so the idiot can brag to whichever lamentable soul he has forced to dine with him that he is so manly he killed the dinner himself! I've never understood it. The sight of blood has always made me queasy and I couldn't eat a thing I'd watched choke on its dying breath.'

But sleep soundly knowing men have been murdered at your word? Gray bit back the angry, incredulous retort and tried to push his understandable prejudices to one side. Not for King and country this time, but for Thea. His friend... The friend his arms still longed to hold. The same friend who was currently making his heart ache in a way that did not feel at all like simple friendship. If anything, it felt alarmingly like...affection. Perhaps more than that. A knot of emotion formed in his throat. Fear and realisation. He was in too deep—but knew he couldn't back away and that had precious little to do with his mission and everything to do with her.

'Tell me plain, young man, so I can prepare. Does the nag stand a fighting chance or are we merely prolonging the inevitable?'

'I think it's just a sprain. Perhaps a bad one. But if I'm right he might recover.' Seeing her so distraught, he'd nurse the beast day and night for a month if he had to. Whatever it took to make her smile again. What was that about?

'I hope you are right.' The Viscount clumsily lowered himself on to an ottoman by the wall, suddenly looking old and frail. 'Archimedes was her father's horse. Her last link to him bar me. I can only assume that is part of the reason she is so upset. She lost her father young. A carriage accident. Such a tragedy. Maybe this has churned that all up?' There was a chance. Her grief was that raw. 'She had nightmares for months afterwards and thoroughly blamed herself.'

'Why?'

'They argued that day. Something which was a frequent occurrence because they were both as headstrong as each other, but which always quickly blew over. He'd lay down the law, she'd rebel and then he'd despair of her wilful nature when she refused to comply. But once they had both cooled off, they would both apologise. My brother and my niece both had twin fiery tempers that matched their fiery hair. Tempers that burned hot instantly, then cooled just as quickly. Except that day, he stormed out in anger and they never got to make it up. She used to dwell on that a great deal, no matter how much I tried to tell her my brother wouldn't have cared. He adored his daughter and, like me, royally spoiled her rotten. But she forgot that in the midst of her grief. I suppose it's easier to focus on the negatives than remember the positives. To lose Archimedes through tragedy...well, that would be a bitter blow indeed.'

As Gray digested that, he realised it was entirely plausible. Those fragile links to the past mattered. He doubted he'd ever set foot in Wales again for exactly that reason. Wales, his mother, Cecily and the hornet's nest his life had quickly turned into were all inextricably linked to that place.

The butler approached on silent feet and coughed politely. 'The post has finally arrived, my lord. Did you want it now?' On the silver salver in his hand was one letter. A letter written in the same, elegant, sloping hands as the ones tied with ribbon locked in the Viscount's desk.

The older man glanced at it and sighed in relief. 'Put it in my study, thank you. I shall read it later.' Just as Gray would read the few he had pilfered from that same study a few hours ago at his earliest possible convenience. In an hour or three. Once he was sure Thea was all right.

Chapter Sixteen

They were love letters. Beautifully written. Poignant and filled with all the angst and longing of a love that wasn't allowed to be, yet managed to survive regardless. The earliest ones were over twenty years old and intimate. The author of the letters described her joy at Gislingham's tenderness alongside the emotional fulfilment the intimacy had created.

I suspected you were the one. Now I know it. I refuse to feel guilty for loving you.

A few years on and the situation appeared hopeless.

I know you are married and that I must be part of your past, but I think of you every single day and what we might have had and curse fate for introducing us to each other too late to change things.

In his haste to grab a decent sample, Gray had missed a decade's worth of the doomed story of the star-crossed lovers, but the next letter had a wholly different tone. Chatty and filled with gossip. Family stories about her mother, her brother and her new nephew.

*Such an adorable cherub with eyes almost as dark
as your Thea's.*

This was a relationship where everything was shared.
Almost as if out of their initial passion, they had found
a way to be friends. Yet the final paragraph discussed a
stolen weekend by the sea where they had been free to be
solely with one another.

*You are my everything. Tonight I shall lie on my
pillow and blow you a thousand kisses. Make sure
you catch them.*

By the date, he was sure Gislingham had remarried by
that time. All their intelligence suggested he had walked
Caroline down the aisle within a year of his first wife's
death. Had he and his true love not reconnected before
then? Was she also married? It seemed a great shame that
these two people were clearly meant to be together, but,
like ships passing in the night, never came quite close
enough. He wished he had taken more of the letters to
know the full picture, but was also glad he hadn't. The
Gislingham on the page was too likeable. Too much like
the old man who had fretted about his niece yesterday
and who loved to laugh.

The accounts Gray had taken from the Viscount's desk
were also surprising and thankfully thorough enough that
Gray had no cause to break into Thea's bedchamber. Her
fortune was quite staggering and diligently managed. She
did have stocks in ships—but a totally legitimate fleet.
You couldn't work hand in glove with the Excise Men
and not know which companies were above board and
which worked hard to appear to be. These were owned by
Quakers and, famously, not only diligently paid all their

levies and tariffs, but also eschewed transporting any items which had links with slavery. She also had shares in a successful pottery, several banks and a publishing house. None of which seemed even slightly dubious.

More curious were Gislingham's private investments. He had a similar portfolio to Thea, but a quarter of its size. He was a wealthy man to be sure, but the majority of his money-making efforts—on paper, at least—appeared to be on her behalf. Almost as if he really was securing her future after he was gone, but was perfectly content to live comfortably within his means himself.

Completely incongruous with the man Gray suspected Gislingham to be—and more like the devoted, loving man in these letters. Unless those accounts were all the clever ruse of a genius who had known that someone would one day come looking and had constructed a legitimate façade which he hid behind. The Boss wouldn't be stupid enough to keep any evidence of his criminal dealings at home. But were these love letters faked, too? He glanced back down at the one in his hand and cast it aside. The private emotions spilling on to every neatly written page made him feel ashamed to read them. Voyeuristic, even. Perhaps because he knew what it felt like to love deeply and then to lose it.

Unlike the Viscount's, every heartfelt letter he had sent to Cecily before her marriage had been returned unopened. Something he was glad of now. She had ripped his young heart from his chest and trampled it. That was enough. She didn't need to know exactly how much her betrayal had hurt him or how much he had wanted her back. The same day she married his brother in Wales, Gray had stepped on a merchant ship in Bristol bound for the Orient, strangely embracing the weeks of horrendous seasickness because it numbed the pain in his heart.

Then he had banished her from his thoughts until he had arrived here in Suffolk, knowing the mere memory of her face, her voice and their shared childhood would stir it all up afresh.

Except it *was* different. Time had taken the sting out of the memories. He had to concentrate hard to conjure an image of Cecily. That face he had adored was hazy and blurred. He couldn't hear her voice any more. Didn't feel that sharp pain in his ribs when he pondered what might have been, because for some reason it no longer mattered—because she no longer mattered.

Why that was, he wasn't inclined to examine—suffice it to say that it was an entirely different woman who consumed his thoughts now. And as he approached the stables at Gislingham Hall, he felt his blood fizz with excitement at the prospect of seeing her. Another thing best not examined. He was here for Archimedes and to catch The Boss. Those were the only two tangibles he would focus on in a swirling sea of variables and he would cling to both like a piece of driftwood in a storm.

The big horse was munching hay, apparently quite content to have the ceiling bear most of his weight and not the least bit bothered by the peculiar harness supporting his belly. Without asking permission from the stable hands, he made a huge fuss of the brute, then crouched down to unwrap the poultice from his fetlock. Last night, to give his mind something else to do rather than worry about how badly Thea had taken the injury, Gray had visited the stable again late and reapplied a fresh one. Now the joint was still swollen, but less so. He was able to run his hands over all of it without Archimedes flinching once. A very encouraging sign.

Seeing as his unlikely treatment appeared to be working, Gray repeated it, bathing the leg in ice, then wrapping it in another cooling poultice, then took himself off to report the progress to Thea.

'She's gone off to lick her wounds.' The Viscount had insisted Gray eat breakfast with him in his private sitting room. 'Came down this morning apologising for carrying on, checked on Archimedes and I haven't seen her since. She does that, does Thea. She's one to mull by nature. Ponders everything far too long and then pretends to everyone she is fine and dandy, when we all know she isn't. She's always been the same. I never quite know what's going on inside her head.'

'Was she the same when her father died?'

'Worse. Bottled it all up inside. It took more than a year to see smatterings of the old Thea return.' He chewed thoughtfully on his bacon. 'Heartbreaking.'

'What happened?' Because all the King's Elite intelligence had focused on Gislingham's past, Thea's was a grey area. He watched the older man slump a little in his chair at the memory, then felt guilty for dragging it up. 'It's really none of my business. I'm sorry.'

'No… You of all people should probably know.' What did that mean? 'They were staying here. They always came down from Cambridge to rusticate here over the summer. It's a short journey back and my brother would sometimes return to attend to whatever business he had to attend to. They'd argued. I told you that. Over something nonsensical, as was their wont, and he'd stomped out, muttering about being cursed with the most wilful daughter any man had ever been cursed with while she haired up the stairs like a banshee and slammed her bedchamber door. An hour later, the constable came. The brake on his gig had failed as he'd tried to avoid something in the road. I can't say I know exactly what happened that dreadful morning, suffice it to say his gig overturned and his neck was broken.'

Thea watched her feet swish backwards and forwards in the water, feeling both stupid and guilty. The logical, adult half of her brain knew that what had happened to Archimedes was a fluke. Out of anyone's control and just one of those awful things that happened from time to time when you least expected it. But Impetuous Thea's brain still remembered the crushing guilt she had felt as a child at angering her papa so that he had driven away for the last time in a temper. A memory which might have been forgotten, had her uncle not had his stroke within an hour of another blazing row brought about by her wilful, rebellious nature and selfish intention to do exactly what she wanted—regardless of what he wanted.

Somewhere along the line, those two tragically similar events had become intertwined and she had promised herself never to behave like that again, just in case they were linked and she was entirely to blame. It was nonsensical, yet she couldn't shake it. She had always shouldered much of the blame for both her father's untimely death and her uncle's stroke—and always would. Carried both events around in her heart daily while trying, and ultimately failing, to behave better than that wilful girl she had been. Digging her heels in, shouting and slamming doors were largely a thing of the past.

But as Gray had warned her, leopards didn't change their spots. As much as she tried to curb Impetuous Thea, sometimes it was just too hard. Yesterday, she had allowed herself to be tempted again by forbidden fruit and it had ended in tragedy. Or at least near tragedy. Another similarity, which in her distressed state had petrified her and rendered her senseless for a good hour.

Then common sense and reality had prevailed and she was heartily ashamed of herself. It was one thing to think nonsense in the private confines of one's own head. It was quite another to allow the world to see it. Thea had worried her poor uncle when he didn't need the stress, dominated all of poor Aunt Caro's afternoon with her wailing and probably sent Gray running for the hills.

Lord only knew what the poor man had thought. One minute she had been shamelessly pursuing him and the next she was a snivelling, grizzling mess against his chest. At the time, it had been the only place she had wanted to be. Still did, truth be known, and that didn't frighten her half as much as it should, if at all.

Gray had chiselled his way into her thoughts and occupied far too many of them, just as he had since she had first encountered him.

Here.

The exact spot where she had headed at the crack of dawn to lick her wounds. That was only partly what she had been doing for the better part of two hours, when she couldn't glance at the water without picturing him in it and had probably come here with the express intention of doing so. Unhindered, unwatched and unjudged for her outrageous, lustful fantasies in which there was just her and him, cool water and a shocking absence of clothes.

'There you are.' He strolled into the clearing, making her jump, and stood a little awkwardly, eventually settling with his hands on his hips, taking in the whole clearing as if seeing it for the first time. How splendid. They were both beyond uncomfortable. 'Archimedes seems well. It's early days, of course, but so far so good. He has made excellent progress in just one day.'

'Yes. I saw. Thank you. Even our pessimistic stable master is hopeful.' She should probably apologise for her out-of-character and childish outburst, but had no earthly idea where to start without looking like a complete fool. Instead she stared back at her feet in the water, cringing, willing him away.

'I suspect we need to have one of those honest conversations you're so fond of.'

'I suppose so.' She couldn't look up, but sensed him move closer. Then heard him tug off both boots before he lowered himself on to the bank next to her. He sat quietly, his bigger feet idly swishing next to hers, clearly assuming she should start. It was time to bite the bullet.

'I'm sorry about yesterday. I got myself in a fluster.' A hysterical mess more like. Clinging on to him like a ninny. Irrationally inconsolable.

'A fluster?' She could hear the smile. She didn't need to humiliate herself further by looking at it. 'If that's what a fluster looks like, I'd hate to see you in a state. You scared the hell out of me. Do you want to tell me about it?'

'Not particularly. It was a shocking bout of useless self-pity that I am heartily ashamed of.'

'We all have our moments, Thea. Your horse was hurt and for a while things seemed grim.'

'And in the midst of the crisis, I was a hindrance rather than a help. I hate that.' Almost as much as she hated the hideous display of histrionics she had subjected him to.

'I disagree. It was you who suggested the cart. You who fetched it and organised the grooms. In the midst of the crisis you were a rock.' His hand found hers where it sat in her lap and he closed his fingers around it, instantly making her warm. 'Only once the crisis was past did you falter. Something you are entirely entitled to do. Nobody can be a rock all the time. I just came to check you are all right now. I hated seeing you so upset.'

'It's silly having such an attachment to a horse. He's just a horse.'

'I'd be devastated if anything happened to Trefor. I adore the useless mutt. And Archimedes isn't just a horse. He was your father's horse. I understand how much the things which link you to a lost parent matter. My mother's ruby means the world to me. I could never part with it. Fortunately, I never have to watch it age and die. Such attachments merely make us human, Thea, and, in case you were wondering, I certainly don't judge you for falling apart at the prospect of losing him yesterday. Grief is also human. It's real and it's visceral and it hurts.' Something he would understand more than most. 'What does concern me is the way you blamed yourself for what happened, when you were blameless and it was the droning, spitting Colonel who shot the gun. He just came around to apologise, by the way. I left your uncle reading him the riot act.' His other hand gently tipped her face to him. 'Why would you blame yourself for a freak accident?'

'It's ridiculous. You really wouldn't understand.'

'You understood how I lost my fortune thanks to my momentous fluster all those years ago. What makes you think I won't be equally as sympathetic?' Those unusual silvery-blue eyes were unwavering and kind. 'I am assuming it has something to do with your father... Your uncle told me the last words you exchanged on the day he passed were said in anger.'

'They were.' Thea considered lying, then discounted it. He would know if she lied. He was that perceptive. 'He wanted me to spend an extra hour with my governess perfecting my times tables. I wanted to climb Uncle Edward's apple tree. I told him I hated him and he never came back.'

'You were a child. He knew you didn't mean it.'

'Did my uncle also tell you that the last words I said to him before his stroke were also said in anger? Just like that awful day when my father was killed, I had given the rebellious part of my nature free rein and as a result my uncle and I butted heads worse than we ever had before. The eerie similarities are not lost on me.' He frowned, disbelieving. Who could blame him? To her own ears what she was trying to articulate sounded daft.

'There was a man. An officer. He was a few years older than me, handsome, dashing and charming and like a dolt I believed all his flowery words. Uncle Edward saw right through him from the outset, but I wouldn't listen. Even when I was presented with evidence of the man's many debts I refused to consider such an experienced and intriguing gentleman would be so shallow to want only my money when he sounded so sincere. To cut a very short story shorter, being underage, I was forbidden from seeing my dashing soldier again and in response I was a total horror. I accused my uncle of being jealous, because his relationship with my aunt was so hideous he couldn't bear to see me find true love.' The next part was the bit she was most ashamed of, so turned her head away in case he also judged her as harshly as she judged herself.

'My uncle is not one to lay the law down, so the fact he had was unusual and I should have heeded him. But against his express instructions, I sent my *beloved* a note and crept out that night to meet him. He tried to seduce me, promising he would happily marry me once my virtue was gone, and alarm bells began to ring. We barely knew each other—three dances over two separate assemblies was the full extent of our acquaintance and already he was suggesting marriage? I was a dolt, but clearly still a suspicious one. It didn't ring true. I tested the theory by lying and telling him that I wouldn't receive a penny of my fortune till I turned thirty.'

'If he had loved you, he wouldn't have cared.'

'I know. But instead he said something which proved me to be the stupidest of fools and the most wilful of idiots.' She mimicked the scoundrel's overly sincere voice. 'Your uncle won't see you in the poor house, *my darling*. I am certain the terms of your trust can be altered.'

'Ah.'

'Ah, indeed. I ran home with my tail between my legs and walked through the door to chaos. My aunt was wailing about what was to become of her. Bertie was beside himself with grief and the physician said my uncle wouldn't survive the night.'

'Ergo, in your mind, you were somehow responsible for his stroke just as you were your father's carriage accident? When you weren't present for either event, nor witnessed the particular circumstances?'

'Both times I was lured by forbidden fruit.'

'Did your uncle know that you had disobeyed him?'

'No. He still doesn't.' Gray was using logic when all the tangled emotions inside her were completely illogical. 'I told you it was daft. But perhaps if I hadn't roused both of their tempers, neither tragedy would have happened?'

'And perhaps they still would have. None of us can fully control what fate has in store for us. How old were you?'

'Barely twenty and too green for my own good.'

'It's a dangerous age, twenty. You think you know it all when really you understand nothing of the world. As I know to my cost.' His foot brushed hers in the water and he stared down at it for a few seconds before moving it away. 'I suppose there were echoes of what had happened before. Enough for a vivid imagination to combine and jump to superstitious conclusions. But that doesn't explain yesterday's reaction. You never once lost your temper or rebelled. Did it churn all that misplaced guilt up again? All we did was have a perfectly pleasant morning ride to the village.'

'That Impetuous Thea orchestrated.'

Chapter Seventeen

'Impetuous Thea?'

'The part of me that refused to learn my twelve times table the morning my father was killed. The part that gorged on apples instead. The same part that ran off to meet the soldier. Was letting him kiss her at the exact moment my uncle was struck down.'

'The part that is obviously *entirely* responsible for two completely unlinked events, a decade apart, neither of which you were there for.' He smiled, his thumb tracing lazy circles on the back of her hand that were playing havoc with her pulse despite her misery. 'So you indulged in a bit of kissing? That doesn't make you evil, merely human. And the fact that you were not compliant and sought a little adventure hardly justifies fate punishing you. It makes you interesting. Flawed, as we all are. You were twenty. Barely an adult. And unlike your father, your uncle didn't die. If fate had truly wanted to punish you, that stroke would have killed him. It would have broken Archimedes's leg in two. Have you considered that?'

She hadn't. That night and yesterday could have been so much worse. 'Perhaps they were warning shots across the bow?'

'Or more likely it was an unfortunate coincidence. As so much of life is.' He leaned closer so that they touched from shoulder to hip. 'I am intrigued to know how Archimedes's sprain fits into this picture. What nefarious deed did Impetuous Thea do to make Colonel Purbeck fire off his gun at precisely that moment?'

She tugged her hand away because his touch was waylaying her from her guilt. 'I never should have been there in the first place! Impetuous Thea wanted to...' Thea sighed, feeling thoroughly embarrassed and ridiculous. 'The implausible long and the short of it is, I think fate punishes me for my wilfulness. That's why I keep Impetuous Thea locked in her box.'

He didn't laugh. That was something. But he was quiet for the longest time. 'If you were being scientific about it, you should probably test that theory.'

'Test it?' The idea was as daft as her fears were. 'How do you suppose I do that?'

'Tempt fate. Let Impetuous Thea out of the box for a month. Live in the moment, be a slave to her whims. Enjoy yourself. Eat every piece of forbidden fruit. If you are correct, then you are in for a horrendous few weeks and you can lock her up for good. If not, then life will continue much as it always does. There will be good things and bad things—because there always are. But unless there are significantly more bad things than usual, then I think you can safely and *scientifically* say it makes no difference if you cage the beastie or let her run riot. Life is far too short not to be yourself or to worry about what fate might throw at you, because in my experience it throws things at you regardless.'

'You make it all sound simple.'

'Not simple exactly, more philosophical. I'm all about leaving the past in the past where it belongs. It can't be changed, so onwards and upwards. Embrace the moment and follow the path it sends you on. That is what makes life exciting.'

'Is that another one of your mottos?'

'It's a bit long to be a motto in the strictest sense of the motto, more an edict to abide by. Let's take what happened with Cecily as a classic example. It was all very tragic at the time and losing my fortune was an act of desperate stupidity—but if those two awful things hadn't happened, I never would have joined the merchant navy. Then I never would have travelled the world and done all the things I've done. I wouldn't have Trefor and I wouldn't be here now. And you'd have been riding all alone with Archimedes and Colonel Purbeck might still have fired his gun—and without my hare-brained idea to truss him to the ceiling, the stable master would have put your old horse out of his misery and you'd be mourning him today instead of feeling sorry for yourself.' He laced his fingers in hers and sighed. 'My convoluted point is this, Thea. Things always happen for a reason, even if the reason for them is not immediately apparent. And if I may say, the last thing a woman with an imagination as vivid as yours should be doing is wasting time over-thinking things. Nothing good can come of it.'

He stood and pulled her up with him. 'Out of interest, what *did* Impetuous Thea orchestrate yesterday?' She instantly felt her face burn with the shame of it all. Hell would have to freeze over before she admitted she had only wanted to see him.

'I can't recall.'

'That's such a pity. Because from the ferociousness of that blush, it's bound to be good. Never mind, I shall interrogate you all the way home to see if I can provoke...' Thea planted both her hands in the centre of his chest, pushed and giggled as he went flying backwards into the water. He emerged, coughing and spluttering, but smiling. 'What was that for?'

'Don't blame me! You're the one who told me to give Impetuous Thea free rein.' Then she picked up her skirts and ran.

Gray found himself smiling as he fixed his ridiculously early morning coffee, then frowned when he realised he was smiling because of her. Again. Over the past week, he had been doing that a lot. Every morning he sprang out of bed at the crack of dawn filled with purpose, went to check on Archimedes, then used that as a flimsy excuse to call on her. Although yesterday she had been waiting for him at the stables and, instead of drinking tea in the company of her uncle, the pair of them had ended up chatting for more than an hour tramping across the meadow with Trefor as he followed whichever sniffing trail took his fancy in between adoring Thea as only a besotted dog could.

Lord Fennimore was delighted with Gray's progress, assuming he was ingratiating himself into Gislingham's circle diligently for the sake of the mission, when the mission had nothing to do with it. It was Thea he was actively seeking out and, while he asked the odd pertinent question which would help the King's Elite, the bulk of his time was spent getting to know her.

It was all very proper and platonic. All roughly within the parameters of their truce, but the fact that he didn't flirt with her did not in any way reflect how much he wanted to or how hard he had to work not to. Although yesterday there had been a moment, when she had been smiling and he had been walking alongside her trying to make her laugh, when their eyes had locked for far longer than they should have and he had almost kissed her before he'd stopped himself. Since then, he had given a great deal of thought to that moment and still wasn't entirely sure that *not* kissing her had been the right thing to do.

A sound outside pulled him out of his pleasant musings a second before Fennimore came through the back door and stopped dead at the sight of Gray.

'You're up early.'

He took in his superior's guilty-looking appearance and his face split in a grin. 'And you're apparently home late.' By the lack of cravat, ruffled hair and the crumpled evening clothes, the old man had either spent the night in a gaming hell—unlikely in this quiet corner of Suffolk— or unbelievably he'd spent the night with a woman. 'How was dinner at Lady Crudgington's?'

'Very pleasant.' But Lord Fennimore was glowing crimson. 'But all that rich food gave me indigestion, so I decided to take myself off for a walk this morning. Early. Very early. As it was dark, I pulled on the first clothes that came to hand.' It had been the old man himself who had taught Gray the art of spotting a liar. Liars, he was often prone to drone, always overembellished with too much detail.

'Of course you did.' Gray winked saucily. 'Rich food. A pre-dawn stroll and wearing the first clothes you could grab. Such excellent embellishment and so early... You *old dog*!' It had the most spectacular effect.

Clenched fists at his sides. Blinking and stuttering. 'Keep your filthy accusations to yourself, Gray! I went for a walk, damn it. I haven't seen her ladyship since I left her last night!'

'Of course, sir. And let's not forget the indigestion. Did the exercise help it in any way?'

The sound of horses outside prevented Gray's immediate murder. Two agents burst in without knocking and got straight to the point. 'There have been developments, sir. The Excise Men have captured a ship at Leiston! It's full to the brim, sir.'

'Do we have the crew?' Lord Fennimore snapped into action, his embarrassment and indigestion now miraculously cured.

'Every single one of them. And there's more, sir. Within the last half-hour, an express arrived at Gislingham Hall. The rider must have been minutes behind ours on the road from the coast.'

Nobody needed to mention how significant this coincidence was. It was their first tangible clue that The Boss and Gislingham were one and the same. 'I assume you are planning to check on Archimedes this morning?'

'I was heading there straight after breakfast.'

'Good. Observe the lay of the land, but tread cautiously. I'll head to Leiston to interrogate the crew.' The light of battle was in Lord Fennimore's eyes. 'The net is closing in, gentlemen. This is the most perilous time. Keep your wits about you and don't make any mistakes. One wrong move now and we destroy a year's worth of work.'

Less than an hour later, Gray trotted casually into Viscount Gislingham's stable yard with Trefor in tow, expecting to see some hint of uproar, but instead nothing appeared out of the ordinary. He dismounted and went directly to Archimedes, who was gingerly putting some weight on his newly strapped leg as he munched on hay. Only after he had given the animal a thorough going-over did he risk heading to the house to report the good news to Thea.

To his surprise, the ancient butler immediately invited

him upstairs to the Viscount's private apartments where the old man was sat eating a jovial breakfast with his niece as if he hadn't a care in the world. 'Lord Gray! Sit! Sit. Cook has outdone herself with the coddled eggs this morning. You won't be disappointed. Will it be coffee or chocolate today?'

Next to him, Thea beamed and, despite his important mission, everything else went out of Gray's mind as he basked in her smile. He sat in the chair directly opposite, allowing himself a surreptitious inhale of her sultry jasmine perfume as she lent down to make a fuss of the bouncing Trefor at her side, then caught the Viscount eyeing him with interest. 'Coffee, if you please.' He needed his wits about him today of all days. But, lord, she looked lovely this morning. 'How are you this fine morning, my lord?'

'Cannot grumble, young man. I slept like the dead and woke with the lark. And today promises to be most entertaining. Harriet is coming around to paint my portrait.' He chuckled, nudging Gray with his elbow. 'Is it wrong that I find myself delighted at the prospect? There is a disastrous inevitability about it, which appeals to my warped sense of the ridiculous. I am determined to hang the finished monstrosity in the gallery next to my father's portrait. Purely to vex the old tyrant. He always took himself far too seriously.'

Concentrating proved difficult as Gray felt Thea lean to pour his coffee and his eyes involuntarily flicked to hers. Locked. Held. They did that a lot nowadays. Lingering glances and knowing looks that negated the need for words. All very worrying, but equally as special. All seemingly as natural as breathing. 'I hope you two youngsters aren't going to waste this glorious day inside.'

'I have a basket to deliver in the village if Trefor would appreciate the walk?'

He needed to stay close to the hall. 'Trefor always appreciates a walk. And a good sniff. We'll happily accompany you.' He really needed to work harder at being a better spy. 'At least for a little while.' Where he would use the time to subtly interrogate her as well as thoroughly enjoy her company. He watched her rise and prepare a plate for him and tried not to wish she could be there for every breakfast.

'I suppose at some point I should ask you about your intentions, young man.'

'I'm sorry?' His head whipped around to find the Viscount grinning.

'One of those cringingly awkward man-to-man conversations which have been laid down in the statutes, where I stand like an admiral inspecting the fleet, rocking on my heels and piercing you with my overprotective and fatherly glare.' Gray felt the colour drain from his face, not at all liking the direction things were going. 'I shall enquire about your prospects and be generally intimidating.'

'Er...well...' Exactly how did he get out of this without hurting Thea, insulting the Viscount and jeopardising the mission? The plate of coddled eggs appeared in front of him alongside Thea's hand on his back. He felt that touch everywhere. Didn't want it to end.

'He's testing you. For his own wicked amusement. And you are failing abominably.' She sat down, her own cheeks a little pink, he noticed. 'He's been doing the same to me since you knocked me into the brook.'

'And I've got precious little out of her. It has both me and Harriet intrigued. The pair of you have been the source of much speculation.'

Thea pointed at her uncle with her fork. 'Desist or I shall tell Bertie you have been very lax with your exercises and I caught you smoking that cigar.'

'Talk of the devil and the devil appears.' The Viscount's manservant suddenly filled the door frame, still in his travelling clothes.

'Bertie! You're home early!' Yet another pertinent coincidence this morning. Thea tossed down her napkin and greeted the servant like a dear friend, kissing him on the cheek. 'We didn't expect you for another week at least.'

The manservant and his master shared an odd look, one that spoke volumes. 'I knew I was needed, so cut my visit short. Lax in his exercises, you say? Then I am glad I came home…'

Aside from that look, nothing else untoward happened in the next hour. Bertie disappeared and then reappeared just as quickly in fresh clothes. Neither man seemed in a hurry to do anything or seemed particularly perturbed. Harriet arrived with her easel and among much hilarity she began to paint. As they left, Gray took his time, watching the servants, the outbuildings and the drive for signs that something was amiss. But if The Boss was bothered about losing a ship loaded with brandy as well as its entire scurvy crew, he did a very good job of hiding it.

Chapter Eighteen

Gray was unusually quiet for the rest of breakfast, something Thea entirely blamed her uncle for. Intentions and prospects indeed, when neither of them had discussed anything vaguely romantic since their truce! Although the past week had been romantic as far as she was concerned. She had never spent so much pleasant time with a man. And although he never instigated any of their casual walks or rides after he had attended to Archimedes, he had never turned a suggestion down either. Which she had decided to take as a very good sign, despite the dire lack of flirting or touching or incendiary heated looks.

If anything, he had been the perfect gentleman. Rigidly sticking to the parameters of their truce but allowing their new friendship to blossom. She was glad for that—but wanted more. Especially since Impetuous Thea had been out in the wild for seven whole days now, too, and nothing untoward had happened at all. She never curbed her in front of Gray or Harriet and had twice told her uncle off quite forcibly. Once for the sneaky cigar she had caught him with and then briskly confiscated, and once for his shameless cheating at chess. Both times he had bristled and bit back, and neither time did he keel over. It encouraged her to be bolder, which in turn made her feel lighter and happier than she had in years. It also made her wonder if that boldness might be just what was needed to give Gray a gentle nudge to let him know she was open and receptive to more should he feel inclined. The more she got to know him, the more it seemed a shame that such a warm and passionate man was so averse to allowing himself to love again.

His was a big heart, filled with joy, and it was increasingly playing havoc with hers. With each meeting, a little more of her wariness melted away and she became more convinced he wasn't forbidden fruit, but the man for her. And she was the woman for him.

Yesterday, she had almost kissed him. They had been walking along, chatting amiably and laughing, then her eyes had locked with his and lingered. She had instinctively licked her lips and watched those wolf-like irises darken, found herself leaning towards him in invitation. Then lost her nerve at the last moment, fearing she had misread the signals or might push him away because he was adamantly wary of anything involving hearts. Particularly when one of the hearts was his.

They had discussed that a little this past week also, always at Thea's instigation, too, and although it was still clearly a very sore topic, he had opened up. Enough that she was now convinced it was the fear of heartbreak that made him keep his heart at arm's length, rather than his continued deep and abiding love for the awful woman who had broken it. In fact, he had confessed yesterday also that he now had to concentrate hard to properly recall Cecily's face. Something which had apparently surprised him, but made Thea's heart soar.

Because her wary heart was waning. Instead of being instantly suspicious or worried about his motives, she found herself thoroughly enjoying each and every moment in a way she never had before. She got butterflies before she saw him, tingles once she did and a delightfully warm feeling deep inside simply knowing they occupied the same planet. As well as a completely different sort of warm feeling every single time she looked at him or pictured him naked in the brook.

'Fetch the ball, Trefor!'

Shamelessly she feasted on the sight of him pulling back his arm and throwing the tattered ball, admiring the way the muscles in his shoulders and back bunched. He really was a very fine specimen of manhood. Once she plucked up the courage to kiss him again, she was going to allow Impetuous Thea to thoroughly explore those muscles. He glanced back, then paused to wait for her, his eyes fixed on Trefor as he bounded through the tall grass after his beloved cricket ball. 'I meant to ask— one of the grooms mentioned your uncle received an express early this morning. I trust it was not bad news.'

'He did?' That was news to her. 'He never mentioned anything, so I doubt it was of much importance.'

'Perhaps they were mistaken. He seemed in perfectly good spirits. It was good of Bertie to come back early, although I am not certain your uncle was as surprised to see him as you were. He looked relieved, though—as if he had wanted him back.'

'Bertie is his right arm. Always has been—but more so since his stroke. He's worked for Uncle Edward for all the years I have been alive and longer. Although I have no idea how many years. I've never thought to ask. Dear Bertie is the only person truly able to make my stubborn uncle do what he is supposed to.' Without his diligence, he might have died in those first dreadful weeks after the stroke.

'Really? He holds that much sway?'

'Much more than me, I'm sorry to say. But then Bertie doesn't have my fiery temper or my uncle's pig-headedness. He simply issues calm instructions and miraculously we all comply. It's his gift.'

'I wish I could manipulate people to do my bidding.'

'Me, too. Perhaps we both need to be more overt in our manipulations? Perhaps that is the secret. It certainly seems to be working for Harriet.' Something Thea was becoming more and more envious of. 'She seems to have your dour cousin Cedric eating out of her hand.' Gray grinned wickedly, then chuckled, but didn't elaborate as he picked up his pace. 'You know something, don't you?'

'I do.' Gray bent to wrestle the soggy ball out of Trefor's jaws and threw it again into the trees that hid the brook. 'But daren't tell you.'

'Daren't? Is it a secret? For if it is, I have to tell you Harriet will tell me herself.'

'I doubt that. It's not for delicate ears.'

'My ears are hardly delicate! And it shows how little you know Harriet if you think she would censor something. I have been privy to some eye-opening confessions.' Harriet was a great fan of *bed sport*, as she called it. 'Besides, it strikes me as grossly unfair that you should know something that I don't.' He had jogged on ahead after the dog, forcing her to sprint after him and catch him by the arm. 'Tell me, you wretch! Did you catch him stealing a kiss?'

He grinned and shook his head. 'So *innocent*... Worse!' He was laughing, the deep sound doing odd things to her nerve endings.

'Worse?' He watched her puzzle it through, making no attempt to hide his delight when shock replaced curiosity. 'Oh, my goodness! They are...' She felt her cheeks heat as she struggled to find the polite term for the act she suspected.

'The word is *lovers*, Thea.' He raised his dark eyebrows suggestively. 'In truth, I've been itching to tell you all morning, because nobody is as shocked or thoroughly entertained by the situation as I am. But there is no doubt. He came home at the crack of dawn this morning, attempting to creep in in the exact evening clothes he went to hers to dine in last night—minus his cravat.'

'There might be a perfectly innocent explanation...' Harriet was incorrigible. She knew that in her bones. Although scandalous, part of Thea—the impetuous and wilful part—couldn't help but be impressed. Her friend didn't waste time with doubt or overthinking. When she wanted something, she leapt.

'There was nothing innocent in his guilty, convoluted excuses or the brilliance of his beetroot face. Consequently, I am left in no doubt that our older and wiser companions have...'

'Seen each other *naked*.' He roared with laughter and Thea found herself giggling. 'Oh, my goodness. Cedric and Harriet...do you think this is just an affair or something more...serious?'

He paused as if considering it for the first time. 'I have no idea. Cedric keeps his cards very close to his chest. They have been spending an inordinate amount of time together.'

'So have we.' The words had popped out before she could stop them and then she saw his shoulders stiffen. 'By which I mean, they might just be friends. As we are.'

His shoulders relaxed. 'Yes, but they have seen each other naked. There is a difference.'

'I've seen you naked.' What was the matter with her? Why was she intent on spoiling a perfectly lovely walk by pushing him into discussing something he really did not want to discuss.

'Again, there is a difference. You saw me in the altogether from a polite distance. Their nakedness was up close.' There had been nothing polite in the way her eyes had greedily drunk in the sight.

'Do you know, I was secretly rather jealous of you and Trefor that day? It's been so hot and that water looked so cool. Then, of course, thanks to Trefor, I got to enjoy it.'

'Fully clothed is hardly the same. You should give it a go one day when there's nobody around. A naughty bit of nude bathing sounds exactly like the sort of pursuit Impetuous Thea would enjoy.' She would. Except Impetuous Thea wanted to do it with him. An errant thought which made her suddenly peculiarly warm.

'I suspect it's something Trefor is currently enjoying.' Gray stared at the trees and shook his head. 'His absence suggests he's clearly been waylaid by the water again.' It was exactly then that Thea's toes reached the edge of the mystical precipice Harriet kept going on about and immediately all her friend's advice made sense. If there was any sort of future between her and Gray beyond this lovely friendship they shared, then one of them had to leap.

They found the dog swimming backwards and forwards with the ball clamped in his mouth, his tail swishing from side to side like a rudder. Gray tried to get him to stop, feeling slightly uncomfortable that they were in this intimate, secluded spot when moments ago they had been talking about it and other wholly inappropriate things, and his mind was now filled with images of Thea floating naked in the water. Copper hair unbound and fanned out on the surface.

He never should have told her about old Fennimore and

Harriet. No matter how easy he found her to talk to, how frank and open and honest their conversations were, there were certain subjects a gentleman didn't discuss with a woman who wasn't *his* in the biblical sense. Now all he could think about was what it would be like to know her in a biblical sense and that was playing havoc with his senses.

Obviously, she wasn't similarly affected, because she made herself comfortable on the bank. 'Oh, to be a dog! Leave him be for a little while. I'm in no hurry and I'd hate to spoil his fun.' She patted the ground next to her, a place he really did not want to be. Not when his breeches were suddenly tighter and all he wanted to do was kiss her again—and more.

'I should check on my grooms. They claim they will have the exercise yard cleared by today.' Good grief, he sounded jittery. But his feelings regarding Thea were becoming more complicated with every passing day.

'Then leave Trefor with me. I might just allow Impetuous Thea to join him in the water.' She offered him a mischievous half-smile, peering up at him through her ridiculously long lashes which his rampant body responded to immediately. He really didn't want to know that. Or be beyond excited at the idea. Not when he was failing abysmally at being a better spy thanks to his overpowering need to be with her.

'I suppose I could linger a little longer.' Utter madness, but his feet were already making their way towards her. 'Keep Impetuous Thea on the straight and narrow.'

Gray sat, self-conscious and riddled with inappropriate lust, and decided the most sensible course of action was to change the subject back to what he was supposed to be doing. 'I wonder why Bertie rushed back? Do you suppose he was summoned by your uncle?'

'Uncle Edward isn't one to make demands.' She sat

back on her hands, staring up at the dappled sunshine. The pose did wonders for her figure and served to further torture him. 'I think it's lovely that Cedric and Harriet have found one another don't you? I hope they make a go of it.' Her eyes flicked to his. 'In case you haven't already guessed, and despite my justified suspicion of fortune hunters, I'm a romantic at heart. I believe in true love. I know that you are jaded from the experience, but I like to believe that there is the perfect someone for everyone. I'm glad Harriet has been given a second chance.' She took his silence as disagreement. 'Don't you believe in second chances?'

'Of course I do.'

'Just not for you.' She tilted her face back towards the sun, making the obligatory loose tendrils of hair glow copper and gold to torment him. 'Because your heart cannot mend.'

'It's mended enough.' Unstable ground. 'But it's too scarred to risk again.'

'Liar.' She smiled up at the sky. 'At least be honest about it. This has nothing to do with the current state of your heart and everything to do with your silly fear history will repeat itself. You're no different from me for all your bold claims you like to live in the moment and leave it all up to fate. You claim to be full of life. Claim to embrace all its twists and turns and potholes and peculiarities, yet when you find a woman you are drawn to on a far deeper level than you care to admit—your words, Gray, not mine—you create boundaries and silly truces to guard your precious heart. You're a hypocrite. One who is too frightened to live life to the full.'

'You wouldn't understand.' And they were not having this conversation. He shot to his feet, not caring whether or not he looked outraged, because he was, damn it. This conversation crossed a line. He was not going to discuss them. They were friends. Nothing more. He couldn't allow there to be more. 'I need to get back.'

'Go ahead. Run away.' She was smiling wryly, but otherwise seemingly unbothered by his response. 'You're very good at that. But before you go, at least listen to some advice. It's good advice. Yours, in fact.' She sat forward and sighed, then smiled kindly, her dark eyes filled with an emotion he couldn't decipher. 'You were twenty. It's a dangerous age. You think you know everything, when in fact you are barely an adult. I should imagine what Cecily did, to someone with a vivid imagination like yours, would give you an irrational fear of trusting a woman ever again. But what you had with Cecily was one-sided. You loved her and the awful reality is she didn't love you enough back.'

'I know what the awful reality was, Thea. I lived it. And with the greatest respect, it is a subject you have little experience of. You have never been in love so are not in a position to offer me advice.' His hands had fisted at his sides and his poor damaged heart was thumping in his chest. He turned on his heel and began to stride out of the suffocating intimacy of the clearing and the perilous turn in an otherwise pleasant conversation.

'Then I suppose this odd feeling I have for you doesn't count?' At her words his feet stopped and those invisible cords forced him to turn around. She was stood now, proud but vulnerable. And more beautiful and tempting than he had ever seen her. 'The excitement I feel every time I see you. The overwhelming sense of rightness I feel when I'm with you. The affection. The friendship. The desire. You say I have no experience, but this...' both her hands went to her chest to cover her heart '...this certainly feels like what I've always imagined love would feel like.'

'Stop.' Although there was no conviction in his words. She loved him? Instead of making him want to run away, it tempted him to run to her. She loved him? That was... everything. She saw his hesitation and took a step forward.

'I am not Cecily. I don't care about titles. I have no need of a bigger fortune or greater standing in society. None of those things matter to me. I just want you.' She took another cautious step forward. 'If that makes you want to run, then go now before I humiliate myself further.'

Unbelievably, he was disinclined to run. He had promised himself he would never again allow another woman to get under his skin as he had Cecily. But while half of him was terrified by her unexpected confession, the other half—the half that couldn't resist the lure of the moment or the pull of the woman who stood next to him—was intent on staying exactly where he was. Because she had mined under his defences regardless and inexplicably he discovered he was exceedingly glad for the intrusion. His damaged, scarred heart was bursting with something which felt like joy.

'Oh, Thea...' He wasn't going to spoil the moment by considering the ramifications or all the many reasons why it was a bad idea. She loved him.

Him!

That was miraculous, all things considered. More miraculous was the way both relief and warmth bloomed in his chest. Instead of running, and because he was imprisoned by those invisible cords, he closed the distance between them and gently pressed his lips to hers.

It was an honest kiss. Slow, tender and brimming with all the complicated emotional attachments he had avoided for a decade. When she kissed him back, he wound his arms around her and gathered her close, carefully lowering them both to lie on the bank before he deepened the kiss.

Thea didn't hold back, slowly running her curious fingers through his hair, over his shoulders and down his spine before tunnelling under his shirt to find skin. He felt the dappled early morning sun on his back as she tugged his shirt off, then rolled him to lie beneath her so her fingers could explore his chest. Where they trailed, her lips followed, torturing him. Good grief, it felt perfect.

'This is dangerous.' Gray didn't have the strength to stop her, but then the panicked voice in his head came to the fore as he silently hoped she would come to her senses before he completely lost his. 'I can't make any promises.'

'I don't recall asking for any. I am simply following your advice and giving Impetuous Thea free rein. In this precise moment, she simply wants to kiss you.'

This was madness. He should put a stop to it. But his fingers had gone to her hair and were pulling out pins. 'Best not deny her, poor thing. Not when she's been shut in a box for years.' Not at all what he should have said for the sake of his heart—yet his heart was soaring. Beating with more purpose than it ever had before. What did that mean?

He kissed her again and she kissed him back. A heated, open-mouthed kiss that blasted through what was left of his reserve. Let the cards fall where they may. With that acceptance came more relief and joy, both surging through him with such force they made him unsteady. Holding Thea steadied him and anchored him in the present and he realised his heart had not only mended, but was lost again. He wasn't entirely sure when that had happened, but knew it wasn't recent. Perhaps he had lost it that first day, when she had stumbled upon him in the brook. He didn't remember a thunderbolt, but he had felt a connection. One that had grown and thrived. One that felt perfect. So very different from what he had felt for Cecily.

The woman who didn't matter any more. The woman who paled into insignificance now that his heart had found Thea.

As moments went, it was the greatest he had ever experienced. He found himself smiling against her mouth as he accepted his fate and wrestled with veritable ironmongers nestled in her scalp. 'Exactly how many pins do you have in here?'

'A great many. Otherwise my hair is vertical.'

'I'd like to see that.' All her fiery hair loose; all her alabaster skin uncovered. Utter, utter madness, but those invisible cords were wrapping themselves around them, lashing them comfortably together, and he was powerless to fight them. Not when holding her felt so very right and he never wanted this perfect moment of clarity to end.

'It's not a pretty sight.' But she was smiling as she briskly and methodically plucked each pin out, then bent her head forward to shake out the curls. 'I have wayward hair, too.'

It was the first time he had seen it completely unbound and the sight of it had more impact than those few fallen tendrils he had glimpsed before that she was forever attempting to tame. He ran his fingers reverently through a long, copper ringlet, tugging out the curl until it was completely straight. To his delight it stretched way past her hips. 'It's beautiful. You're beautiful.' His hands smoothed their way back up her hips, briefly pausing to span her waist before moving up to cup her breasts. 'You've haunted my dreams, Thea. Have since the first day I met you. I am severely sleep deprived.'

'Me, too.' He loved her earthy giggle. Loved everything about her. Loved that the mere thought of loving her didn't make him want to run. 'But we are young and can sleep when we're dead.'

He kissed her again, their tongues tangling until his body wanted more. Far more than she might be prepared to offer. But he would wait...

Wait? That sounded ominously like he was ready to make plans. 'We should stop. Before this gets out of hand.'

'Very sensible. Is the brook cold?' She chewed her lip shyly before boldly glancing up at him from beneath her lashes. 'Only in my dreams, you're back in there and I am swimming with you.'

There was no doubt he wanted her. Always had, but this was more than lust and so much more than one reckless moment. Unconsciously, he rubbed the spot in the middle of his ribs. Was she worth the risk? 'I'm not sure I can do this, Thea. Not again.' But the voice in his head urged him to gamble once again. It was tempting. She was tempting.

'I don't want to break your heart, Gray. I want to possess it. There's a difference. Unlike her, I shall treasure it and look after it.' Her fingers went to the laces at the back of her dress. He watched, helpless, as the front of her bodice loosened and fell to hang off her shoulders. 'Although don't take my word for it. To be completely sure, you should test the theory. Scientifically, of course. If I break your heart, you'll have the satisfaction of knowing you were right all along. And if I don't...' She stared at him intently. 'Onwards and upwards. It's your motto after all. Leave the past in the past where it should be...' She wiggled her shoulders and the bodice slipped down further, barely covering her breasts. 'And live in this wonderfully unexpected moment with me.'

Chapter Nineteen

Suddenly in a hurry, they both stripped off their clothes. Having never been naked in front of another person before and feeling self-conscious, Thea jumped in the water first, dipping quickly beneath so it covered her to her chin, and shamelessly watched him do the same.

His body was so different from hers. Broad where hers was slight. Angular where she had curves—and hard. The skin on his shoulders and flat abdomen covered intriguing muscles. He had thighs Harriet would approve of, she realised with a giggle. Strong and taut, as if he had spent many an hour in the saddle, but it was the wholly male part of him which appealed to her more. That, too, was hard. For her. And the prospect excited her and terrified her at the same time.

Should she be doing this? They barely knew each other, yet she wanted to be intimate with him. It would be the ultimate grand gesture. For the first time in for ever she had found a man she could trust. She felt giddy and euphoric and overwhelmingly glad she'd had the courage to leap.

Was it too soon?

Her heart said no. He was, bizarrely, everything she had ever wanted. And if she tweaked her essential attributes list, he ticked every one. Gray was prudent in his own way and gave sensible advice. For a purported scoundrel he was delightfully proper. In fact, he had been more of a gentleman to her than all the gentlemen she had encountered since her come out. Cautious with his heart, but adventurous in all else. It went without saying he was trustworthy and, while he wasn't completely above reproach, there were reasons why he had behaved as he had in the past. They had both been young and foolish and lived to rue the day. And they had both survived the experience and emerged the stronger for it. She didn't care if he had no fortune because she knew in her bones he had no interest in such things. He embraced her wayward nature. Enjoyed it. With him, Thea could be herself. He had always brought that out of her, even as she had tried to fight it. When you met the right person, fighting that powerful, all-encompassing emotion was pointless. She understood that now. It was deliciously liberating.

And he wore his breeches well—although she much preferred him out of them.

He climbed in and swam towards her, then caught his arm around her waist, pulling her close for a searing kiss. Wet bare skin next to wet bare skin was a revelation. Her body seemed to fit perfectly against his as if it had been made to do exactly that. Thea curled her arms possessively around his neck, flattening her breasts shamelessly against his chest, and enjoyed the way her pebbled, water-chilled nipples tingled at the contact.

He took his time kissing her. His big hands sliding over her body with aching slowness. Learning its shape and caressing the sensitive places she had not known she possessed until he touched them. Unable to stop herself, Thea's hands also went exploring, marvelling at the feel of the smattering of dark hair on his chest and the way he shuddered when her fingers grazed his nipples. It emboldened her to allow her palms to journey south, until she could tentatively trace the hard, hot shape of him with her fingertip. She watched his eyes close and his Adam's apple bob as he fought for control, until he could stand no more, wrapping his fist about her hand as he schooled her in how to hold him properly. Boldly.

Then he kissed her again, filling his hands with her needy breasts which were screaming for his touch, his thumbs doing wicked things to them which made her cry out in a voice she didn't recognise. A carnal, desperate sound that wanted more. So much more.

As if sensing that, he lifted her so that her over-sensitive nipples came level with his face and took one scandalously into his mouth, flicking the tip with his tongue and smiling against it as she moaned and writhed against him. Suspended in the water, all she could do was cling on to his shoulders as he thoroughly worshipped that breast before he moved slowly to the other. Torturing her with unspeakable pleasure until her legs were locked wantonly around his hips, her body throbbing with need, his hardness jutting against her with all the forbidden promise she had always secretly craved. So close, but yet so far from where she desperately needed it to be.

Of its own accord, her body positioned herself to take him, feeling the whole length of him harden further at the encouragement. 'There are other things we can do...we don't have to do this.' He voice was gravelly and breathless, laced with desire.

'Don't you want to?' Because she did. Thea had passed the point of no return and was ready to commit herself completely. There was no point executing a giant leap of faith to falter at the end. That wasn't a *grand gesture* when she was in the mood to be scandalously grand and shamelessly bold. She wanted to experience all of the things Harriet had alluded to. Wanted to feel such passion that she lost her head and he lost his.

'Of course I want to. But there are implications…'

'Forget them.' She moved her hips to caress him shamelessly, felt his fingers flex against her waist. Heard his laboured breathing as he fought the inevitable. 'Just make love to me, Gray.'

He hesitated for a second, clearly at war with himself. She recognised the second the lure of the moment won, because his beautiful, silvery, wolf-like eyes darkened and locked intently on hers. He watched her as he entered her, as he slowly lowered her body in the cool water to take all of him. His eyes closed only briefly as she winced slightly at the intrusion, as if he shared her pain, and she loved him for that, his strong arms holding her steady as the slight discomfort passed.

'I'm sorry.'

'Don't be. I trust you to make it right.'

He kissed her with such tenderness then that she knew she had made the right decision. 'I will. I promise.'

'I thought you could make no promises?' She didn't wait for his answer, knowing that it might not be at all what she wanted to hear or was ready to accept. Instead, she ignored his brief hesitation and the wary look in his eyes, kissing both away, then losing herself in his kisses and the blissful sensation of him moving inside her.

Neither spoke then. He offered her no promises and no flowery compliments, but he loved her body with such determined and sustained intensity, it didn't matter that so many important things were left unsaid. This was as daunting for him as it was for her. Nothing needed to be settled in the heat of this glorious moment—although for her so much was.

As the last rational thoughts fled from her head, she told him how she felt. If he was not ready to hear the words that was too bad, because she was ready to feel them and say them. 'I love you, Gray. I want to spend for ever with you.'

His answer was a kiss so intense it sent her over the edge. As she tumbled over the second, unexpected precipice, she wrapped her arms and legs tight around his body and dragged him with her. Through the roaring chaos in her head and through the powerful sensations which had possessed her body, she heard his voice. The quiet whisper so close to her ear, choked with emotion and desire.

'God help me, but I love you, too, Thea.'

It was late afternoon before he ventured home. Stunned, unsteady and shaken to his core. He was in love again and cautiously delighted to be so. He recognised all the signs, although despite some of them feeling familiar, they also felt different. It was that difference which occupied his mind now that he was alone and he tried to quantify exactly what had caused it in order to understand it.

Gray had always thought he had loved Cecily with every fibre of his being—but they had never been intimate. They had dabbled in pleasure—in an inexperienced and guilty way—but he had never seen her completely naked or been given the privilege of taking her innocence. In many ways, that lack of intimacy had been a barrier. With hindsight, he could see now that it was her insurance in case something better came along. Back then, he had accepted her reluctance to fully share her body with him as the way things were. They were both saving themselves for their wedding night because propriety dictated they did so. Similarly, as childhood had given way to adulthood, he could now see that his relationship with Cecily had been unbalanced. It was Gray who had done all the running and Cecily who controlled things.

It had always been Cecily who had stopped things getting out of hand, because as much as she had enjoyed his touch—and she had been quite selfish in the pursuit of her own pleasure—she had still had the rational and pragmatic ability to stop. In private she had used his affection and desire to manipulate him to bending to her will, so much so that in public in the latter stages of their relationship she had convinced him to behave as if there was nothing serious between them at all. She had rationed them to one dance at balls and happily allowed him to watch as she was twirled around the room by other men.

Now that he thought upon it, how many times had he watched her waltz with his brother? Certainly enough that he had come to think nothing of it.

In contrast, Thea had given herself with complete abandon. He had given her plenty of opportunities to hold back and she had dismissed every single one. Her trust and complete commitment had humbled him. Initially, it had been daunting. Terrifying, even, because he had known that the physical act of love between them was as much of a declaration as the words had been. She had been the first woman he had made love to with his heart as well as his body and the experience had been earth-shattering and earth-changing as a result. With entirely unscientific motives, he had made love to her twice more and both times the intensity of emotion had been there front and centre throughout.

What had really shocked him was how easy it all was. They had not only made love in the brook, on the bank and then back in the brook again—but they had laughed and chatted and relaxed with each other in between. She

never asked him about the future, nor did he venture anything about it, but she had shared her body with impunity and delighted in sharing his. They had lived entirely
in a moment that had lasted hours, both stripped naked
in more ways than one and, despite not discussing what
would happen next, Gray accepted they would have to.
They would have to because he wanted to.

There was no turning back now. They were in love and
there were plans that needed to be made. All he had to do
first was work out how to remove the giant fly from the
ointment. The enormous elephant in the room. Whichever path he took now was positively littered with potholes and, frankly, he had no idea what to do about it.
Because it didn't take a genius to work out that Gray's
mission, and all the secrets he was keeping from her, had
the power to destroy it all and leave him alone and heartbroken all over again.

That horrendous prospect had occurred to him about
an hour ago and had plagued him the second he finished
their lingering goodbye kiss at the stables and he still
hadn't worked out a way of fixing it. Casually dropping
the fact that he was a spy into the conversation, one who
had lied to her about a number of important details, one
who happened to be searching for enough evidence to
see her uncle hang for his crimes, wasn't an option. Nor
was failing to do his sworn duty for King and country.
Waiting for the cards to fall where they may, his usual
answer to all life's problems, was also unappealing. He
wouldn't trust fate with something of such importance.
Somehow, he would find a way to negotiate the potholes
because he couldn't and wouldn't live through all that
misery again.

Trefor's barking interrupted his thoughts and it was
then Gray saw the subtle signs—the amassed forces of

the King's Elite had made it to Kirton House well before an agent came to tell him.

'Lord Hadleigh is waiting for you inside, sir.'

Of course he was. Now that an arrest was imminent, the lawyer would be chomping at the bit to get started. 'Is Lord Fennimore back?'

'Not yet, sir. We've received word he's staying overnight to continue his interrogations and see the prisoners secure. I'm to tell you that you are in command in his absence.' A responsibility which had now lost all of its appeal. One that meant he might be called upon to hammer the death knell into his and Thea's relationship. 'And to give you this.' The agent handed Gray a burned piece of what once must have been a letter. Remnants of a wax seal still adorned the charred back while on the other side were words which now made no sense because the rest of the sentences were missing, written in neat, tight handwriting.

Men will meet...
...payment in full...
...do not

'The captain of the vessel was in the process of burning this letter as the Excise Men found him. They managed to salvage this. It's not much, but Lord Fennimore wants you to do some subtle digging to see if you can find who wrote it.' A task easier said than done. It wasn't as if he could blithely stroll up to Gislingham and Bertie and demand they write something for comparison.

Wearily, because the full weight of the world now seemed to rest entirely on his shoulders, Gray headed to the kitchen where Hadleigh was calmly drinking coffee. 'What's going on at the Hall?'

'Nothing. To all intents and purposes, Gislingham and

his right-hand man are behaving as if nothing is amiss at all.'

'His right-hand man?'

'Bertie. Or Albert Frederick Walsham, to give him his full name. Ostensibly his manservant but there's more to it than that. I can feel it.' The secretive behaviour. The knowing looks. Instinct told him there was something there. Something more than the bond between a master and an invaluable servant. 'The man watches everyone like a hawk and was the only person to dash back after the express arrived. He was *needed*, apparently.'

Gray shared everything they knew thus far, which was not a whole lot more than they had known when they had first arrived a few weeks ago. But at least they now had this tiny fragment of charred paper and the handwriting of somebody significant, even if they had no earthly idea whose. Then he gave Hadleigh all the papers he had taken on his midnight raid. The lawyer scanned each one silently and thoroughly before pushing them to one side on the old, battered table.

'There has to be more. The man never leaves the house! Did you search everywhere?'

'Of course not. It was too close to dawn, so I focused only on his study. I've thoroughly searched downstairs and, believe me, there is nothing of any interest down there.'

'What about the bedchambers?'

'Never set foot in one of them.' For very good reason. 'All of Gislingham's private apartments are on the first floor. Thea and the Viscountess sleep on the second.'

'Thea?' His friend quirked an eyebrow. 'That's very *informal*.'

They were long past informal. Gray had kissed every

beautiful inch of her. 'Things are more informal here in the country.' Especially down by the brook.

'Do you think his niece is involved?'

'No.' And nor was he prepared to even discuss the possibility that she might be. 'But *dear* Bertie is in it up to his neck. And unlike Gislingham, he *does* leave the house. He's been gone weeks.'

'I concur. Maybe Bertie's room holds the key? I assume it is within the Viscount's private apartments. We need to urgently procure a sample of the man's handwriting.' The lawyer's eyes lit up. 'And in view of recent developments, I suggest we do that sooner rather than later. We don't want evidence destroyed.'

'Impossible. The man has eyes like a hawk. We can't go rifling around in his private quarters in broad daylight. Believe me, I've tried. I haven't even been able to return the letters I took from his desk! The Viscount is very particular about his privacy and Bertie is the hawk that guards it.'

'Even hawks sleep, Gray. And the longer we wait, the more chance we give them to cover their tracks. We have one tangible piece of evidence. This note.' He tapped the burned missive with his index finger. 'This could be our only chance to categorically link it to Gislingham.'

'You want me to break in again? Tonight? The day after his ship has been seized and they will be on their guard? That's utter madness. I won't do it.'

'Fair enough. I'll do it alone. I am an unknown entity here. I'll have a good poke around the bedchambers and if I'm discovered you'll be completely in the clear.'

Chapter Twenty

Several hours later and against his better judgement, Gray found himself picking the lock to the French doors while Hadleigh stood guard. Because the lawyer had the bit between his teeth and wouldn't be dissuaded and, because he had expressed his intention to investigate the trunks in Thea's room to sift through those accounts, too, Gray had reluctantly become involved. To his friend he hoped it looked like diligence and a desire to return those damned letters rather than a primal need to protect the woman he loved from the unsupervised gaze of another man as she slept. In fact, Hadleigh didn't stand a cat's chance in hell of setting one foot in her bedchamber. If that made him an irrational, jealous fool, then so be it. She was his and that was that. Irrational, protective jealousy went hand in hand with being in love.

God help him. This had been the most trying twenty-four hours!

Beneath his fingers, he felt the barrel of the lock click into place and tested the handle. The door swung open silently on its blatantly well-oiled hinges. They crept inside and diligently checked the hallways before moving on.

'There is a distinct lack of guards, don't you think?' Hadleigh whispered as they crept down the hall.

'There's a distinct lack of anything, if you want my humble opinion. Guards, papers, suspiciousness, motive...'

'You doubt Gislingham is The Boss?'

'I think there's as much chance, if not more, of him *not* being the man we suspect as there is the chance he is. Something doesn't add up.' Or he was becoming so desperate for a way to prevent the inevitable implosion and awful aftermath affecting him and Thea that he was purposely, yet unconsciously, missing things. 'I cannot shake the feeling that Gislingham is far too nice to be a master criminal.'

'That's what he wants you to think.'

'Yet if this house was his lair, the centre of all his nefarious deeds, then it might look like a house on the outside, but it would be a veritable fortress within.' To prove his point, they were able to slip up the stairs to the Viscount's private apartments completely unseen with not so much as a sleeping servant at the front door in case they were visited in the night.

They made a search of the sitting room Gray had happily sat in almost daily during the past week and found nothing one would not expect to be in a sitting room. Behind every picture was nought but blank walls and beneath the giant Persian rug every floorboard was secured with sturdy nails. There were no secret compartments, no hidden escape hatches, no nothing. Harriet's half-finished daub stood proudly on an easel near the window. A sorry effort which was little to show for the hours she had doubtless spent on it. Thea's unfinished book lay on the table. *Pride and Prejudice.* A romance, because his Thea was a romantic at heart, he now knew. When Hadleigh wasn't looking he traced his finger along the spine and allowed himself a little wistful smile. He hoped their romance had a happily-ever-after. She deserved it and perhaps so did he. If he could only navigate those blasted potholes.

They then searched the study where Hadleigh hastily stashed the rest of the love letters into his satchel and sat in the window seat, scrutinising the large leather account ledger by the light of the moon, with the burned note held aloft for comparison, while Gray hunted for hidden compartments in the furniture and floors.

'Anything?' Time was ticking along. They had been here an hour already.

'Nothing.' Hadleigh closed the book and returned it to its exact spot on Gislingham's desk. 'The handwriting is all the same, very curly and flamboyant, and very definitely not this.' He pocketed the charred remnant looking peeved.

'Thea acts as his secretary. The writing is probably hers.' She was curly and flamboyant, too. There was nothing staid or average about his Thea. 'Did you see anything amiss in the accounts?'

'He lives well—but well within his means. Exactly as you said.'

The next door led to a messy dressing room. A testament to Bertie's lack of talent as a diligent servant. Piles of Gislingham's bright silk waistcoats lay on a chair. Cravats hung from doorknobs. Plainer waistcoats that looked far too sedate and too small to still fit the Viscount sat folded on an ottoman in the corner. His plethora of cufflinks and stickpins jumbled together in a deep glass dish. Gray pressed his ear to the bedchamber door and heard the soft, rhythmic sounds of snoring. As there was no other way forward, they had to risk it.

He opened the door a crack and peered through. The large lump under the bed covers suggested the Viscount was sound asleep on his side. His two canes were propped haphazardly by the nightstand, their gold tops shining silver in the single sliver of moonlight that seeped through the tiny gap in the curtains.

In case they were spotted, Hadleigh went first, his pocket stuffed with a silver candlestick and a diamond stickpin. If caught, he was going to claim to be a common, opportunist burglar so that Gray could escape with his cover intact. It wasn't much of a plan, but as he had point-blank refused to allow anyone to creep around Thea's bedchamber but him, it was the best they had and would jolly well have to do.

Hadleigh skirted the edge of the room, then stopped dead, frowning at the bed. Then he gestured and Gray followed and couldn't quite believe his eyes.

The Viscount was not alone.

Curled up next to him, their limbs intertwined in the tangled bedcovers, was Bertie.

Bertie!

Suddenly feeling guilty for the intrusion, Gray grabbed Hadleigh's sleeve and dragged him back to the dressing room as so many things fell into place. The secrecy. The knowing looks. The determined protection of his privacy. The dire state of the Viscount's sham of a marriage. The love letters that told the sad story, not of love lost, but of forbidden love. The most forbidden love.

I suspected you were the one. Now I know it. I refuse to feel guilty for loving you.

Homosexuality could still be punishable by death, so this illicit love affair had had to be conducted well away from prying eyes.

It made him feel sad. Life couldn't have been easy for

either of them, yet their love had survived twenty years of potentially giant potholes. But that didn't excuse smuggling and murder—if indeed they were smugglers and murderers. Yet stranger things happened, as this revelation was testament to.

'Well, I wasn't expecting that.' Hadleigh raked a hand through his hair as they both stood back in the sitting room, stunned. 'I think it's fairly safe to assume from the dressing room Bertie doesn't have his own room and if he does he rarely uses it.'

'We should go.' Gray felt queasy. Not at what he saw, because he had seen worse on his travels than that touching, affectionate display of what he now knew was enduring love, but at the ramifications for Gislingham and Thea on the back of it. Society, not to mention the authorities and the church, would be unforgiving. Ruthless even. He doubted even Thea knew exactly how much Bertie truly meant to her uncle.

'Not until we've searched that trunk in the niece's dressing room.' Hadleigh was already through the door before Gray could pull him back. 'We need to match that handwriting!'

'Only the dressing room! You do not set one foot in her bedchamber.'

'All right...' Hadleigh eyed him curiously. 'Any particular reason why?'

'This has nothing to do with her.'

'Is that based on feeling or fact?'

'I know her. And you don't.' Gray's feet took him to the third door along the landing, guided no doubt by those invisible cords and the intoxicating scent of jasmine. 'Her dressing room is the next door along.'

Hadleigh gently tested the door and poked his nose inside before turning to regard Gray blandly. 'Intuitive. It is indeed. And from a man who claims never to have set foot in any of the bedchambers here before...'

As there was no response that wouldn't condemn him, Gray set his jaw and followed the lawyer inside. Instantly, he was overwhelmed with her. The chemise and corset he had helped her back into only hours before lay on top of the trunk and he hastily moved them out of the way before Hadleigh touched the garments. Beyond the door he could sense her. Feel her breathing, her tender heart beating, his beating stronger as a result. Messy, complicated, wonderful feelings he was nowhere near getting used to.

While the lawyer searched through the discarded reports, Gray tried and failed not to drink in the intensely personal sight of her belongings. The huge pot of pins on the dressing table to tame her wayward, vertical curls. The fat hairbrush she must use to rid it of the inevitable tangles. The pretty perfume bottle filled with her imported fragrance from the Orient. He could picture himself here. Watching her dress or undress, comfortably chatting about their day. Their life. Perhaps even their children. The image so vivid and perfect he *had* to make it a reality.

The creaking sound next door had them both standing to attention. 'Gray?' The soft voice beyond the door was filled with sleep, but she sensed him, just as he had her. The bed creaked again, the mattress shifting as if she had sat up. '*Gray? Is that you?*'

In seconds she would come to the door and check. He knew that with the same certainty that he knew she would likely never forgive him for what he was about to do. He gestured frantically for Hadleigh to leave, feeling sick to his stomach and riddled with guilt at the only option fate had left him with, then answered, 'Yes, my love. It's me. I crept in. I hope you don't mind.' What else could he do but lie? As the lawyer hid in the shadows he grasped the handle and opened the door at the exact same moment as she did. She was smiling. Beautifully rumpled in the moonlight. 'You crept in?'

'Don't hate me.' He hated himself enough. This was the worst sort of betrayal. One she would likely never forgive him for if she ever found out. Their goodbye. 'But I missed you.'

'I missed you, too.' Feeling like the worst sort of chancer, ne'er-do-well and scoundrel, he opened his arms and she stepped into them, and in doing so he fell into the biggest, deepest pothole of his life.

Thea woke late and Gray was gone. She wasn't surprised. He was a gentleman despite his impulsive ways and he would want to protect her modesty. She could still see the indent his head had made on the pillow, still smell the lingering scent of his spicy cologne, so she wrapped her arms around it and hugged it close. It was a poor substitute for the man. She smiled as she pictured him unable to sleep and then doing the outrageous and coming to her in the night. It was such a spontaneous, devil-may-care, live-in-the-moment, Gray-like thing to do and hopelessly romantic. She still couldn't quite believe it.

Then he had climbed into the bed beside her and, at her instigation, made love to her with such aching, impassioned tenderness that it had brought poignant tears to her eyes. His final words before she had drifted blissfully back off to sleep in his arms had also been heartfelt.

'Just remember I love you. Always. No matter what. No matter how dire things are or how bad they seem.'

They made her sigh just thinking about them.

With an undisguisable spring in her step, she dressed and allowed her maid to fix her wayward hair loosely. Gray loved all her mad curls, so she would forgo the usual plethora of pins for him. She practically floated into her uncle's sitting room to find him sat on a chair striking a pose as Harriet stood behind her easel, measuring his angles with her outstretched paintbrush while Bertie stood by, looking highly amused at the ridiculous tableau.

'You look lovely today.' He eyed her up and down appreciatively. 'You've changed your hair. It's softer. Suits you.'

'Thank you. I feel lovely.' She did. Warm and ripe and thoroughly loved.

'Tuesdays will do that to a person.' Bertie's face was deadpan, but his eyes were dancing as if he knew she'd been thoroughly ruined and was happy to have been so. 'Tuesdays...and handsome gentlemen with soppy black dogs.'

'I don't know what you mean.' But her cheeks were heating at the memory of exactly how splendid her Tuesday had started. Harriet had never mentioned *that* particular bit of bed sport in all her descriptions, but it had been most enlightening. Her man had a very talented mouth.

Her man.

She wanted to sigh again at how marvellous that sounded, but withheld it because Bertie was grinning at her. 'How is the portrait going?'

'It's at a critical stage. Frankly, I think it's beyond saving. Your uncle, though, is quite delighted with it.'

'Good heavens, then it must be bad.' She wandered behind the easel and looked over Harriet's shoulder. It was a definite face—that was something—not her uncle's, but at least it had discernible features.

'What do you think, darling?' Her friend stepped back to admire her work, too.

'Fabulous colours.' The bold striped waistcoat jumped off the page, making her uncle's vivid choices seem tame, but part of Uncle Edward's hair was also apparently blue. Prussian blue, to be exact. She met his eyes and watched him stifle a chuckle. He really did have the most warped sense of humour. 'I think you've really captured his essence.'

'I've already had some footmen clear space in the gallery opposite dear old Pater. I decided he'd be able to avert his eyes if I was hung next to him and there's no fun in that. He can glare at me in disappointment for eternity now.' The chuckle escaped then and soon turned into raucous laughter. 'The old grouch will be spinning in his grave.'

'Has Lord Gray been to check on Archimedes yet?' Any hope that she had made the question sound casual died when she watched the three of them share a very unsubtle, but pointed look.

'Not as yet, darling. I'm sure he'll be here presently. He does seem rather devoted...to poor Archimedes, of course.' Harriet studied her thoughtfully. 'You look different.'

Thea drifted to the sideboard to fix herself some tea. 'It's the hair. I've decided to give my scalp a holiday and stop nailing my coiffure to my skull.' Once she was out of view of both her uncle and Bertie she couldn't resist beaming at her friend, then walked two fingers along the edge of the sideboard. Two fingers which hesitated at the ledge, then leapt off the end. 'Today, I am a quite different Thea from the one I was yesterday.'

Harriet grinned back, instantly understanding. 'How positively splendid. Did you *sleep* well?'

'I am thoroughly *rested*.' Although now that she thought about it, she wouldn't mind a passionate kiss to start the morning properly. 'I might wander down to the stables to check on Archimedes.'

But Gray wasn't in the stables and nor had he been

there, which might have been odd considering he was usually up with the lark like Thea was, but, seeing as they had both used the bedtime hours for pursuits other than sleep, she wouldn't blame him for sleeping in. She had, after all, and *she* had worn him out. Alone, she made no attempt to stifle the grin of achievement and decided to saddle a horse to ride to Kirton House instead and be unapologetic about the reason. She wanted to see him. Wanted to kiss him. Wanted to drag him back to the brook for more shamelessly wanton lovemaking.

But as soon as Kirton House came into view through the trees she saw something wasn't right. There were strange men everywhere and lots of horses. Several wore uniform—she recognised it as that of the Excise Men—but Gray was nowhere to be seen. That made her panic and, recalling the overheard conversation from Ipswich, set her old, suspicious mind whirring.

Instinctively, she tied her horse to a branch out of sight and quietly picked her way through the copse by the brook to come level to the house without being seen. It was then she saw the guns. Big ones. Shotguns and pistols. So many of them in a huge crate, all being loaded and passed around like port after dinner to the forty or so strange men in the stable yard who appeared very confident handling them.

'Hurry up, you fools! We don't want to alert the whole of Suffolk to your presence. Unload and get inside!' She recognised Lord Fennimore's impatient bark and tried to pick him out from the crowd to no avail. Beyond, within the confines of the stable, were more men. She was certain she recognised the back of Gray's aged cousin as he quickly disappeared through the wide door frame, but she was too far away to be certain.

Sensing something was now very wrong, Thea crouched low, darting across the meadow from ragged bush to ragged bush, getting as close to the outbuildings as she dared without leaving the safety of the tall grass. When that proved fruitless, she darted towards the rear of the stable, sinking her bottom to the ground and pressing her back against the slatted wood to attempt to hear what was going on inside, while castigating herself for her suspicious nature. Gray was different. She felt it in her bones. He was good and kind and...

'I expressly warned him not to seduce the chit!' Lord Fennimore again. Angry.

'Well, if you don't mind me saying—' A new voice. Aristocratic. Deep. '—it's a damned good job he did. Their passionate little romance saved our bacon. We'd have been done for last night without his quick thinking.'

'Something that would not have been necessary if you had stayed put last night and not risked the entire mission with your carelessness!'

'Do you think it's a real romance?'

'Hard to say...' Two more strange males, their tones teasing. 'But from the look of him, there's something there. I've never seen him quite so angry.'

'Angry! Why, he's positively seething. He looks ready to punch one of us at any second.'

'Back off!' Gray's voice, accompanied by the noise of reins and buckles jangling.

'I think he's a bit taken with Miss Cranford.' Thea's hand covered her mouth a second before the wounded cry burst forth. She was the chit he had seduced? 'He called her *my love*...'

Bile rose in her throat as the world shifted on its axis. Last night had been a lie? It had all been lies! The two slices of toast a winking Harriet had forced her to eat to keep up her strength threatened to make an instant reappearance at the bitter aftertaste of forbidden fruit. She could hear fate laughing at her in the background. Realising Impetuous Thea had fallen for another vulture. A bounder. A ne'er-do-well. A scoundrel who would make calculated, premeditated love to her to cover up whatever it was he was really doing.

She stumbled, half-running, half-crawling, back to the trees blindly, silent, bitter tears streaming down her cheeks at the universe's cruel punishment. Her heart ripped callously in two.

Chapter Twenty-One

Gray had just slammed Hadleigh against the wall when he sensed her, then bolted from the stables like a man possessed to try to fix the unfixable. He frantically scanned the yard and the meadow, knowing she was there and that she was in pain, then saw the unmistakable glimpse of fiery copper hurtling through the trees. He tore after her, oblivious of the odd looks he was getting from his men and his friends. Nothing else mattered but reaching her and trying to limit the damage of whatever she had potentially seen, or, God help him, overheard.

'Thea! Wait!' He plunged into the trees, ignoring the branches that caught and tore his clothes and skin. 'Thea! Let me explain!'

She was fast. His lungs burned with the effort it took to come within touching distance. He reached out his hand, his fingers grazing the back of her dress. 'Please let me explain!'

She skidded to a halt then and finally turned to face him, small fists clenched, her face leached of all colour, the awful evidence of his betrayal etched plainly on her lovely face. 'Explain? What is there to explain? You are a liar! A barefaced, shameless, heartless liar!'

'I'm not...' Yet another lie when she deserved the truth. 'All right—I've lied, yes... But I had to... But not about the important things. I didn't lie about us.'

'Really? Then last night wasn't a lie. There wasn't someone with you when you claimed you couldn't bear to spend another second without me? When you climbed into my bed? Made yourself at home in my body?'

'There was, but...'

'How could you!' Her face crumpled, but she held back the sob. 'I trusted you! I gave myself to you believing you were genuine, yet you played me all along! Your own cousin forbade you from seducing me, because clearly you do this sort of thing a lot. How you must have laughed when I did your dirty work for you! Gave myself freely! What a stupid, ignorant fool I am!'

He reached out to touch her and the stinging slap across the face caught him unawares, although it wasn't anywhere near as painful as he knew he deserved. 'Don't touch me, Gray! Never touch me again!' She hugged her arms around her body and put six feet of distance between them. He couldn't blame her for that either. If he could have left himself standing somewhere and marched off in disgust, he would have, too. 'Why me? Was it sport? My fortune? The challenge?'

'I work for the government.' The least he could do was give the whole truth, no matter how unpalatable it was. 'For a covert agency called the King's Elite. Lord Fennimore is my superior, not my cousin. We created that story as a cover, to attempt to infiltrate a dangerous smuggling ring and bring the ringleader to justice. I wish I could have told you all that, I really do, but I couldn't. My mission had to take precedence over everything else—except it didn't. You kept pulling me away from it. I've always been drawn to you. That part wasn't a lie. All my background, everything about Cecily, all that is the honest truth, too. I've never lied to you about any of that.' His voice was desperate. 'In fact, I doubt you'll believe me in light of what you now know, but you are the only person on this earth who knows me that well. But I was tasked with befriending your uncle. Ingratiating myself into his circle.' He was spilling state secrets, breaking the law, but she was worth it. They were worth it. *If* he could make her understand.

'My uncle?' There were tears on her cheeks. More silently spilling over her long lashes. Tears he had caused. Each one like a knife to the chest.

'We have intelligence which leads us to believe he is the leader of that smuggling gang.'

She baulked, her face paling further. 'The cut-throat who murdered those men in Newgate?' She staggered backwards towards the brook, her head shaking with denial. 'That's preposterous!'

'Yesterday the Excise Men intercepted a smuggling vessel at Leiston.' The words felt like dust in his throat, but they now had a direct link to Gislingham Hall. The warrants had been issued. Her uncle's arrest was imminent. Sooner, seeing as she had overhead things their planned midnight raid would have to be brought forward. 'An express arrived at the hall within two hours of the raid. At roughly the same time, we were able to link the ship to a storehouse in Ipswich. It was heavily guarded. A few hours ago, we raided it and took every man within it prisoner. I am sorry to tell you that, as we suspected, it was filled with illegal French brandy.' The pretty, trusting mouth he had kissed just hours ago hung slack, disbelieving. 'But there was more. Guns, tea, tobacco...money. It hasn't all been counted yet, but we estimate there is in excess of twenty thousand pounds in coin alone.' There was no point sparing her from the most damning connection. The one he still struggled to come to terms with himself. 'According to the landlord, the storehouse is rented by a Mr Walsham.'

'Bertie?'

'And he's seen a carriage bearing the Gislingham crest there on more than one occasion in the last few weeks. Late at night. But while the witnesses cannot describe the passengers' faces, they all clearly remember the two canes he needed to lean on as he was helped out of the coach.'

'I don't believe it. I *won't* believe it! This is just more deception piled on your lies! Neither my uncle nor Bertie would ever do such things. They are not criminals!'

He rifled in his pocket for the charred piece of note, knowing she needed to see the proof with her own eyes. 'Do you recognise this handwriting?'

She stared at it, then flinched, recoiling at the sight, circling around him warily. He held it out. 'Look at it closely. It is a matter of national importance.' She took it and stared, her features frozen but her eyes tragic. She knew it. It went no way to making him feel better. 'Men have died. Too many of them. It's my job to see that nobody else does. Please, Thea—tell me. Do you recognise this handwriting?'

'No!' Then he felt her palms flat against his chest as she lunged, sending him flying backwards into the water. By the time he hauled himself up the bank, he heard the horse's hooves kick into a gallop and, sopping wet and utterly devastated, was forced to watch her ride like the wind towards her house, the precious, tiny, damning piece of evidence gone with her.

Thea had no memory of the short journey home. Not when her mind was reeling and the ground had been pulled from beneath her feet in more ways than one. But she miraculously made it in one piece and headed to the sitting room blindly.

'How could you?' Her temper so hot and bubbling above the surface, she swept her hand violently across the mantelpiece, sending all the tawdry silk arrangements flying.

Her aunt stared back at her blankly. 'Is everything all right, dearest?'

Thea held out the damning charred fragment. The one covered in her aunt's small, neat writing. Needing to piece together some sense out of the tempest of chaos swirling in her head. 'I know! I know all about your warehouse and the smuggling.'

Caro gently grasped the toxic piece of paper and stared at it silently. 'How did you get this?'

'The Excise Men retrieved it from a ship they boarded yesterday.' Her aunt sat up straighter. 'They've impounded all your brandy!'

All those meaningless lunches, all those shopping trips. Just lies. So many lies and all from people she cared about.

'But how did you come to have this?'

'They asked me if I recognised the handwriting! They caught the Captain trying to burn it.' Her aunt's calmness was staggering. Thea was accusing her of hideous, criminal acts and she hadn't even left her chair. Hadn't looked outraged or denied any of it. 'I snatched it and came here to confront you. I can't believe it...'

'Did you tell them it was mine?'

'No. I ran. I didn't want to believe it... But they can't be far behind me. They have a small army.' Good grief, this was all so surreal. Why didn't her aunt deny it? 'Is it true? Have you killed men?'

'Not personally.' Her aunt stood and began to pace, her eyes oddly blinking as she tapped the burned piece of paper against her other hand. 'This is all very unfortunate, but not entirely unexpected.' She sighed, as if it was of no matter rather than the most catastrophic and devastating news Thea had ever heard. For a woman who stressed about every wrinkle, her composure at the bombshell was staggering. 'Are you certain you never told them whose writing this is?'

'Not yet. I wanted to look you in the eyes. I wanted to understand.' But she didn't. Why anyone would stoop so low? And were Bertie and her uncle also involved? 'He said the warehouse is rented by Bertie. Is that true?'

'As it's in his name, legally it is.'

'What sort of an answer is that?' Thea gripped the other woman's arm hard, not caring that her nails bit into her skin. Caro tugged her arm away.

'Have they seen your uncle at the warehouse? The carriage?'

How did Caro know all this? 'Yes.'

'Yet only you know this handwriting is mine?' Her face contorted into an ugly expression. Calculated. Cruel. Completely mad. 'Interesting…'

'Interesting?' Thea's world was falling apart. Blown to smithereens. And it was just *interesting*? For the first time, Thea saw through the brittleness and the self-absorption to the woman beneath the ageing face she fought so hard to keep youthful. Her uncle might well be a criminal, too, something she still couldn't quite believe, but he had been right. Her aunt was every inch the cold, callous, self-serving and unfeeling witch he had always accused her of being. 'All this time, I tolerated your vanity and made excuses for your affairs, yet they were apparently the tip of the iceberg. You're a criminal. A murderess…'

Her aunt caught her expression and snarled, 'How dare you judge me, Thea! You are the last person in the world who can judge me! I had no alternative. Not when you and your uncle forced me into it.' She saw it then. Blind, unadulterated hatred burning in the other woman's eyes. Hatred for her. Hatred that made no sense.

'Forced you?'

'He ruined everything. Years of planning. Years of sacrifice…yet he gave you everything and left me with a pittance!

'Everything that isn't entailed or cannot be nailed down was legally bound to you in trust the day before we married! Out of sheer spite! When he dies, which he will sooner rather than later, this house will go to some distant, faceless male relative and then where would I have been left? All the money has already gone to you! It was Edward's petty act of revenge. One I should have foreseen!' Out of nowhere her hand shot out and something hard and blunt struck Thea on the temple.

She saw stars and staggered backwards, catching herself on the sideboard before she crashed on the floor. Dazed, it took several moments before she could focus properly on the pistol pointed at her. 'You're a *monster*!' Why hadn't she seen it before? 'But they are coming for you!'

'No, dearest. They are not. They are coming for Bertie and Edward. I have made very sure of that.'

Chapter Twenty-Two

The King's Elite stormed Gislingham Hall within twenty minutes of Thea's mad dash home. Thanks to his carelessness, they had little choice. Powerless and ravaged with guilt and wretchedness, still soaked to the skin, Gray rode silently alongside Lord Fennimore and Hadleigh. His friends Seb Leatham and Jake Warriner rode close behind along with fifty agents and half of Suffolk's Excise Men. He supposed they made an impressive sight. They were all fully armed and prepared for a full-scale battle. One he was more than happy to die in if he couldn't make Thea understand.

Except, when they thundered up the drive, the grooms and the gardeners all stopped work to come and investigate what all the fuss was about. They dismounted and were met at the front door by the equally perplexed ancient butler, still clad in his brown apron, a silver candlestick in one hand and his polishing rag in the other. He took in all the strange new faces and then settled on Gray. 'Has something happened, Lord Gray?'

'Where is his lordship?'

'I believe he is resting, my lord. Bertie insisted he take a nap before Lady Crudgington returns this afternoon to finish his portrait.' It felt rude to simply barge past him when the man had never done a thing wrong, but before he could reply, both Leatham and Warriner were half-way to the stairs. 'Wait! You cannot go up there now! His lordship won't be decent!' But it was too late. They had.

Gray followed, taking the stairs two at a time in his haste to catch up. Although to do what, he wasn't sure. His duty, probably, but he had stopped caring about that the second he had seen Thea's tears. Now, all he cared about was her. Her and him, and whatever dregs of their love he could salvage, dreading the thought that there was noth-ing left to salvage and already mourning the loss of her.

He arrived at the door to the sitting room where he had been such a welcome guest seconds before Leatham flung it open. It crashed hard against the panelling.

Bertie stood alone in front of a chair, blinking at the unexpected intrusion. The book he had been reading hung limply from his hand. 'What the blazes is going on?'

'Albert Frederick Walsham.' Hadleigh's deep voice boomed over Gray's shoulder. 'I have a warrant for your arrest.' Every bit of blood drained from the servant's face as he backed towards the farthest door. 'Where is Gis-lingham?'

The door opened and the man himself appeared. Hair on end on one side of his head, shirt-tails untucked, but leaning proudly on his two canes. Something about the scene didn't sit right. In fact, it made loud alarm bells clang in Gray's mind. 'What is the meaning of this, gen-tlemen?'

'Where's Thea?'

'I thought she was with you.' Gislingham stared Gray dead in the eye. Unwavering. But accepting. 'And I shall ask again—what is the meaning of this rude intrusion, gentlemen?'

'It's all right, Edward.' Bertie used his body to shield the Viscount. 'It's me they want.'

The older man tossed one of his canes to the ground and took his lover's arm. 'Over my dead body. If we are to hang, then we'll hang together. We always knew this day might come.' They smiled at one another. Wistfully. It was the single most poignant display of affection Gray had ever seen. 'Yet I would not have a changed a second of it. You were worth it.'

Bertie's hand closed around his. 'As were you.'

'Gentlemen, it is not your unconventional relationship which brings us here.' Hadleigh stepped forward with the papers in his hand. 'These arrest warrants are for high treason. There is one for each of you.'

Neither Gislingham nor Bertie said a word. If their flabbergasted expressions were anything to go by, the power of speech had temporarily left them both.

'Treason?' Both men seemed to Gray to be genuinely confused.

'We have evidence you have been smuggling brandy into these isles for years.' Hadleigh had no sympathy for their denials. 'Furthermore, we suspect you have colluded with subversive French nationals, paying them in guns in return for your contraband. Contraband you have had your minions distribute with impunity while you reap the handsome rewards.'

'You are mistaken, sir.' Gislingham's tone was measured, reasonable, but it was obvious he was scared. 'We might be criminals in the eyes of the law, but I can assure you, neither one of us has ever smuggled a thing.'

'Furthermore, you are both charged with murder in the first degree.'

'Murder? Who has been murdered?' As the Viscount wobbled, then crumpled, Bertie supported his weight and guided him to a chair. The Viscount then gripped Gray's arm, the mobile half of his face a mask of grief. 'Not my Thea? Please God, not my Thea!'

'No, of course not Thea!' At Gray's impassioned answer the old man slumped in his chair with relief. Not at all the behaviour of a selfish, callous man who had just been charged with treason. 'Excise Men, government agents. Viscount Penhurst and the Marquess of Deal.'

'The two men murdered in Newgate?' Gislingham shook his head in denial. 'I've never even met them, let alone murdered them! This is lunacy! On what evidence are these scurrilous charges brought?'

'We have witnesses.' Again Hadleigh's tone was matter of fact. 'The lease to your storehouse in Ipswich. And that is just what we have managed to find in the last day. Once news of your arrest spreads, I'm sure more poison will seep out of the woodwork.'

There was a shriek downstairs and what sounded like a scuffle. Lady Crudgington's outraged voice. 'I have every right to go upstairs! Unhand me, sir! Or you will answer to my fiancé!' Lord Fennimore instantly went to the door in time to see her frogmarched in. 'Cedric!' She shrugged off the agent and clung to the old man. 'What's happening? What's going on? Has this got something to do with you being a spy?' Unlike Gray, his superior had at least been honest if he had confided that much.

'There, there, my dear.' Leatham, Warriner and Hadleigh all stared open mouthed at the sight of the old curmudgeon kissing Harriet's hair. 'I shall explain it all in due course.'

'We've been arrested, Harriet,' said Gislingham, still shaking his head in disbelief. 'For *treason* and *murder*.'

'I don't understand? That's…ridiculous.'

'We know. The world has plainly gone mad.'

'Have you seen Thea?'

'I thought she was with you, Lord Gray.'

'She went to find you.' Bertie was still soothing the Viscount with a calming hand on his arm. 'At least an hour ago.'

'She found me.' In the worst way possible. Lord only knew what she had heard or thought. 'She learned all about this and fled home. In a state. I expected to find her here.'

'Then perhaps she went to Caro? She dealt with her last upset quite well...' He turned to Bertie with obvious concern for his niece when he should have been thinking about himself, casting more doubt in Gray's mind as to his ability to commit the heinous crimes he had been accused of. 'Is the *boss* here today?'

His blood ran cold. 'What did you say?'

'That for all her many faults, my wife managed to calm Thea after Archimedes's accident.'

'Not that. The name. Why did you call her *The Boss*?'

Bertie and Gislingham shared a look, before Gislingham shrugged. Defeated. 'Well, I suppose the cat is well and truly out of the bag regarding Bertie and I... You should know she's been blackmailing us for years. Since well before I married the witch. It's our private name for her. Makes us feel better about dancing to her tune.'

Thea had been constantly aware of the cold press of the pistol throughout the short walk across the deserted lawn. She had expected to be dragged to the stables and the carriage, not across the boundary meadow to the old and disused ice house at the back of Colonel Purbeck's estate. Now, sat on the damp, cold floor, she kept one eye on her aunt and the gun while the other scanned for objects to use to aid her escape. The choice was limited to a rickety table and a three-legged milking stool. Both well out of reach.

Caro was agitated, despite her claims to the contrary. And as every minute passed she became more so. She might have her own escape planned to within the last detail, but it all hinged on her men carrying out the plan to the letter of her instruction and Thea doubted cut-throats could be trusted on their word.

But as her aunt paced, waiting to be rescued, Thea kept asking her questions, hoping that she would have enough time to give someone—anyone—the shocking answers that would save her uncle, before her aunt put the promised bullet between her eyes. The witch wanted no messy loose ends linking her to her crimes once she was safely ensconced in France with all her ill-gotten gains.

Yet, as bizarre as it all was, Thea had heard too much to be shocked any longer. One dreadful crime after another had been unveiled. Unspeakable things that made no sense, but peculiarly made perfect sense to her crazed aunt.

'Does Uncle Edward know you murdered his first wife?' Something Caro had apparently plotted and meticulously planned for years before she carried out the crime because she had always had her heart set on huge wealth and a title. And after some scandal during her one and only Season involving a married French *comte*, there was no chance of her snaring a suitable candidate in the capital. That's when she had turned her greedy eyes on the only viable option while she had languished in virtual exile in Suffolk—poor Uncle Edward.

'Of course not. He still thinks it was a mystery illness which killed her.' As opposed to the arsenic their then young neighbour had slowly fed her during her frequent social visits. 'Your uncle can be very naïve sometimes.'

Because clearly, poisoning a man's wife to take her place was the most natural thing in the world. Especially to a woman who had then used blackmail to force the grieving husband down the aisle. Caro had had lofty plans of birthing his heir swiftly and then dispensing with him, too. Except he had thwarted her on that score and never set foot in her bedchamber. Hardly a surprise, really, in view of the other revelation.

She still couldn't quite believe that her uncle and Bertie were lovers, although alongside today's other earthshattering and tawdry discoveries, it was the secret that bothered her the least. At least he'd had the wherewithal to transfer the bulk of his fortune to Thea before he had been forced into marriage, something which her crazed aunt was clearly still enraged about. She had hoped to retain the entailed half upon the birth of her first son, but despite the many lovers she had taken to her bed over the years to provide her with one, Caro's womb had remained as barren as her cold, black heart.

Her aunt smiled, regarding Thea in an odd, detached way as if the madness which consumed her had now completely taken over. 'Nor has he any idea that it was me who facilitated his brother's accident either.'

Fresh betrayal and grief ripped through Thea. All these years, she had blamed herself and all these years her aunt had let her. 'You murdered my father?'

'It was necessary.'

'Necessary?' Poor Papa! Every second of that awful day surged to the fore, making Thea relive each moment with agonising clarity. The argument. The dreadful news. Aunt Caro comforting her afterwards, knowing full well his blood stained her hands. She lunged, an animalistic cry coming from her lips.

'I'm going to kill you!' Her nails bit into her aunt's

cheek until Caro pressed the gun to her temple and forced her back down to the floor, the barrel digging into her temple painfully.

'Now, now, dearest. Go sit down. There's a good girl. You cannot die yet, I might need you as insurance.'

'What did my father ever do to you?'

'He was in the way. He'd met a woman. He thought himself in love. After everything I'd suffered, I couldn't allow him to remarry and father a son before I did. Another hideous brat to inherit what should have been mine.' She shrugged. Once again flipping to the cheerful assassin devoid of any and all conscience. 'Once I had a son, I knew it wouldn't matter, but then your uncle exacted more petty revenge and had his stroke.' As if her poor uncle had almost died on purpose! 'With the clock ticking, I had to have a contingency plan.'

Tick-tock. Tick-tock.

'And wide-scale smuggling, treason and more murder was the obvious choice?' Thea wanted to laugh at the absurdity of it all, except nothing about it was even remotely funny.

'I had the connections.' Caro never had stopped seeing her scandalous French lover. 'And it's not as if everybody doesn't buy from the free traders.'

She wished Gray were here. She hated him, but he was strong and resourceful and she still loved him despite her broken heart. He worked for the government. His mission was to have the perpetrators brought to justice after all, except they were going to hang two innocent men for her aunt's many crimes. Because Caro hated Bertie and her uncle more than she loved money.

Chapter Twenty-Three

They had searched everywhere. Scoured every inch of the grounds and the surrounding countryside. Nothing had passed through one of their road blocks and nobody had seen a blasted thing. To all intents and purposes, Thea and her aunt had disappeared off the face of the earth.

As Leatham and Warriner turned their horses back to the hall to regroup with the others to plan their next move, Gray couldn't bring himself to turn back. She was close. He could sense her.

'It'll be dark soon. We won't find her in the dark without lanterns.' Leatham's accurate assessment was unwelcome.

'You go back and get lanterns. I'm going to check the grounds again.'

'Gray—this is madness. We are going round in circles. If she was here, we'd have found her if...' His friend's voice trailed off. He didn't need to finish the sentence. Gray had been wrestling the awful possibility to the back of his mind since the search had started. *If she was still alive.* 'I'm not suggesting we give up. I know how much she means to you. I'm just suggesting we take a break and fetch lanterns.'

Fetch?

Before pausing to reconsider the unlikely idea that had popped into his head, Gray kicked his horse towards Kirton House, leaving his friends to trail clueless in his wake. Trefor had a nose for Thea. He adored her. Was besotted. He always knew where to find her.

He burst through the door to find his dog jumping with excitement. 'Trefor—fetch Thea!'

The dog tilted his head and Gray repeated his desperate instruction again, swiping away the errant tear which was making its way down his cheek. As if understanding his master was heartbroken, Trefor nuzzled his hand. Licked it. 'Please fetch Thea, boy. Fetch Thea!'

Finally, the animal seemed to have an epiphany and dashed out the door, his black nose inches from the ground. Miraculously, he started moving and Gray followed, trying not to hope, but praying for a miracle regardless. When they came within sight of Gislingham Hall, Trefor sped up and then bounded towards the door.

He was sat patiently on the threshold as the three friends finally caught up with him. His tail wagging. Proud of himself that he had understood such an important instruction, while not understanding it at all.

'It was worth a try.' He felt Warriner's hand on his shoulder. 'Come on. Let's get those lanterns.' His friend's enforced optimism was not mirrored on his face.

Inside the house, it appeared everyone was back and, judging by the grim expressions, nobody had located her. Someone pressed a glass into his hand. 'We'll find her.' Harriet's voice, lacking its usual certainty, cut through the silence of the room. 'Remember, Thea is fearless.'

She was. She'd been braver than him. And now, thanks to him, she was in danger. His eyes wandered around the room. Gislingham sat with Bertie, utterly distraught. Hadleigh, Warriner and Leatham in the corner, talking in hushed voices. Trying to spare him from hearing the potential truth. Harriet...

'What the blazes!' Lord Fennimore almost fell over Trefor, who was sat in the middle of the room. 'Why does that blasted dog always sniff the air?'

'Come here, boy.' But Trefor refused to budge. His head was tilted back, his shiny black nostrils were twitching and he was inhaling deeply almost as if he was in a trance. 'Trefor!' Gray patted his thigh. 'Come here, boy.'

Instead of obeying, the dog began to bark. Agitated and pawing the ground, he stared at Gray for several seconds, then he was off like a shot down the stairs, barking all the way. Trying not to hope, Gray followed him to the Viscountess's sitting room, watched the dog circle the room with his nose to the rug, then sit and whine outside one of the concealed servants' doors in the panelling.

Praying for a miracle, he pulled it open. 'Fetch Thea, boy!' He watched transfixed as the dog hurtled along the passageway as if he knew exactly where he was going, when Gray knew for a fact neither of them had ever set foot here before. 'This way!' he bellowed the instruction to Hadleigh, who had followed them downstairs. 'Bring lanterns! And guns!'

Alone, Gray followed his dog, trying not to get impatient each time the animal paused and quietly sniffed the air, instead making a fuss of him while repeating the command, *Fetch Thea*, in case he got waylaid by any other scent or distraction as he was prone to do. At the boundary of the spitting Colonel Purbeck's vast estate, Trefor sat, then began to pace a slow circle, his sensitive nose never leaving the ground.

As the others all arrived bearing light and weapons, and, in the Viscount's case, canes, he motioned for them to stay well back, not wanting their scents to contaminate whatever trace of Thea's intoxicating jasmine remained.

After an eternity, during which Gray's heart loudly hammered in his head because he was too frightened to breath out, Trefor set off again. He ran for a good quarter of a mile towards the strange house, then Gray watched the animal disappear down what appeared to be a genuine pothole.

Caro froze at the sound of an animal's whining. 'What's that?'

'A fox, I think.' Or, please God, a dog. A black one with floppy ears and an irritating, deceitful master who Thea had been silently willing to find her since she had been frogmarched out of Caro's cloying, soulless sitting room. Now that it was dark outside her aunt was becoming more twitchy, craning her ears at every sound and constantly unlocking the heavy oak door, checking outside for her rescuers.

'It's a long way from midnight. They won't be here yet. Why don't you sit down?' They were apparently coming along the brook, an irony that was not lost on Thea, and would smuggle Caro out on the water. A plan that had been made over a year ago. A plan that had been rehearsed repeatedly. How could such things happen in such a quiet corner of Suffolk and someone with as suspicious a nature as Thea's not notice? Clearly, she had atrocious instincts all around.

Caro began to pace again, her finger never leaving the trigger. 'I hate foxes. I wish the damn thing would shut up.' Absently she tossed the heavy key on the rickety table where the only lamp burned. The key Thea had been desperate to get her hands on since they had arrived. 'They'll be here! It's more than their scurvy lives are worth to double-cross me! They know that.' Another mantra the woman kept repeating, as if reassuring herself of her own power. 'I'll have the lot of them killed!' She pulled out the timepiece again, stared at the dial and then snapped it shut, oblivious to the scant few inches Thea had managed to move closer to the table in the brief bit of time. 'They'll be here. They'll be here.'

The animal whined again and her aunt instinctively started towards the door to investigate, allowing Thea to shuffle closer to the key.

'Not so fast, dearest!' The barrel raised again as her aunt spotted what she was up to. 'Sit still and stop being a nuisance, there's a good girl.' The key disappeared back into her pocket again accompanied by a smug smile.

'Gray will come for me.' Despite wanting to hate him, Thea knew that in her bones. 'His men have probably blocked every road. They will search every property.' At least that is what she guessed government agents did. 'They'll have boats on the water, too. I've never seen so many Excise Men.'

'He'll be too busy clapping your uncle and his molly in irons to give you a second thought and, by the time he does, I'll be long gone. You were a means to an end, dearest.'

True, but aspects of his behaviour last night kept niggling. The fervency. The selfless passion. He had thoroughly adored every inch of her and not allowed her to repay him. The intense emotion swirling in those troubled, wolf-like eyes. Almost as if he hated himself for lying.

Just remember I love you. Always. No matter what. No matter how dire things are or how bad they seem.

Well, things were about as dire as it was possible for them to be, so dire that she was now clinging on to the pathetic hope that he at least cared enough about her to come looking. In the meantime, all she had to do was stay alive and find a way to get either that key or the gun.

'If Gray doesn't come, then Mr Hargreaves will. He's in love with me.' Seeing as patience, cunning and obedience had failed to give her any chance to escape, she might as well try riling Caro. The woman was already quite irrational. In anger, she might make a mistake and provide an opening. Thea knew only too well how irrationally an angry mind behaved. 'He told me so only last week at your garden party. He wants to marry me. Which is odd, considering he warms your bed, don't you think? Perhaps it's your age that's putting him off?' A gentle kick in her Achilles heel. 'Men always prefer a younger woman. Especially as they all want to sire a son.'

'Shut up!'

'Why? I have nothing to lose, do I? Seeing as you are going to kill me regardless, I might as well be honest in my final hours. I have no cause to spare your feelings now, nor am I particularly inclined to. Let's face it, you were a means to an end to Mr Hargreaves. He wanted a way to get close to me and your pathetic desperation to be adored by any man in possession of a pulse allowed him to do it. He mentioned he hated your wrinkles...'

'I said shut up!' Her aunt had stalked forward, the pistol pointed menacingly. Refusing to be cowed any longer, and mindful that she couldn't make any sort of move glued to the floor, Thea stood defiantly.

'Do you know you're pitied by all our neighbours? They all whisper about you behind your back. The *poor* barren Viscountess. How *sad*. Nothing going for her except that *once*-pretty face. If only they knew the whole truth. That the only way you could get any man to marry you was by blackmail! Do your loyal men know that? I'll bet none of them turns up to save you. Why would they? You were nothing but a means to an end.'

As Caro lunged, Thea went for the gun, holding her aunt's arm to the side to avoid getting shot. She felt the other woman's fingers in her hair, felt them twist and pull hard, heard the ominous click before the trigger was squeezed, then saw bright light as her head was smashed against the wall.

Except the bright light never went. Out of it came Gray. He barrelled into her aunt and sent her sprawling on the floor amid what sounded like frantic barking alongside the ominous gunshot.

Thea couldn't see what happened next through the streaming army that followed him into the icehouse. Lanterns, noise, more barking as she swayed, struggling to focus on the sea of moving faces swarming in front of her.

'We've got her!' A stranger. Her aunt's howl as she struggled. Muffled as they overpowered her.

Trefor's pitiful howling.

'Good grief, is that blood?' Her uncle.

'He's wounded!' Lord Fennimore. 'Leatham! Get a physician!'

Finally, the scene came sharply into view.

Gray. Face down. Unmoving.

Time stood still.

Chapter Twenty-Four

Thea threw herself on the ground to get to him. 'Gray! Wake up! Wake up!' A crimson circle of blood was blooming through his coat at his shoulder. He groaned and it was the most perfect sound she had ever heard. 'He's alive! Somebody help him.'

Two men stepped forward who seemed to know what they were doing far more than she did and reluctantly she stepped back and watched impotently as they gently cut off his coat and turned him around. Twice his eyes fluttered open and twice she watched them close again, his normally tanned face waxy pale.

'Is he dead?' Please God, don't let him be dead. Not when it had taken so long to find him.

'Not yet.' But Hadleigh's expression didn't hold out much hope as the man she loved was loaded on to a stretcher and carried away, his loyal dog practically glued to his side.

'The bullet has gone straight through.' Lord Fennimore patted her hand reassuringly on the sofa several agonising hours later. They had locked her out of the bedchamber. For the best, with hindsight, because Thea had been an inconsolable mess.

'Is that a good thing?'

'In my experience, they're better out than in.'

'But will he survive?'

'He'd better. I'm too old and too busy to command the Invisibles.' He turned as the lawyer stepped into the room. 'How's the patient, Hadleigh?'

'Awake and in high dudgeon. He wants to see you.' The blond man gestured for Thea to come closer, pointing to his ruined cravat. 'He demanded it, actually. Quite forcefully. He's been in a dreadful state since you went missing. Something he will undoubtedly blame himself for when it is me who should shoulder it all. It was my idea to break into the Hall last night. Gray was dead set against it and only came to protect you. It was also my clumsy, disrespectful words you overheard this morning. I was playing to the gallery and had no idea how he felt about you or that you would ever overhear. I apologise wholeheartedly for all the distress I have caused you, Miss Cranford. If it is any consolation at all, I think he loves you.'

'Oh, I know he does,' said Harriet with a dramatic sigh. 'The man leapt in front of a bullet meant for her. A true leap of love. He was prepared to sacrifice himself so that Thea lived. As grand gestures go, they don't get much grander than that.'

'Indeed they don't. Don't you remember what I've always said? True love is the greatest joy in the world and worth all the hideous turmoil in the long run.' Uncle Edward gripped Bertie's hand and the pair smiled a little watery-eyed at one another, still not quite over the trials of the day, but obviously relieved they would not have to stand trial themselves. Lord Hadleigh and Lord Fennimore had given their word. 'He loves you, Thea. Trust me—nothing else matters more.'

Thea dashed from her uncle's sitting room to the bedchamber beyond, emotion clogging her throat as she saw him propped on pillows, deathly pale but thankfully alive. Their eyes locked and then his dropped.

'I'm so sorry. For everything.'

He reached for her hand and squeezed it hard, reassuring her that he had plenty of life left in him, thank goodness. 'Don't be.' It had been a grand gesture after all. The grandest. The sort that melted away all doubt. 'Things always happen for a reason, even if the reason for them is not immediately apparent. If you hadn't lied, then we wouldn't have fought. And if we hadn't fought, my uncle and Bertie would have been accused of crimes they didn't commit and you wouldn't have caught the true criminal.'

'I don't care about any of that. All I care about is you... And me. If there is *still* a you and me.' He tugged their entwined hands to rest possessively on his chest. Beneath her palm she could feel his heart beat, sure and steady, secure in the knowledge it beat solely for her.

'You lied to me.'

'I had to. That doesn't make it right. If I could do it all again...'

Thea silenced him with a kiss.

'You forgive me?'

Her uncle was right, true love was the greatest joy in the world and worth all the hideous turmoil in the long run. That didn't mean she couldn't make him sweat a little. She sat back and disentangled her hand from his. 'Lord Gray, I have found no reason to reappraise my initial assessment of you. You are a chancer and a ne'er-do-well. A man with scant regard for the proper rules of society. A man who lives wholly in the moment without any thought to the consequences. A disgraceful scoundrel of the first order...and I speak for both myself and Impetuous Thea when I say we wouldn't have you any other way.'

She watched her words sink in. Watched him smile that cocky smile he did so well. 'Then I have a question for you.'

Her heart danced. 'What sort of question?' He was going to propose. She could feel it in her bones.

'An important one…' As his voice dropped to an intimate whisper, Thea found herself leaning closer. 'One that frankly terrifies me… One I've been running away from for the better part of ten years…but the thing is, I've recently had cause to re-evaluate everything I've come to believe, face my fears and…'

'And?' Her lips were inches from his, so close they heated with awareness and longing.

'I was wondering if you would…?'

'Would what?'

'Consider…' She had dreamed of this moment. A perfect proposal from her perfect mate. 'Consider making some plans?'

'Plans? *Plans?*' His eyes were dancing with mischief, the wretch, because he knew exactly how to vex her. 'I want more than plans, you scoundrel. At the very least, I want promises. Blood-sworn, granite and solemn promises. Of the forever kind.'

A wet black nose appeared from nowhere and sandwiched itself between them. Two big, manipulative chocolate eyes gazed adoringly up at them before he wiggled on to the mattress and presented his belly to the ceiling for a rub.

'And I want Trefor. That is not negotiable. And a summer wedding. And babies. Plural. Disgraceful dark-haired boys and fiery redheaded girls. And I want to see some of the world. Have a few adventures. With you, of course. And I want an exercise yard full of horses. And long summer days filled with laughter and long winter nights wrapped in your arms.'

'That's a great many ands. Is that all of them?' His finger had begun to wind itself in one of her vertical curls.

'And I'd like to see you naked and cavorting in the brook again, but I'm prepared to make Impetuous Thea wait till you're better for that one.'

'I might struggle with the brook, but I can't deny poor Impetuous Thea the rest of her request. Not when she's been shut in a box for years.' Despite being pale, weak as a kitten and clearly in no fit state to be indulging in anything energetic, her man always found tremendous joy in the moment. To her delight, he whipped back the sheet and then lay back with a wolfish grin, mirroring his charming mutt's scandalous pose. 'For the record, in case there is any doubt whatsoever, I would be delighted to have her vouch for my credentials whenever she sees fit.' Something she did as soon as he was better. Rather a lot.

* * * * *

THE DETERMINED
LORD HADLEIGH

For Frankie and Shell.
Thanks for all your support since I started my writing journey.
You are awesome!

Prologue

The Old Bailey—May 1820

She had attended every single day of the trial. Alone in the gallery, her face pale, sitting erect, her slim shoulders pulled back as she stared straight ahead. Her hands were hidden among the folds of her skirt. It had taken Hadleigh almost a week to realise that she hid her hands because they provided the only clue to the way she was truly feeling as they twisted a ruined handkerchief into tight, agitated spirals which she kept proudly from view.

She had a child, he knew. A son who was a little over a year old. Yet she never brought the babe to the court as some did in a bid to elicit sympathy. Nor did she give any indication she noticed the hordes who had come to gloat at her tragedy. The blatant pointing and unsubtle whispering; the shameless newspaper artist who frequently perched himself directly in front of her and sketched her expression incorrectly for the breakfast entertainment of the masses—such was the gravitas of this case that everyone wanted to know about it. And about her.

The traitor's wife.

That quiet dignity had both impressed him and humbled

him because it was eerily familiar. Her honesty, yesterday, had shaken him to his core. In a last-ditch attempt to save her husband and prove his good character, the defence had called her as a witness at the last minute. Unexpectedly. They asked leading questions, to which she could answer only yes or no, then stepped aside so that he could cross-examine her.

'Was he a good husband?'

She had looked him dead in the eye. 'No.' He had expected her to lie, but gave no indication of his surprise. Her gaze moved tentatively to the furious man in the dock. 'No. He wasn't.'

'Why not?'

'He wasn't at all who I had hoped he was.'

'This court requires more explanation, Lady Penhurst. In what ways was the accused a bad husband?' He'd had an inkling. More than an inkling, if he was honest, especially as he had lived in a house where a marriage had become a legal prison, but as the Crown Prosecutor his job was to present the government's case as best he could. The jury deserved the whole truth about the man in the dock, no matter how unpalatable it was. Or how intrusive.

'He was violent, Lord Hadleigh.' His friend Leatham had said as much. Violent and depraved and his heart wept for her suffering. She reminded him of another woman in another time. One who had also endured stoically because she had had no option to do otherwise and had not wanted to burden him with her troubles. The bitter taste of bile stung his throat at the awful memory so long buried.

'He beat you?'

Her eyes nervously flicked to her husband's again because she knew that if he was acquitted, she would pay for her disloyalty today and there was nothing in law to stop that happening. But her spine stiffened again with resolve and she slowly inhaled as if to calm herself and find inner strength. He knew how much that small act of defiance cost her. 'If I was lucky, only weekly.' Her gloved index finger touched the bridge of her nose where the bone slightly protruded. 'He broke my nose. Cracked a rib—'

'Objection!' The defence lawyer shot to his feet. 'My learned friend knows what happens between a husband and a wife in the privacy of *his* house is not pertinent to this case.'

Hadleigh addressed the judge. 'I believe it is pertinent m'lud. It gives the jury an insight into Viscount Penhurst's character.' Because a man who used his wife as a battering ram was rarely a good man, as his own mother had learned to her cost.

'We have debated this many times before, Lord Hadleigh, therefore I know you are well aware the law clearly has no objections to a husband disciplining his wife.' The judge had the temerity to look affronted that it had been brought up in the first place, seemingly perfectly happy that a husband had the right to beat his wife senseless and the courts who supposedly stood for justice would do nothing. 'You will desist this line of questioning immediately and the witness's answers will be struck from the proceedings.'

Hadleigh nodded, his teeth practically gnashing, consoling himself that while the law was an ass as far as the rights of married women were concerned, at least the seeds had been sown. You could strike words from the record, but once said, they took root in the mind. A few of the jurors had looked appalled. That would have to do. 'My apologies.' Hadleigh made no attempt to sound sincere before he turned back to her and the job in hand. 'Lady Penhurst—you lived predominantly in Penhurst Hall in Sussex during your marriage, did you not?'

'I did.'

'Then do you expect this court to believe that you lived in that house and never suspected what was going on in the cellars right beneath your feet?' Her husband had run part of a vast smuggling operation, utilising his estate's close proximity to the sea to receive and sell on thousands of gallons of brandy in exchange for guns. Guns destined for France, and more specifically to the supporters of the imprisoned Napoleon who were desperate to see their great leader restored to power.

'I have eyes, Lord Hadleigh. And ears. Therefore, I knew he was up to something but, to my shame, I had no idea what and nor did I truly attempt to find out.'

'Why to your shame?'

'Because my life was easier if I asked no questions. It is hard being married to a man who answers them with his fists.' Another thing he had learned through bitter experience. 'But with hindsight, I wish I had confided in someone.'

Then, unprompted and in a tumbled rush, she had begun to reel off what she had seen and heard which she had thought suspicious. Things she had neglected to mention the first time he had interrogated her fresh from her husband's arrest, doubtless because she didn't dare say a word against him then in fear of his retribution. Hadleigh had had no intention of calling her to the stand for precisely that reason—wives, even grossly abused ones, rarely turned against their husbands or even testified at all—so her sudden extensive and embellished testimony surprised him.

The guards in the cellars, the menacing servants who watched her every move and reported it back to her spouse, the odd messages which arrived at the house at odder hours which Penhurst always burned after reading, the new and endless supply of money that he spent like water. Most significant were the dates she freely shared. Dates when her husband had been home which coincided with the same dates the Excise Men had recorded sightings of smuggling ships on the Sussex coastline. Dates Hadleigh had already appraised the court of during this significant and well-discussed trial. All in all, it had been a damning testimony, an incredibly detailed and courageous one, and one he was of the opinion she had come to the court room determined to share despite being a named from the outset as a witness for the defence.

Lady Penhurst was a very brave woman.

As a reward, she was subjected to the most spiteful rebuttal from both her vile husband and the defence that Hadleigh had ever heard in all his years in the courtroom. Horrendous mudslinging which highlighted the gross disparity between the law for men and the law for women. He had been reprimanded by the judge for bringing up the way she was beaten by her husband, but that same judge had blithely ignored all Hadleigh's objections to her haranguing because the court deserved to know what sort of a woman the witness was before they chose to believe her.

She was a liar. Who had lain with a succession of men for money. Deranged. Cold and frigid. A drunkard. Unfit to be a mother. Throughout the litany, she had stood proudly, her clasped hands shaking slightly, her expression pained but defiant. Grace in the face of the contemptible. He admired that, too.

By the end, Hadleigh hated his profession and himself more for not adequately defending her, even though it was neither his place nor his job to do so. But as it had been his intrusive questions she had answered with more detail than he could have possibly dreamed of, he knew she was suffering this contemptible onslaught thanks to him.

Knew, too, that she had helped him by hammering the last few nails into Penhurst's already rotten coffin regardless of the inevitable cost to herself.

As she left the witness box, she held her head high, but her eyes had dimmed. He knew it wasn't the first time she had been whittled down and belittled by his sex. He'd seen that same expression many times and, while he could never ignore it, he had played along with his mother and pretended he hadn't seen it. That nothing was amiss. That all would be well. A flimsy lie that had never come to fruition. Oh! To be able to turn back time and do things differently...

Hadleigh couldn't shift his immense sense of guilt and shame throughout his closing arguments, although bizarrely that painful, niggling, unprofessional emotion made them sound stronger than any closing speech he had ever made before. Perhaps because he had argued for her. Used his voice in an arena where she had none. Treason aside, more than anything he now wanted Penhurst to pay for what he had done to the quietly proud and stoic woman sat all alone in the gallery.

Then the jury were sent to huddle in a private room to discuss their verdict, away from the circus in the gallery. They came back unanimous in less than ten short minutes.

Guilty.

Of high treason.

Her face had blanched then. Her blue eyes filling with tears and for the first time she stared down at her lap as her husband was dragged screaming from the court. He had hoped she didn't regret her part in the verdict. It had been small, but largely insignificant, because Hadleigh had done his job well. But then he had no emotional attachment to Penhurst, so could regard the man's inevitable demise through a detached and pragmatic lens. For her, there would be complicated ramifications as well as the release from her suffering. Penhurst had fathered her child and been her husband. There were many in society who would judge her unfairly and she was unlikely to ever be welcomed within its hypocritical ranks again thanks to the sins she had not committed but which branded her nevertheless.

While the judge retired for the night to consider the punishment, she had left the court alone as always and gone who knew where, not realising that more machinations far out of his sphere of control would occur before morning which would make her future life undeservedly more impossible than it already was.

Hadleigh learned it had been a reporter for one of the scandal sheets who had blithely informed her that her husband's title and estate had been transferred back to the Crown, his ill-gotten fortune and all his assets seized. It was a petty act of revenge as far as Hadleigh was concerned, designed to put the fear of God into his yet unknown co-conspirators. A stark reminder of what a traitor could expect for his crimes against England and its King even in this enlightened day and age. But Penhurst's infant son was no traitor and nor was the child's abused mother, yet now both of them would also pay for his crimes and for much longer than the crooked Viscount would. Their entire lives had been ruined with one vengeful stroke of a pen.

That was not his concern.

Or at least it shouldn't be. But looking at her now, sat all alone in the gallery waiting to hear her violent and odious husband's fate, he found he couldn't seem to take his eyes off her or not feel partly responsible for all she was about to suffer. Not a single family member had accompanied her on her daily trips to the court. Nor had a single family member leapt to her defence in any of the hundreds of newspaper stories that made outrageous and wild accusations. Was that because they had disowned her or because she had wanted to do this alone? Or perhaps she was alone? And why the blazes should he care about this woman when he had brought many a criminal to justice and not given two figs about any of their family, when the family were ultimately irrelevant when justice needed to be done?

While pretending to study a document in front of him, he found his gaze wandering back to her hands. As usual, they were buried in her dull skirt, out of sight. Her outfit today was austere, as they all had been this last week, but he noticed that, even though she was seated, the brown spencer hung from her frame. She had lost weight. Rapidly, if he was any judge, and the dark circles beneath her eyes were testament to the insomnia she had clearly suffered in the few scant weeks since her husband's arrest. How would she sleep after today? Would she ever sleep again?

That was not his concern!

She wasn't his responsibility and neither was her child. Doubtless someone would crawl out of the woodwork and take them in. If she had any sense, she would move to the opposite end of the country and change her name. Perhaps he should tell her as much once this was all over?

He sensed her looking at him and realised he had been openly staring. He schooled his features into the bland, emotionless mask he always wore and allowed his eyes to meet hers unrepentant. There was something about Lady Penhurst's eyes which disarmed him and called to him in equal measure. He found he wanted to keep looking at them, as if within their sapphire-blue depths was something he needed, except the inexplicable guilt which had sat heavily on his shoulders for days got the better of him and he hastily looked away.

Not that he had anything in this instance to be guilty about. Penhurst was a traitor. He had robbed the Crown of taxes, as a minion of the infamous and still-unidentified mastermind known only as The Boss, he had willingly consorted with England's worst enemies and had blood on his hands. Lots of blood. Too many innocent men had died thanks to that smuggling ring and it was hardly his fault the evidence had been so plentiful and compelling the man had got his rightful comeuppance. Hadleigh had no earthly reason to feel guilty at doing his job well. None whatsoever.

So why did he? Those eyes perhaps?

'All rise.'

Putting his misplaced guilt and odd mood aside, he stood with the rest of the chamber and forced his gaze to remain fixed on the judge as he entered. The judge sat and so did the rest of the chamber, while Penhurst was brought in to hear the sentence. He appeared terrified and rightly so, his eyes darting around the room nervously while the whole indictment was read. Then, as Hadleigh and most of the baying crowd had expected, the clerk placed the black-silk square atop his wig as an eerie hush settled over the room.

Hadleigh's gaze flicked to her and she was ashen, those lovely eyes swirling with emotion, his heart lurching painfully at the sight. All he could think of was what she might be thinking and what in God's name was to become of her. No husband. No home. No money. None of it her fault.

Professional detachment be damned! Once the judge was done he would offer some help. He wouldn't leave her all alone to be fed to the wolves today. He would escort her home. Give her money. A chance to start afresh. Something—anything—to make his misguided conscience feel better.

'William Henry Ashley, formally the Viscount Penhurst and the Baron of Scarsdale, the court doth order you to be taken from hence to the place from whence you came, and thence to the place of execution, and that you be hanged by the neck until you are dead, and that your body be afterward buried within the precincts of the prison in which you shall be confined after your conviction. And may the Lord have mercy upon your soul.'

'No!' Penhurst broke free of his guards, scrambled over the dock and lunged at the bench. Instinctively, Hadleigh stepped forward to stop him and the Viscount's fingers gripped his robe with all his might. 'I'll tell you everything I know. Everything!' The genuine fear in the man's expression was visceral. 'You have the power to appeal! To respite my sentence! Transport me. Imprison me. Flog me. Do whatever you see fit, but surely I am more use to you alive than I am dead?'

Around them, the gallery had jumped to their feet and surged forward to get a better view. It took two clerks and four men to restrain the panicked Penhurst and several minutes to drag him kicking and howling from the melee of the court room before order was resumed. By the time it was, her chair was empty. The ruined, twisted handkerchief lying crumpled on the floor, still damp from her tears.

Chapter One

Cheapside—five months later

'You are mistaken, Mr Palmer. I promise you I haven't yet paid the account. I came in here today specifically *to* pay the account.' Penny once again held out the money the pawnbroker had given her for her mother's jade brooch only minutes before.

The shopkeeper smiled kindly, but made no attempt to take it. ''Tis all paid, Mrs Henley. In full.' He turned around the ledger and pointed to the balance. 'There is no mistake, I can assure you.' His eyes wandered over to another woman in the corner who seemed perfectly content examining the rolls of ribbon all by herself. 'If there's nothing else I can help you with, Mrs Henley, I'd best see to my other customers.'

'But I didn't pay you, Mr Palmer!'

'Somebody did, because it's been noted down and I shan't be taking the money twice. That wouldn't be honest now, would it? And I pride myself on my honesty. Spend it on that little lad of yours, eh? I dare say he needs something. Growing boys always need something.' He closed his ledger decisively. 'Will there be anything else you need, Mrs Henley?'

He didn't strike her as a stupid man, but it was obvious he was a stubborn one and too proud to admit his error. Perhaps his wife would be more accommodating? 'Please send my regards to Mrs Palmer. I had hoped to see her today.' She cast a glance over his shoulder to the little anteroom beyond the counter. 'Unless she's here so I can do so in person?' The shopkeeper's wife was meticulous and would find a way to gently correct her husband's blatant accounting mistake.

'She's gone off to visit our daughter and the grandchildren, I'm afraid. I shall pass on your regards when she returns next week.'

Not wanting to argue further in public, Penny decided to come back then and attempt to pay her debt to the Palmers' shop. She said her goodbyes and, mindful of the time, walked briskly up King Street to the home of her landlord, Mr Cohen, fully intending to pay in advance for her next month's rent, only to find that, too, had been paid. Unlike the cheerful shopkeeper, Mr Cohen was a humourless individual who didn't like to waste words.

'I tell you it's been paid, Mrs Henley. A full twelve months' rent!'

'But that is impossible! I haven't paid you.' But the coincidence was not lost on her and she found her teeth grinding at the suspicion as to who might have. 'Who paid it?'

'That I can't say. Nor will I, as much as I don't like it. Your benefactor wants to remain anonymous.'

'Benefactor?'

The old man scowled and shook his head. His rheumy eyes burning with accusation. 'That's what I'll call him for now, Mrs Henley—because he assured me he wasn't your fancy man and I choose to think the best of my tenants, no matter how new they are to me or how implausible their stories.'

'Fancy man?' Penny didn't need to hide her outrage at the suggestion. 'I can assure you...' The old man rudely held up his hand.

'And I can assure you, rent or no rent, I'll toss you out on your ear if I get so much as one whiff that he is. I won't tolerate any scandal in one of my buildings, Mrs Henley—if indeed you are or have ever been a Mrs. If you hadn't been vouched for personally by Mr Leatham, I never would have accepted you in the first place. I wonder what he'd have to say about a strange man paying a year's worth of rent?'

An interesting question indeed. Exactly what would Seb Leatham have to say? He was a man of few words, but one used to blending into the background and doing covert things behind the scenes. Never mind that he would walk on hot coals if Clarissa asked him to.

Suddenly, a nasty suspicion began to bloom in her mind. This was all a little too contrived and convenient. Less than twenty-four hours before she had had a disagreement with Clarissa, the only friend she had left in the world and wife to the aforementioned Seb Leatham. It had been about her decision to seek employment somewhere as a governess or housekeeper or some such to make ends meet which had so thoroughly outraged Clarissa. She had been very vocal on the subject before she had backed down. Her friend had claimed she respected Penny's decision even if she did not agree with it. Yet now, by some miracle, her rent and her household accounts were miraculously all settled by a mysterious benefactor. Twelve months gratis in Cheapside kept her close enough so her well-meaning friend could continue to keep an eye on her and Penny would have no need to sully her poor, pathetic hands with work in the interim.

'I insist you give the money back whence it came, Mr

Cohen! I'll pay my own rent, thank you very much.' She wasn't that pathetic woman any longer. As much as she had grown to hate her husband, she had hated the woman she had been during their marriage more. A scared, spineless and stupid girl who had ignored everyone's cautionary words about the man she had set her heart on marrying who had lived to rue the day. Oh! How she had hated being powerless and subservient, and because it went against the grain of her character she was determined to be a different woman now. She was neither worthless nor useless. Nor would she be beholden.

Because accepting charity and feeling beholden allowed others the opportunity to control her life and she was done with all that. How was keeping her in Cheapside any different from keeping her in Penhurst Hall? And just because her friends meant well, that didn't give them the right to use their wealth secretively to get their own way. After three interminable years of being powerless and controlled, the only person who had any say about her life now was her son, Freddie. As he was still unable to talk, there was nobody else who held that power.

To prove her point, Penny began rummaging in her reticule for the money. What was the matter with working for a living anyway? Perhaps such a prospect daunted an aristocratic woman like Clarissa, but it didn't faze Penny. She had come from trade, spent her formative years working within it and had enjoyed every second. Her mother and father had worked all their lives with her on their knee. Why, her father had built his business from scratch, from the ground up, and those same principles of hard work and honest enterprise were as ingrained in her as good manners. There was no shame in honest labour and she wouldn't be deterred from finding a way to stand on her own two feet after everything she had endured. After three years she was finally free and intended to remain so. Making her own living, living her own life, was something she was looking forward to rather than dreading and just as her dear parents had, she would find a way to make it work around Freddie. A fresh, clean slate that left her shameful past firmly in the past.

'*He* made me promise not to allow that—and paid me over the odds to ensure I complied.' Old Cohen crossed his arms. 'But if I find out there's any funny business going on between you and him...'

'For any funny business to be going on, *Mr Cohen*, I would first have to know who *he* is, don't you think?' Although whoever he was, he was linked to Seb Leatham somehow. The man was a high-ranking government spy, one who had a legion of subordinate spies to do his dirty work for him. She was going to strangle Clarissa. How dared she?

How dared she?

Not caring that she was being rude to her mean-spirited landlord, Penny turned on her heel and began to march home, imbued with the determination and outrage of the self-righteous. How dare Clarissa use her husband to go behind her back like that? When her friend had explicitly promised to support her in her endeavours and claimed she understood why Penny wanted to leave her old life and all its horrid memories well behind.

What other choice did she have? Her parents, God rest them, were dead and the distant relatives who still lived had disowned her before the trial had even started. Either she earned her own living or she lived on Clarissa's charity again as she had during the humiliating trial. Because Lord alone knew there wasn't enough of her mother's old jewellery to pawn to keep her head above water for more than a few months at most. There certainly wasn't enough of it yet to buy Freddie and her a cottage of their own in the wilds of the country.

And *yet* was the operative word, because one day she would have one. That was her dream. The only thing which had sustained her these past months. A pretty place to call her own where she could finally put the past three years behind her. Of that she was determined. If those dreadful years married to Penhurst had taught her nothing, it had taught her that it was long past time she needed to stop being dictated to by others and take control of her own destiny in whatever shape she chose to make it.

Her respectable lodgings in Cheapside were only ever meant to be temporary. A place to lick her wounds in private while she considered all her options. She had happily taken Seb Leatham's advice on that. Aside from the fact she had spent the first fourteen years of her life living here before her father could afford Mayfair and had always loved it. It was a busy area of the city which allowed a person to hide in plain sight. With all the businesses, merchants and transient visitors from far and wide, nobody looked twice at a well-heeled woman with a child in Cheapside. Nor did any of the upper crust of society venture here. They might send their servants, but they would never be seen dead on the same streets as those in trade.

Heaven forbid!

Any more than they would consider continuing their acquaintance with the widow of a traitor.

She stopped dead outside her building and sucked in a calming breath. Perhaps she shouldn't be too hard on Clarissa? Her friend had stalwartly stood by her throughout everything. Quite openly. She would have sat with her through every minute of the trial if Penny hadn't stopped her. She had claimed at the time she wanted Freddie to be with someone he knew, someone who cared for him, rather than admitting she didn't want to taint or ruin her friend's good reputation by well-meant association. Even now, months after Penhurst's death, Penny refused point blank to darken Clarissa's door in Grosvenor Square. That wouldn't be fair, no matter what her friend said to the contrary. That hadn't stopped her coming here and stepping into the breach when Penny needed somebody to watch her son and for that, she was in Clarissa's debt.

This wasn't worth losing her only true friend in the world for.

Wearily, she took the two flights of stairs slowly and tried to think of a more tactful way of voicing her annoyance at what was obviously meant to be a kindness. Especially as her life had been devoid of such niceness for so long.

She found Clarissa in the tiny parlour sat cross-legged on the floor helping Freddie build a lopsided tower with his wooden blocks, his current favourite toy. 'You're back early. I thought you had heaps of errands to run.'

Penny hadn't confided to her friend that she was visiting the pawn shop and didn't intend to. 'I did—but something peculiar happened and I thought I'd better come back.'

'Peculiar? You weren't recognised, were you?' Her only friend looked concerned at the prospect. People had been quite cruel during the trial. The press had positively hounded her.

'No. Nothing so terrible.' She untied her bonnet and placed it on the table with her gloves, then stalled for more time by carefully hanging up her cloak on the peg by the door, needing to give herself a stern talking to in order to be that better, stronger, independent version of herself.

Be tactful. But be assertive. This is your life and you can now live it exactly as you choose. Something you have yearned for. For three long years. 'However, I did learn something niggling. Something probably best discussed over a cup of tea.' More stalling, which irritated, although was annoyingly typical when one considered she had always shied away from conflict—even before Penhurst. It didn't matter. All this self-flagellation at her supposed flaws was misplaced and pointless. One could still be fundamentally nice and assertive at the same time. It was not as if Clarissa would punch her.

She kissed her son noisily on the cheek before walking to the fireplace to grab the kettle and prepare the teapot. The lack of servants was another thing Clarissa worried about, but Penny genuinely rather liked her new privacy. It wasn't that much work to clean up after herself and her son. Preparing meals was getting easier, but was certainly not her forte, yet a small price to pay for proper privacy. Besides, she still wasn't completely over the sheer joy of being able to spend unrationed and unmonitored time with her boy. Proper time where she could be his mother rather than the scant few minutes her husband had allowed each day before her little cherub was taken back up to the nursery to the paid sneak, Nanny Francis, and out of her control. Penhurst's servants had been her gaolers. Good riddance to the lot of them. She wouldn't mourn their loss any more than she mourned his.

Clarissa took charge of pouring the tea a few minutes later, while Penny settled down with Freddie in her lap. Once done, her friend placed the steaming cup in front of her, then stared at Penny intently. 'What's happened?'

Best to get straight to the point. 'I know you *mean* well, but you shouldn't have paid my rent.'

Her friend blinked, then frowned. 'I didn't.'

'Perhaps not in person, you're far too clever for that, but you arranged for it to be paid behind my back and you settled my account at the shop as well.' She smiled, softening the admonishment, but was quietly pleased that she had given it.

'I didn't. I wish I had…because heaven only knows you need someone to help you and I can well afford it. But honestly, Penny, I didn't. I value our friendship too much to go against your express wishes and I meant it when I said I *would* respect your wishes. After everything, you of all people deserve to be mistress of your own life.'

'Then Seb arranged for those bills to be paid without your knowledge.'

'He wouldn't do such a thing behind my back. Or yours for that matter. I know you have a justifiably jaded view of men and marriage, but Seb is an honourable man and he would never do anything without my knowing. He loves me.'

Penny picked up her tea and tried not to be irritated at her friend's naivety. Men always did what they thought was best irrespective of the woman's feelings. 'Then how else do you explain twelve months' worth of rent miraculously paid on my behalf?'

'Twelve months!' Her friend seemed genuinely shocked. 'Someone has paid an *entire* year of rent? Who? And, more importantly, why?'

'Oh, for goodness sake, Clarissa—let's not play games.' She wouldn't feel bad for losing her temper. A line had to be drawn somewhere and her overprotective friend had pushed the boundary between concern and downright interference too far. 'I appreciate I've been the biggest of fools, that I married a man you had the measure of from the outset and cautioned me against, that I put up with Penhurst and did his bidding like a quaking dolt for three years! I am walking proof of how stupidly trusting, misguided and downtrodden a woman can be! But I'm not an idiot. Not any more, at any rate. You directly or indirectly paid my rent without my consent or knowledge to stop me applying for work.'

'No. I didn't. I swear it. I had every intention of having another long chat with you about the topic today in the hope you might reconsider. That I will freely admit. I see no earthly reason why you continue to isolate yourself here in this tiny apartment in Cheapside when you could live with us comfortably in Grosvenor Square. And I was jolly well prepared to shake you by the shoulders if you continued to be stubborn, but I respect the fact that only *you* can make the decisions concerning you and Freddie. After Penhurst, and all the dire and wicked things he did to you, I would never dream of robbing you of free will.' Her friend leaned forward and clasped her hand, looking worried. 'I swear to you, Penny, I did not pay your rent.'

'Then who did?' It didn't make sense. She had two distant cousins left, neither of whom wanted anything to do with her. They had been very specific on the subject in their final letter to her during the trial. No other friends. They had all been shamefully quick to desert her, too. Rats hurling themselves from a scuppered and sinking ship. It had hurt, but she understood it. Aside from Clarissa and her husband, she had no one.

'You don't suppose one of Penhurst's old *friends* paid it for you?'

A cold chill skittered down Penny's spine at the thought. 'Why would they?' Surely those cutthroats hated her? 'I testified against him...' Before those same cutthroats had violently murdered her husband in his cell. 'And they've all been rounded up. Haven't they?' The ringleaders were all in gaol—but what if the government had missed someone? Would they wish her, a woman who knew nothing outside of what had happed within her own four walls, harm or malice? By the look on Clarissa's suddenly pale face she suspected they did. 'I thought nobody bar you, Seb and the authorities knew my new name and address.' If her new lodgings and identity had leaked outside the safety of her minuscule intimate circle, to people who could feasibly perhaps want her dead, then she would have to take Freddie and leave tonight. Lord only knew where or how. She was down to her last five guineas—thanks, bizarrely, to the money she had not been allowed to pay to those to whom she owed it, six pieces of her mother's jewellery and the clothes on her back.

Clarissa saw the fear and her tone instantly became reassuring. 'Believe me, if those people wanted to punish you and knew where you were, they would have done so. Swiftly and mercilessly. It makes no sense they would offer you charity. Besides, they've arrested the leaders. Those crooks beneath them would have long fled if they have any sense. Staying in the capital is tantamount to a death sentence if they are caught. Whoever paid your rent doesn't mean you harm, Penny. We can be certain of that. On the contrary, I suspect. They want to see you safe and well cared for.'

'I don't want anyone else's money or their help. Especially if they are linked to my husband in some way.' And even if they weren't, she only had two friends left in the world and Freddie. Being beholden to a complete stranger, no matter how benevolent, made her feel uneasy. 'But what if it *is* one of his criminal contacts?' All manner of dire scenarios flitted through her mind, making her unconsciously tighten her hold on her son.

'There's nobody of importance left, dearest. All the authorities are convinced of it. What if I talk to Lord Fennimore or get Seb to investigate it? I'm sure he'll get to the bottom of your mystery benefactor in no time and then we'll set them straight as well as put your mind at ease. As soon as they realise their well-meaning interference is unwelcome, I'm sure they'll leave well alone.'

Chapter Two

Hadleigh placed the little jade brooch in his desk drawer alongside the dented gold locket, well-worn cameo and the delicate ruby earrings, then locked it and pocketed the key. He was no expert on woman's jewellery—or women's anything, for that matter—but he doubted they were worth a great deal. They lacked the sparkle of the gems he saw glittering beneath the chandeliers at the few society events he was forced to attend when he couldn't find the right excuse to get out of them. If anything, they were a sad, meagre collection of jewellery as far as he was concerned, but they were of great personal value to her. He had witnessed that with his own eyes this time as he had watched her dither outside the pawnbroker's, staring at the brooch for the longest time lovingly before swapping it for a few coins.

Thanks to the Bow Street Runner he had assigned to watch her since she had moved to Cheapside three months ago, the detailed weekly reports had made it easy to see there was a pattern to those heart-wrenching visits. On the first of the month, every month, she pawned a trinket and used the proceeds to pay her bills. Today, he had paid them all before she left the house and retrieved the latest item within minutes of her leaving the pawnbroker's shop, supremely thankful that she had not noticed him loitering in that convenient doorway as she had briskly bustled past within a hair's breadth of him. A little too close for comfort, truth be told, when a man in his position shouldn't be anywhere near a witness from a prior case.

But the same thought processes which had kept him up at night since the Penhurst verdict still plagued him. Continually worrying about her had compelled him to see her for himself today for the first time since the trial. He had needed to see with his own eyes exactly what was going on in her world and if her situation was as dire as the Runner had intimated it was. Solvent people, he had said in last week's report, didn't sell off the family silver.

For a gently bred lady to stoop that low, things had to be dire. She must be at her wits' end with worrying about how to pay for things. He sincerely hoped she would sleep easier tonight knowing she no longer ran the risk of being evicted. Hadleigh certainly hoped he would sleep sounder. He also hoped that single act of benevolent charity would appease his niggling conscience. A conscience which bothered him the most in the dead of night when he should have been snatching enough hours of rest to keep his legal mind fresh. He was plagued with insomnia and desperately needed proper sleep. And now unburdened, would grab some—just as soon as he finished today's mountain of paperwork.

He cast a glance at the stack of case notes and witness statements on his desk, next to yet another cold and unappealing candlelit supper his valet had left out for him and allowed himself a pitying groan. There was at least another hour's work there, perhaps two, before he could even consider heading to his bed.

There was no doubt this was the biggest case of his career. For over a year, the King's Elite had been seeking the criminal mastermind behind a dangerous smuggling ring. A few weeks ago, they had finally found the person and, as the appointed Crown Prosecutor, Hadleigh's current and enormous quest for justice had truly started. The infamous, well-connected and dangerous Boss, who had been the scourge of the hallowed halls of Westminster as well as turning more peers than the odious Viscount Penhurst traitor, had finally been unmasked and arrested. And to everyone's shock, including Hadleigh's, the man they had been seeking was in fact a woman.

Viscountess Gislingham was now safely under lock and key in the most secure prison in the country—the Tower of London. Six other peers were similarly incarcerated in Newgate. It was Hadleigh's job to build a watertight case against her and her fellow traitors so they could crush that evil smuggling ring once and for all. Months of painstaking work lay ahead of him, work that would need his full attention. Already Lady Penhurst had occupied far too much of it, when he desperately needed his rest and was tired of mulling over and fretting about her situation. Paying her debts had been an act of charity to himself as well as to her. How was he supposed to be on top form when he spent night after night tossing and turning? Dreaming of knotted handkerchiefs, proudly set shoulders and pretty blue eyes swirling with heart-wrenching emotion.

The question brought her image starkly into view and he ruthlessly banished it as he sat down.

Enough! She was not his problem!

This case was.

He tore a chunk of bread from the half-loaf near his elbow, sawed off a slice of ham and chewed both dispassionately as he reread the meticulous interrogation notes he had made only this morning during another interminable stint with the traitors at Newgate. Five were still pleading their innocence. One had broken and was blabbing everything he knew. Whether or not the information he had given was enough to justify lessening the man's sentence was still in doubt. But in his experience, once a criminal committed to turning King's evidence, they committed wholeheartedly. Tomorrow could be interesting, but he needed to be fully prepared.

Within minutes, Hadleigh was so engrossed, the sound of a fist pummelling his front door had him jumping out of his skin. People didn't bang on his door. Especially not this close to midnight. One of the main reasons he continued to live in bachelor lodgings at the Albany, rather than his own house less than an hour's carriage drive from the capital, was that there was always a porter at the main entrance to dissuade unwelcome visitors from calling at unsociable hours—or any hours, for that matter—and bothering him. That was his excuse and he was sticking to it. He was a solitary beast by nature, partly because his work made it difficult to have unguarded conversations with most people and partly because he had been on his own for so long he was used to it. The Albany, close to his work, made perfect sense. That haunted house down the road didn't.

The fist bashed the door again, reminding him that Prescott, his valet, always took Thursday afternoons off and rarely returned before Friday morning. It also told him whoever was pummelling his woodwork with such vigour was probably known to the porter, hence he had been let in. Something important must have happened since he left chambers. 'I'm coming!'

He had expected it to have something to do with the government, so was not surprised when he flung open the door and Seb Leatham strode in, looking furious.

'What's happened?' Immediately his mind went to the

prisoners and his case. Experience had taught them that The Boss's smuggling gang had no respect for the law or its institutions. Viscount Penhurst and another conspirator, the Marquis of Deal, had been brutally murdered in their cells in Newgate a few days after their sentences had been issued in case they made any final confessions. The bloodthirsty crew of assassins had also ruthlessly sent three prison guards to meet their maker that same night. It had been a grim and stark reminder of exactly how powerful the group of criminals they were dealing with were. 'Please tell me nobody else is dead!'

'Not yet. But the night is young and as I'm royally furious I shan't rule it out.' His friend barged past him and stalked into the only room with a light burning— Hadleigh's study. He tossed his hat on the desk, folded his meaty arms across his chest and glared.

'I am not entirely sure I follow...'

'I made allowances for the Bow Street Runner.' Seb's eyes bored into his, his tautly controlled stance quietly terrifying. 'After everything she has suffered, and in light of the dangerous people her husband dealt with, I reasoned the more people who had eyes on her the better.'

He knew about the Bow Street Runner?

Oh, dear. All ideas of anonymously appeasing his niggling conscience with a secret act of charity swiftly disappeared. 'This is about Lady Penhurst?'

'You're damn right this is about Penny!' One pointed finger prodded him right in the breast bone. 'What the hell were you thinking, paying her debts off like that?'

Confused that Seb had so swiftly traced it back to him and even more confused that the man was angry about his obvious thoughtful and noble generosity, Hadleigh grabbed the still-prodding digit and made a point of pushing it away. 'Not that it's any of your business, but *I reasoned* she would be pleased not to have to struggle to make ends meet after the Runner informed me she was struggling.'

'Then clearly you don't know Penny very well. And clearly you know nothing whatsoever about my wife!' Seb began to pace, his hands waving in annoyance. 'Good grief, man! Talk about taking a mallet to crack a nut! What were you thinking?'

'After the Crown abandoned her, I was trying to help.'

'Well, you've gone and made a splendid hash of it. What the hell am I going to tell Clarissa?'

'As it was meant to be an anonymous gesture, you will tell her nothing, because it has nothing to do with her either.'

At that, Seb finally sat down with a huff in Hadleigh's chair and shook his head. 'Spoken like a true bachelor. Unfortunately, as it was Clarissa who expressly asked me to investigate her *best friend's* mystery benefactor, and because your ham-fisted attempt at being a Good Samaritan has spectacularly served to scare the living daylights out of both women, I have no choice but to tell her.'

'Why would they be scared?'

'You really have no clue, do you? Which is exactly the reason why you should leave the spying and covert machinations to us trained spies and stick to barristering.'

'I don't think barristering is an actual word.'

'And still you fiddle while Rome burns!'

'The Devil is in the detail...' Words he lived by. He was good with details, although clearly he had missed one here.

'Shall I spell it out to you in simple terms?' Seb did not wait for a response. 'Firstly, think about the particular circumstances of your good deed. Only a few months ago, that poor woman's vile husband was arrested on charges of treason. Your own investigation linked him to a whole host of unsavoury characters. Cutthroats. Smugglers. Cold-blooded murderers. When Penny testified against him, she testified against them, too. We assume we've rounded them all up now that we've captured the ringleader—but what if we haven't? It is entirely reasonable to assume any stragglers might have an axe to grind with her. It is one of the main reasons I actively encouraged her to assume an alias!' He stood then and began to pace. 'Furthermore, in paying those debts covertly, you have also alerted a very proud and determined woman to the fact she is under close watch at all times.'

'A gross exaggeration. The Bow Street Runner does not watch her at all times. He has quite specific instructions as I do not want to alert her to his presence.'

'That I am well aware of. Fortunately, my Invisibles have had her on continuous watch since the moment her husband was first arrested.' And hence the reason, no doubt, that Hadleigh's generosity had been quickly traced back to him despite his best intentions of keeping his guilty secret. The Invisible branch of the King's Elite specialised in blending into the background and watching unseen. Worse, the angry man in front of him had personally trained every last one of them. 'However pragmatic, logical and well meaning it was meant to be, Penny is not going to take the news well. Not when we've had the devil of a job keeping her near us in London and not when she was constantly watched for years on her husband's instruction. She is adamant she is entirely done with all that nonsense going forward. And who can blame her? You should have consulted with me!'

'I do not answer to you, Leatham. Or Lord Fennimore. I answer to the Attorney General.'

'Did you consult the Attorney General?'

Of course not. Had he have done, he would have been reprimanded for even considering helping a traitor's wife.

A barrister was supposed to keep his professional life entirely separate from his personal one. They wore wigs and gowns to avoid being recognised out of court by disgruntled receivers of justice or their families or being tracked down by the press and goaded into discussing cases. The Attorney General would take a very dim view of Hadleigh's overwhelming urge to rescue the woman they had callously ruined with one stroke of a pen. 'I wanted to help her.'

'Then you went about it in a very poor manner and have undone months of work. I am actually tempted to strangle you!'

'What work?'

'For the first time in years, she has proper freedom and independence—and even though we know that independence comes courtesy of the pawn shop every month, it is still an achievement. A point of honour and pride. One that we will destroy the second she learns a whole host of people have been working behind the scenes to create the illusion she is coping perfectly well all on her own.'

'She isn't?'

'I think she puts on a good front. She's a good mother and seems to enjoy being mistress of her own house, but it worries Clarissa that she's all alone. That bastard knocked all the confidence out of her and such things take a long time to heal, but that aside, she has nothing. She is nowhere near ready for the harsh realities of life yet, especially one she will be forced to start from scratch. Not that she'll hear it. It's almost as if she's embarrassed by the situation she has been placed in and blames herself a great deal for it, when we all know she was a victim of cruel circumstance. Clarissa has been trying to support her to no avail. Penny point-blank refuses to live with us and is unbelievably stubborn about accepting what she sees as charity.

'She has two perfectly good feet, apparently, and thinks it's long past time she stood on them, regardless of her empty purse. London is expensive and she has a mind to move somewhere cheaper and far away from the *ton* before she is recognised. I can't deny the risk of her true identity being revealed is greater here than anywhere else in the country. That worries me, of course, but if nothing else, here I can ensure she is safe and my wife can be there for her. Recently, she's even started talking about seeking employment, for heaven's sake, in a big house or school somewhere, so she's clearly concerned about her future. Yet she is so proud she prefers to sell her mother's jewellery to make ends meet. Again, something she has no idea we know or have blatantly interfered with. Thanks to you, she might discover Clarissa and I have surreptitiously been giving her money all along.'

'You have?'

'Of course we have! We couldn't see her struggle! Penhurst sold everything her parents left her of value. Those trinkets she sells every month are pinchbeck and paste at best and all of them in total would barely have raised enough to scrape six months' rent. I've been bribing the pawnbroker to give her an excellent price for them to keep her from leaving any time soon.'

'Ah.' Hadleigh would not mention he had paid more than market worth to buy them back each month. He was going to have stern words with that wily, conniving pawnbroker on the morrow.

'Ah, indeed. I dread to think how she will react if she ever finds out how Clarissa and I have been quietly interfering.' Seb let out a long, laboured breath. 'That's not true. I know exactly what she'll do. She'll feel betrayed and she'll leave. To go and stand on her own two feet. One lone, proud woman with nothing bar a small child, no money and a past that could come back to bite her at every turn. Believe me, the world is a hard place for a woman like that...' Seb's broad shoulders seemed to deflate as he exhaled.

'Which brings me to my final point, the most sensitive and delicate of all the points, and one which a sad bachelor like yourself will have little experience of—my wife *trusted* me to find Penny's mystery benefactor.' Seb slapped his own chest hard. 'She trusted me! Knowing that I would sort it quickly and make it right. Put poor Penny's mind at ease and stop her fleeing out of the sphere of our covert and careful protection. Your actions could destroy months of our good work, a lifelong friendship and ultimately leave Penny vulnerable. So, you see, I *have* to report it all back to Clarissa tonight. I made a promise.'

Yes, perhaps Hadleigh had unintentionally made a delicate situation worse, but Seb was being overdramatic about it. 'Surely you don't have to report everything back to Clarissa? Be selective. Lie if need be. Isn't that what spies excel at? You lie for a living.'

Seb smiled winsomely, his eyes softening for the first time since he had stormed into the place uninvited. 'That I do—but I would never lie to my wife. She is my everything.'

Hadleigh wanted to roll his eyes, but didn't. Seb was newly married and still head over heels in love. It was all a bit bizarre and he didn't understand it. Apart from his mother growing up, he had managed to sidestep any emotional attachments or strong bonds in his life. Largely because emotions in general made him uncomfortable, especially his own. He kept friends at a polite distance, too, preferring the reassuring company of his work more. He could socialise and enjoy it, he didn't suffer from a lack of confidence or shyness around people as Seb did, yet he was still always oddly relieved when a gathering came to an end so he could retreat back into his own space again. Even his sporadic and discreet affairs were with women who were wedded to their independence. Getting too close to anyone made him uncomfortable.

He had always been the same. A little detached. Naturally solitary. A typical only child, he supposed. *Lonely.* Where had that thought come from? Good grief, he needed some proper sleep. 'Then tell Clarissa the truth and have *her* lie to her friend. I meant well and I have no intention of taking the money back when she obviously needs it.' That route would only lead to more tossing and turning and vivid dreams involving soulful blue eyes, when he needed to be on top form till this trial was over.

'You have placed me in an impossible position.' His friend raked his hand through his hair in agitation. 'I'll be honest and say, I cannot promise Clarissa will not unmask you. She and Penny are very close and Penny is *very* upset. Ultimately, we will do what is best for Penny and continue to do whatever it takes to keep her close by.'

'I understand.' At least he thought he did. Seb didn't want Lady Penhurst to know he was protecting her. Hadleigh could sleep better knowing that someone was. 'If you think it would help, I am happy to tell her it was all down to me if it comes to it.' Which he sincerely hoped it wouldn't. Her poignant expression and sorrowful eyes outside the pawnshop this morning had haunted all his waking thoughts since. Given the strange hold the woman seemed to have over him, meeting her again, actually conversing with her, was exceedingly unwise.

'That should keep your own machinations on the lady's behalf out of it.' Not ideal, but he could see he had rather put Seb in an awkward and potentially untenable situation. And he didn't want to be the cause of Lady Penhurst either fleeing the safety of their care or taking menial work which was beneath her. That, certainly, had never been his intention. But then, neither had he intended to ever have to speak to her. A conversation which was bound to be awkward, all things considered. Definitely unprofessional in the extreme. He had prosecuted her husband, for pity's sake! 'Perhaps once I explain my actions were borne out of genuine concern, based on irrefutable fact—' alongside an unhealthy and guilt-fuelled obsession with her '—I am hopeful she will see sense and accept the gift in the spirit in which it was intended. Clearly the woman needs help.'

He used reason for a living. If it came to it, once he stated his case, plainly, and backed it with logical evidence, the truth would become apparent. Failing that, he would use the quick wits he had been blessed with and his innate ability to read people to convince her to accept his financial help. She shouldn't have to struggle alone. Not when he could easily right that wrong at the very least.

'And clearly, my learned friend, you don't know much about women if you think that will be the outcome.' Seb appeared amused as well as appeased as he walked to the door. 'But I shall pass all this on to Clarissa and see what she thinks. As long as it keeps both of us above suspicion and still allows me to keep a vigilant eye on Penny, I am more than happy for you to suffer all the consequences.'

Chapter Three

'Try not to be nervous. Now that we know who the culprit is and that it was meant well, there really is nothing to worry about.' Clarissa offered another one of her reassuring smiles of encouragement which Penny returned half-heartedly when the truth was she was still reeling from the revelation hours later.

While it was a relief to know that she wasn't in any immediate danger, to learn that the man responsible for paying all her debts was the same man who had doggedly pursued her husband through the courts was bizarre. Why would he do that? It made absolutely no sense.

She was nothing to him. Just another face in an ever-changing sea of faces on the busy witness stand of the Old Bailey. Their interactions had been brief and impersonal. Or at least his interactions with her had been impersonal. He never once showed an ounce of human emotion in all the many long hours of the trial. For her, those hours had been deeply personal and life-changing. One minute she had been unhappily married to a brute and the next unwittingly married to a traitor who had been sentenced to death. Now, suddenly, out of the blue, the prosecution lawyer decided he needed to pay all her rent... Why? And more importantly, what the blazes was she supposed to say to him on the subject when he imminently arrived at her small apartment.

'It is peculiar though…isn't it? Why would he do it?' Penny asked. Clarissa had asked the same question at least sixty times since Seb had told her the news just after dawn. What exactly had motivated him to be so unwelcomely generous? Guilt? Penny sincerely hoped not. 'And what possessed him to set a Bow Street Runner on me to watch my every move?' Knowing she had been under surveillance when she had assumed she was safe—completely incognito—really bothered her. Aside from the unpalatable fact that it was reminiscent of her years under watch during her awful marriage, if the Runner had easily found her, would the press? Or her horrid husband's criminal friends? That was the trouble with London. In a vastly overcrowded capital, it was too easy to hide in plain sight. She had become complacent and, in so doing, had stayed far longer than she had originally intended. A situation she needed to quickly remedy for Freddie's sake.

'I don't think he did that for anything other than noble reasons. In many ways, I would actually find it a comfort that somebody cared enough to want to ensure my safety and…' Clarissa's voice petered off as Penny glared and the fraught silence settled between them once again.

They had spoken about this most of the morning. While Clarissa seemed of the opinion it was perfectly acceptable to take the man's money now that they knew who it came from, because it made her life considerably easier, Penny found the idea of his or anyone's charity abhorrent. Again, it felt uncomfortably familiar. Penhurst had made her jump through hoops for every farthing she dared ask for and then used it to his advantage afterwards. You need a new dress? Wear this one… Freddie needs toys? He can have them if you stop bothering Nanny Francis… Your mother is dying and you need to take the post to visit her? If you do as you are told for the next week, and beg convincingly, I might give you the fare...

Such experiences scarred a person.

Besides, never a lender or a borrower be. Her father's old motto rung in her ears and was too ingrained to shift. She had marched blindly into a marriage with a shameless borrower and her life had been both miserable and embarrassing as a result. Before he began his career as a criminal, it had been Penny who had had to deal with the debt collectors and the awkward conversations with friends who had lent him money in good faith when Penhurst knew full well he was in no position to pay it back.

Just thinking about how her life had been made her muscles tense and her toes curl inside her shoes. She would not start her new life beholden to anyone.

How did one explain all that to Clarissa?

Nor could Clarissa possibly empathise, particularly as their perspectives were so at odds. But then Clarissa had not had every aspect of her life controlled and Penny had. What she had initially assumed was her besotted groom's eagerness to have her in his life had quickly turned into a rigid and oppressive life which his penchant for ruthless violence ensured she adhered to. Simple, everyday activities like walking to the village to buy ribbons were restricted unless expressly sanctioned by him. Not that she ever did buy ribbons. To buy ribbons, one needed pin money and despite bringing a significant dowry to the marriage, Penhurst never gave her a farthing unless it had many strings attached.

Control like that made you crave the opposite. Freedom and independence like she used to have. Which was why Penny was eager to start afresh. A new life. A new place. A new, improved and better her, shaped by her past certainly, but not tied to it. Rightly or wrongly, she saw her current situation as a second chance and one she refused to squander. Well before his arrest, her life shackled to Penhurst had become a wretched existence. That that had ended, regardless of the circumstances, had to be viewed as a blessing and she was not inclined to mourn its loss.

Her friend wanted to anchor her here where the past hovered ominously to haunt her for her own well-meant but ultimately insulting reasons. Poor, mistreated, misguided and fragile Penny. A label which was probably well deserved, but now galled, because it reminded her too much of the woman she had temporarily been, but now loathed. Much as she loved Clarissa and would be forever grateful to her, her overprotectiveness now was stifling and, when they clashed on any topics involving Penny's future, felt alarmingly like control once again and instinctively that made her chafe against it. Like her awful husband and her oppressive sham of a marriage, the green, anxiously compliant and tragic Lady Penelope Penhurst was dead and good riddance to her. Long live Penny Henley! Whoever Penny Henley was.

They had both lapsed back into their own quiet thoughts, the brittle peace broken only by the ominous ticking of the second-hand clock on the tiny mantel, until the polite tap on the door had her practically jumping out of her seat.

'Finally!' Clarissa stood with the innate grace her plainer friend had always envied and smoothed down her dress, the action highlighting the first beginnings of the tiny baby bump forming in her normally perfectly flat tummy. The bump which she had yet to formally appraise Penny of, no doubt not to give her another excuse to want to stop being a needy burden on her generous friend's time. 'Sit straighter. Pull your shoulders back. Don't smile. Remember, you want to keep the upper hand.'

Clarissa had staged the room to put the lawyer at a distinct disadvantage. Penny sat in the tallest and most regal chair, one which her friend had had delivered from her own house less than an hour ago to give the illusion of a gravitas she did not feel. Both Clarissa and Seb were to sit on the small sofa near the room's only window, there for moral support and to ensure Penny did not allow herself to be walked over. This was well meant, but it galled. As if she would continue being a doormat after all the times Penhurst had metaphorically wiped his muddy feet on her back!

Lord Hadleigh got to sit in the short, hard chair next to the roaring fireplace. Being mild by October standards, the unnecessary fire would also serve to make the interfering lawyer feel uncomfortable. Clarissa intended the man to bake like a crusty loaf while he sweated out his apology. While Penny thought all her friend's staging was taking things a bit too far, she did hope the searing heat would encourage him to leave swiftly. Hopefully with a polite flea in his ear, put there by the new, assertive, improved version of herself and after promising to acquire a refund from Mr Cohen for the rent. Because Lord only knew Penny stood no chance of scrabbling together a year's worth of rent any time soon to repay him.

Clarissa opened the door and the lawyer positively filled the frame. An unpleasant surprise, when she had worked hard to convince herself he had only seemed imposing in the courtroom because of his austere barrister's attire, and she had been entirely intimidated by the proceedings and the intentional, dramatic theatre of the Old Bailey.

He stepped in, his sharp eyes taking in the whole room, and only then did she notice Clarissa's enormous husband behind him. Heavens, the barrister really was tall! And handsome, in an aristocratic and detached sort of way. She hadn't noticed that before—probably because of the wig and gown. The intimidating staging of the legal system.

'We shan't beat around the bush...' Clarissa gestured specifically to the tiny chair '...seeing that you clearly have some explaining to do and we are keen to hear it.'

He walked straight past the chair and stopped in front of Penny, inclining his golden head politely and taking her hand. 'Lady Penhurst—my humblest of apologies. Leatham here tells me my clumsy gesture caused you angst and for that I shall never forgive myself.'

For some reason, she had not expected an outright apology straight away. Nor such a pretty one. Nor had she expected his gloveless hand to be so warm or his touch so reassuring. As if he had read her mind, his other hand came to rest on top of hers in what she assumed was meant as a friendly gesture, but in actuality made her feel a little odd. Not in an unpleasant way, but those large, gentle hands, combined with the way his unusual burnt-amber eyes locked and held with hers, set her pulse jumping.

She recognised the sensation from long ago. That frisson of awareness and excitement she remembered only too well from those initial heady days of her first and only Season, when a dashing new suitor showed an interest and flirted. Her former hopelessly romantic heart would begin to race as her vivid, naive imagination began to conjure up scenarios of a future with him. Because then, despite all the teachings of her sensible and hard-working parents, she had abandoned good sense for unrealistic dreams of romance and love. What a foolish girl she had been then!

Instinctively, she disentangled her hand and buried it with the other safely within the folds of her skirt. She watched his eyes dip to them before he smiled and her stupid pulse quickened further. She had never seen him smile. It suited him. 'It was not my intention to cause you concern.'

'What exactly was your intention?' Annoyance at her own body's reaction made her tone irritated and for that, at least, she was glad. She had fallen for pretty words once before and look where that had got her. Annoyed was decisive. Penny Henley was decisive.

He took a step back, but appeared perfectly content to stand. Uncharitably, Penny decided he was avoiding the chair on purpose to deny her the chance to take control and she instantly bristled. 'I imagine, given our limited and professional acquaintance, my actions do seem a trifle odd, but believe me, they truly were well meant. After the Crown saw fit to render you homeless, I could not in all good conscience allow you and your innocent son to struggle.'

He considered Freddie? That was nice... *Good grief, girl, grow a backbone! You used to have such a fine one. He took it upon himself to make a decision for you when he had no right. None whatsoever.* She wasn't a wife any longer. Not a chattel nor a charity case.

'Do prosecution barristers regularly pay the household bills of defence witnesses?' He blinked, the only sign her forthright words had been unexpected.

'Under normal circumstances, the Crown would not take the archaic decision to strip a family of their title and assets.' They agreed on that at least. Losing her home had ripped the floor from under her feet, hurting far more than losing her distasteful husband. 'I was merely attempting to make some small amends for that travesty in my own ham-fisted and clumsy way.'

A plausible answer. A charming and disarming one. But not to her direct question and Penny felt her hackles rise further. He was being the unfazed and convincing lawyer she had seen every day at the Old Bailey, attempting to play her like a violin. She had seen him in action. He was charming and decisive. Used to commanding the ears and then the thoughts of those who found themselves listening to his clever arguments and well-chosen words. A man who had reluctantly come here today with one purpose. To justify having her put under surveillance for months and then anonymously settling her debts—apparently for her own good.

Despite all of Clarissa's careful staging, he now thoroughly commanded the room. He had ignored the tiny chair. Avoided the sweltering fire. And instead of regally looking down her nose at him, Penny was forced to look up. A long way up. Another professional trick he had clearly done on purpose. She stood, hoping she appeared partially regal despite the vast difference in their heights, and allowed her irritation to show plainly on her face. Money aside, no matter which way one looked at it, having her followed was a gross invasion of her privacy, one she had every right to feel angry about.

'Did the Crown also sanction the Runner you had spy on me?'

He blinked again, frowning slightly. 'No. Of course they didn't. My actions have nothing to do with the government or the Crown in any way.'

'But you are such a noble man, such a seeker of justice, that you simply decided to right a wrong regardless? Or do you merely have a guilty conscience about what transpired?'

'Not at all.' He took another step back and his normally inscrutable expression dissolved briefly into one of outrage. 'I had no part in their decision.' The bland barrister's mask slipped back in place. 'If you must know, I petitioned the Attorney General on your behalf.'

That she knew. Clarissa and Seb had told her as much that dreadful night in their house in Grosvenor Square once she realised she no longer had a home to go back to. Those had been the darkest and most hopeless days of her life. The press had huddled outside the house like vultures, doing whatever they could to catch a glimpse of the traitor's wife—soon to be traitor's widow. No peer of the realm had been stripped of his title *and* his estates in decades. Neither had any peer been sentenced to death for any crime—let alone treason—since Lord Lovat after the Battle of Culloden two generations previously. Meanwhile, inside her friend's house Penny had been too stunned, too broken down after years of her oppressive marriage, to do anything other than weep or stare, catatonic.

What was she going to do? What was to become of her son? *Oh, woe is me!*

When news came days later that her husband had escaped the hangman's noose only because his criminal associates had decided it was safer to have him murdered in Newgate than risk having him make any deathbed confessions which might implicate them, an intrepid reporter had broken into Seb's house. The intruder had successfully climbed three stairs before he was tackled and removed by the guards. Those had been three stairs too many for Penny and strangely galvanised her into action, awaking a part of her which had lain dormant for too many years. She was so tired of being the helpless victim.

Weeping and lamenting *Oh, woe is me* was not going to change a single thing and it certainly wasn't going to protect her son. Only she could do both—yet could do neither while feeling pathetically sorry for herself when she only had herself to blame. The signs had been there from the outset. Clarissa had warned her. Even her father had offered to help her flee the church on the morning of her marriage despite spending a king's ransom on the gown, the elaborate wedding breakfast and the marriage settlements, and despite knowing her mother would also be devastated to have encouraged the match. But blinded by the belief she was madly in love and madly loved in return by her handsome, titled, ardent suitor, she had positively floated down the aisle towards her groom, regardless of the niggling voice in her head which cautioned she was making a huge mistake.

It had been a revelation to finally accept the fact she had made her own bed, through her own foolish weaknesses, and now had to lie in it—and just because her new bed was hard and uncomfortable, it didn't make it a bad bed. If anything, it was a significantly superior bed to the one she had been lying in. Only this time, she could make it exactly as she wanted.

The next day she had gone into hiding, in plain sight at Seb's suggestion, to live independently for the first time in her twenty-four years and she had not looked back or wallowed in one drop of pointless self-pity since. Her new life had started and she found she rather enjoyed it. The past was the past. Done. Dead. She had come to terms with it all and was well shot of it. Didn't allow herself to think upon it any more.

Yet now the past was back in the most unexpected and unforeseen way. Not from the press. Not from being recognised. But from the man still stood proudly in front of her. Too proudly when he was the one clearly in the wrong here. What gave him the right to assert change on her life when he'd had a professional hand in creating her current situation? Did he feel guilt at proving her husband guilty?

Perhaps that was the problem? That awful possibility had been niggling since she had learned the truth this morning. What if his guilt about the trial ran deeper than he was letting on? If so, then it kicked a veritable hornets' nest she was only too content to leave well alone.

For five months, there had been no doubt in her mind that Penhurst had been guilty of all the charges levelled against him and probably more. Penny had realised as much the moment the King's Men had stormed into her house and arrested him. Later, the lawyer's case had been convincing and thorough, and while she felt stupid at her own ignorance and ashamed of her own cowardice to question that ignorance, so many things she had seen or heard during the final year of her marriage suddenly made perfect sense once all the pieces of the puzzle were finally slotted together.

Lord Hadleigh had done that. So much so, it had given her the confidence to stand up to her husband by telling the truth and she had resigned herself to hearing a guilty verdict.

Resigned was the wrong word.

It suggested she was dreading the verdict, when the opposite was true. While she had not expected a peer of the realm to receive the death penalty, she had anticipated a guilty verdict and a life blessedly free from Penhurst afterwards. Looked forward to it eagerly—something which caused her guilt late at night when sleep eluded her. Whatever Penhurst had done, he was still the father of her son. Something she knew she would one day have to explain to her little boy.

Was it wrong to be completely relieved to be free of him? Or to have helped him on his way by testifying against him the moment fate had given her the chance? For five months, she had consoled herself that she had done the right thing for Freddie's sake so that he could grow into the man he was meant to be rather than one tainted and poisoned by his sire's warped morals.

The lawyer's guilty conscience suddenly made her question the validity of the trial. Had Lord Hadleigh embellished the truth or lied? Covered important and pertinent details up? Fabricated evidence? She sincerely hoped not. Penny did not want to have any of her relief at the tumultuous end of her marriage dampened. She had hated Penhurst and was glad he was dead. Felt no guilt at his violent passing whatsoever. But guilt might well explain why the lawyer had paid her rent for an entire year.

'I don't want your blood money!'

'Blood money?' Her harsh words took him aback. 'I can assure you, madam, my gift was nothing of the sort.' Hadleigh raked an agitated hand through his hair and began to pace. The very idea was as preposterous as it was insulting and he wanted to loudly proclaim his utter disgust at the suggestion. He was a principled man who believed in right and wrong. Good and evil. Justice and truth. A man who righted wrongs, not caused them. How dare she even suggest his motives were fuelled by...what? Malpractice? Deceit? Wrongdoing? And on what evidence was his good reputation so unfairly besmirched?

But as he paced the worn old rug on the hard, scuffed wooden floor, took in the mismatched furniture, the cramped and basic surroundings alongside the proud and clearly frightened woman stood before him, he couldn't help but remember a similar scene years ago. And another time when he had attempted to rescue a woman who flatly refused to be rescued because there was nothing she needed to be rescued from.

Absolutely nothing.

Hadleigh realised that losing his temper now, just as it had done then, would not help her at all. Better to stick to reason, logic and the truth and keep emotion well out of it.

'I can see why you would jump to that conclusion, so please allow me to reassure you. My actions had nothing to do with guilt regarding your husband or the way his trial was carried out. I am sorry if you find that difficult to hear, but on that score I am remorseless...' Good grief! Hardly the best way to win her over and accept his benevolence in the spirit it was intended. 'I acted as I did more out of a sense of regret that you had to suffer more than was necessary and completely unjustly. If the Crown refused to see you right, then someone needed to. I am a wealthy man, so it was no hardship for me to help. Consider it my penance for failing to get the Crown to see sense.' He was righting a wrong. It was that simple.

'That does not explain why you saw fit to have me spied upon these past months.'

'I didn't have you spied upon.' So much for sticking to reason, logic and the truth. Hadleigh found himself wincing. She had a perfectly valid reason to be angry with him and now that he was seeing it all through her eyes, he had made a royal hash of it. 'All right... I suppose in a manner of speaking I did, but again it was not done with any malice. After you had been left with nothing—through no fault of your own, I might add—I needed to reassure myself you and your child were coping all alone. When the Runner informed me you were selling your jewellery...'

'Insignificant pieces to which I had no attachment.' Her pretty face flushed as she resolutely avoided her friends' sympathetic eyes and he realised he had inadvertently put his big, fat foot in it again. Like his mother, she was too ashamed of her situation to accept help despite none of it being her fault. 'Things given to me by a husband which I would prefer to forget and mine to dispose of as I see fit.' Despite the fact that both her friends, and he, knew she was pawning her mother's jewellery to pay her monthly bills, she was still labouring under the misapprehension that her friends, at least, didn't. 'I no longer wanted any reminders of him in *my* house.'

She was proud in the face of defeat and his heart wept for her. His hands wanted to touch her, tug her into his arms and hold her close. What was that about, aside from the bone-deep exhaustion which came from weeks of sleeplessness? No wonder his emotions were a tad frayed and close to the surface. 'A perfectly understandable reason to sell them and one which makes me sorrier my heavy-handed and unnecessary response has caused you both worry and embarrassment.'

'I am not in need of charity, Lord Hadleigh.'

'That I can plainly see, my lady.' Blast it all to hell, he had gone about this all wrong. Pride always came before a fall and, like his mother, this one would rather suffer in silence than allow the world to see her pain. He, of all people, should have pre-empted such a reaction. 'And once again, I humbly apologise for insulting you. It was well intentioned, although, I concede, highly inappropriate and misguided.'

It was time to make a hasty retreat before he was backed into a corner of his own making and forced into rescinding his gift before she had had time to mull over the many benefits of it. Given a little time, and the obvious easing of her financial burdens, she might be convinced to keep it.

'I really meant no offence, or to cause you worry of any kind. Although I can see that my ham-fisted, overbearing and overzealous attempt at helping you has done exactly that, and for that I am sorry. This has most definitely not been my finest hour. But know that I am on your side whether you want me to be or not.' From his pocket he produced a calling card which he gently pressed into her hand, making it impossible for her to refuse it. For some reason, his fingers longed to linger so he quickly snatched them away.

'What I should have done all those months ago, rather than put a watch on you, was simply this. Should you need anything…anything at all…money, help…a ham-fisted but well-meaning friend…all you need do is ask. Whatever it is, whenever it is, send word to this address and I will move heaven and earth to see it done.' Before she could respond he bowed. 'Good day to you, Lady Penhurst. Thank you for allowing me the chance to explain and to see for myself the error of my ways. You have been most gracious.' Then, with the swiftest and politest of nods to the room in general, he promptly turned and marched swiftly out the door.

Chapter Four

Three days of silence lulled him into a false sense of security, so Hadleigh wasn't expecting his clerk to inform him she had turned up at his chambers unannounced, wishing to speak to him. While the clerk went to fetch her, he braced himself for another difficult conversation and was not disappointed. She arrived ramrod straight and proud, only her eyes giving him any indication she was nowhere near as confident as she wanted to portray. They were wide and restless, darting every which way before finally settling on him stood politely behind his paper-strewn desk.

'Please forgive the intrusion, Lord Hadleigh, but I needed to speak with you.'

The gaunt, pale woman from the courtroom was gone and clearly her appetite had improved in the intervening months, as the same dull spencer which had once hung from her frame was now filled with gloriously feminine curves. She might be petite in stature, but there was no disguising she was all woman. Something he had no right noticing considering the circumstances.

'It is no intrusion at all.' He gestured to the chair opposite and she sat daintily on the edge, gripping her reticule for all she was worth. Her errant hands, once again, saying much more of the truth than he was likely to get out of her pretty mouth. 'What did you wish to speak to me about, Lady Penhurst?'

Her dark brows drew together in an expression of what he thought might be distaste as her fingers toyed with the ribbon handle of her bag. 'I am not Lady Penhurst any longer and, if you don't mind, I would prefer not to be addressed as such. I go by Mrs Henley now, which was my mother's maiden name.' Her troubled blue eyes flicked to his briefly as she shrugged an apology. He found himself drowning in their intense, stormy depths. 'There is less chance of my being recognised with a run-of-the-mill name and I would prefer not to use my real married name any more…for obvious reasons.' And there it was again, that flash of distaste, although whether it was at the thought of her husband or her situation, he had no idea.

'Of course…very wise.' He settled back in his chair, hoping his posture would help her to relax, calmly waiting for her to proceed. It didn't. Only the smallest fraction of her bottom was on the chair, her knuckles quite white as she continued to nervously fiddle and twist the ribbons further.

After a few seconds ticked by awkwardly, she sat up straighter. 'The thing is, I went to visit my landlord, Mr Cohen, this morning…and was informed you have made no attempt to contact him since our last meeting…to retrieve your money.'

'Mrs Henley, might I speak plainly?' She nodded, eyes widening once again as if fearing his words. 'I think we would both agree our last meeting was a little awkward. I believe we both left a great deal unsaid.' How to frame these next words in the most gentle and appeasing way and leave her dignity intact? 'For my part, I realised that neither

Clarissa nor Seb knew you were selling your jewellery, so I quickly backtracked to avoid further embarrassing you.'

'I explained about the jewellery, Lord Hadleigh.' Two charming pink spots began to appear on her cheeks which called her a liar. 'They were gifts from my husband and I no longer wanted them.'

Pride always came before a fall. 'I beg to differ. I saw you that morning outside the pawnshop.' It had done odd things to his heart.

'You did?' That seemed to surprise her and set her expressive eyes blinking. She had lovely long lashes. Dark and thick. The sort that waylaid a man's thoughts from the important task at hand, much like the way she filled out that spencer.

'Indeed I did, so I saw for myself how difficult you found it to part with them.' Should he tell her he had the brooch? That it was safe with all the other trinkets necessity had forced her to sell and hers again whenever she wanted? Probably not. It would make her feel more beholden, when clearly beholden was the state which caused her the greatest discomfort. 'I also went in and questioned the pawnbroker who showed me the piece. It was old and well-worn. You were married only three years, were you not? Hardly long enough to cause the deterioration I witnessed in that brooch. Which lead me to believe it was hardly the sort of piece of jewellery a husband would give to his wife.'

'My husband was not a generous man...'

'Mrs Henley, we both know that was your mother's brooch or your grandmother's. It was a sentimental item. Worth more to the heart than the purse.' He had similar items himself. The handkerchiefs his mother had embroidered for him. Her letters sent while he was away studying. The last one filled with no hint of the nightmare she was living or the absolute fear she must have been feeling in the days before her death. If only he could turn back time.

'And what if it was?' The sudden affected bravado was brittle and unconvincing. Eerily familiar. 'It was still mine to do with as I wished.'

He mentally took a step away from those old emotions which had suddenly decided to plague him to focus on the here and now. An unfair wrong he could easily right and the woman his soul appeared to demand he rescue. 'The Runner said you took the money from the jewellery each month directly to the shops and used it to pay your accounts.' Hadleigh decided to present her with irrefutable evidence in the hope she might realise further lies were pointless. 'You always go to Palmer's Shop of All Things first because it is closest to the pawnshop. Then you walk to your landlord Mr Cohen's place next, followed by Shank's the butcher and Mrs Writtle's bakery. I can even tell you how much you paid to each of these merchants and how much you received for each precious piece of your mother's jewellery that was sold.'

She blinked rapidly, her mouth opening to speak before she closed it firmly. For several moments, she seemed smaller and he realised now might be the best chance he had of appealing to her logic. 'You see, I had a very clear picture of your finances, Mrs Henley, before I took it upon myself to assist you with them.' He exhaled slowly and waited for her dipped eyes to pluck up the courage to rise back up to meet his. 'You were barely making ends meet and unless you have a jewellery box stuffed full of old earrings and brooches to sell, I also knew your reserves would likely soon run out. That is why I stepped in...or stomped in more like.' He smiled to soften the blows he had just dealt her. 'I wanted to take that worry away from you. I still do. That is why I have not, nor will I make any attempt to get the rent money back from Mr Cohen. Allow me to help you.'

She was silent for an age, sat perfectly still. Only the occasional movement of the fingers now buried within the folds of her skirt made her appear less like an inanimate statue. 'Your Runner really was thorough, wasn't he?'

'I made sure I engaged the best.'

'Except he didn't know everything, did he?' Her head tilted and she gazed at him down her nose, her slim shoulders rising proudly. For some reason, he liked that version of her more. She wasn't broken. She had gumption. 'I am leaving Cheapside soon to take employment elsewhere. That has always been my intention. So you see, Lord Hadleigh, your decision to pay a year's worth of my rent was quite pointless.'

He didn't believe her. 'Perhaps—but at least it gives you the option to decide whether or not now is the right time to take employment. You have a young son, do you not? Is he old enough for you to leave him?'

'I shan't be leaving him. He will be coming with me.' Her nose rose a notch higher. 'Therefore, you have wasted a great deal of money.'

'It is mine to waste, my lady.'

She briefly chewed on her bottom lip, drawing his eyes to it, before she caught herself and feigned nonchalance. 'Have it your own way.' She stood quickly, looking as though she was about to break into a run, then surprised him by rifling in her reticule. 'I anticipated your refusal.' She placed six guineas in a neat stack on his desk. 'I believe that covers half of the debt I owe you. I will begin reimbursing you for the rest as soon as I receive my first month's wages.'

He hadn't been expecting that, she could see, because he stiffened and frowned at the coins. Finally, after what felt like an age, his penetrating gaze fixed on her. He had unusual eyes. Golden brown, almost amber in colour. Unnerving and perceptive. They matched his hair which was a tad too long and curling above his collar and austere, simply tied cravat. Pompous and handsome. The all-too-familiar combination. His prolonged scrutiny unnerved her, but she stood proudly. She had made a plan, a good one, and all she had to do was stick to it.

'There is no way I will accept it.' To prove his point, he slid the column of coins back towards her. She ignored them.

'As our business is now concluded, I shall bid you a good day, Lord Hadleigh.' She had hoped to appear formidable as she said this before turning and striding decisively towards the door.

'Oh, for goodness sake! Stop being so stubborn when it is patently obvious you need it!' He stood, his palms flat and braced on his desk as he quashed the brief flash of temper and replaced it with an expression which was irritatingly reasonable. 'The Crown, in its lack of wisdom, did you wrong and I am simply making it a little bit right.'

'That is your opinion and you are entitled to it, just as I am entitled to be stubbornly opposed to your unwelcome interference in my life.' An awkward silence hung and she let it. There was no point in arguing with the man. He was used to getting his own way, as men were, and she needed to get used to being the new improved Penny who was mistress of her own destiny. Besides, it felt empowering to take a little control back from this man who was clearly used to owning it.

The overbearing lawyer stared, then for the first time since she had encountered him he appeared awkward in his own skin. He glanced down at his feet, then raked a hand through his hair before those unusual eyes locked on hers, the emotion in them unfathomable. But there *was* emotion. And it wasn't anger at her rude behaviour. 'Why won't you allow me to help you?'

'I have no need of anyone's help, my lord.'

'I think you do. The life you now have is no life for either you or your son.'

That was insulting. It might well not be much of a life yet, but it was infinitely better than the one she had had and she was committed to making it better. What right did he have to judge her? To do what *he* thought best and enforce *his* will? 'My life is none of your business.' Another rude outburst which she wasn't the least bit sorry for. Clearly, a tiny bit of her spine had already grown back to so plainly voice her outrage.

'I cannot, in all good conscience, allow you and your son to continue living like that when I have the means and the desire to help you. Is a life of poverty, pawnshops, scrimping and saving...' he scowled again as if the cosy little oasis she had lovingly made was somehow abhorrent '...truly the life you want for your son?'

'Was it your intention to insult me and the life I have worked hard to make for myself? For if it was, you have succeeded, sir.'

'I meant no offence. I am merely trying to help to make your lot in life better after the grievous injustice you have been made to suffer.'

'By bullying me into your way of thinking? By accepting your money to make yourself feel better about whatever it is that has put a bee in your bonnet?' She watched his golden eyebrows draw together a second before his eyes dropped to stare at the ground. 'If you really want to help me improve my lot, my lord, then you can start by sparing me the continued ordeal of your presence or interference.' Realising her feet had taken her back towards his desk during her impassioned speech, Penny briskly walked back to the door, strangely enjoying the sensation of being angry at a man and not fearing his retribution, although bewildered as to why she didn't fear it with him when he was so annoyingly overbearing.

It made no difference that his broad shoulders were slumped or that his normally piercing gaze was rooted to the floor as if he was miraculously unsure of himself. As if a man like him would ever know what it truly felt to be uncertain about anything. He deserved one more parting shot and so did she. 'I have spent three miserable years being dictated to by a man. Three years being bullied and lectured.'

'You cannot compare my actions to his.' He appeared hurt at the suggestion.

'Can I not? You had me spied upon, just like him. You are trying to enforce your will upon me—just like him. And ultimately, whatever your intentions, noble or otherwise, you are using my weaknesses to control me. You just belittled me to my face. Just…like…him.' She sounded like her old self, the one before Penhurst she still liked. It was a heady feeling and she was proud of herself. This was the Penny she wanted to be again. Brave and undaunted. Unapologetically marching to the beat of her own drum.

'You are not my master, sir. I cannot begin to tell you how relieved I am that nobody is any longer nor will anyone ever be again. Nor do I need a benefactor. What you see as for my own good to right a wrong, I see as unwarranted and insulting interference now that I finally have my freedom back. If I want money, I will earn it. My labour in return for wages! Because that is an equal transaction, one I am entirely familiar with. One both parties can terminate whenever they see fit.'

Head still bent, his eyes lifted, seeking hers almost

tentatively. 'I find myself again in the awkward position of having to offer you another heartfelt apology, for if you misconstrued any of my actions as bullying then I am mortified. I abhor bullies and it is humbling to realise that in attempting to enforce my will, I inadvertently became one. You are quite correct—you have every right to be angry at me. If it is any consolation at all, I am furious at myself.' He looked pained and awkward as he slowly picked up the six guineas from the desk and placed them in the drawer. Only once he had pushed it closed did those unusual perceptive eyes lock with hers again. They were swirling with an emotion she couldn't quite fathom. Regret? Sadness? Shame? Whatever it was it made him seem more human. 'But for the record, despite all the mounting evidence to the contrary, I swear to you on my life I am nothing like *him*.'

Chapter Five

The pews in St George's in Hanover Square weren't meant for big men, yet for some inexplicable reason the ushers at Lord Fennimore's wedding had decided to seat the two biggest together in the middle of a row. Seb Leatham's ridiculously burly shoulders were encroaching into his space on one side and a strange woman's ludicrously large bonnet inhabited the other. In silent, tacit agreement, both men were twisted at the same obtuse angle to try to make the best of it.

'Dear God, I hope the bride arrives soon!' Leatham hated social occasions and was already getting twitchy.

'It's the bride's prerogative to be late, so please try to sit still.'

'My leg is going to sleep. My backside is already numb!'

'Then it shouldn't be long till your leg joins it and you won't feel the pain any more.' If only all pain could be so easily desensitised. The dull, constant one in his conscience had taken permanent root since she had held a mirror up to his face. What had he been thinking? Acting like the Admiral of the fleet, snapping out orders and expecting them to be followed, when any fool with half a brain would know a woman who had suffered at the hands of a dictatorial, brutish husband was never going to respond well to such behaviour. Common sense would tell them that the reaction would either be cowering fear or bristling outrage. He was heartened that her response to his I-know-better-than-you tactics had been to fight back. He doubted he could live with himself if he had caused a woman's fear. No matter how much he worried that the man in the mirror that day might be a little too much like his father for comfort, to be that much like his father made him feel physically sick.

'The bride is certainly milking her prerogative to be late! There is late and then there is just plain self-indulgence.'

A scowling society matron offered them a pointed look, one which clearly said shut up. Hadleigh lowered his voice further, because he couldn't pretend even to himself any longer that he didn't need to know. 'How is she?' A very touchy subject, seeing as Leatham had threatened to break his idiotic, ham-fisted and worthless neck over the guineas incident three weeks ago.

'How the blazes do you think she is?' Seb offered him his most withering of glances. 'Applying for every blasted housekeeper or governess job from here to John O'Groats to no avail to pay you back what she owes you. Hell-bent on leaving London as soon as possible regardless. Scrimping on food for herself to make the last pennies she has stretch further. Clarissa is beside herself with worry! I hope you are pleased with yourself. If she ends up working for some robbing scoundrel for farthings in the back of beyond, I give you fair warning, I've promised my wife I'll give her your *jewels* as earrings.' His friend threw up his hands despite the confined space. 'I just don't understand it. You are normally such an affable fellow. Charming, even. Upright, upstanding—normally annoyingly very sensible. Yet in all your dealings with poor Penny you have been a total oafish idiot!'

Hadleigh couldn't argue with that description. 'Surely I can do something to help? I could try talking to her again...' Something he had desperately wanted to do since she had given back his now-tainted six guineas and left him with a heavy heart and his tail between his legs. He only wanted to make things right and it was driving him mad that he had been thwarted in that noble quest.

'Stay away from her!' Seb's elbow jabbed him hard in the ribs. 'Unless you know some generous toff with an estate that needs a very well-paid housekeeper, you've caused more than enough trouble already!' Hadleigh had an estate... She wanted to trade her labour for honest wages...*that* might just work...

No! Bad idea... A very bad idea. For so many reasons.

'Hallelujah!' Seb's cry had the stern matron frowning again. 'I do believe it's finally time for the off.'

Hadleigh settled back in the pew as the organ began to play and fixed his gaze firmly on Lord Fennimore waiting nervously at the altar in an attempt to stop his mind whirring. There was no point in attempting to meddle again. She wouldn't take well to it and Seb would kill him. Clarissa, too. Lady Penhurst probably hated him. Another depressing thought. Not that he wanted her to like him, but still...she thought him a bully. No better than her awful husband. He felt an ache form between his eyebrows and realised he was scowling, something which was hardly fair on the bride, so he stalwartly banished all thoughts of saving the proud and exasperating woman who didn't want rescuing to focus on the unlikely wedding about to take place in front of him.

The Commander of the King's Elite was close to sixty and, up until recently, had been a confirmed bachelor wedded solely to his profession. Yet, like Warriner, Leatham, Flint and Gray, he had also fallen victim to the parson's trap. All five men—Hadleigh's friends and comrades—had succumbed in quick succession this past year. Like dominoes, lined up just to fall, there had also been an inevitability about it. The ladies they had fallen for were all perfect for them. But out of the five of them, only Lord Fennimore's impending nuptials had surprised him. Not because his choice of bride was wrong—Hadleigh had developed a soft spot for the indomitable Harriet and wished them all the happiness in the world—but because he saw a great deal of himself in old Fennimore. More, he hoped, than he saw of his father.

They shared the same set of values, had a defined and unwavering moral compass and the same determination to see things through no matter what. It was a solitary path, but a noble one. A vocation even. Nothing was more important than getting the job finished and seeing justice done.

Righting wrongs.

That single-minded, driven determination was what made them the men they were and why they had climbed so quickly to the pinnacle of their careers. Nothing else was more important.

Except, apparently, now the soon-to-be Lady Fennimore was equally as important, or perhaps more so, and that was a state of affairs Hadleigh simply couldn't fathom. He had never been in love. Never come close to it and couldn't imagine why he would want to be. Despite knowing he was capable of experiencing powerful emotions, because Lord only knew they had plagued him since the blasted trial, they had never been something he had been comfortable with. He buried them, hid them and, if the situation warranted it, hot-footed it as fast as he could to escape them. Anger was destructive. Fear knotted the gut. Grief was too painful and shame gnawed at you from the inside as it was right now.

He'd had indigestion for a week thanks to his spectacular error of judgement and his insomnia concerning a certain former witness had got so bad, he rarely managed a few hours of broken sleep before his troubled conscience woke him up. The strange nightmare was cyclical and went nowhere. Stormy, proud blue eyes with ridiculously long lashes haunted his dreams. Fevered dreams where her expressive, elegant hands kept trying to hide the truth in his tangled sheets as his own tried frantically to hold one again. Or hold her. But she was always out of reach. It was driving him mad and he hated all the foggy-headed confusion which inevitably followed for hours afterwards.

If shame and his initial misplaced guilt was capable of doing all that, one didn't need to experience romantic love to know that its power could be unbelievably destructive and he knew enough about it from observation to be certain it required far more effort and time than he was prepared to spend on it any time soon.

The old man saw his bride in the entrance to St George's and visibly relaxed, his permanently scowling expression softening into a smile for once at just the sight of her. When the ceremony was over he proudly stood with her on his arm, basking in the congratulations of the guests and later in her company during the interminable wedding breakfast.

Interminable because, despite the crush, the laughter and the presence of good friends, Hadleigh felt alone. As if something was missing. An odd thought when he always preferred his own company and, being an only child, had lived like that for as long as he could remember. Both self-reliant and usually contentedly solitary. Yet that alien feeling refused to go away no matter how much small talk he exchanged with the other wedding guests at the wedding breakfast or how many times he reminded himself he was perfectly at ease with his life exactly as it was as the party whirled on around him.

Alongside that was the annoyingly persistent melancholy which he was usually very adept at burying in work, but which had bothered him unrelentingly since the Penhurst trial first began. Probably because Lady Penhurst's situation reminded him too much of his mother's. That, and the enormous hash he had made in trying to help her.

Rationally, he knew that. He dealt in evidence and truths, so it was impossible to ignore the stack of eerie coincidences piling inside his troubled conscience. Like his mother, Lady Penhurst had been subjected to both physical and mental abuse during her marriage. Exactly like his mother, she was an innocent suffering thanks to an overbearing man. And because history enjoyed repeating itself, both women were destined to suffer for ever for their spouses' sins when they had had no hand in them themselves. The law gave no rights to wives. While Hadleigh was determined to uphold the law until his dying breath, he was also prepared to concede that as far as women were concerned the law was an ass, too, and desperately needed changing.

On this occasion it had been the biggest ass of all. A big, fat, clumsy, vengeful ass which he hadn't been able to prevent or overturn despite his being entirely in the right. Which, in turn, had led him to be a big, fat, clumsy, ultimately domineering ass himself. Just like his father and her foul husband. History repeating itself again, yet that still didn't make the truth any easier to swallow.

Logically, his legal brain also recognised it was no coin-

cidence that the timing was significant, too. The Penhurst
trial had taken place exactly one decade since his mother's
tragic death. Ten years was a significant anniversary and
one which had lurked darkly for months long before the
blasted Penhurst trial. It had been the first thing he had
thought of when he had awoken on New Year's Day and
would doubtless lurk until the bells signalled the turning
of another year in a few months' time. Yet, exactly like
that year, this one was a defining one in his life. This year,
he would try the biggest case of his career. Back then, the
year had culminated with his call to the bar.

He should have deferred that year. As his health declined, so too had his father's temper become more erratic
and explosive than it had ever been before. Irrefutable evidence he had witnessed with his own eyes ten years ago,
yet he had preferred to listen to the untruths his ears had
heard come from his selfless mother's lips.

Everything was fine. She could cope.

Good grief! All this pointless pondering on his own
befuddled emotions created by the past twisting and tangling and confusing with the present was exhausting. No
wonder he couldn't sleep!

'How is the case coming along?' Lord Fennimore's
voice snapped him blessedly back to the present. 'Is it as
cut and dried as we'd hoped?'

'Perhaps not cut and dried.' Because in a British court
of law anything could, and did, happen. 'But certainly
promising. Now that we have the ringleader, I've been
able to dig up all manner of things.' Lady Gislingham's
co-conspirators were beginning to panic. 'Unsurprisingly,
already two of her former associates have felt compelled
to turn King's evidence to save their own sorry skins
and each day more damning evidence spews out of their
mouths.' The two had pleaded guilty and accepted a lesser

sentence of life imprisonment in exchange for their testimony. 'Although the circumstances by which it comes still galls me.'

'Irritating—but we must sacrifice a few minnows for the shark. Though I dare say after a few years in that stinking gaol they'll regret saving themselves. If they avoid the diseases for that long…' Lord Fennimore cast a quick glance to his new wife who was holding court in the corner. Harriet was a vivacious and entertaining woman. An unlikely match for his serious and brusque superior. 'I promised my wife I wouldn't talk shop till tomorrow. Do you have a date yet?'

The dedicated commander of the King's Elite was postponing his own honeymoon until the case was over. 'The Crown want it done and dusted quickly—however, to put forward a thorough and conclusive case I'm tabling the first week of January.'

'Capital. Two months is a good buffer. I shall be sure to speak to the Attorney General and the King's advisors, endorsing your suggestion. Like you, I want to be sure that woman and her minions get exactly what's coming to them. As keen as the government are to get this over and done with, a hasty trial may well backfire. However, Flint won't like the extra delay. He's understandably reluctant to bring his wife to London after the circus of the Penhurst trial…and just in case there are a few wrong 'uns still at large who we've missed.' The old man rolled his eyes.

Flint's new wife was Hadleigh's key prosecution witness. Not only had she been forced to work with the Comte de Saint-Aubin-de-Scellon, the crazed leader of the French side of the smuggling ring, she had also written encoded messages to all the British traitors, which categorically implicated them in the treachery. She knew each one by name.

'Do you think she is still in danger?'

'I don't—but then she's not *my* wife. If it was Harriet, I'm not sure I'd want her in the capital either until absolutely necessary. Too much risk…what with the press and all.' His eyes drifted to his new spouse again and his serious, professional expression curiously disappeared for a split second before he scowled again. 'But I suppose you need her here for the good of the trial.'

'I need to go through everything she knows again with a fine toothcomb. Every day turns up something new which will need corroborating. I want to leave no stone unturned and no loophole open.'

'A fair point. I'll strap on some armour and put it to Flint. Although I dare say he'll insist on using all the resources of the King's Elite and perhaps all the King's cavalry regiments to guard her, too, if I demand she has to venture out of his castle. Have you seen how many people he has guarding this wedding? I had the devil of a job convincing him to leave Cornwall to come today—and I was his father's oldest and dearest friend. But he is a man besotted and there is no reasoning with such a man.'

'Perhaps he'd find it more palatable if we hid Jessamine somewhere not too far from London?' The idea was forming again. No doubt a foolhardy one, but his emotions had apparently taken hold of his reason and no matter how much he tried, he still couldn't shift his misplaced guilt or his ridiculous need to rescue that woman who had been wronged so grievously on his watch. 'Somewhere private enough to avoid any suspicion and easily secured. A place owned by an honorary member of the King's Elite…'

'I'm listening…'

'Well, I have an estate in Essex which would work perfectly if the government would care to borrow it.'

Don't open Pandora's box!

'You do? You've never mentioned it.'

That's because he preferred not to remember it and all the bad memories within it. 'My work here keeps me too busy. I rarely go there.' Around nine years ago had been the last time—to put his father in the ground. He'd had it boarded up four years ago when the butler, the last-standing indoor retainer, had finally acknowledged Hadleigh was never coming home and had taken his pension and his wife to move closer to their son. 'It's spacious. Walled and sits on a hill in the centre of its five hundred acres. Flint, his wife and all the guards he can muster could live there until the trial. It wouldn't take much to make it habitable.' Aside from removing four years' worth of dust and cobwebs, ripping off the dust sheets and hiring a whole host of new servants to bring it back to life. Nothing a small fortune and a good housekeeper who could start immediately couldn't sort out—

If he could find a way to convince her—because he had the small fortune a hundred times over. She did want to work for wages, after all.

He could lie, he supposed. Pretend the house was Flint's... As soon as that thought popped into his head, he sent it swiftly packing. No more well-meaning deceptions and schemes as far as Lady Penhurst was concerned. An offer of genuine employment wasn't charity, so she could hardly refuse it on that score. She either took the job above board, knowing who the real owner was, or she didn't. And perhaps this time he should allow her to meet the real Hadleigh, too. The charming one who had a way with people, not the self-righteous oaf who used a mallet to crack a nut and behaved like a cretin. Either way, at least he would have tried everything within his power to help her rise above the government's unjust punishment and his prickled conscience would have to find a way to cope with that.

There were other benefits to having her take charge of his unwanted house. Genuine benefits which had nothing to do with his own need to right a wrong. Firstly, as a good friend to Clarissa and by default Seb, she knew about the King's Elite so they would not have to creep around covertly in case she overheard something. She was bound to have been kept abreast of developments, even if the Leathams had been sketchy on the details and so far nothing had leaked. Therefore, it stood to reason she was trustworthy. That was a practical consideration. As was the fact she knew what it was like to be a witness in a high-profile case. She could help better prepare Jessamine for the ordeal ahead. Most practical of all, was that it was far enough outside of London to allow Flint and his bride to hide from any perceived danger, but close enough that Hadleigh could travel back and forth in a day, therefore never having to sleep in the damned place.

Two birds. One fat stone. *And Pandora's blasted box!*

'That might work, Hadleigh.'

He could see that Lord Fennimore was already enthused by the prospect because he wasn't scowling, yet instead of feeling the elation at having convinced him, dread settled like lead in the pit of his stomach. He would have to go home. *Good grief! He would have to go home!*

'It would certainly keep the blasted press away.'

'A blessing indeed, as they have already started to pester me.' Bands of panic had already began to wrap themselves around Hadleigh's neck. Squeezing. Why was he doing this? He knew the answer, but didn't quite understand it. *Her.* And his ongoing and debilitating insomnia.

'Then let's make it so and I'll give Flint no choice in the matter. He's never been very good at disobeying direct orders. Besides, we want you to build a conclusive case, Hadleigh, and this timely solution allows us to do it. After all the effort and lives it took to stop The Boss, we cannot allow anything to get in the way of seeing proper justice served.'

Chapter Six

She pulled open the door impatiently. 'I didn't expect to see you again.' Although bizarrely Penny was not surprised to find him on the other side of it when all hell had just broken loose in her apartment. When she had heard the knock, she didn't dither. Didn't bother asking who it was, because she knew it was him. She could sense it.

'Yes, I know. But I have a proposition.' As she glared he raised both hands, palms up in surrender. 'Not from me—I wouldn't dare—but from the government.'

'The government?' She hadn't expected him to say that and wasn't entirely sure she believed him. 'And pray what do *the government* want with me tonight?'

'An important service which they will happily pay you handsomely for—if you can spare them a few months.' His eyes wandered from her suspicious face to the utter carnage beyond. How typical he would turn up now when she was at a distinct disadvantage, looking exactly like a woman who couldn't cope. She had turned her back for two minutes to make herself a well-earned cup of tea after a taxing day and her son had found the small sack of flour she had bought on the romantic and foolish whim of baking biscuits. All by herself. To cheer herself up after re-

ceiving yet another rejection letter. The third this week.
Nobody wanted to employ a woman with a child in tow,
so she would never be able to pay this man back.

Now, all that flour which her son wasn't currently wearing coated the entire floor. Instead of looking aristocrat-
ically appalled at the mess, he smiled sympathetically.
'Although I see I have called at a bad time.'

'A very bad time.' But for some reason, she didn't
slam the door in his face as she should have. 'Since Freddie started toddling, I apparently have to nail everything
down. Even things locked away in a cupboard.' She didn't
need to justify herself to him, except her nerves were frazzled and after a day spent trying to soothe an unreason-
able baby who flatly refused to be soothed or give her
any indication as to why he was so fractious, she was pathetically pleased to see someone. Even if that someone
happened to be the sanctimonious, self-righteous lawyer.
Parenting alone was hard work. Especially at the end of a
long day when she hadn't spoken to a single other human
being over the age of one.

'I looked away for a second…perhaps a whole minute…
and he has wreaked complete destruction.' Suddenly she
wanted to cry. Crumple to a heap on the floor, roll herself
up into a ball and wail in complete, impotent frustration.
When the hideous trial or the imminent prospect of financial ruin hadn't beaten her spirit, clearly another stupid
rejection letter and a bag of spilled flour could. She must
have looked as utterly miserable and fed up as she felt because he immediately stepped over the threshold and reassuringly squeezed her arm.

'Then allow me to help before you dismiss me again.'
Once again, she found his warm touch strangely reassuring, except this time, although only the lightest and brief-
est of touches, she could still feel it after he took his hand

away. 'It is the least I can do after everything. Besides, I am exceedingly good in a crisis. It is one of my strengths.'

'There is no need for you to help me. I can manage...'

'Perfectly well on your own. Yes, I believe I have heard that speech.' He was still smiling. It was a nice smile. An extremely human and genuine one. 'And while I am prepared to concede that under perfectly normal circumstances you can—without my overbearing interference— this hardly constitutes a normal circumstance and helping you to clean up a bit of flour hardly leaves you for ever in my debt, now, does it? If it squares things up in that proud head of yours, I shall have flour strewn all over my office on the morrow and you can come and help clear it up to make us even.'

Not waiting for her response, he headed straight to her tiny kitchen and began to look about. 'Do you own a broom? A dust pan, perhaps?' She hadn't expected that and pointed ineffectually to where they were kept in the furthest corner as she closed the door. Before Freddie caused more chaos, she picked him up. Something which didn't please him because he struggled and whined, smearing flour all over the front of her dullest, most shapeless house dress.

Not that she should be ashamed of that, when she had not expected visitors and certainly never him again, but up against his fine clothing she did. His outfit today was more suited to a fancy dinner party than an official visit to Cheapside.

'Have you ever had cause to use a broom?'

'I've brushed down a horse and mucked out a few stables in my time.' From the amusement radiating from his unusual eyes, he was plainly not insulted by her lack of faith in his domestic abilities. 'I'm sure the principal is similar, but I'm happy for you to give me pointers.'

He swiftly shrugged out of his greatcoat and tossed it over the sofa, then stalked back towards the kitchen to retrieve the tools. Then, in a surreal spectacle she had never dreamed of witnessing, she stood by stunned as he began to wield the broom with economic precision. The wretch had clearly used a broom before. Of course he had. 'Really, I can manage well enough and you are hardly dressed for the occasion.' Freddie chose that moment to begin to howl, push and twist his back over the cage of her arms. His small, angry handprints making a haphazard pattern across her bosom.

'Why don't you sit down and try to distract your son from his ill temper while I remove the worst of it?' His amber eyes were kind for once and out of frazzled necessity she found herself complying, despite not wanting him to witness her continued current ineptitude. Doubtless he would enjoy seeing stark evidence of her inability to cope all on her own.

He picked up her smothered embroidery hoop and frowned as he handed it to her. 'I fear your sewing might be ruined.'

'Believe me, it was ruined long before the flour got to it.'

As Freddie's fidgets became less enthusiastic, she could do little else but watch her rescuer. Lord Hadleigh didn't look much like a lawyer now, nor did he seem half as intimidating. He did well to tame most of the flour into a tiny heap in the middle of the parlour, but puffs of it floated around regardless, clinging to his highly polished boots from heel to shin. Something he either didn't appear to mind or even be aware of when they were clearly expensive boots. She had never seen him without a billowing greatcoat or barrister's gown before, so the sight of him in boots and breeches was unexpected. Without those extra layers he was still a large specimen of the male species.

Tall and surprisingly broad, he would have topped Penhurst by several inches in height and significantly more in width. There had to be at least two feet of man between his arm sockets, maybe more.

As he knelt to sweep the pile of flour into a pan, she got to study the sight of those breeches in profile unwatched. He wore them well. Because of his height, she had assumed his legs would be thin and gangly. However, the thighs which perfectly filled out the buff kerseymere stretched taut around them had been honed on horseback rather than by sitting behind a desk. They had to be. A gentleman might pad his jackets as her husband always had, but never his breeches. That would only look silly... Why was she thinking about a man's breeches? Not that she needed to feel guilty about contemplating an impressive pair of thighs now that she was a delightedly unmarried and independent woman. But *his* thighs! When she hadn't shown a single jot of interest in any man's anything in years! Clearly, she was overtired and overwrought this evening to be so befuddled. An unanticipated flour storm could do that. 'Really, thank you... I can clean up the rest once I put Freddie to bed. It's late and he is tired.' Polite code for leave. Now.

'I suspect your little man could do with a bath before bed. Why don't you see to that while I finish up with the mess? Then we can talk business unhindered.' Making it plain he had no intention of leaving any time soon, he went to the heavy kettle and grabbed a nearby rag to test its weight before topping it up from the jug as if he had spent his life in tiny kitchens. 'Where do you keep the tub?'

In her bedchamber. A place Lord Hadleigh was most definitely even less welcome in than her parlour. 'I will fetch it.' She bustled off with her grumpy son balanced on one hip and closed the door firmly behind her. No sooner has she deposited him on the rug, an unwelcome tap on the door made her realise the lawyer had no respect for boundaries.

'What?' She practically snarled the word at the wood and felt instantly guilty for her tone when he genuinely was only trying to help.

'It seems silly dragging the bath out here when there is still flour everywhere and I can just as easily bring in all the water. Then I'll have everything spick and span before you finish.'

While his suggestion made sense, she still did not want him setting one foot into her most private of spaces, nor did she feel particularly gracious. 'Kindly leave the water outside the door once it's ready. I don't want Freddie accidentally scalding himself.'

'Ah...yes. I never thought of that. My experience with children is limited.' She heard his boots retreat over the hard, wooden floor, heard the sound of flour being swept into the dust pan and sighed with relief. If he wasn't leaving, then seeing to Freddie in private gave her pause enough to compose herself properly. Clearly, he had pondered their last interactions and decided he was unhappy with losing. She had seen his technique in court—whittle away until there was nothing left to whittle. Whatever he was intent on *proposing* needed to be digested with a level head, not a frayed one. The lawyer had a fundamental problem with the word 'no' and her nerves were too close to the surface to have his clever arguments wrap her in knots designed to encourage her to comply. Besides, making him wait would make her feel a tad more in command of the situation.

Penny took her time preparing everything she needed. Soap, towels, Freddie's nightgown. She stripped her son and hugged his adorable, wriggling cherub's body while she dusted as much of the flour as she could out of his hair. Finally, she placed the half-bath near the glowing fireplace in time to hear the water arrive outside.

He had taken himself back to the kitchen out of sight by the time she opened the door, so she set about filling the tub with all the boiling kettle water and a generous amount of the cold water he had also left in a large pail. The warm bath seemed to improve Freddie's mood and he allowed her to wash him from head to toe while he splashed about giggling.

His eyes were drooping as she gently towelled him off, brushed his damp, brown curls and bundled him into his bedclothes. Some warm milk and he would be out like a light for the rest of the night. She left him lying on his back on the rug, examining his small feet as they shamelessly waved up in the air, while she tried to repair the damage done to herself. It was little more than Clarissa's staging again, but it would make her feel better. When the dampened edge of the towel failed to remove the flour handprints from her bosom, she quickly retrieved another dress from her limited selection in the wardrobe and hastily put it on in case the man beyond the door decided to barge through it.

The silence beyond suggested Lord Hadleigh had finished bringing order to floury chaos and the time for avoiding him was now past. Hopefully projecting a confidence she didn't feel, she scooped her child up and decisively opened the door, only to find the current bane of her life not in her now-spotless parlour at all. No evidence of the flour explosion remained anywhere. He must have beaten the rug as well as washed down the floor. A few wet smears on the dull polished floorboards bore testament to the latter.

He poked his golden head out of the kitchen and smiled.

'Perfect timing. I've just made an entire pot of tea...*all by myself.*' Was he mocking her lack of faith in him or being self-effacing? Penny was too jittery to tell. 'I thought you might need it.' To prove it, he held a laden tray aloft. It ominously held two cups. 'Everything is better after a cup of tea.'

'I need to warm some milk for my son.' She couldn't quite bring herself to say thank you just yet, although a thank you was deserved regardless of her belligerent mood. He had restored her life to calm order at a time when her nerves had taken about as much as they could. Penny lowered Freddie to sit with his now neatly tidied blocks and bustled past Lord Hadleigh as he carried the tea over to the table, mentally rehearsing exactly how she could thank him while still appearing as if she had not needed his help at all.

Like her parlour, the kitchen was also as neat as a pin, so he hadn't only managed to make a pot of tea all by himself—he'd cleaned up after himself as well. Uncharitably, his thoughtfulness irritated her. She didn't want him to be thoughtful and helpful. She wanted him gone. Put in his place. As she sloshed some milk into a pan and set it to heat, she listened to the china clatter beyond. 'Do you take milk and sugar?' Now he was apparently pouring the tea, too. There was no end to his domestic talents or his thoughtfulness tonight.

'One spoon, please.' The *please* came out reluctantly through gritted teeth. 'With just a splash of milk.'

This would be the first time any male not a servant had ever made her tea. Penhurst would never have done such a thing. Nor would her dear father, come to that. Pouring tea was women's work. Childishly, she hoped the brew was either pathetically weak or so strong you could stand a spoon up in it. Just something she could feel slightly superior over, seeing as the dratted man was clearly good at every-thing and this evening he had found her on the back foot.

The milk began to hiss a little as it frilled against the edge of the pan, so she tested it with her finger and, sat-isfied, poured it into Freddie's nursing bottle. She should begin to train him with a proper cup, she knew, but as one of the last things the horrid Nanny Francis had tried to do, much to her darling boy's distress, she couldn't bring herself to do it yet. Not when he was six months away from two and still really a babe. The dour and judgemental nanny Penhurst had grown up with was all about sparing the rod and spoiling the child. If Penhurst was the end re-sult of her heartless attitude, then Penny could think of no good reasons to pick up the rod and much preferred to continue spoiling her darling boy and smothering him in love. And she didn't care what anybody else thought of it.

She snatched up the bottle and turned, then stood frozen to the spot at the sight of her little boy stood holding the barrister's knee with one chubby hand and offering him a block with the other. Bemused, but friendly, he lowered his face to Freddie's and took it, ruffled the boy's curls gently, then added it to the tower which the pair of them had begun building next to his chair. It was a strangely arresting sight and one she was not entirely sure what she felt about. When she sensed her heart softening a little, she decided it was likely a ploy to disarm her, so she decided to double her efforts to remain righteously peeved at him.

Lord Hadleigh looked up as Freddie clumsily dashed to retrieve another wooden block, completely unfazed by the overfamiliarity of her child. 'He seems to be in better spirits now. I bet you had the devil of a job getting all that flour out of his hair.'

She had. The flour and water had made a paste which took three separate lots of lathering and rinsing to shift.

But unwilling to make small talk, because small talk was friendly, Penny simply nodded, then intercepted her son and took him to the sofa. Something Freddie made sure she knew he wasn't particularly happy about when he had a new building playmate. 'Drink your milk, darling.' She snuggled him next to her and began to stroke his head, something which never failed to make him drowsy. Knowing that, her son decided to fight her all the way. Something that made her feel inadequate once more.

A steaming cup of perfectly brewed tea appeared at her elbow.

'Thank you for your kind assistance this evening, my lord.' Continued avoidance of basic good manners was petulant. Her eyes finally lifted to meet his and she immediately regretted it. It was as if he could see right through her, past the determined and proud façade, to the uncertain and lost woman beneath. 'It is much appreciated.'

'No, it isn't.' He grinned, his intuitive eyes dancing, and the sight did funny things to her insides. Why couldn't he be wearing his bland and inscrutable expression tonight? She knew where she stood with that. 'You would have rather walked over hot coals than have me help you and I cannot say I blame you. I behaved poorly on both our last encounters. Boorish, high-handed and arrogant with a healthy dose of sanctimonious mixed in. I had no right to attempt to force my will upon you or to assume I knew what was best. I've mulled it over long and hard since and chastised myself repeatedly for my crassness.'

Another pretty apology. Why did he have to be so good at apologies when she wanted to remain annoyed at him? Being righteously annoyed justified overt formality.

'You have flour on your face.'

'I do?' Her free hand swiped at her chin.

'Here…allow me.' His fingers brushed her cheek and

Penny swore she felt it all the way down to her toes. She found her breath hitching as he dusted it from her skin, not daring to breathe out in case it came out sounding scandalously erratic. Which it suddenly was. As if sensing the new, potent atmosphere between them, his unusual, insightful amber eyes locked with hers and held. They both blinked at each other before he severed the contact and took several steps back.

Did he realise that the dormant female part of her body had suddenly just sprung to life? That her pulse had quickened or her lips tingled? Damn him and his well-fitting breeches and perfect cups of tea!

'You are now here on the behest of the government— *apparently.*' Better to keep things polite but distant. Matter of fact.

'Indeed I am. With a proposition.' He settled himself back into his chosen chair, the large one left by Clarissa which only served to make him seem bigger and more in command, crossing one long, booted leg over the other as he reached for his own tea. 'I'll get to the point, as I can see you want to be rid of me...' To her shame, Penny's cheeks instantly flushed at his perceptiveness, followed swiftly by embarrassment with his next, damning statement. 'I know you have been actively seeking decent employment with little luck.'

'I have been offered positions, my lord. None have suited.'

'I should imagine it is hard to find a decent position with a little boy.' His eyes drifted to where Freddie was now finally beginning to relax, then seemed to soften before returning to hers. 'Which is why I immediately thought of you when this opportunity presented itself—because in this case, your unique skills outweigh the fact they come with a child in tow.' He leaned forward, his gaze holding hers intently. 'Would you accept a position as a house-keeper if Freddie was allowed to come with you? Only the government and I find ourselves in a bit of an unusual situation.'

Suspicion made her frown. He had neglected to mention thus far that he was also involved in the proposition. 'What sort of a situation?'

'I assume you are aware of the case I am working on?'

'The Gislingham case.' Much as she had tried to avoid it, it had been hard to miss and she was too inextricably linked to it all to avoid it with the necessary detachment such avoidance took. Her husband's shameful involvement aside, both Clarissa and Seb were also part of the proceedings. Both would be witnesses again. 'I think every man, woman and child in Christendom knows about that case.' Much as they had known about Penhurst's scandalous trial and aftermath. 'What has that to do with me? Apart from the obvious connection, I mean...'

Chapter Seven

She was already bristling, patently ready to decline whatever he was about to suggest. How he worded this next bit was crucial, especially as he was still a little unsettled at his body's peculiar reaction to one brief and innocent touch. His fingers still itched to caress her skin again—properly. Despite the lack of floury smudges decorating her bosom in the new dress, it took a great deal of effort not to allow his eyes to drift back to that magnificent area and feast. Or picture her peeling off that previously soiled garment mere feet away from where he had been when she had removed it and imagining what lay beneath it. Was every inch if her skin as soft and velvety as her cheek? Probably.

What the hell was he doing lusting after a woman while she was rocking her child to sleep? 'May I speak plainly?'

'I wish you would.'

'Do I have your word that anything I tell you now never leaves this room?' He watched her dark brows furrow as suspicion gave way to curiosity.

'Of course.'

'The key prosecution witness in the case is a woman. Lady Jessamine is now the Baroness of Penmor, but she used to be the proxy daughter of the Comte de Saint-Aubin-de-Scellon, the man almost entirely responsible for running the French side of the smuggling operation. When her mother died, Jessamine was imprisoned and forced to write and translate the coded messages which passed back and forth across the channel between the Viscountess Gislingham and her co-conspirators. She holds within her head a vast wealth of damning evidence. Perhaps unsurprisingly, that has made her a target once she escaped to England. My friend and King's Elite agent Lord Peter Flint was tasked with protecting her. The Comte hired assassins to silence her and when they failed he came himself. I cannot deny it was a near-run thing at one point.'

There was no need to tell her that it had been his bullet which had dispatched the evil Saint-Aubin. He didn't want to scare her by appraising her of the fact he had killed a man in cold blood despite his conscience being entirely clear on the matter. Saint-Aubin had been a murderer and tormentor of women. Had Hadleigh's bullet not hit its mark, then his friend Flint would be dead and Jessamine would have been dragged back to a life of cruelty and imprisonment in France.

His only regret was that he had failed to be as decisive all those years ago when similar opportunities had presented themselves—a memory long forgotten, one of the first consigned to the sealed box in his mind. Yet since saving Jessamine, that buried memory had resurfaced and plagued him constantly since. Why had he been able to pull the trigger for a woman he barely knew, yet not for the one who had birthed him?

Clearly both the rattling skeletons in the dark recesses of his mind and the inappropriate lust were symptomatic of how hard he was working.

That had to explain it.

'Suffice to say, good triumphed over evil as it always should and the Comte de Saint-Aubin is now dead. However, even though the Viscountess Gislingham and the rest of her accomplices are safely under lock and key, Jessamine's new husband—the aforementioned Flint—is overprotective. He is reluctant to bring her to London because he still fears for her safety. While I am confident the spectre of further assassination attempts are highly unlikely, I cannot deny I share his reservations about dragging her here to the capital until it is absolutely necessary. As I am sure you can entirely empathise, the press will have a field day.'

'An understatement, Lord Hadleigh.' Her face clouded as she nodded. 'They will make her life unbearable.'

'I knew you would understand...' How to broach the next part delicately? Because he suspected it would all hinge on this. 'In many ways, Lady Jessamine's situation tragically mirrors your own. Saint-Aubin was a violent man and she suffered horrendously while he forced her to do his bidding.' He doubted he would ever erase the haunting and shocking image of Jessamine's scars from his mind. 'Like you, she was an innocent victim of a callous monster and, like you, I fear she will suffer the petty and harsh judgement of the society which abandoned her.'

'He beat her?' Her eyes were wide, awash with pity, and he had to lock his fingers together tightly in his lap to prevent reaching out to comfort her.

'Among other things.' His eyes drifted to the tiny bump on her otherwise perfect nose. The perfect nose she had stated under oath Penhurst had broken and felt anger bubble at both of the men who had used pain and cruel mental manipulations to subdue Jessamine and the brave, stoic woman in front of him. If Penhurst wasn't dead, he might have been tempted to visit him and give him a taste of his own medicine. Except he wouldn't stop at the bastard's nose. 'Her life was not her own for many years well before her imprisonment. He used the health of her dying mother as a tool to blackmail her.' Injustices which made his blood boil. 'Hardly a surprise her devoted new husband is keen to protect her still. But this presents the Crown with a challenge. We need her here while the case is prepared.'

Hadleigh found himself rising to his feet and pacing. To her it might appear he was doing so because he was agitated about the case, when in fact it was all the wrongs he couldn't right which gnawed at him. 'I need Lady Jessamine close. As each day passes, I learn more and more from the suspects. A couple seem eager to spill everything. Others sling mud, hoping to save their own skins. Corroborating what they are saying and separating the fact from the lies is becoming increasingly arduous—especially when Lady Jessamine is the only witness who can categorically confirm or dismiss the majority of their claims.'

'I still do not understand what this has to do with me?'

'We have found a compromise which Flint is willing to agree to. A way to have his wife at hand when I need to consult with her and a way for him to be able to guard her privacy. I have an estate just a few miles from London to the east—less than an hour's ride away...' *Pandora's box.* Fear of revisiting it warred with his overwhelming desire to help her.

'Your estate?' She didn't look happy with that detail. He waved it away as if it was inconsequential, when it wasn't. For either of them.

'Who the estate belongs to is by the by because I have lent it to the state for the duration. It is the location which has led to us selecting it. I've not used it in almost a decade because my work keeps me here.' And he loathed the place and all its ghosts. Would have sold it had it not been entailed. 'It's been boarded up for years and will be boarded up again once this is over. However, its situation and design make it the perfect place for Flint and Jessamine to live while we await the trial. In view of your own unique *experience,* and no doubt the many sympathetic insights you might be able to add, combined with your close connection to Leatham and his wife and this case, the government wondered if you would be willing to run the house in the interim.'

'The *government* wondered?'

'At my suggestion, I cannot deny—because you instantly sprang to mind when I discussed it with my superiors. Who better to ensure the privacy and care of a witness than one who has lived through the experience?' She didn't appear convinced. 'This is a state matter, my lady. The Gislingham trial is the single biggest treason trial in England in a century. Justice not only needs to be done, that goes without saying, but it also needs to be *seen* to be done properly. We cannot afford any speculation or criticism on a job completed poorly, nor do we want any misinformed sympathy for the traitors involved—especially as the ringleader is a woman. And we need to learn from our previous mistakes. I would not wish the way you were treated by the press on anyone. You can help us do that.'

'I suppose I am familiar with all their tricks…'

'Indeed you are, alongside all of the pressure and concerns Lady Jessamine will have to endure. You and she have a great deal in common.'

Her scepticism had given way to thoughtfulness, which in turn meant he had argued his corner well and convinced her that this was about more than her. Or at least that is what he had told himself when he had concocted this complicated and uncomfortable justification for offering her a job. He had almost convinced himself the undeniable benefits also justified him having to face the house again.

'I only have a few months to construct a conclusive case. With time of the essence and the house barely habitable, we need someone trustworthy who can start straight away. Instinctively, I thought of you because I know you are actively seeking such a position, but by no means do you need to feel you have to take it. It is a temporary offer of employment. But as I said, in view of the gravitas of this case, and the unusual circumstances and particular duties such an important position will entail, you will be compensated generously. We suggest an amount of ten guineas per month and a further hundred guineas at the end of the tenure as a bonus for your sacrifice and eternal silence.'

A staggering amount no matter which way she looked at it. Enough, he hoped, to lure her into accepting without questioning the tiny lie he had just told her.

'*One hundred guineas!*' Hadleigh saw her eyes widen and her lips part in shock. His gaze was apparently magnetically drawn to those lips until he caught himself staring.

'And obviously, you will leave here with glowing and unquestionable references from myself, the Attorney General and Lord Fennimore, which will ensure a lifetime of similar employment should you need it and firmly establishing *Mrs Henley* as the *crème de la crème* of housekeepers.' Now he was in danger of over-egging it. 'You will manage a small staff which we will recruit the bulk of, however, because of the delicate and secretive nature of the conversations which will inevitably have to take place—only you will be privy to some of the rooms in which those sensitive discussions will occur. The fewer people who overhear, the less chance there is of those conversations being repeated outside the house. We cannot risk anything leaking to the defence or, heaven forbid, the press, before the trial. Therefore, recruiting from scratch is, as I am sure you can see, problematic.'

'But you want *me* to be the housekeeper? A convicted traitor's wife?' She sounded incredulous.

'He was the traitor, my lady. Not you. To my mind, you have proven to be an asset to the Crown before and we have been impressed with the way you composed yourself both during and after your own ordeal in the courtroom. You are discreet and honourable. Leatham and Clarissa have always vouched for your good character.' Thank goodness he had had the good sense to discuss things with them in front of Lord Fennimore at the wedding party.

Both were all for it if it meant keeping their friend close and safe from the sort of vultures who preyed on single young mothers left all alone in the world, or the key defence witness who also happened to be married to one of their closest friends. 'What better choice than a person who already knows of the government's covert machinations? Or the ridiculous lengths the press will go to in order to get their story? You might seem an unconventional choice in the first instance, but your recent experiences actually lend themselves perfectly to such a sensitive task.' He almost had her. He could practically see the cogs spinning in her mind as she digested everything he said. His instincts warned him not to give her too much time to ruminate or himself any more time to act upon his unwanted and inappropriate impulses. He had come here to rescue her, not stare at her lips with longing, although he had no earthly idea why he was suddenly so consumed with the latter, other than something about her called to the man as well as his conscience. Something that transcended his noble quest and had absolutely nothing to do with pity or guilt or righting wrongs.

'Everything to do with the running of the inside of the house will be down to you. Unhindered. There will be only essential staff. I see no need for a butler as he would interfere with your decisions. Neither I, nor Lord Fennimore, will have the time or the inclination to attempt to interfere either. The grounds and security will be overseen by the King's Elite as you would expect. You will liaise with them on how the security is organised within the house or how to deal effectively with any potential breaches...not that we envisage any. The location of Flint and Jessamine will be of the utmost secrecy, known only to a select few who need to know. That is Flint's express stipulation.'

'Only Lord Flint and Lady Jessamine would live there?'

'As I have said, my work necessitates me staying here. But I will make regular trips to meet with Jessamine, although I have no plans to stay overnight.' The mere thought made his gut clench. Nothing short of an earth-shattering catastrophe would ever have him sleeping under that godforsaken roof again. 'So you will barely have to suffer my presence. Which, alas, I fear you might have suffered quite enough of already this evening.'

He unfolded himself from the chair and grabbed his coat, making his intention to leave crystal clear, despite not having yet received her answer. Years of courtroom experience taught him that sometimes it was best to assume rather than ask. Seeking forgiveness was always easier than asking permission. And, it went without saying, he really didn't want to have to properly clarify anything, knowing that the whole truth and nothing but the truth would likely result in a firm no. There was a sharp and clever brain behind those beautiful blue eyes and he had learned to his cost how blunt and cutting those enticing lips could become when given just cause. 'If you could begin some time next week, that would be marvellous. I'd like the house to be ready for Flint and Jessamine to move in by the first week of November.'

Penny's definition of barely habitable and Lord Hadleigh's were poles apart. An hour after arriving at Chafford Grange, and despite the icy chill created by the cold walls and the myriad eerie cobwebs, she could see it was a grand and sumptuous house. It wouldn't take much to bring it back to life. The gardens were immaculate and had obviously always been tended, while the house had been lovingly put to bed. Before it had been closed all those years ago, the former servants had taken great pains to protect it. Heavy dust sheets covered every stick of furniture and were wrapped carefully around the curtains draping each window. She had lifted a few on her solitary tour of the house and been pleasantly surprised by what lay underneath.

Comfortable brocade sofas, glossy marquetry end tables, ormolu clocks, Sèvres vases, enormous Venetian mirrors, a huge and imposing mahogany dining table which would not look out of place in a royal palace—it was a veritable treasure trove of exquisite taste and ultimate luxury. Oddly incongruous with the professional government servant who spoke with such assured and convincing eloquence in the Old Bailey or the perplexing man who had swept her parlour clean before making her the perfect cup of tea.

Because it was calling to her, she used her foot to roll open a large rug in what she assumed might be a sunny morning room, as its floor-to-ceiling arched windows overlooked the garden and undulating parkland beyond. It was stunning. The bold turquoise base was woven with a wide band of gold interspersed with subtle colourful flowers.

Similar yet larger flowers swirled with golden leaves in the centre of the carpet. It was a beautiful piece that oozed class, one that would make a statement in this otherwise sedate and plain room. Although in this case, plain did not mean stark. The walls had been kept white, but covered in the most subtly patterned silk damask to bring texture and warmth, a luxurious touch so subtle it served to showcase the magnificent Persian. The only other splashes of colour came from the curtains. Turquoise again, the exact same shade as the carpet, held back with chunky golden-rope tie-backs. Understated, yet in being so made far more of a statement than anything fussy and patterned.

Class was a commodity no amount of money could buy. Something Penny knew only too well, having learned it at her mother's knee. She had never understood Penhurst's taste at all. He had been of the school that the more gilded and ostentatious the item, the more he coveted it.

All flash and no class.

A statement her mother would often utter in disdain when a merchant attempted to sell their emporium crass and showy furniture, but which summed up her former husband perfectly. He had no class. Ironic, really, when he had always lamented at marrying so far beneath him. Had she been allowed to decorate her former home, it would have resembled something like this rather than the tawdry monstrosity her husband had created.

Her mother would have approved of *this* carpet. Her eye for such things had been impeccable, one of the main reasons she and Penny's father had made such a success of their business. He had dealt with the financial side while her mother had hand-picked the stock. A match made in heaven in more ways than one.

Unable to help herself, Penny knelt and ran the flat of her hand over the thick pile. As she had suspected it was densely woven from the finest gauge of the softest wool mixed with just enough silk to give the fibres a lustre.

Class.

And clearly very expensive. The very best quality Persia was capable of creating. Superior craftsmanship, elegant, timeless... Words she would have used to describe it had it been on sale at Ridley's. Clearly once a shopkeeper's daughter, always a shopkeeper's daughter.

That thought made her smile. It was the sort of high-quality rug her father had imported for his well-heeled clientele many moons ago, back when their emporium and catalogue had been thriving before he sold it and retired on the proceeds.

She missed those days, the hours spent with her beloved parents in their fancy Bond Street shop learning the trade, or years before that in their larger emporium in Cheapside or the original draper's shop in Clerkenwell. But like all the most precious things, she had not appreciated them properly until they were gone. As her father's fortunes had rapidly increased, so too had their standing in the community. They might well have come from the wrong end of trade, but with an impressive dowry like the one her parents had accumulated for her, Penny had been destined for a life within the aristocracy they had once served. That was her mother's dream and she had allowed herself to become swept away in it. Once upon a time, she had foolishly thought life would only get better and had spent far too much time dreaming about her future than living in the now.

More regrets.

Another classic example of what she would change if she could turn back time. Yet there was no point in harking back to those halcyon days of her girlhood or lamenting them at the same time. That route only led to dissatisfaction when she found herself quietly satisfied with the way things were turning out in the here and now. Ten guineas a month for at least the next three months and one hundred more thereafter! Good heavens, that felt like a fortune. Enough money certainly for her to lease somewhere decent in the home counties. A nice little cottage with a garden for Freddie to play in... If only she could clear her mind of the reasons it had come about and her nagging doubts as to the validity of it all.

But she had a contract, therefore it did all seem to be exactly as he had outlined. The meticulous and thorough document had arrived the morning after Lord Hadleigh's impromptu visit alongside six guineas and a note from Mr Cohen, her old landlord, acknowledging he had refunded a portion of the year's rent money. The very legal language in the contract stated her exact duties and stipulated the *government's* precise terms. In a nutshell, it was Penny's job to see to the smooth running of the house while ensuring the strict privacy of its important inhabitants—Lord Flint and his wife Lady Jessamine alongside whichever high-ranking government or King's Elite official might also be involved in the Gislingham trial.

Any breach in the strict secrecy clause on her part would result in making the agreement null and void, with instant dismissal without payment or references. Not that she ever would talk to the press or confide the details to anyone outside the clearly defined inner circle. The only two friends she had left in the world were part of that circle and beyond that Penny was determined to remain entirely Mrs Henley. A young widow who had lost her husband at sea and who had never been tainted by a speck of scandal in her entire life—although she still wasn't entirely comfortable with that version of her because it felt like an ill-fitting suit. But she would make it fit in time and then there would be no stopping her.

No, indeed. This temporary stint as a housekeeper meant she could and would strike a line through the last three miserable years and truly start afresh. Why else invoke such a strict clause unless the deal was entirely genuine?

Something she really had to thank Lord Hadleigh for. Whatever his initial motives, he had given her the chance to earn her own living and do so without having to leave Freddie. For that alone, she would make more of an effort with the man. Perhaps she was even starting to like him a little? Or at least the version of him who made tea and wasn't too proud to hold a broom. The inscrutable, emotionless lawyer was a separate entity entirely. She doubted she would ever warm to that Hadleigh at all.

One hundred and thirty guineas! And all for relatively light organisational duties she could do in her sleep and all with a household budget so vast she could spend with impunity every day for a year and barely make a dent in it. Not that she would, nor would she let such a budget allow her to overspend when she could haggle for cheaper prices. Once a shopkeeper's daughter and all that. Organising and management had been her forte, not that Penhurst had allowed her to do much of it. But her parents had. Accounting, negotiating prices for services, arranging staff and planning events. All the things which had made their business run like clockwork all those years were akin, in many ways, to the skills necessary to run a great house.

However, Penhurst had never allowed her to run his house and was very secretive about his household accounts, chose staff not for their ability to do the job but to spy on his wife or keep any outsiders from poking their noses into his business. The only leeway he had allowed her to be mistress of the house was in the planning of the frequent parties.

Penhurst had loved a house party and, as his fortunes mysteriously improved, loved hosting regular soirées to show off his wealth. Penny had organised the entire events, especially fun entertainments for the ladies, knowing that those unfortunate women would need something to take their minds off the debauchery which her horrid husband would inevitably lead them into from almost the first moment they arrived at Penhurst Hall. That was, after all, the main reason those men came...

'The staff are arriving, Mrs Henley.' The King's Elite agent who had brought her to Chafford Grange seemed to appear out of nowhere, giving her a start. Something she supposed she needed to quickly get used to in this house of government secrets and government spies.

'Thank you. Have them gather in my sitting room and I will be there shortly.' Part of Penny's contract had stated she had her own contained apartment within this grand house. It had been the first suite of rooms she had elected to see and was still amazed by their sheer size and situation. A cosy first-floor sitting room-cum-study leading to a staggeringly large bedchamber for her and a smaller bedchamber for Freddie. It was nearly twice the size of her rented lodgings in Cheapside, lighter, brighter and certainly more cheerful, although she would need to replace the fine-quality rug in the main room with something more robust for her son. And throws for the lovely furniture, too. If he spilled something on any of those fine pieces she would never forgive herself and did not want to live on permanent tenterhooks that he might.

For now, her darling boy was staying with Clarissa and Seb in Mayfair, no doubt having a whale of a time being spoiled rotten as the pair of them practised being parents.

Not that they had confessed that detail to her still, but to Penny it was obvious and she was delighted for them. Perhaps now that she was earning her own money doing something they approved of they might cease attempting to mollycoddle her and entrust her with their secret. It would be so nice to have Clarissa as just her friend again, rather than her self-appointed nursemaid. These past months had been trying on their friendship.

But all that was behind her now. This was exactly the kind of fresh new start she had wanted. A few months here and then the world was her oyster! How marvellous that was. Her best friends were bringing Freddie to join her in five days, which meant she had four days to get this beautiful house shipshape and shining like a new pin. A stocked kitchen, decent spirits in the cellar, fresh linens, a thorough spring clean and airing, roaring fires in every fireplace to take the chill out of the walls. They would need a veritable forest of chopped wood, candles, flowers... As she ticked off each thing on her extensive mental list of things to do, she couldn't help but notice that for the first time in for ever she was walking with an excited, almost giddy spring in her step. Almost like the old Penny.

Chapter Eight

There was no getting away from it, Hadleigh felt nauseous. The queasiness had started before he turned his horse on to the drive and had increased with every yard he had travelled. Now, still sat in the saddle and staring at the house, his head was spinning, his chest so tight it made breathing an effort and the last remnants of the breakfast he had choked down was roiling in his stomach. He was intentionally opening that securely sealed box.

What had he been thinking? What had started as a means to help a woman who refused to be helped had spiralled out of control to become his worst nightmare. Aside from being a handy hideaway for the main prosecution witness, Lord Fennimore and his team were determined to use it as their base. Which in turn meant Hadleigh had to spend much more time here than he had originally bargained for and was certainly unprepared for—if his body's tumultuous reaction was any gauge. The temptation to turn his horse around and gallop away was overwhelming. Typical, really, when he had always preferred to run from the demons of his past like a worthless coward rather than face them.

Hell, he'd been running for days already. She had been

there for three whole days and he'd made a plethora of pathetic excuses not to visit, until he had realised sometime around three this morning as he had awoken in another cold sweat that he needed to do so before Flint and the others arrived. He didn't want them to see that mere bricks and mortar could render him so sick and panicked he could barely function. He needed to harden himself to the place before he was in any fit state to work collaboratively with others within its haunted walls. This *had* been *his* idea.

One of his stupidest.

In the distance, someone stepped out of the stables and waved. There could be no turning back now. That simple wave would start a flurry of activity within the house. Servants would be warned, scurrying to welcome him. The new housekeeper, the woman who had prompted him to make this foolhardy decision in the first place, would be at the front door to greet him.

A cold trickle of fresh perspiration made its way down his spine. He didn't want her to see how much this place panicked him either. Perhaps if he kept this first visit short and sweet, he could wear his detached lawyer's mask for the duration?

And perhaps pigs might fly.

The second he stepped into that cavernous marbled hallway he would be confronted with the staircase. Then the events of that dreadful day a decade ago would all come rushing back. The anger, then the numbness which still shamed him. That caused the oppressive guilt he always carried with him but buried in work. He'd buried it so well with so much work, he had barely thought about it in years.

There would be no burying it today because there was no way of avoiding that blasted staircase. Even if he blindfolded himself he would sense it. Picture her last moments before she plunged helplessly to her death.

'Good morning, my lord.' Closer, he recognised the new groom as one of Lord Fennimore's agents and raised his hand quickly in an approximation of a cheery wave. A little too quickly because it made him instantly bilious.

This was nonsense! A man halfway through his thirtieth year shouldn't be so petrified of visiting an empty house. And it was an empty house and not Pandora's actual blasted box, so he needed to stop thinking about it in those terms. What was done was done. Dusted.

Buried.

Hadleigh gave himself a stern talking-to as the agent took his horse and he walked on alone the short distance to the house. Near the entrance he dithered, considering if for this first visit he shouldn't ease himself in by entering through the back via the kitchens or, if by some miracle they were unlocked, the French doors leading into the morning room. That had been his mother's favourite room and the place they had spent many a happy hour. Just the two of them. Avoiding talking about his father or the increase in his erratic behaviour because it was easier to pretend everything was fine...

'Lord Hadleigh!' Her voice stopped him staring resolutely at the gravel and made the distasteful decision for him. 'I wondered when you might make an appearance.'

Reluctantly he looked up. She was stood at the top of the colonnaded steps which led to the enormous front door, smiling. Wearing a pretty blue dress unlike any of the dour dresses he had seen her in before. The colour suited her. The style suited her more. The demure, long-sleeved bodice fitted her trim figure perfectly, showing off her splendid bosom to perfection. A bosom, which to his shame, he had contemplated a great deal since he had seen it dusted enticingly with flour. The blustery autumn breeze plastered the skirt to her body, giving him a tantalising hint of the rest of her figure properly for the first time. A petite hourglass finished off with a very shapely and surprisingly long pair of legs. For a split second the sight made him forget where he was.

Then reality came crushing back like a tempest.

'My lady... I mean, Mrs...' Good grief, with all the stress of being here he had completely forgotten her new alias. *Hendon? Henry?* It began with an 'H', he was certain. She must have seen him floundering.

'Under the circumstances, with the lines between my old life and my new still so blurred, maybe it would be easier to simply call me Penny.' She was smiling again, attempting to stand still, but practically bouncing with a suppressed energy he had never seen in her before that warmed his heart. She was happy. He might be in hell because of it, but he had made her happy. 'Come in! I've been itching to show someone. I think you'll be delighted with our progress.'

Like a man headed to his own execution, he slowly took the short steps to the threshold of the house and then took a deep breath. Penny—he liked that name, liked the sound of it on his lips—had skipped on ahead and was stood in the centre of the cavernous atrium. Behind her, on either side, were the stairs. Two unyielding marble flights, flanked with the intricately carved ebony banisters his mother had once helped him slide down, curved around in a sweeping arc before meeting at the landing above.

She was everywhere, his mother. He could hear her echoing laughter in the walls, picture her dashing down those stairs to greet him. Arms wide, smile wider. Picture the grisly scene of her body broken on the hard marble floor at the base. Neck broken. Dead eyes staring lifeless.

He shivered.

'It's still a tad cold in here, isn't it? I think it will take another couple of days at least to heat the walls properly.' She touched his arm and that anchored him to the present. He wanted to grab her hand, absorb her strength and stay there. 'Especially here in this vast space. Marble is notoriously cold and unforgiving.' Indeed it was. Catastrophically unforgiving. 'Would you like some tea or some refreshments before we take the tour or after?' Despite standing next to him, she sounded so far away.

'After.'

Best to get the hideous experience over and done with before he did part ways with his breakfast.

She led him down the hallway and he waited for more hideous memories to batter him, but bizarrely none came. His arms and legs felt leaden, his breathing shallow, his emotions numb. Something which bothered him more than anything. In all these years, he hadn't grieved. Hadn't shed a single tear. The tragedy had happened, he had calmly dealt with the aftermath in what he would later realise was a detached haze, then he had focused on his studies. Just like his callous father he felt nothing whatsoever. Neither of them had mourned his mother properly.

As if she sensed his disquiet, Penny never said a word or, to her credit, expected him to say anything. They stopped at the door to the drawing room and, before he could remember his manners, she opened it for him. 'We have focused on what we presume will be the most used rooms first.' The old ormolu clock on the mantel was ticking loudly. The familiar, but long forgotten, noise sounded hollow to his ears. Other than that, Hadleigh had no visceral reaction to the space. He was able to glance dispassionately over it as was expected.

It smelled of fresh beeswax mixed with the faintest whiff of lavender. The windows shone, letting in the crisp early November sunshine and making the room feel bright and airy. He recognised every stick of furniture, but perhaps not their exact position. She must have moved things around, he supposed, although to his eye, it all now appeared to be in exactly the correct space.

He found his gaze fixated on the thick woollen blanket draped neatly over the arm of a chair and decided he had no recollection of it ever being there. As if reading his mind, she explained its presence. 'Big rooms like this can get chilly even when the fire is roaring. I thought Lord and Lady Flint might appreciate a few cosy, homely touches while they are residing here. I hope you don't mind.'

Mind? Why would he? He had no opinions regarding this house other than complete abhorrence. He wouldn't be here now if it weren't for her. His eyes listlessly lifted to meet hers and he saw her confusion. He'd allowed the silence to stretch too long when she was clearly seeking his approval. 'Everything looks perfect.' And he couldn't wait to leave.

She beamed then and the numbness lifted.

She had dimples. Two adorable matching indents which framed a smile that turned her quietly pretty face into something quite beautiful. 'Oh, I am so glad! On the one hand, I didn't want to tamper with what was here when this house is *so* lovely, but on the other, I couldn't resist gilding the lily with a few tweaks here and there... Come—I bet you are dying to see the rest.'

He was slowly dying inside, more like.

Everything he was, everything he enjoyed about life, was being slowly sucked out of him just by standing within these walls. Leaving a vacuum...of numbness. Odd, really, that he should feel so detached when everything that had happened here was so intensely personal—or at least should have been.

The next few minutes passed painfully slowly as

she led him from room to room, pointing out her subtle changes or appraising him of how much work it had taken to bring the space back to its former glory. He managed to grunt one or two responses and hoped they were appropriate. Speech was hard when dread was strangling his vocal cords.

But, in truth, the rapid progress she had made surprised him, as did his reaction to it all. Hadleigh had expected to feel horror at everything, as the sights and smells of his childhood home conjured up all manner of uncomfortable memories. His calm detachment came as a relief. They were just rooms after all. Just furniture. Aside from his first glimpse of the staircase, the ghosts of his past remained blessedly silent and the lid remained firmly closed on the terrifying box of unpleasantness in his mind. To such an extent that the queasiness he had suffered since setting out at the crack of dawn began to wane and he started to believe he *could* do this after all.

'This is my favourite room...' She flung open the door to the morning room, then stood aside so he could enter first. 'There was no need to tweak anything in here. Just a good dust and an airing...' Every thus-far silent ghost suddenly bombarded him as they screamed and exploded out of the woodwork, so swiftly they caught him off guard. The pain was instantaneous and all-encompassing. 'And of course these magnificent windows needed a significant amount of cleaning.'

In his mind's eye he could picture his mother there. Hear every damned word of their last conversation. Stood staring sightlessly out of the window, the weight of the world on her shoulders, her posture shielding the faded, ugly bruise from his gaze. One palm flattened against the glass.

'Leave! Come back with me to London.'

'Out of the question. Your father needs me here.'

'He is becoming dangerous. More dangerous than usual.'

'He's ill, darling—not dangerous.' She had turned then and smiled in reassurance, all hint of the burdened woman banished solely for his benefit, touching the bruise and then brushing it off. 'Let's not confuse my innate clumsiness with anything more dramatic.'

That had always been her answer to every injury and bruise over the years. *'Silly me. I walked straight into an open cupboard door. Would you believe I tripped over my own feet...my skirt...a floorboard?'*

No. He hadn't. Not once. Except while those occasional bouts of violence which occurred only when his father was home could be readily glossed over by his mother and to his shame he had let her, things had taken a more sinister turn and Hadleigh had been scared. 'Besides, he needs me here. The physicians really don't see him lasting long—no more than a year at most.'

There had been no love lost between his mother and his father, nor between father and son. His sire had been a difficult man to love. Dictatorial, aggressive, cold and unfeeling. Free and handy with his fists, especially after a drink. Nothing anyone did was ever good enough, but until his health had declined he had been largely absent from Chafford Grange and their lives.

But then he had spent longer stretches at home and things began to change—more for her than Hadleigh. He had his mother to thank for that. She did a splendid job of keeping the pair of them apart until he had learned fairly late at what cost. He had been fifteen. No longer a child, but nowhere near an adult. He had tried to intervene once he realised the awful truth, planned several ways of permanently stopping his father from raising his hand to her again, but ultimately had always fallen short of succeeding. Just a frightened boy attempting to be the bigger man, but never quite rising to the challenge.

Right and wrong.

Good and evil.

The law and the lawless.

That was the problem with all his solutions. They jarred with his fundamental beliefs, all the things that made him...*him*. With hindsight which came from a decade of seeking justice, he should have shot his father that awful summer of eighteen hundred and five. The man had been all alone on the turnpike which clipped the furthest edge of the estate. Roaring drunk after another night of hedonism. The moon was full. He had a clear line of sight. Thanks to their close proximity to the capital, this busy road was a notorious spot for footpads. And despite practising hundreds of times for this exact opportunity until he could hit anything dead centre the first time with his first shot, squeezing the trigger of his gun to kill a flesh-and-blood man rather than an inert, lifeless target proved to be too difficult.

Instead, he had run, thrown his stolen pistol in the lake and by the time he had come home, his father had taken his drunken anger out on his mother again. He had found her weeping in the kitchen, a cold cloth pressed against her blackening eye.

'I should have lit a candle before I came downstairs... silly me. Would you believe it? I hit my head on a sconce.'

A lie he should have spared her, simply by taking that shot.

Instead, that fateful day had taken his feet down a different path. If he couldn't *break* the law to protect his mother, he would *use* the law to do it. From then on, he had been single-minded in his pursuit of that lofty goal, losing sight of the here and now while he chased the all-consuming promise of the future he intended to shape. That was why he had chosen to be a prosecutor rather than a defending attorney. In the decade since her death, he had used the system to defend other defenceless women, whether that be to seek proper justice after their deaths or to help free them from the prison of a toxic marriage or, at the very least, ensure they received adequate financial compensation for their suffering. Penny wasn't the first woman who had received some of his father's fortune and he sincerely doubted she would be the last. Whatever it took to right the wrongs.

'I cannot leave him to die here all alone. He's scared. It's so sad to watch. The illness is confusing him.' She always called it *the illness*, preferring that to the truth. But then syphilis sounded so distasteful and his mother had not wanted the servants to know why their master could no longer control his own bladder or recall where he was.

'Then I'll stay home. I'll help you.'

'What? Defer your studies? Out of the question. Everything is fine, darling. Or at least as good as can be expected under the circumstances. It's not as if you can do anything which will alter the course of things and most days now he doesn't remember his own name, let alone yours. I promise I will send word as soon as the end is close.'

She had walked to the chair he was sat in, cupped his face with her hands and kissed him on the forehead. 'It was lovely to see you today, Tristan. An unexpected and wonderful surprise. But it's getting late and you know I hate to think of you riding back to town in the dark. Be a good son and don't add to my worries. Besides, I am sure there is some lovely young lady desirous of your swift return.' There was. There always was. Although the lusty widow who had warmed his bed that year was a good decade older than he had been. 'I am sure she's missing you terribly. And do stop fretting about me and your father. There are servants watching his every move, the physician comes every other day and I am never left alone with him.'

Because it was simpler to accept those lies than deal with the truth and upset with his stubborn mother, he had left and put it out of his mind as he always did. That was the easiest and simplest option. Bury himself in his studies so he could fix things for her and every other voiceless woman properly—legally—for ever once he was qualified.

A week later, he received word of her death. Ostensibly an accident, but he knew in his heart of hearts that his father had pushed her down those stairs because the servants had heard his sire's nonsensical shouting in the small hours shortly before they found her. He also knew that he could have prevented it simply with his presence. An extra pair of eyes and ears to protect her. But he had been too eager to hurry down the path that called to him, when his studies could and *should* have been deferred that year for obvious reasons.

'Is everything all right?' A voice, not his mother's, dragged him out of the pit.

'*Yes*... Yes, of course.'

'I think you do need that cup of tea now. You have had a tiring journey.' Penny was regarding him with confusion. Had his lawyer's mask slipped? Had she witnessed the terror and disgust on his face when he had been trying so hard to keep it bland? 'I'll send for some. Why don't you sit down?'

'No!' The atmosphere and the newly settling numbness were suffocating him. 'Please...don't trouble yourself.' He needed air. Miles of open road. The ability to turn back the clock. Cold settled in his spine while hot perspiration suddenly appeared on his skin.

'It's no trouble at all. And I absolutely insist. A wise

man once told me everything is better after a cup of tea.'
She threaded her arm through his and, as if realising this
room had something to do with his current state, tugged
him back into the hallway, closing the door and trapping
the ghosts inside. 'I'll have it brought to the drawing room.
If you don't mind, I will join you as I have some questions
regarding Lord and Lady Flint and the overall organisation for the next few weeks.'

He found himself manoeuvred away, distracted, enveloped in the soft, lilting sound of her voice as she deftly
rescued him from his past and delivered him back safely
to the present.

Chapter Nine

Penny instantly took to Lady Jessamine. There was so much in her that was like looking in a mirror that they had instantly developed a rapport. They were both survivors in their own way and both only too happy to leave their pasts in the past. Jessamine wanted this trial over with so she could draw a veil over hers. Penny wanted it over so that she could have the funds to bury hers. Only three days in and she felt more like her friend and confidante than her housekeeper. It was so lovely to be able to discuss those things with someone who *knew* exactly what it did to a person. They both suffered from misplaced self-loathing at their supposed weaknesses, yet completely understood why the other had had to conform as they had.

Lord Flint was nice enough, but preoccupied with keeping his new wife safe from whatever imagined threats lay outside the quiet estate's outer wall, so they didn't collide much. The Dowager Baroness of Penmor, his irrepressible mother, was a breath of fresh air in what could have been an oppressive situation. A tad eccentric, a tad overdramatic, nosy to the point of outrageous and absolutely hilarious. She made sure that laughter became part of every day.

'He sounds like an absolute brute!' Penny had brought the ladies some mid-morning tea and now found herself the main topic of their conversation. The Dowager had insisted on a full rundown of her awful marriage which had been strangely cathartic, much as the in-depth recollection of the entire trial yesterday had allowed her to begin to view it with some distance and new perspective. Time was beginning to heal the wounds and purging her soul, as the Dowager was prone to point out whenever Penny tried to sidestep the most awkward questions, and felt so much better than bottling it all inside. 'There must have been one good reason you chose to marry the man? You did *choose*—didn't you?'

'Alas, I did, so I cannot blame anyone for that folly other than myself.' She picked up the pot again to refill the cups seeing as this latest friendly inquisition was bound to last a while. 'I thought myself in love with him and foolishly convinced myself that feeling was mutual.'

'But he only loved your dowry.'

'Mama!' Lady Jessamine quickly interjected to spare her feelings. 'I am sure he initially saw more in Penny than that.'

'And I am quite sure he didn't.' Penny smiled as she passed the cup back. She had been reconciled with her feelings concerning her hasty and regrettable courtship long ago. 'I was young and naive and quite out of my depth. To be brutally frank with you, ladies, I was also pathetically shallow. I was so delighted a viscount wanted to court me I never took the time to consider why that was, when I wasn't a particularly good catch in the eyes of the *ton*. I came from trade, you see, had no aristocratic connections and had to learn quickly how to behave like a proper lady. What I was, ultimately, was an easy target for a fortune hunter and a desperate fortune hunter found me. Very quickly.'

The Dowager leaned forward conspiratorially. 'How quickly?'

'We were married within three months of our first meeting.'

'A perfectly acceptable amount of time. I met and married mine within two and my son married Jess in just one.'

'Perhaps, but in truth I barely knew Penhurst at all. Before I skipped blindly down the aisle, I do not think we spent more than a few hours in one another's company overall and certainly for no longer than a scant few minutes at a time. I had no clue then that *anyone* can pretend to be somebody else entirely for a few minutes. Over a few hours the first cracks began to show and the true blackguard I had shackled myself to emerged swiftly afterwards. I knew within weeks I had made the worst mistake of my life and by then, of course, it was too late. I should also state for the record, in case you are feeling sorry for me, I had been warned about him from the outset. Clarissa cautioned me not to marry him, as did my own dear father on the wedding day itself.'

'No...'

'Yes. He had discovered Penhurst was up to his neck in debt and had his suspicions as to his motives, but I wouldn't listen. I was too caught up in the romance alongside my ailing mother, who so wanted to leave this mortal coil with the happiest of memories. A viscount wanted to marry *me*. Penny Ridley. A shopkeeper's daughter.'

'Ridley's was hardly a shop, my dear. It was an institution. A fine one. People used to brag about owning a piece of Ridley furniture. I always spent a few hours there perusing its treasures whenever my dear husband,

God rest him, dragged me to London. And always such fine quality! Why, I still have a pair of mahogany end tables which I must have bought over a decade ago and they are just as good as when I first bought them. I miss Ridley's.'

'My mother and father would be delighted to know that.' Both ladies already knew her parents had passed. Thankfully, they never got to witness the full extent of the huge mistake Penny had made in marrying her Viscount. 'As am I. Once a shopkeeper's daughter, always a shopkeeper's daughter. I am tremendously proud to have been part of Ridley's.'

'Are you ever tempted to resurrect it? Because that would be marvellous!' The suggestion caused a bubble of unexpected excitement before reality quickly popped it.

'Alas, if I were to open a shop now it would have to be Henley's and it couldn't possibly be in London. For obvious reasons.'

'Damn Penhurst. I've decided I loathe him doubly now, for treating you abominably and for depriving me of good shopping. When did you realise you loathed the brute rather than loved him?' The Dowager had a canny knack of asking the most intrusive questions outright and would not be waylaid from the main topic at hand. There was no point in trying to avoid the question. Three days in the Dowager's company had taught Penny that she could teach the meticulously thorough Crown Prosecutor a thing or two about interrogating a witness.

'Quite quickly.' She had been a delirious bride for almost the whole day and then Penhurst had shown his true colours. It had been their wedding night and he had been drunk. Too drunk to do what her mother had whisperingly promised a wedding night involved. He had stumbled into her bedchamber in the small hours, dropped his trousers, roughly hoisted up her nightgown and then blamed her for his lack of passion. He might, he had castigated in a slurred and spiteful voice as he had attempted to caress his own body into life, have been able to overlook the fact she was a lowly *cit* if she had been a real beauty, but beggars couldn't afford to be choosers. 'Which in some ways I am grateful for as it allowed me to quickly learn to loathe him with a vengeance.'

'I'll wager he was an atrocious lover, too.'

Penny almost choked on her tea.

'Mama, that is none of our business!' Poor Jessamine looked appalled.

'Why ever not? We are all married women here, Jess. It perfectly acceptable for *married* ladies to discuss such things in private.'

'I am *so* sorry, Penny. She is incorrigible. You do not need to answer.'

'She is incorrigible—but we adore her for it.'

'I *knew* he was an atrocious lover! Villains like him always are. Was he selfish? Rough? Lacking in the correct equipment?'

All of the above, alongside repugnant. The only way to endure Penhurst's impersonal and unpleasant intrusions had been to close her eyes and imagine she was somewhere else. Somewhere so far away she could completely detach—like the moon. Fortunately, he only cared about his own gratification, so the act was over quickly and then he always left her bedroom straight after.

'All I will say in response is that I was exceedingly relieved when I learned I was carrying Freddie, so that he stopped visiting my bedchamber and thankfully never bothered to return. I am not sure I could have withstood many more months of *that* chore.' The marital bed had been nothing like her mother had promised, not that she had ever confessed as much to her. Far from it, in fact. Her mother had promised tenderness, passion and pleasure, not a drunken, grunting lecher. In the days and weeks after, Penny had pretended she was ecstatic to be married—solely to please her romantic mother—when the opposite had been true. Straight away she had felt trapped. Straight away she had bitterly regretted her folly. Without thinking, she made a face of disgust. Then, remembering she was trying to keep the tone of the conversation light-hearted, shuddered for effect. 'He was an all-round sorry excuse for a lover...'

'I hope I am not interrupting...' At the sound of Lord Hadleigh's deep voice behind her, Penny did choke on her tea. She made a delicate attempt not to retch out a cough, but when it became apparent she would likely turn purple unless she did, had to suffer the further embarrassment of the Dowager whacking her on the back until the wayward tea finally dislodged itself.

Penny immediately shot to her feet and tried to look more like a housekeeper than a gossiping lady. 'Let me take your coat. Did none of the footman greet you properly at the door?' In her embarrassment, she was babbling. 'We did not expect you till later this afternoon, my lord.'

She hadn't seen hide nor hair of him since last week when she'd practically had to drag him around his own house before he had dashed away. He had been aloof and uninterested, not at all like the charming fellow who had helped her with the flour explosion the week before. At the time she had put the change down to the shift in their statuses. She was no longer a peer's widow and was now a servant and technically, despite it being commandeered by the Crown, this grand house was his so that made her his servant.

But upon reflection, his manner and demeanour on that visit had bothered her to such an extent that he had occupied a great deal of her spare thoughts since. She had never seen him so out of sorts or so...uncommanding. He had been positively monosyllabic for the entire tour. Penny had had to prise every word out of him and, once or twice during that short half-hour visit, when he was not being terminally detached he had even seemed almost vulnerable. Not so now, though. The confident barrister had come visiting today. He stood in the doorway still clutching his hat, looking windswept and handsome. Perhaps, on a second glance, he still seemed a little bit awkward to be there now, too, if she was honest.

Good heavens! Had he heard her discussing intimacies?

'Do not let it trouble you.' He could barely meet her eye, which suggested he *had* heard her. 'I came around the back. Through the kitchens. I didn't mean to startle you.' Although if she had been doing the job she was being paid to do rather than sitting around sipping tea and discussing her disappointing history with marital congress, she wouldn't have choked on it in the first place.

He shrugged out of his greatcoat, sending a waft of something delicious her way as he handed it to her. A subtle, spicy cologne mixed with the crisp autumn air. She took the garment, trying not to be so aware that it was still filled with the warmth of him as he greeted the other ladies with much more affection than she had expected.

'Hadleigh! How are you?' Lady Jessamine smothered him in a hug.

'I am well.' He held her at arm's length and grinned his pleasure at seeing her, something which shouldn't have bothered Penny in the slightest—but did. She wanted him to be the charming man for her again, too. 'But look at you! Marriage clearly suits you.' Then he held his arms open to the Dowager. 'Lady Flint! I had no idea you were coming.'

'As if I would leave dear Jess to suffer *you* alone.' She kissed his cheek affectionately and then neatened his cravat. 'You have form, young man. Somebody needs to be here to make sure she is allowed to eat at civilised times.'

'I didn't realise you all knew each other so well.' And Penny felt oddly left out despite knowing she had no reason to. She was a servant here, not really one of the ladies and certainly not part of this affectionate reunion.

'Indeed,' said the Dowager, still obviously thrilled to see him, 'Jess endured many *arduous* hours being interrogated by this scoundrel. But he *did* save her life, so we all feel duty-bound to be nice to him.'

'He did?' The man in question appeared discomfited by this admission.

'I can assure you, they are exaggerating my part in it all.' Before anyone could elaborate, he was all business once more. But only to her. 'Is the room readied as I instructed?'

'Of course.' Although why he had insisted setting up a new study in what had been the music room she couldn't fathom when there was a perfectly serviceable study further along the hallway containing everything he had requested she buy again from scratch. But she had purchased a new sturdy desk exactly as he had asked for, a comfortable chair to go with it, paper, quills, ink. Organised the furniture to catch the daylight as well as moving in a few homely touches to make it seem less sparse now that all the instruments apart from the beautiful pianoforte had been relegated to the attic. 'Everything on your list is ready and waiting for you.

'Then if you will excuse me, ladies, I need to head there directly and prepare. And might I have a word, Penny?' As he was already striding purposefully towards the door, she had no choice other than to follow, quietly dreading any potentially awkward conversation about her place in his lovely house or the sort of conversation she had just been having within it.

Chapter Ten

Hadleigh had been mulling over what he should say for days. A brief apology for his odd behaviour the last time they met which would include a tiny, dismissive nod to the painful memories this house had conjured in him, swiftly followed by his heartfelt thanks that she had readied it so quickly. Something he should have done on his last visit before he had fled the estate as if his breeches were on fire. Not his finest hour.

He had been sorely tempted to flee the house again a moment ago—but for entirely different reasons. That would teach him to cowardly sneak into the back of his own house like a thief and then spend several illicit minutes eavesdropping on a conversation that really didn't concern him. In his defence—although blatantly such behaviour was wholly indefensible—he had been intrigued to hear about Penny's marriage. She had been so open to the Dowager and Jessamine, admitting to her own folly in hastily marrying the man and inadvertently appraising him of details he had not known. Like the fact her time with her son was strictly limited or that he used that time to blackmail her with. No wonder she had adhered to all his demands when she had been threatened with banishment if she stepped out of line. Having seen her with her little boy, seen the palpable love she had for him shining in her eyes, being wrenched from his life like that would have destroyed her.

When she had told him that she had lived with a controlling man, he had assumed she had lived with someone like his father. His word had been law—but even he had not attempted to control all aspects of his mother's life. She had been able to come and go as she pleased, visit friends, do exactly what she wanted with the house and bring up Hadleigh in whatever way she saw fit. His father always had more pressing things to do than care two figs about the running of the house or being a parent to his only child. He much preferred spending all his time with his current mistress, or, more often than not, *mistresses.*

Yet Penny had endured more than that—her entire life had been rigidly controlled, which went a long way to explaining why she was so adamantly determined to control her own future without any outside interference now her husband was gone. Aspects of her character now made more sense. The stubborn pride was a sign that Penhurst hadn't broken her spirit—or if he had, it was recovering. Hadleigh was glad he had overheard she felt no inclination to mourn the man because she was well shot of him. He wasn't entirely sure what he felt about overhearing that snippet about what had gone on in the marital bed, though.

Pity had been the first emotion he had experienced, rapidly followed by a whole host of clamouring emotions he had not been the slightest bit prepared for. The anger had been so sudden and explosive it shocked him. He had wanted to pummel Penhurst's smug face with his fist for treating her with such brutish carelessness. Intertwined with the anger had been something which was worryingly akin to jealousy. It had been that surge of irrational, wholly male possessiveness which had prompted him to either make his presence known and put an abrupt end to the confession or storm out of the house again. Because if she had elaborated, with actual specific detail of those lacklustre intimacies, Hadleigh wasn't entirely sure how he would have reacted, truth be told. Not when he had been dreaming about intimacies with her himself since the fateful night with the flour.

He'd had the same dream every night for a week. She stood at the top of the steps in front of the front door, her dress plastered to her body by the wind just as it had been the last time he had come here. Only in his dream, the house beyond didn't bother him because she was there waiting for him, so he had sprinted up those steps and taken her in his arms, kissed her. What happened next in the dreams varied from night to night, depending on how much cheese he had had at the interchangeable, unappetising but reliably cold suppers he had eaten before falling exhausted into bed. But they always reliably ended up in that same bed and he awoke hot and bothered, a little ashamed and a great deal hard.

He had suspected that, on top of everything else currently clouding his mind, he was seriously attracted to her. Now, thanks to the undeniable knot of jealousy he couldn't seem to shift, he knew he was.

He blamed this house. He'd opened Pandora's box to right a wrong when his mind was at its most occupied and the pressure resting on his shoulders was the greatest. And, if he was honest, he blamed himself, too. He could and should have walked away when she had politely sent him packing, heeded Leatham's order to leave her well alone, but something about her called to him and he hadn't been able to resist. He had gone out of his way to find a solution to help her. Gone out of his way to visit her. Allowed his wayward hands to touch her cheek and his wayward eyes to look their fill when he should have been focusing all his energies on the trial.

It was a good thing he hadn't been stupid enough to give the object of his nightly fantasies a job in his own house! Oh, the irony! Of all the stupid decisions he'd made in the last month, that one had to reign as the stupidest. His only consolation was the poor woman had no idea of his raging lust now that she was here. He sincerely doubted she would have taken the job if she had.

He reached the music room and took a deep breath. He had spent hours here growing up. Mostly on his own, but occasionally with his mother. Conscious of Penny waiting behind him made procrastinating impossible, so he gripped the handle and flung open the door.

Nothing. Only numbness.

Splendid. Exactly why he had chosen it as his temporary study for the duration.

'Is everything to your satisfaction?'

Hadleigh instantly regretted his quick glance sideways, because she was worrying her plump bottom lip with her teeth when he really didn't want to have to think about her lips any more than he wanted to think of her in bed with Penhurst. Or the silky, bouncing, dark curl which had dislodged itself from its sensible coiffure in her haste to keep up with him. Dragging his eyes resolutely from temptation, he took in the room.

It was a tableau of ordered perfection. Uncluttered. Simple. Eminently practical. Alongside the excellent, high desk she had chosen to accommodate his long legs and the well-upholstered high-backed chair behind it that could have been crafted with his exact measurements in mind, there were now a row of deep and sturdy bookshelves he had most definitely not requested lining the back wall.

All empty. All awaiting his detailed and meticulous notes which would doubtless soon fill them in the precise alphabetical order he found easiest to work with.

How had she known he was incapable of functioning in anything less? Unless she thought him stuffy and staid, which rankled, before he reassured himself that was probably for the best. Better to be seen as a crusty, emotionless, rigidly organised nitpicker than a man who had apparently been suddenly and catastrophically consumed with lust. Hadleigh strode to the desk and practically threw himself into the chair in case that lust decided to immediately show itself.

Good grief, what was the matter with him? Had he become so overly tired that he now no longer had any control over his animal urges? 'It is exactly as I wanted it. Thank you.' Hardly a gushing compliment when he had barked it at her, so he tried to immediately make amends. 'You have a canny eye for good furniture. Your parents taught you well.' And in that single, desperate sentence, he might as well have just told her he had been lurking in the hallway, eavesdropping for a good ten minutes, because they had never had a single conversation about her parents or their blasted emporium. He knew the exact moment she realised because she quickly glanced down at her clasped, busy hands before they buried themselves in the folds on her skirt. A sure sign he had made her feel completely uncomfortable.

'Thank you, my lord.' Her eyes didn't rise, but that only served to give him a better view of those beautiful long eyelashes as she chewed once again on that lush bottom lip to torture him. He needed to stop looking at her lips! 'I take it you overheard my conversation with the Dowager.'

'Well…er…' Perhaps he could still save face? His talent with words was legendary, after all. 'Er…' Clearly, like the unmistakable bulge in his breeches, he had lost control of his vocal cords, too. For that he would blame the new dress. Where had all the dour ones gone?

'Oh! I am *so* sorry!' Her eyes finally lifted to meet his and they were swirling with emotion. It turned the pretty blue irises a deeper, stormier cobalt. 'The Dowager asks a great many personal questions and it is almost impossible to avoid answering them!' He watched a blush stain her cheeks, forcing him to remember that it was those exact cheeks which he held entirely responsible for his current predicament. Alongside another pretty new dress which drew his blasted eyes to the fine bosom encased within them. If he hadn't stupidly brushed those inconsequential specks of flour off those cheeks, then he never would have realised how soft her skin was and he certainly would not have begun to fantasise about its texture beneath her clothes. 'Although I realise it was highly inappropriate in this instance for me to answer all of them with such… candour.'

Good grief! She was alluding to the bedchamber part of the conversation. The part he most definitely did not want to discuss with her at all, because ever since he had overheard what a chore she had found it with Penhurst, God help him, he wanted to show her what it could be like between a man and a woman. Or more specifically what it would be like with him.

'The Dowager was most insistent that it was acceptable for married ladies to talk about such things and I forgot my place and should never have allowed myself to be lured into talking about my husband's—'

'Please!' Hadleigh held his hands up, supremely conscious that the tips of his own ears had begun to redden. 'For both our sakes, I beg you, let us leave it unsaid.' He smiled, or he attempted to smile and feared it might actually be more akin to a weird grimace. 'I should have informed you all of my presence sooner. It's entirely my own fault. And that is not at all what I wanted to talk to you about now.' He needed to stop snapping. The poor woman was stood at his desk like a naughty pupil awaiting punishment. 'Please…take a seat, Penny.'

She did, but once again was perched on the edge of the chair, ramrod straight. Beautiful blue eyes wide. Gloriously soft cheeks still flushed. That distracting coil of hair still dangling, drawing his eyes to her neck now and the acres of alabaster skin on show above the scooped neckline of her forest-green gown. The deep colour suited her. It complimented her pale complexion. Unfortunately, it also gave him the smallest glimpse of a tiny bit of cleavage as her chest rose and fell with her breathing. 'The thing is…' His mouth was suddenly as dry as the Sahara. 'I wanted to apologise to you for last week.'

Her lips parted and stayed that way long enough for his to get entirely inappropriate ideas. 'Apologise? Whatever for?'

Just say it as you rehearsed it. Get it over with. 'My behaviour here last time was…well, a little odd,and I might have come across a tad abrupt. I did not mean to be rude, especially as you had done such a good job. Nor did I mean not to compliment you on a job well done. Being here…' he gestured lamely to the walls and ceiling '…in this house after such a prolonged absence was a little overwhelming.' Not at all what he meant to say, because being overwhelmed made him sound pathetic and despite being entirely pathetic as far as this godforsaken place was concerned, he did not want to appear that way in front of her. 'What I mean is, this house brings back lots of memories… I was not prepared for the full extent of them.' Time to wave it away as if it was of no matter, exactly as he had rehearsed. 'So, how is Freddie settling in?' A safer topic. He even managed to steeple his fingers on the table casually.

'Freddie is doing well. I wanted to thank you for sending Gwendoline.' He'd interviewed fifteen potential nursemaids, all highly recommended, until that kindly old lady had arrived at his chambers armed with a glowing pile of references. References he had diligently and thoroughly checked to ensure they were genuine. 'He already adores her and so do I.'

He brushed that away, too. 'I am glad.' Which rather left him at a loss as to what else to talk to her about, but as he had asked her to sit, realised he needed to think of something. 'How did you know I would want all these neat bookshelves?'

She offered him a half-smile which made her eyes sparkle. 'I have watched you work, remember. You are an organised person by nature. So very *thorough* and *meticulous*.' She gave a little shrug. 'The notes in front of you in court were always neatly arranged and you seemed to know exactly where to find something when you needed it and could immediately put your hand on it. While the defence lawyers were always shuffling papers.'

'And a predictably *thorough* and *meticulous* person needs shelves.'

She seemed very pleased with herself. 'Lots of them. And with all the work you have to do in the next few months, I suspect they will fill quickly. Although I sincerely hope that not all aspects of your life are so rigidly organised. A little noise and chaos enriches life, or so I've found. At least that is how I justify the noise and chaos Freddie brings to mine.' She was smiling, making small talk. Extending the olive branch of friendship.

'I get quite enough noise and chaos in the courtroom.' Why had he said that? It sounded like a criticism when he had intended to grasp the proffered branch with both hands. Now his mouth as well as the bulge in his breeches was refusing to listen to his head.

There was an awkward gap as he racked his brains, trying to think of something, anything, to say to her to make the awkward situation feel better.

Sensing his discomfort, she stood. 'Luncheon is at one and will be served in the dining room.' He nodded and she made to leave, turning at the last moment with a quizzical expression. 'Were they good memories or bad?'

'A bit of both.' As he said it, he realised that was true. Not everything that had happened here had been bad. When his father had been away, in many ways his childhood and youth had been idyllic.

'But it is always the bad our mind presents us with first, isn't it?'

'I suppose it is.' There had been laughter here as well as tears. Good memories lurking in these walls, too long forgotten. His eyes drifted to the pianoforte still sat in its original place near the furthest window. Remembered playing it for his mother all the time. *Mozart.* Always Mozart—her favourite—while she sat on a chair close by embroidering something which would make its way into his bedchamber at some point to hide among his things. Handkerchiefs, his initials woven into a flourishing swirl on all manner of clothes—cravats, shirt tails and, entirely to vex him, his drawers in case he lost them at university. With that recollection his fingers flexed and he had the sudden urge to play a tune. How long had it been since he had done that?

'The good memories will win in the end. They always do, or at least I like to think that is the case. As you say, good should always triumph over bad.' Words he lived by. 'Shall I send in some tea?'

'Yes. Tea would be lovely.' Hadleigh waited till she

had gone to walk to the pianoforte and trace his fingers lovingly over the keys. Glad he had one good memory to treasure again in the swirling sea of bad.

Chapter Eleven

Now that Freddie was fast asleep, Penny left the new nursemaid watching him while she did her final evening round of the house. The Flints and the Dowager were happily settled in the drawing room, dinner had been cleared and the dining room was spotless, and the daytime servants had retired to their own quarters now that the Invisibles had taken their posts for the night. The fact that a group of men known only as the Invisibles now seemed the norm made her smile, because not in a month of Sundays would she ever have imagined in her wildest dreams that one day she would work hand in glove with a whole battalion of government spies. She still had moments where she had to pause and wonder what a bizarre twist in the path her life had taken, when at this time last year she had still been trapped in a loveless union with Penhurst. Yet, despite the bizarre twist, things had settled into a routine over the past two weeks.

Every other day, Lord Hadleigh would turn up through the back of the house after breakfast, take tea in his new study alone which Penny always brought to him. Their exchanges were brief but pleasant. He enquired after Freddie or the Flints, appraised her of his plans for the day so that she could time luncheon and dinner properly, then he would get an odd look in his unusual amber eyes which always signalled it was time for him to bury himself in his work. On these days, he sat with Jessamine for hours upon end, asking questions, meticulously going over her answers. Her new friend came out of these sessions mentally exhausted, but Lord Hadleigh never seemed to stop. After Jessamine, he would always work alone for several hours unless he had someone else lined up to talk to. Flint or the other regular visitors—Seb, Lord Fennimore and Gray.

While those visitors nearly always stayed the night, Hadleigh never so much as stayed for dinner in his own house, preferring instead to leave as it was served at seven to ride his horse alone in the dark for the hour it took him to return to London. That bothered Penny.

Now that the November weather was starting to bite and it was pitch-black outside from four in the afternoon, she had started to worry about him all alone on those deserted roads where anything could happen. Then, of course, it was his health which concerned her. He looked more and more exhausted with each passing day. Dark circles shadowed those perceptive eyes, no doubt from exhaustion. Aside from the unnecessarily long journey he undertook twice each day he was here, the pressure of the case was obviously taking its toll. He worked too hard, cared too much about the case, and if he wasn't careful he was going to make himself ill.

She had discussed both of these worries at great length with Jessamine and the Dowager, but no amount of their talking to him made a jot of difference. Lord Hadleigh was a stubborn man and flatly refused to listen. What she had never discussed with those ladies was the thing about it all which bothered her the most. The case and his heavy workload aside, she was coming to believe his continued stubbornness was not borne out of his belief that he knew best, but fear. There were parts of his house he deftly avoided like the plague—the morning room and anything involving stairs.

When she thought back over his first visit, those had been the places where he had been the most rigid and aloof. How could a man own such a magnificent house so close to the capital and fail to visit it for years? Nearly ten years according to the old gardener who diligently tended the flower beds. Flower beds he had carefully looked after when the rest of the house had been boarded up. However, he flatly refused to elaborate as, apparently, it was not his place to say and he always managed to leave Penny with the impression she should be ashamed of herself for asking.

Yet that only made her more curious.

His obvious reluctance to live under the same roof as his work made no sense, unless she weighed it with Lord Hadleigh's brisk and throwaway apology on his second visit. She had known the second he had said it that he had let on far more than he wanted anyone to know.

This house brings back lots of memories... I was not prepared for the full extent of them.

She had pondered both that sentence and his expression as he said them a great deal since, because for the first time since she had known him, his inscrutable lawyer's mask had developed a crack. One that had allowed her to see, if only for a moment, that those unusual amber eyes were a little lost and sad. Frightened, even. But she might have imagined that. Despite his tired demeanour he had certainly displayed no cracks since, although he quite obviously stayed away from certain rooms and, of course, the front door which he deftly avoided like the plague. Aside from those foibles, he was every inch the determined and tenacious seeker of justice his reputation proclaimed. She dreaded to think how many hours in a week he dedicated to this impending trial, or, more worryingly, how many hours he failed to dedicate to his self instead. He was working himself into the ground.

But if he wouldn't listen to his friends, he certainly wouldn't listen to her. Not that she'd attempted to reason with him. That wasn't her place and since she had commenced her employment here, the dynamic in their relationship had changed significantly since the night of the flour. They maintained a polite distance—or at least he did. Probably because he didn't want to muddy the waters now that she had stepped back down into the class she had been born into.

She headed to the music room to carry out her last duty, one he hadn't asked her to perform, but which she did anyway. He worked so hard, she didn't want him to have to concern himself with time-wasting chores such as refilling his ink pot or replenishing his neat stack of foolscap in the top drawer of his pristine desk. Most days she sharpened his quills, too. If he noticed, he never mentioned it, so she never did either. It was a small and insignificant gesture for a man who grafted so tirelessly and wouldn't be helped.

But as she turned into the long, dim hallway which lead to her destination, she hesitated at the sight of the thin shaft of light bleeding out from under the closed door. As he should have been long gone, she assumed one of the maids had simply forgotten to extinguish the lamps, but knocked just in case before she opened the door.

He was sat hunched at the desk, his dishevelled golden head propped on one hand as he turned and appeared shocked to see her.

'What are you still doing here?' A quick glance at the mantel clock confirmed it was nearly nine. 'I thought you'd left hours ago.' Several documents were strewn across his desk in a manner most unlike him.

'I have some things to finish.'

'Things that couldn't wait until tomorrow?'

'If I left them, they would niggle at me and then I wouldn't sleep. I need to work through this conundrum.' He pointed to the sheet of foolscap in front of him that was divided into two long columns. 'When I cannot see the wood for the trees, I always list things side by side— evidence versus conjecture, motive versus circumstances, pros and cons...' He offered her a half-hearted smile which didn't touch his troubled eyes. 'I'll be done shortly. Just as soon as I work out which column tells me the answer. The one with the majority is always the right course of action.' As if dismissing her, he turned his weary head to stare at his lists. Perhaps it was his posture—usually so straight, it was now slumped. Or the disorganised clutter on his desk, or the bleak, burdened nature of his expression.

Penny hovered instead of leaving.

'Have you eaten?'

'I will eat once I get home.'

'You are home. And if you are determined to continue working then you need something in your stomach.'

'I'm fine... I'll be leaving soon. But I wouldn't say no to some coffee.' He looked up again and he appeared so lost and alone she decided not to take a blind bit of notice. Coffee! He seemed to live on the stuff. Someone had to look after his health and well-being if he was going to continue to neglect them.

'Very well.'

She strode out of the room, leaving the door ajar, and headed directly to the kitchens. On the stove, slowly bubbling away, was the hearty stew that the cook had prepared to sustain the men on watch through the night. She ladled a healthy portion into a bowl. Sawed off two thick slices of bread which she buttered, then retrieved the remains of the apple tart that had been served for dessert which she finished with a huge dollop of cream. In deference to his request for coffee, she poured him a large glass of milk instead, then balanced the whole lot on a tray.

She practically kicked the door open as she marched back into the room and deposited the whole lot noisily on the sideboard. Lord, she was fuming at him! His head had snapped up and he was staring at her confused, but by that time she was in no mood to be trifled with. Like a mother tested to the furthest limits of her patience, she briskly went to his desk and scooped as much of the paperwork to one side where she hastily gathered them up into a pile, then snatched the list from under his fingers. 'You are going to make yourself ill, you silly man!'

'Silly man?' If he was angry at her rude outburst, she neither noticed nor cared.

'Yes! Silly man! You are being so stubbornly *thorough* and so determinedly *meticulous* you are working yourself into the ground. And neglecting yourself horribly in the process!' He went to defend himself, and she found her forceful mother's finger had attached itself to her hand from beyond and started to wag itself in front of his stubborn face. 'You ought to be ashamed of yourself! This is the biggest trial of the century! The government are depending on you! And you risk it all with your own disgraceful carelessness! What good will you be to anyone if you are laid up in bed?' Now that the papers were all gone, she fetched the tray again and dropped in unceremoniously in front of him. 'I was employed to ensure the smooth running of this house and the comfort and safety of all of its occupants. While you are under this roof, that also includes you! There will be no more work until you have eaten a proper meal, Lord Hadleigh.' She folded her arms for good measure. 'So eat!'

He stared down at the food and then back up at her, his expression as unfathomable as it always was. She watched him take a deep breath in and then wondered what had possessed her to be so direct and so loud. She needed this job. Needed the money and the references that came along with it. He was well within his rights to give her a jolly good carpeting for her insubordination. Had she dared speak to Penhurst like that, he'd have hit the roof. But just as she was about to cave in and issue a grovelling apology, he picked up the spoon and sighed.

'Well, that was a well-aimed kick up the backside. One I suppose I deserve.' He dipped the spoon into the bowl and stared at the thick stew. 'I was going around in circles anyway... This case is sending me mad.' Then he took a mouthful and chewed thoughtfully until his eyes locked with hers once more. Amused this time. 'If you are going to keep watch to ensure I comply, you may as well sit while you're doing it.' He gestured to the empty chair with his spoon.

Penny sat, feeling both relief at his reaction and that he was finally putting something wholesome in his belly. When sitting and watching made her feel awkward, she decided to make conversation. 'What has you going around in circles?' It was a bad question and she winced. She had no right to ask about the case. 'What I mean is...'

'It's—how did you put it?—gilding the lily. I have built the case and as it stands it's a solid one. But because I am doggedly *thorough* and *meticulous*, I'm trying to mitigate against the defence tearing Jessamine's testimony apart. As the main prosecution witness, there is a chance they can call hearsay on some of the details. That's what I would argue in their shoes. The word of one person against another is not conclusive proof of guilt. What I want to establish, and which I am failing to do in the case of some of her co-conspirators, and prove is a direct link between them and Viscountess Gislingham to knock those arguments down with. Three have already laid the blame firmly at her door and have put forward tangible evidence or witnesses who can corroborate their version of events. One was a childhood neighbour, the other two regulars in her… social circle.'

Polite code, she assumed, for the Viscountess's bed.

'The remaining three are refusing to talk at all. Lady Gislingham herself is pleading complete ignorance of any of the charges laid against her. While the state has a great deal of evidence to the contrary, including all the evidence we have been able to glean from the three turncoats, there is a slim chance that with the right counsel, one or two of those other peers will escape justice because the evidence we have is circumstantial. We can prove the smuggling— but not the treason. The long and the short of it is, I wish I had more names on my witness list for Jessamine's sake. That is a heavy burden to rest entirely on her shoulders.'

He spooned up another mouthful, looking despondent. 'Were the other traitors her lovers, too?' Penny asked.

'They could be. She was rather free and easy with her favours and we know for certain she had an affair with Saint-Aubin during her first Season. That was quite the scandal at the time, because of the wars with France and his links to Old Boney. That scandal forced her out of London society then and years later that damning link couldn't be overlooked, seeing that it was Saint-Aubin who provided all the smuggled brandy in the first place. But proving she seduced the other men into treachery won't be easy if they refuse to admit it.' He picked up the milk and frowned at it. 'What made you ask that?'

'Because Penhurst and Lady Gislingham were also lovers—both before we married and after.' One of his earlier indiscretions in their short marriage, back when his affairs had still hurt.

The lawyer's eyebrows rose and he sat forward. 'How do you know they were intimate?'

'He told me.'

Penhurst had found pleasure in parading his virility in front of her while listing her many failings. Usually her prolonged barrenness was his chosen emotional stick to beat her with, when he needed an heir and her womb remained defiantly empty, but he wasn't restricted to just that hurtful barb. Her figure was disappointing, her personality lacklustre. She wasn't pretty enough, enthralling enough, alluring enough. Her breasts weren't anywhere near big enough, she lacked the passion he enjoyed in his other lovers' beds and he had only married her because of her dowry. Never mind that it was hard to feel passion for a man who ruthlessly pursued his own pleasure to the detriment of everything else. From that first night when he had swiftly and roughly taken her innocence at the start of their marriage to the last time he had drunkenly demanded his conjugal rights a few days before she learned she was carrying Freddie, Penny had felt debased and disgusted by her husband's touch.

They had only been wed a few months when she came to welcome his frequent affairs. While he was laying with another woman, he wasn't laying with her. Thankfully, as soon as he had made his heir, he never visited her bedchamber again. 'My husband never saw the point of keeping that sort of secret. Ironic, really, when so much of his life was kept hidden. Beyond his nocturnal relationship with the Viscountess, I am afraid I know nothing more to aid your conundrum.'

'That you have proved there was a link between them is enough for the purposes of my investigation. It does prove a theme...and suggests the Viscountess had a tried-and-tested modus operandi as a seductress. It might be exactly what I need—if I can find witnesses to the infidelities.'

'Have you spoken to the wives of the men who refuse to talk?'

'I confess, I am reluctant to speak to the wives.' He had not spoken to her after Penhurst's initial arrest either.

'Why ever not? Nobody knows better her husband's affairs than the poor little woman left at home.' She watched him look down at his food blandly and then realised exactly why he had left her alone. 'Are you are trying to protect them?' While that was noble, it was also foolhardy for his purpose.

'Legally they are exempt unless they choose to speak out and I am going to be sending their husbands to the gallows—surely that is humiliation enough after all they have endured? If they want to come forward, they know where to...'

'Do they? Have you explicitly offered them the opportunity?' Penny reached across the desk and touched his hand, a huge mistake because she found she didn't particularly want to let go. 'If you had asked me about Penhurst again before the trial, once the shock had worn off and reality had settled in, I would have told you everything I knew. I felt so angry, so betrayed and so terrified he would be released into my life again. Instead, I had to wait and hope his lawyers would call me to the stand to say my piece. And in leaving me—and please do not think I blame you—I was left all alone feeling impotent and aggrieved and ashamed of who I was. My voice was stolen from me during my marriage, but I found it again in the witness stand. Perhaps their husbands weren't monsters at home and perhaps they might refuse to co-operate. But unless you give them the opportunity to speak, how do you know those women don't feel the same?'

Chapter Twelve

She had left him to eat. The stew proved much easier to digest than her insights. The way Penny told it, being part of the proceedings had been the start of the healing process for her, a way to fight back and matter again. With the clarity which only came with hindsight, he realised that perhaps her life during those weeks leading up to and during the trial might well have been easier if she had been named as a witness for the prosecution. A traitor's wife still, but publicly seen to be both brave and honourable herself because she had chosen her side.

Hadleigh had also grossly underestimated her. In blindly honouring the law and allowing her the right not to testify against her husband as was the norm, he had cast her as a victim who needed cosseting rather than giving her the chance to prove her mettle. He should have asked her. Should have granted her a voice sooner.

He was ashamed of himself for not treating Penny with the same rigour as he had treated all the other witnesses during that trial, something he had avoided because he had known beforehand she had suffered Penhurst's violence. Ashamed, too, that part of his reticence came from his own experiences. His mother had not wanted to speak of her turmoil, therefore he had wrongly assumed Penny—and every other abused wife out there—would feel the same. He had assumed they would all be like his mother and deny any wrongdoing from the monsters they had married for fear of what? Judgement? Retribution? Shame?

Did it also follow that he took it upon himself to shield them from having to admit it because he had failed to protect his mother all those years ago? That uncomfortable truth left a sour taste in the mouth, because, whichever way you looked at it, he was tarring every abused woman with the same brush when he prided himself in always seeking the truth—no matter what. Yet he had purposely left stones unturned.

That knowledge was preventing him sleeping.

That knowledge and the fact he had agreed to the unthinkable and was currently attempting to sleep at Chafford Grange.

To be fair, she had ambushed him when his mind was still reeling. She had come back to collect his tray and announced she thought it careless and foolish to ride home so late, especially when he was intent on returning on the morrow. That it made no sense, which of course it didn't unless he confessed to his guilty conscience. She also reminded him that his friends were worried about him and that the Flints had better things to concern themselves with at the moment than his selfish insistence to put himself unnecessarily at risk of footpads. Then she had played her trump card, one which tugged at his emotions more effectively than any other argument possibly could have.

I worry about you, too.

Five words which had done odd things to his heart. Her solemn blue gaze had instantly dipped as soon as she said them, as if she was bearing a little bit of her own heart and was embarrassed by that, yet his soared gratefully at the admission.

So he had said yes. He would stay the night just this once and take better care to leave before dark in the future. Then hastily concocted a series of unbelievable excuses why he couldn't possibly stay in the family wing tonight, when the truth boiled down to two things. Firstly, there was no way he would ever set foot in his father's bedroom which she had readied weeks ago for him as the designated master of the house. Flint and Jessamine were already in his mother's while the Dowager slept in his old bedchamber. There were too many memories in both those rooms, too, so he was relieved they were taken. And secondly, and perhaps most importantly, he wanted to avoid the main staircase. None of those were things he would tell her—or anyone. He might well be a pathetic coward, but hell would have to freeze over before he admitted it out loud.

Perhaps Penny had worked that out, because she hadn't argued and had, of her own accord, led him up the servants' stairs to the row of guest rooms located at the front of the house. Not only did that allow him to avoid the stairs which had killed his mother, they didn't come with walls crammed with ghosts either, so he had assumed he might be able to snatch a few hours of rest.

How wrong he was.

After hours staring hopelessly at the ceiling, he had decided enough was enough. If his mind was whirring from Penny's revelation and the way his body had reacted when she had briefly touched him, he might as well work! He could snatch a few hours before the first servants woke and sneak back up here before Penny was any the wiser. He flung the covers angrily aside and shoved his feet in his breeches. The blasted woman had got under his skin and was making him rest when he had better things to be doing! Like preparing the single biggest case of his career! He grabbed his shirt before he stormed out of the room and tugged it over his head as he retraced his steps down the dimly lit servants' staircase once again.

As he made his way down the narrow corridor to the rear of the house, he noticed a light coming from the kitchen. One he would have ignored had he not heard a child's fractious cry as well.

'Shh, Freddie darling, or you'll wake up the house.'

Hadleigh stopped, then shook his head. It didn't matter that his first instinct was to rush to her, it was none of his business and she probably wouldn't appreciate him barging in on her while she was trying to calm the child. Besides, at this ungodly hour, there was every chance she was in her nightgown and he really didn't need to see that any more than he needed to be willingly alone with her in the cosy intimacy of the kitchen. More distractions in a head already crammed with them!

Furthermore, in his haste to escape his mattress prison, he had neglected to put anything on his feet. Wasn't wearing either a waistcoat or coat. No cravat. He really wasn't decent himself. And what did he know about crying babies?

Nothing.

'Please, darling…try to calm down…shh.'

Penny's voice was soft and soothing, but like a siren's it called to him. Rather than let his bare feet take him to the music room where his overly occupied mind had intended to go, they transported him quietly to her instead.

At his first sight, she had her back to him. The glowing fire at the furthest end of the kitchen gave the room its only light, but that light floated through the gauzy linen of her nightdress and cast the contours of her body into a dark silhouette, forcing him to watch her delectable round bottom undulate as she rhythmically rocked the grumpy child in her arms. Her feet were bare, too, while her dark hair fell between her shoulder blades to the middle of her back in one thick, loose plait. That, too, swayed as she did, giving him alternate views of both sides of her swan-like neck. Beautiful and seductive.

Utter torture. Exactly as he had known it would be.

Yet for several moments he still stood transfixed, simultaneously panicked that she would turn and see him loitering while wondering what the hell he was going to say when she inevitably did. His throat had gone so dry and tight with unexpected longing, he feared whatever he said would come out in a strangled croak and he'd look foolish and guilty at being caught red-handed. Or worse, look utterly charmed and bewitched.

Better to pre-empt the embarrassment. 'Is there anything I can do to help?'

Despite his whisper, her head whipped around and her expression was alarmed. 'I am so sorry, my lord, I didn't mean to wake you!'

'You didn't.' And his wayward feet were off again, walking directly towards her. His mouth was smiling. His eyes drinking her in. 'Like Freddie there, I couldn't sleep. I'm afraid sleep and I have not been bedfellows for a while.' Bedfellows! What a horrendously appropriate word which hinted at the direction his thoughts were headed.

Her lovely face softened and her body turned around to him. 'Poor you. Insomnia is awful, isn't it?' As she rocked her child innocently in her arms, she had no idea that the firelight gifted him with the willowy shape of her legs, the steep, alluring curve as her trim waist flared to hip. Nor was she aware how the embers added copper and red tones to her dark hair or deepened the colour of her eyes to make them seem more sultry.

'It is.' But it had its benefits. His feet scandalously took him to stand right in front of her. They were clearly marching to their own agenda now and had formed an alliance with his overactive and lusty imagination. 'What's wrong with your little man?'

'I have no idea. The last of his teeth, perhaps? Not that they have shown themselves. He has no temperature either and his appetite is hearty, so he is not ill. I cannot even blame the change in environment for his temper tantrums either, because he was like this a good month before we left Cheapside as you saw the night of the exploded flour.'

Mention of the flour reminded him of the flour on her bodice that night and the womanly breasts that filled that bodice. Breasts that would be unbound tonight in that nightrail. Only one layer of linen separating them from his gaze. His groin tightened at the thought.

'Gwendoline claims that even the most even tempered of children turn into beasts in their second year. According to her that is what ails him regardless of the fact he is not two for five more months.' Penny gave a put-upon shrug, then shifted her son from sitting on one arm to the other. Was Hadleigh a beast for lusting after her when she clearly had her work cut out? Probably. 'I came down here to make him some warm milk, but as you can see, he is stubbornly refusing to allow me to make it. Noise and chaos in action.'

He needed something to focus his mind rather than the inappropriate ideas suddenly racing through his head and in case his hands decided to mutiny like his feet. Under the circumstances, it was best not to watch her. Aside from the fact it was a gross invasion of her privacy, he knew already he would suffer horrendously from this night forward with more fevered dreams. Dreams which would take his mind further away from his work and drive him mad with yet more unslaked lust. How long had it been since he had lain with a woman? Months? A year? A bit longer... Good grief.

Far too long than the male body was designed for if his overwhelming carnal reaction was any indication. 'Then why don't I hold him while you do?' He could have offered to heat the milk for her, but reasoned that dealing with a squalling child was the perfect antidote to all the inappropriate things he was feeling.

'Would you mind?'

'I wouldn't have offered if I minded. Besides, you are clearly in the grip of a crisis and you already know that is when I can be most relied upon. Noise and chaos is my forte.' Hadleigh held out his arms, then wondered what the hell he was supposed to do when the fidgeting boy was placed in them. He had never held a child. Had no idea *how* to hold a child. Instinct had him supporting his bottom with one hand while the other held his back as he had witnessed her do, but conscious his big hands might harm the child, he was undoubtedly holding him far too limply if Freddie's sudden acrobatics were any gauge.

She smiled at his ineptitude. 'He is not made of glass and is certainly much stronger than you could imagine.' He was heavier, too. A positive, wriggling dead weight with no personal boundaries judging by the annoyed little hand which was now pushing hard at his chin in his eagerness to escape. Hadleigh adjusted his hold which lessened the wriggling, but not by much. 'Sometimes, the tighter you hold him, the more likely it is he will give in to Morpheus.' She bent to fetch a pan. 'Although sometimes it just makes him worse.' Pan in hand, she shrugged as she filled it with milk from the jug. 'My best advice is do whatever you think is best. That has worked for me so far. Or hasn't.' Hardly reassuring.

While she heated the milk, he dedicated all his energy into keeping Freddie still. He jiggled him. Rocked him. And when neither worked, dragged the boy's moaning head to his shoulder, stroked his hair and began to pace up and down in the kitchen, whispering encouraging nonsense into the boy's ear. Miraculously, that appeared to work, because the wrestling stopped. Then the squalling became the odd moan and by the time she was filling Freddie's bottle, the child's head lay heavily on his shoulder and his small body was finally limp in his arms.

Mindful that any sudden movements might end the blissful peace, he gingerly lowered himself into a chair and arranged the pair of them so that Freddie could lay across him unhindered with just the lightest support from his arms. The boy's thumb went to his mouth and he snuggled against his chest, almost as if the sound of Hadleigh's heart beating was like a lullaby.

Penny picked up the bottle and the two steaming mugs of milk and turned, then faltered. The sight of her son sleeping soundly on Lord Hadleigh's chest and Lord Hadleigh cradling him as if he were the most precious thing in the world made her heart stutter. Why hadn't she had the good sense to pick a man like that to father her child? One who was clearly born to be a natural father...

Where had that thought come from?

As if he sensed her errant and romantic imaginings, he looked up, his dark amber eyes flecked with gold in the firelight, smiled, and her silly heart did somersaults against her ribs. Good heavens, he was a handsome man.

More handsome tonight, for some reason, than he had ever been before.

Perhaps because he was the most human she had ever seen him? Certainly the most relaxed. Over-long hair mussed from his pillow, his long legs stretched out and crossed at the ankles, big feet bare. The loose linen shirt both untucked at the waist and open at the neck. Even his jaw was informal, shadowed slightly with a day's growth of beard. The overall image he presented made her feel odd and unsettlingly fluttery inside. It also made her supremely conscious of her own body in the most peculiar way and, scandalously, she seemed suddenly very aware she was entirely naked under her sensible nightgown.

'I don't think Freddie wants the milk any more.' His voice was soft and low, the deep, intimate timbre sending a shiver down her spine. 'I think he is out for the count.'

'Never mind.' To her shame, her voice sounded strange. Breathier than normal. 'I made you some milk, too... To help you sleep.'

She placed the mug within his reach on the table and quickly retreated to the opposite end with her own drink which she was clutching tightly as if her life depended upon it. This all felt very naughty. Both of them here in the small hours, all alone. Not properly dressed. Her body humming with what she assumed was need.

How bizarre? She had never experienced it, but knew exactly what it was. Her breasts felt heavier and more sensitive than they ever had. Her skin felt almost on alert, not quite like her own and gloriously alive. Certain parts tingling, longing to be touched. All in all, quite the revelation as she approached her quarter century, as she had never experienced anything vaguely similar with her horrid husband. Not once.

She cradled her own mug and stared into it rather than

at him, in case her needy body leaked out clues, hoping she appeared nonchalant as she sipped the warm milk. But she could feel the force of his stare before she risked returning it. It made the tiny hairs on the back of her neck dance with wanton abandon.

'I've been pondering everything you said earlier and you are right. Tomorrow I will approach the wives. I am so sorry I never afforded you that same chance.'

'I didn't tell you so you could castigate yourself over it. In truth, I was so confused and overawed by the whole thing, I didn't realise that saying my piece was exactly what I needed to do. Hindsight is always a wonderful thing.'

'Even so, it was wrong of me. We men are brought up to take care of women.'

'Not all men.'

His face clouded. 'No. Not all.'

'But your father taught you well.'

His expression became bland again, a sure sign he was about to hide something, then he surprised her by shaking his head, allowing bleak sadness to show instead. Gifting her with the truth. 'Alas, my father was a man exactly like your husband... He was violent and cold. If he taught me anything, he taught me the exact sort of man I never wanted to be.'

'He beat you?'

He shook his head, causing a lock of deliciously mussed hair to fall boyishly over his forehead. 'No...never me. I escaped that. To be frank, most of the time he barely noticed me which suited me fine. But he took his temper out on my mother throughout their marriage—although she attempted to shield it from me even when I was old enough to know full well it happened. Denied it flat out as if she were ashamed. Every injury was apparently caused by something other than my father's hand, usually inanimate objects she had walked into or tripped over, when I never knew a person move with more grace than she did. But it was easier if we both accepted the lie she was clumsy, because then we could ignore the awful truth.' He took a thoughtful sip of his milk then stared at her over the rim. 'My bitterest regret is that I allowed her to do that. I should have challenged her and I should have prevented him—but then it was too late.' His irises swirled with emotion. Frustration. Anger. Self-loathing. 'I should have been there.'

'We mothers are brought up to protect our children. Do not be hard on yourself. You *are* far too hard on yourself. In everything.' She wanted to go to him and comfort him, wrap her arms around him. 'How old were you when she passed?'

'I had just turned twenty. I was away when she died. Cambridge...' His voice trailed off and the shutters immediately came down, dimming all those telling emotions like a bucket of iced water on a flame because they had stumbled into territory he did not want to discuss. He gave a dismissive half-smile she didn't believe and his overly cheery voice came out insincere. 'But enough of all this maudlin talk. I think it's time this little man went to bed.'

Penny set aside her mug, not wanting this enlightening conversation to end. 'Here—I'll take him.' Perhaps then he would linger and she could find a way past the defences he had suddenly raised.

'And risk waking him up? Not a chance. I can carry him up to bed just as easily as you can.' He carefully unfolded them both from the chair, ensuring he escaped all further questions or the temptation to answer them. 'You lead the way.'

It was awkward walking ahead of him in her nightrail when her traitorous skin still wanted his touch and her mind was alight with curiosity about his past, but she hoped she feigned serene calm as she slowly took each of the steps on the servants' staircase. She paused outside her door, wondering if he would relinquish his burden, but when he didn't she experienced a rush of nerves at the thought of him entering her private space. A space that, thanks to Freddie, lacked the organised neatness she maintained throughout the rest of the house. What would such a meticulous man make of the clutter? She flicked her gaze towards him and saw his own staring down the long landing towards the guest rooms. 'I see we are neighbours of sorts.'

'Yes.' Why did that suddenly thrill her? 'Perhaps a bad choice on my part, seeing that Freddie is currently so troublesome at night.' She practically flung open the door and scurried across her sitting room, wishing she had had the foresight to pick up the building bricks still littering the carpet, then opened the second door belonging to her son's bedchamber.

Lord Hadleigh carried him in, his big, capable hand gently cradling his neck as soon as Penny pulled back the blankets, before carefully using his entire body to lower Freddie down. Her son murmured, let out a half-hearted cry, then lapsed soundly back to sleep as Lord Hadleigh gently stroked his hair. She carefully covered her son and found her eyes inexplicably drawn to the man opposite. The complicated man who she now knew hid more from the world than he was comfortable with it seeing. His locked with hers as he smiled and her own hearted melted.

All those years she had wasted believing that ardent suitors, bouquets and waltzes were romantic, when the singular most romantic thing she had ever known was this.

This simple domestic chore shared with him topped each of those foolish ideals instantly.

One man. One woman. Bent over one sleeping child in his crib. A romantic moment which would have been utterly perfect if the sleeping child were his.

A foolish thought! Penny straightened, alarmed at the way her silly imagination was running away from her. She shouldn't be having romantic thoughts about him, despite her wayward body's current wild ideas to the contrary. They were pointless. She was just his housekeeper. She would always be a traitor's widow.

He followed her to the door and waited for her to softly shut it. Then leaned close to whisper, 'Success! Between us we can conquer a terrible almost two-year-old.' She wished his warm breath hadn't caressed her cheek. Wished her nerve-endings hadn't tingled as a result. Wished he wasn't still smiling. That infectious, handsome smile played havoc with her senses. And his eyes... gracious, they were making her swoon, when she hadn't swooned in years. Nor had she ever swooned with the same ferocity as she was in danger of doing now. Something about him tonight had thoroughly seduced her already and she was powerless to stop it.

Panic made her retrace her steps to the door before she realised she was being impatiently impolite. 'Thank you for helping me. And once again, my apologies for waking you up and dragging you to the kitchen.' Minimise it. Don't allow him to see what a wonderful time you had in that kitchen. Just the pair of them. Being themselves...

'It was naught but a detour to the kitchen.' Another intimate whisper, far too close for comfort. She could smell the faint traces left of his cologne, see every tiny golden whisker on his jaw and his throat. 'I was heading to my study to work. I confess I was hoping to sneak a few more hours in without you knowing.'

As if it had a mind of its own, her hand went to his cheek. 'No work… You need to sleep. You look exhausted.' She made the mistake of locking her gaze with his, then couldn't find the strength needed to tear it away.

'Have you made it your mission to look after me?'

'Somebody needs to.' Her thumb was scandalously tracing one of the shadows under his eyes. They fluttered closed for a second, but when they opened his irises seemed to have changed once more. Gone was the sadness and the regret. Now the golden flecks positively burned.

Then, as if they were both caught under this night's same, all-encompassing, intoxicating spell, they closed the distance between them at the same time. His lips brushed hers softly and Penny sighed, hers opening in response. One of them deepened the kiss, she wasn't sure who. Nor would she later recollect whose arms had wrapped themselves about the other first. All she knew in that loaded moment with any certainty was that their kiss felt right. The passion which rapidly grew out of it felt right also.

Her hands found their way into his hair, anchoring his mouth to hers. His smoothed down her back, her hips, tugged her close so they stood touching from head to toe. Rested possessively on her bottom. She felt his desire through the flimsy barrier of her nightgown and it didn't repulse her. She revelled in it. Revelled that he wanted her and she wanted him. Revelled in the kiss until it was he who dragged his mouth away. Still holding her, his breathing as ragged as hers, his expression confused, they simply stared at one another until he let go. Stepped back.

Raked his hand through his hair.

'Perhaps I should bid you goodnight?'

She didn't want him to go. Wanted to ask him to stay, but had no idea how to. 'Promise me you will try to sleep.'

'After that kiss, Penny, I doubt I shall ever sleep again.' Then he left her hugging herself, bewildered, thinking the exact same thing on the opposite side of the door while he walked the scant few feet to his bed down the hallway.

Chapter Thirteen

He'd kissed her! And, blast it all to hell, it had been a kiss which exceeded all the heated kisses he had imagined nightly in his fevered dreams. He'd kissed her, ran his hands greedily over her body, then practically floated to his bed thoroughly overawed by it all, where he then slept like the dead for hours.

Now he could hear the sounds of the house in full swing beyond the bedchamber door and realised that not only had he slept, it sounded as though he had overslept to boot. He felt clumsily for his pocket watch on the nightstand and glared at the dial. Nine o'clock.

Nine o'clock, for pity's sake, when he should have been up at six! Worse, now he would have to dress, take himself downstairs while breakfast was doubtless in full swing, be sociable with Flint and his family—and face her, too. She'd be there. Diligently doing her job as usual.

What exactly did a man say to a woman in his employ he had shamelessly ravished the night before? One he would have ravished further if his conscience at his own rampant and obvious lust hadn't brought him to his senses, the evidence of the former quite apparent, pointing at him in accusation beneath the blankets. Rock hard and showing no signs of deflating any time soon despite the inappropriateness of his behaviour towards her.

Penny was a woman who under all normal conditions would still be in the midst of mourning!

She was a woman whose entire life had recently been turned upside down. One who was undoubtedly still very vulnerable from her ordeal. A woman who at his insistence now worked in his house!

Had she kissed him back because she feared for her job? He sincerely hoped not, because that made him something he really didn't want to be.

But she hadn't seemed reluctant...

She had kissed him back. He was sure of that. She had burrowed her hands beneath his shirt, run them over his back. He could still feel where her touch had lingered like a brand before she had moaned against his mouth and the last vestiges of his reason had temporarily flown away. Until they had come crashing back and he'd needed her consent to continue and, in so doing, killed the magical moment between them stone dead. Because she had happily bade him goodnight.

What was he going to do?

An apology went without saying. A great big fat grovelling one, explaining he had been...what? Overwrought? Overtired? Overwhelmed? When the truth was it had just felt like the right thing to do in that precise moment despite him being all of those things. And, God help him, if she was similarly inclined, it would be something he would happily do again.

In a heartbeat.

Kissing Penny had been a revelation. She had felt so damn good in his arms. Tasted so damn fine on his lips. That delectable, womanly body of hers fitting against his to perfection, so soft...so seductive. Despite the layer of his shirt and her nightdress, he had enjoyed the way her breasts had flattened against his chest, the way he had known exactly where the tips of her nipples rested against his body, rousing his passions further and driving him mad with need. It had been a miracle he had managed to stop himself from hoisting up her nightgown and filling his greedy hands with those breasts, tracing for himself the hard, pebbled shape of her nipples. Instead, he had made do with dragging her hips to press against his, showing her in no uncertain terms exactly what effect their illicit kiss had had on him.

Recollections which really weren't helping his current state of confusion or arousal one jot.

With a groan, he pushed threw back the covers and stared at it in disgust. Then, when that didn't work, stalked over to the vanity and sloshed the chilled water from the jug into the basin before sluicing it roughly over his face and body.

What was it about Penny that affected him so? Passion aside, he'd allowed her to convince him to stay the night—with very little fight, all things considered—he'd willingly gone to her assistance in the kitchen, stared at her body shamelessly without her knowledge and thoroughly enjoyed being alone with her once the staring was done. Then, told her things about his parents he had never confessed to a living soul. Private things. Intensely personal things which could never be taken back and then he had blithely given in to temptation and kissed her. A whole other and equally as terrifying Pandora's box, except he had practically ripped the lid off this one and had no idea where he had carelessly tossed it.

He stared at his still rampant privates miserably. Lord Fennimore was arriving at ten and would expect a thorough summary of his progress on the case since last week.

How was he supposed to do that when his mind was stubbornly lodged elsewhere?

Miserably, he shoved his feet in his breeches and did his best to make his crumpled shirt from yesterday seem more presentable. If only the damn thing didn't still carry the lingering scent of her subtle floral perfume. Or happen to be the same shirt her hands had wandered beneath. Had he not overslept, he would jolly well get on his horse now, ride like the wind back to town, and swap the guilty garment for another. Preferably the stiffest, most starched shirt in his wardrobe. Or a hair shirt, if such a thing existed beyond the annals of history. So he could repent properly.

With leaden feet, he took the servants' staircase down and followed the sounds of the voices. He could hear the Dowager laughing. Then, to his horror, he heard Lord Fennimore's wife, Harriet, laughing and accepted it was probably fitting that his abject mortification should be witnessed by all and sundry. He undoubtedly deserved nothing less—unless fate would take pity on him and present him with Penny before he entered the dining room.

But typically, the hallway was ominously empty as he walked through it, forcing him to stop outside the door and take one last fortifying breath before he stepped inside.

'Good morning, Mr Lazy Bones!' At the Dowager's exclamation, poor Penny sloshed hot chocolate over Lord Fennimore's hand.

'Ouch!'

'Oh, I am so sorry, my lord!' Her lovely face glowed beetroot red as her eyes flicked to meet Hadleigh's before they hastily looked away. Because the world was cruel, she looked particularly lovely this morning. She had done something different with her hair. A looser, yet more intricate style. Yet another well-fitting new dress he had never seen before did wonders for her figure and, once again, his throat dried at the sight.

'Thank goodness I have another hand I can use now that this one has been burned to a crisp.' Lord Fennimore's curmudgeonly response snapped him back to the present, reminding him that Penny didn't look particularly pleased to see him. If anything she was horrified, which further compounded his shame at taking advantage of her.

'Pay him no mind, Penny,' said Harriet, swatting her husband's arm. 'Cedric is a dreadful grouch in the mornings. Unlike our handsome barrister here, he clearly didn't get a good night's sleep.'

Hadleigh felt the tips of his own ears redden, trying to brazen out his entrance for Penny's sake as well as his own, because, frankly, she was doing a very good job of looking as guilty as sin. Trust him to ravish a woman who was incapable of lying! She might as well be carrying a placard.

'Good morning, everyone. I apologise for my tardiness. Sorry for startling you, Penny.' She nodded, then practically sprinted from the room, still clutching the chocolate pot.

'Did you have a bad night?' the Dowager asked innocently. 'Or was it a particularly good one?' She and Harriet exchanged a knowing look thanks to Penny's jittery behaviour and he feared the blush might spread to his face, too, branding him as the guilty party responsible for it. Another loaded look passed between her and Harriet, except this time, they included Jessamine and his friend Flint.

'I slept like the dead.' Which was true, but felt like a lie with everyone suddenly watching him. Stalwartly ignoring them in case his guilt gave him away, too, he took himself to the sideboard and began to load a plate, taking his time in the hope they might actually forget about him.

It was only when he had dished up a veritable mountain that he realised he would now have to choke it all down. Something good manners dictated needed to be done with more decorum than panic wanted to allow. Desperately strapping on his lawyer's mask, he decided to grasp the bull by the horns and direct the conversation at the person he reasoned was likely to be the least interested in speculation and gossip. Lord Fennimore.

'I am going to visit all the wives later and see if any of them would be willing to testify.'

'Against their husbands? Is that likely when all six have already been named as witnesses for the defence?'

'It is worth a try. One or two might feel aggrieved enough or ashamed of their spouses' treachery to feel the urge to vent. If nothing else, it will give me an idea how best to question them in court. Perhaps find clues to their Achilles heels. How goes your side of the investigations?'

Fortunately, never one to miss an opportunity to talk about business, Lord Fennimore gave him an extensive rundown of everything the King's Elite agents had been working on all week. He barely paused for breath, which meant that Hadleigh could pretend he didn't sense Penny as she came back into the room, nor did he have time to allow his gaze to linger as she filled his own cup with coffee and he managed to mumble his thanks. In fact, by the time old Fennimore was done, the servants had cleared the plates, the ladies had all left and only the pair of them and Flint remained.

Penny walked past the dining room for the third time and for the third time that hour had to resign herself to not speaking to him any time soon. He was thoroughly engrossed in his work and attempting to interrupt him to have a word seemed trivial, when she still had no earthly idea what words to use.

What exactly did one say to the master of the house after shamelessly plastering herself against him and kissing him with such enthusiasm her lips were still swollen from her fervour?

Excuse me, my lord, but did you mind me kissing you?

Mortifying. Because of course he had. He had put a stop to it.

Shall we draw a veil over last night? We were both tired...

Her toes were cringing inside her slippers at the lie, because she had never been particularly good at lying. She *had* been tired. Then she had been wide awake and willing. Shockingly willing.

She had lain awake for hours, her body all aquiver and positively throbbing with need, trying to think of a believable reason to knock on his door on the off chance he might want to continue what she had patently started. Or had he? The start of the kiss was a bit of a blur, it was all so overwhelming. The middle was a fuzzy haze of scandalous sensations which had fizzed around her body like freshly released champagne bubbles. The end had been awkward. He had said goodnight and she had been left yearning for more. Which probably meant she had instigated the kiss because he had had to extricate himself from it.

Gracious! She had been all at sea. Still was, truth be told. So much so, she barely recognised herself this morning at all. Her breasts still resolutely refused to feel anything like her own. She kept glancing down at them, convinced they had grown twice their size overnight they felt so heavy.

Perhaps the best course of action was to wait for him

to speak first? Simply carry on, pretending nothing what-soever had happened at all. Just as she had when he had walked into breakfast and she had spontaneously com-busted while simultaneously scolding one of the guests under her charge. Yes! A positively spectacular piece of acting on her part that had been! She should have hung a sign around her neck—*I kissed Lord Hadleigh like a wanton*—not that it would hang particularly straight now that her breasts had ripened.

Just as she had ripened.

Obviously, the world had gone quite mad—she was now actively considering inviting another man to her bed, when she had been thoroughly determined to empty it of the first. But she couldn't deny a newly awakened part of her was considering it. If Lord Hadleigh's kiss was anything to go on, it had been nothing like the aggres-sive, intrusive and sloppy kisses her husband had foisted upon her when drunk. Nor had her body felt violated at his touch. Most striking of all the comparisons was that she had been actively part of the proceedings last night and not pretending she was elsewhere during the intima-cies. A first for her as the only way to tolerate Penhurst's intrusions—because she couldn't think of any other word to accurately describe the distasteful, brisk coupling she had suffered with him—had been to be elsewhere in her mind while it was occurring to such an extent, she ren-dered herself numb from the neck down.

There had been no need to do that with Lord Hadleigh. Her body had screamed for his touch. Welcomed it. Craved it still. What was she going to do about that?

Absently, she wandered back down the hallway, com-pletely forgetting she was actively avoiding the ladies after her ridiculous display of gaucheness over breakfast.

'There you are!' The Dowager beckoned to her through

the open door of the drawing room. 'We have been looking for you!'

Penny attempted to paste on her diligent housekeeper's mask. 'Would you like some tea?'

'We have tea,' said Harriet, patting the seat next to her on the sofa ominously, 'What we need is some juicy gossip to go along with it. We are all dying to know what all that was about this morning.'

'I am not sure I know what you mean.' Penny didn't sit. Didn't dare.

'Oh, come on, Penny! You are among friends here. What the blazes was all that?' The Dowager waved her arms about frantically. 'All that stuff between you and the handsome lawyer? You were both blushing...neither of you could hold the other's eye...'

'There was a distinct *frisson* in the air, I thought.' Harriet smiled knowingly. 'The sort of *delicious* frisson which only occurs when a man and a woman have something to feel guilty about.'

'Honestly, he startled me. I am not used to him being there over breakfast.' She felt guilty blotches bloom on her neck at the flagrant untruth.

'Ah...*bon*...of course.' Even Jessamine was clearly unconvinced, although for some reason, with her French accent her agreement sounded like an accusation. 'He never stays the night, so *of course* you were startled to see him. That vivid blush had absolutely nothing to do with the cosy chat the pair of you had in the middle of the night. The one which you wore your nightgown for and Lord Hadleigh attended in a state of scandalous *dishabille*...'

'How did you know about that?' The guilty blush exploded in all its shameful glory, making her uncomfortably warm in her new wool dress.

'In this house of spies, nothing happens without somebody knowing about it.' Harriet patted the spot on the sofa again and, mortified, Penny perched upon it. 'An agent told Flint and Flint told Jessamine.'

'And *obviously* Jessamine told us.' The Dowager giggled. 'Although we all thought it was only a matter of time. The pair of you have been doing a great deal of looking these past few weeks. And looking invariably leads to touching, in my experience, and then nature takes its course.'

'He stumbled across me trying to get Freddie back to sleep and assisted. We drank some hot milk and then went to bed.'

'Together?' Harriet had leaned forward expectantly.

'Certainly not!' This was getting out of hand. 'You are all making gross assumptions about a perfectly innocent conversation.'

'So there was not even a kiss?' The angry red blush turned instantly purple and her mouth hung slack for several seconds before she attempted, too late, to deny it. 'I knew it!' The Dowager slapped both hands on her knees. 'She has the look of a woman who has been recently kissed. That dress, the flirtatious hairstyle...'

'It was an accident.'

'Tripping over a rug is an accident—unless you tripped over the rug and inadvertently found your lips flying towards his as a result.' Harriet patted her hand as if she were a child. 'Why don't you start the story again properly? He stole a kiss...'

'Actually, I think I might have been the one to steal it.' Penny buried her burning face in her hands. 'He ended it. And now I have made everything so awkward I have no earthly idea how to fix it.'

'Oh...' Jessamine sounded sympathetic. 'By ended it, he rebuffed your advances...or did he join in and *then* end it?'

'What difference does it make?'

'Oh, my dear—a great deal!' Harriet wrapped a reassuring arm around her shoulders and hugged her close. 'Men are simple creatures when it comes to women. They can take what they want without caring. Take what they want because they cannot help themselves or deny what they want out of some misplaced belief they shouldn't be taking it in the first place. Does that make sense?' None whatsoever. 'Therefore, the most pertinent detail we need to consider before we acknowledge he ended the kiss, is if he kissed you back first.'

'Well, I suppose he might have.'

'If you have to suppose,' said the Dowager sagely, 'it couldn't have been much of a kiss.'

'It was a lovely kiss.'

'Passionate?'

At Jessamine's question Penny hid her face back in her hands. 'Yes. A little too passionate.'

'There is no such thing as too passionate, darling.' Harriet again. 'A kiss is designed to give your body ideas and by the sounds of things, it gave your body quite a few of them. Should we ask if the ideas were…reciprocated?'

Penny nodded miserably. She had felt his desire and practically glued herself to it. 'Splendid! Then it sounds as if both of you are in the same hideous place. Both mad with lust and longing and not quite sure what to do about it. We have a strong foundation to build upon.'

'There is nothing to build upon.' Despite their delight at her situation, this needed to be nipped in the bud. 'It was a mistake for so many reasons.' Three faces stared back at her blankly, clearly not understanding her dilemma at all. With a resigned sigh, Penny started to list them. 'For a start, I am a housekeeper and he is a viscount.'

'Weren't you once a viscountess?'

'Which leads me to my second point, that being the sordid fact that I am a traitor's widow. Lord Hadleigh was the man who tried my husband! It's all very messy.'

'But you hated your husband. You testified against him.' The Dowager pushed a cup of tea into Penny's hand. 'Why, only the other day you admitted to Jessamine and me that you never shed a single tear when you heard he had been murdered. Good riddance to the brute, you are well shot of him.'

'Which is exactly why I cannot plunge headlong into a relationship with another man! I've been a chattel and I have no desire to be again.'

'To be his chattel, you would have to marry him and he would have to be the sort of man who makes his wife a chattel, which I am entirely convinced he is not.' The Dowager gestured to the other ladies. 'We all know Hadleigh well and can categorically vouch for him being a thoroughly decent man. But you are missing the point, my dear. This has nothing to do with marriage yet and nor does it need to be. One of the biggest benefits of being a widow is the *freedom* it gives you.'

Penny blinked incredulously, not at all understanding the bizarre turn this unwelcome conversation was taking. It was Harriet who said the unthinkable and rendered her totally speechless. 'What she means, darling, is it is perfectly acceptable for a widow to take a lover. Nobody would blink an eyelid. It's positively expected. I certainly enjoyed a few of them after my first husband died—and before I met Cedric, of course.'

The Dowager nodded, raising her eyebrows suggestively. 'What better way to forget the chore of your marriage bed than finding passion with another who is willing. I'll bet Hadleigh will not be an atrocious lover. That man is far too *diligent*. And your position here is only temporary, after all, Penny. Soon you will move on and so will he. And thanks to Cedric and the government's generous fifty guineas it's not as if he even pays your wages. So you see, there is nothing *messy* about your situation at all.'

Chapter Fourteen

By late afternoon that day, when he had failed completely to track her down, Hadleigh had left Chafford Grange in a state of total wretchedness. It was obvious she was avoiding him and had clearly chosen to traipse to the village to run an errand rather than see him and listen to his apology. Therefore, all the awkwardness between them would still be hanging in the air upon his return today. An awkwardness that his three-day absence would only serve to feed.

Not that he had intended to stay away so long. He had meant to return the next day and make things right, but he had approached the first of the traitor's wives, the Countess of Winterton, and, just as Penny had said, the woman had wanted to talk. Her extensive and damning testimony had led to more unforeseen work as Hadleigh had followed up each of the new leads. At least he could tell Penny that and thank her for opening his eyes.

One other wife had also co-operated, perhaps less enthusiastically than the Countess, but now he knew that there were undeniable links between the leader of the smuggling ring and the peers she had lured to be part of it, because both wives had known that their husband and the traitorous Viscountess Gislingham had been lovers at some point. The Countess of Winterton had even given him love letters sent to him by the other woman, although love didn't really feature in the graphic list of sexual acts the Viscountess had promised to bestow upon the man. Just like Penny's husband, he had been seduced to stray.

Although that put the blame wholly at the door of the seductress when as much lay at the door of those unfaithful husbands who were agreeable to straying in the first place.

Hadleigh didn't understand that at all. If Penny were his, he doubted he'd notice another woman if she were sprawled naked on his bed and it went without saying he would honour his marriage vows. His father had taught him that by default, too. Why marry at all if you wanted to live like a bachelor all your days? Besides, if he failed to honour his, he could hardly expect his wife to honour hers and the thought of Penny kissing anyone else made his blood boil!

Had he just thought the words Penny and wife in the same sentence? Yes, he had. Twice, apparently. And, more importantly, why did the prospect not terrify him as it should?

Good grief, this was all spiralling out of his control. When his mind should be occupied with suspected treason and the trial, his was filled with her. Not more than a few minutes went by before she encroached on a thought. Last night, despite being bone weary and despite the lateness of the hour, he had forgone his unappetising cold supper, put away the pile of work on his desk begging for his attention and taken himself to an inn to eat instead. Simply because she had wanted him to look after himself and rest.

He turned his horse on to the drive and was halfway down it before he realised he didn't feel queasy at the prospect of going home. He supposed he had her to thank for that, too. While he wasn't looking forward to stepping inside the house, that was more to do with the humiliating apology he had to make to Penny rather than the usual dread he suffered at the mere sight of those forbidding four walls.

Things were changing. At speed. But, bizarrely, he was keeping up. Last week, he would have rather died than sleep a night under that roof. Yet folded neatly in his satchel were two clean shirts, cravats, drawers and stockings in case he happened to find himself sleeping here again. Or was that wishful thinking? Brought about by one too many fevered and erotic dreams over the last three nights involving a certain brunette who had all too briefly fitted so perfectly in his arms.

So much for his new resolve to redouble his efforts to concentrate solely on the case now the Crown had insisted it be brought forward. Another reason why his return here had been delayed. Against his sound and reasoned arguments to the contrary, the Attorney General had scheduled the Gislingham trial to the second week of December instead of January. Which meant he had two weeks to put it all together now. Two weeks to dot every *i* and cross every *t* and try his hardest not to think about that kiss and that woman at all.

An agent stepped out of the stables to take his horse. 'Where is Mrs Henley?' Because the King's Elite would know her exact movements. Something he perhaps should have thought of before he'd taken advantage of her so thoroughly in her room.

'She took her son for some air in the gardens not half an hour hence, my lord. They were headed towards the lake.'

The fact she was outside came as a relief and Hadleigh set off at pace to find her. It would be easier to apologise to her without the usual audience and he didn't want to worry her by summoning her to his makeshift study where they would be alone, or, heaven forbid, turn up unannounced and uninvited at her rooms again.

He spied her as promised at the closest edge of the lake, holding Freddie's hand as he toddled along beside her. She must have sensed him, as she turned and momentarily stopped as if surprised. Hadleigh raised his hand in greeting and sprinted the last few yards towards her in case she got any ideas to flee before he had said his piece. He had rehearsed his apology throughout the hour's ride to get here and needed to get it out to be able to move on.

'You are back, my lord.'

'Yes, a little later than I would like.' Because she was still walking he fell into step beside her, wishing he didn't feel so relieved to be with her again. It really didn't help his cause. 'But you will be pleased to know I followed your advance and questioned the wives.' He was stalling. Pathetic, really, but he reasoned he was easing himself in gently.

'You did?' Her blue eyes locked with his, curious. 'Was it fruitful?'

'What you mean to say is, were you right?' She merely smiled slightly in confirmation, staring off to the lake. 'And, yes, you were. The Countess of Winterton was very eager to talk. The Marchioness of Nethway less so, but thanks to you I now know both of their husbands enjoyed a particular sort of friendship with the Lady Gislingham. As a consequence of those conversations, I have left both men in no doubt I have enough evidence to link them to her treachery, so I am hopeful they might come to their senses soon and confess to their crimes. I doubt either of them relish the thought of having the ugly truth spilled by their own spouses in court. As we know, juries have a great deal of sympathy for wronged wives.'

She frowned at that statement, her eyes finally locking with his in disappointment. She had to be thinking about the kiss. There was clearly no putting it off any longer. This woman was peeved. 'I came here to apologise for what happened the other night.' The words came tumbling out. 'It was a mistake... I was tired, you were vulnerable...'

'Vulnerable? An interesting choice of word.' Hadleigh cringed at her annoyed tone.

'What I mean to say is, it was wrong of me to take advantage of you as I did. I am heartily disgusted at myself, if it is any consolation. It won't happen again.'

She exhaled slowly and he assumed she was considering his apology. 'Is that how you see me still—the wronged wife?'

What was he supposed to say to that when it had nothing whatsoever to do with their kiss? 'You were wronged...'

'Of course I was. The world knows that...only that is not the way I see myself. It is such a small part of who I am, yet it appears to be the version of myself others are most content with accepting as if it is a fait accompli. Chiselled somewhere into stone in perpetuity. Maybe I should have it written on my forehead to make it easier for people to decide how to view me? Poor, downtrodden Penny! Rather that, than as that brave women who spoke out in the dock. Or the woman who *is* a good mother or *was* a good daughter. Or the diligent housekeeper here at Chafford Grange who has things running like a well-oiled wheel? I was a wife for just three out of my near twenty-five years. For twenty-two of those nobody would have dared call me *poor* Penny at all.' She was staring straight ahead, her expression slightly wistful for a moment, making him wonder if the flash of temper he had just witnessed was gone and she was merely reminiscing. 'I was an heiress. A catch, if I say so myself. When Clarissa and

I first met and became friends, I was vivacious and witty, a little daring, quite outspoken. Certainly not your average debutante by any stretch thanks to my upbringing. Some gentlemen even considered me rather pretty and told me so at every opportunity. They sent me flowers and poems and asked me to dance.

'Before that I was considered resourceful and level-headed by all those who knew me. My father thought me an asset to his business. Until he sold it, of course. In fact, as my mother's health began to decline, I ran Ridley's for a time. Did you know that? I was barely nineteen, but I could negotiate with hardened merchants, balance the books, organise the staff and sell practically anything to anyone. I had her eye, too—I knew which pieces to select, exactly how to price them and they flew off the shelves. Papa said I had the knack for making money. A talent for charming people. An apple which didn't fall far from both the trees which made it.'

She paused again while Freddie kicked some leaves about and Hadleigh tried and failed to come up with a suitable response, completely confused by the strange way the conversation had turned. He had barely uttered a tenth of his apology and, while she had every right to be angry at him for taking advantage, he got the distinct impression it wasn't the kiss that pinched her lovely features with blatant irritation or made her voice positively sharp.

'I am not entirely sure what you want me to say.' Because he had worked out she did expect him to say something. Or at least he thought she did, although lord only knew what about.

'I suppose what I am trying to say is this: simply because the cap fits, a person shouldn't be expected to always wear it when the world is joyously filled with different hats and we, as individuals, have the right to choose, try them on for size and discard them as the mood takes us.' She began walking again, taking the path towards the house which went through his mother's beloved rose garden. He would have attempted to lead her on a different route and subtly avoid it, except he could see she was in no mood to be led. Now he was trapped. Cornered. Petrified. *He wasn't ready.*

'Let us take you, for example. Who are you, Lord Hadleigh? Are you the dedicated and dogged lawyer your reputation claims? Or are you the wealthy Viscount who owns this grand house? The good friend to the Flints and the Leathams and the Fennimores of the world? Or the charming, thoughtful fellow who sweeps up flour and rocks little boys to sleep? Or perhaps you are that remorseful man I met fleetingly in the kitchen the other evening, who wished he had done more to help his mother? The one who fears the memories inside that house more than he cares to admit and feels responsible for all abused women everywhere.'

Her astuteness brought him up short and he realised she had brought him down this path on purpose. His mother's beloved roses now flanked where they stood. The prickly bushes dormant, only a few inches of their barren stems protruding from the ground. 'Which one of those many hats fits you best?'

'All of them, I suppose…alongside a few more.' He took her arm, tried to turn her, but she refused to budge. Although now that she was stubbornly stationary, at least they weren't moving forward.

'Of course! Because people are more than one thing. We are all multi-faceted and complex in our own way. Brave and afraid. Clever and daft. Downtrodden and proud. Stubborn and charming and annoyingly overbearing.'

'This is a very *philosophical* conversation so early in the morning.' Confusing, more like. She was running rings around him but, for the life of him, he couldn't fathom her intention or dismiss the growing unease.

'I am in a very philosophical mood.' She gripped his arm and purposefully dragged him round the bend and there it was.

His mother's grave.

He had placed her here on purpose, he suddenly recalled, so she would be among the flowers she had always tended with such care. Upon it were three hothouse roses, left by the old gardener perhaps, their pretty blooms withered by the biting winter frost. Much like his rehearsed apology and his hope to smooth things over.

'Why is she here when the family plot is on the other side of the lake?'

'She loved this rose garden.' The past was suffocating him. He could barely breathe.

'And your father is safely and symbolically buried on the other side of the lake under a thick block of granite. *She* is out of harm's way.' He didn't deny it. Instead he schooled his features to become unreadable to hide the guilt and pain which simultaneously hit him square in the gut like punches.

'I remind you of her, don't I? That is why you paid my rent and that is why you now heavily subsidise my wages. Do not bother denying it because I have checked.'

'I failed to help her and have regretted it ever since.' His fixed his gaze on the gravestone. The cold, hard rock seemed a safer option than looking back into Penny's perceptive blue stare and admitting she was right. But he felt her stare regardless and wondered if he'd made a total hash of things yet again. Because she had reminded him of his mother once upon a time...

'Tell me, out of interest, when you look at her headstone what do you see? An abused wife...or more than that?'

A little of his rigid composure cracked. Hadleigh felt his eyebrows furrow as she forced him to see more of the past than he was prepared to. 'Because you do her memory a gross disservice if that is all she has become to you, for the woman who put together this magnificent home, filled this garden with summer roses and raised you to be the crusading, vexing man that you are wore many different hats and I'll wager she preferred all of them over the one you have consigned her to eternity wearing.'

Penny had allowed him to stalk off, not caring that he had been obviously angry by what she had said because she was livid at him. And livid at herself for believing him when she should have trusted her nagging doubts about his miraculously convenient and fortuitous offer of employment. What had her father always said? If something appears to be too good to be true, then it usually was. Ugh! She knew that!

Yet instead of squirrelling away the six guineas she had in her hand, she had frivolously spent them, confident she would soon have more than enough to do exactly what she wanted. Freddie had indulgent new toys and she had treated herself to five new dresses. Dresses she adored which were nothing like the shapeless, dull garments Penhurst had forced her to wear because he knew she loathed them. Now she was stuck here, unwittingly beholden and feeling very silly to have been so easily convinced.

Lord Hadleigh had got one thing right, though—he had taken advantage! Although not in the way he thought. He had taken advantage of her desperation for employment and presented her with an offer he had known full well she would have been mad to refuse.

Logically, she knew it was hardly a betrayal in the true sense of the word. She liked it here and there truly was a job for her which the government were still paying her handsomely for. Fifty guineas for less than three months' labour was astonishingly generous for a housekeeper by any standards—and her role was so much more than house-keeper. She was a confidante, an advisor, the essential component to the smooth running of a house filled with government spies and secrets. It was a unique role and not one just any old housekeeper could adequately fill. It needed Penny's unique experience and insight—he hadn't lied about any of that. Nor had he expressly ever told her the government were specifically paying *all* her wages. She had to give him that, too. In part—

But he had certainly omitted telling her the truth he so rigidly claimed he stood for with every fibre of his being. After she had realised he was doubling the ridic-ulously generous salary out of his own pocket, she had gone through the wording of her contract and not once had it stipulated where the money came from either, nor mentioned the exact sum she would receive. But it had certainly been worded to make her think the government were paying '*the sum agreed*'.

Just as his convincing words the night of the flour had heavily hinted at their involvement.

'*We suggest an amount of ten guineas per month... We will recruit the staff... We cannot risk anything leaking to the defence, or, heaven forbid, the press before the trial.*'

A great many 'we's had been flung about to embellish things with the right amount of gravitas to get her to be-lieve him. And procuring the refund from Mr Cohen had been a masterstroke on his part. It had made it appear he had listened to her assertions about standing on her own two feet and respected them. Except, he hadn't believed her truly capable of managing her own life in the long run, what with her being nothing beyond the tragic abused wife who needed rescuing and thus had felt the need to become her anonymous benefactor once again.

Quite frankly, if she hadn't grown to like the man so much, or grown to understand what a complex, wounded and thoughtful character he was beneath the inscrutable lawyer's mask, she would cheerfully roll up that duplicitous piece of legal parchment and bash him over his irritatingly noble head with it!

But she did like him and she did understand his motives, even if she fundamentally found them exasperating at the same time. Somewhere in his irritating and noble head he had decided to appoint himself the rescuer of abused women everywhere, because obviously they all needed rescuing, the poor things. When, in actuality, in doing it the way he had, by assuming control, he'd labelled her as hopeless and stuffed her unwillingly back in the same box she had been desperate to get out of. Couldn't he see that she loathed *Poor* Penny and everything she had stood for? Wasn't it obvious she wanted to take the whitewash to those awful three years and paint them out of her memories, pretending they'd never happened? That was not who she was! She was more like the old Penny again now. Perhaps had always been the old Penny, because despite the enforced subjugation, inside she had always railed against it. Her thoughts and her actions were different, that was all. And only out of dire necessity.

'Penny…can I come in?.' She had been expecting him. So much so, she had even gone to the trouble to indulge in a little of Clarissa's staging in preparation.

'Yes.'

The door to her private sitting room opened and, because she purposely had her back to it and was facing the fire, she made no attempt to turn when she heard him softly click it shut again. He came to stand awkwardly in front of her as she embroidered. He had no choice but to do otherwise as she had dragged the big chair far away from the others, giving him nowhere to sit. She wanted him to stand and squirm.

'We need to talk, I think.'

She dropped her embroidery into her lap, face down in case he saw it, and stared up at him. 'There is no *we* in this situation, Lord Hadleigh. If there is talking to be done in my chambers, then I will do it.'

'Fair enough.' He looked ridiculously handsome and uncomfortable, and she hardened her heart against the way it fluttered at the sight.

'You lied to me. Perhaps not to my face, but certainly by omission. I am not entirely sure where such a deed stands in legal terms—but know that you would call foul if faced with similar deceptions in court. Worse, you wilfully went behind my back again when I expressly asked you not to.'

'I was only trying to help.'

'Perhaps—but dishonestly. Although I am sure you convinced yourself it was for my own good.'

'All I wanted to do was give you and Freddie a decent start after the government saw fit to—'

Penny held up her hand. 'Fifty guineas *is* a decent start and it is all I will take with me once this job is done.'

'Oh, for goodness sake!' He had the gall to look exasperated. 'It was not meant like that and you know it. You are choosing to be offended, Penny, by something that was only well meant.'

'Be careful, my lord, as it sounds as though you are on the cusp of justifying your actions by telling me it was all for my own good, when we both know this is more for *your* own good, ultimately, than anyone else's.'

'That accusation is unfair. I stood to gain nothing from it, nor did I expect anything in return.'

'Really? Nothing?'

'If you are alluding to that kiss and suggesting my motives were—'

'This has nothing to do with that kiss and everything to do with whatever nonsense you choose to believe in your head!' Penny stood then, clenching her fists at her sides rather than grabbing him by his shoulders and shaking him. 'How dare you underestimate me! How dare you trivialise all that I have achieved in the last six months to assuage your own guilty conscience!' His face had paled, hardened. 'You once took great offence at my calling your *benevolence* blood money—yet you are a hypocrite, Lord Hadleigh, for that is exactly what it is! I know next to nothing about your mother and her suffering or your part in that—but I do know that you cannot use mine to try to make amends for your guilt regarding her! Because it will not work. You can give me your entire fortune, spread it liberally among every abused wife and Christendom if you think it will help, but those demons will still be there waiting for the day you finally choose to stop being a coward and face them.'

His body jerked backwards as if she had slapped him. Then he stalked out of the room, slamming her door hard behind him.

Chapter Fifteen

Hadleigh buried himself in his work for two days and avoided the wench. For the first day, he had been outraged. Royally so. That she could take something noble, something well meant and selfless and throw it back in his face with such venom beggared belief. He had ridden home on the cold, dark road to London imbued with the justified anger of the self-righteous and then lain awake all night castigating himself for poking his nose in when, patently, he should have left well alone for all the thanks he received. There was proud and there was stupid.

Why should he care what became of her? She wasn't his responsibility. She was nothing to him... Nothing!

Except he couldn't quite bring himself to believe *that* lie—because she was something to him. He wasn't entirely sure what, or entirely certain what he felt about it, but he did know he hated to think of her co-existing beneath the same sky as him and hating him.

That uncomfortable truth proved to be a gateway for many others and forced him to do a great deal of introspection over the subsequent day while he licked his wounds in town. Hiding again, but this time from a woman who barely reached his shoulder rather than a house he would rather forget he owned, and one who had the power to prick his conscience, prod at his heart and who called to his soul without uttering a word.

Thanks to her, it had been the single most unproductive day of his professional life. He couldn't focus on his pressing case preparations at all, so in desperation had headed to Newgate to see if he could break the last remaining three traitors who were determined to take their chances with the jury. A huge error of judgement, because he lost his temper, when he prided himself on never losing his temper. Yet for some reason, the cool, calm, reasonable lawyer he was had packed his bags and disappeared somewhere on the long road from Chafford Grange alongside the emotional numbness he felt so comfortable with.

He blamed Penny entirely for that. Thanks to her and her blasted hat analogy, he couldn't stop remembering his mother. His mother had loved a hat. Ridiculous confections with wide brims and tall feathers that always matched her vivid gowns. For a woman with sedate tastes in decor and furniture, her vibrant choice of gowns might have surprised some, but they matched her character to perfection. She had been vibrant. Fun, whimsical. He could once again hear her laughter, which he had adored, and her horrendous singing, which had grated on each one of his nerves. Yet despite her lack of talent, she had loved to sing and dance. She had taught him to waltz one weekend when the snow had been so deep outside they couldn't risk going out. He had been reluctant. She had been relentless.

A force of nature.

Much like Penny in many ways. Neither woman had allowed the pockets of bad in their lives to suffocate their spirit. Neither liked to wear the hat of victim. Both were proud and stubborn and not afraid to put him in his place. His mother would have approved of Penny.

Good grief, he missed her. Missed the sight of her in the mornings before he started his working day, missed the quiet way she made him take regular breaks or ensured everyone's comfort. The lilting sound of her voice in the hallway. The glimpses he stole of her with Freddie in the garden every afternoon, where she swung him around and laughed with such joyful abandon he was always tempted to join them, but never did because he didn't want to encroach. The proud set of her shoulders when she refused to budge. The way he could always see the truth swirling in her lovely blue eyes. The way his body reacted to her presence every single time she was near. The way she had kissed him. Made his house feel a lot like home again.

His rooms in the Albany felt so impersonal and empty now. Soulless. He longed for home. He longed for her.

Then Hadleigh had sat bolt upright in bed. Wondering why the blazes he was trying to sleep when he needed to make it right? Hastily, he had pulled on fresh clothes and stuffed more in a bag. Necessity meant he had to head back there in the morning anyway, he reasoned. There was so much work to do, travelling back and forth would only waste time. It was his house, for pity's sake—his *home*—so he was perfectly entitled to stay in it and if he was there, constantly under her nose, they would have to muddle through all the awkwardness anyway and reach an accord. Besides, he had things to tell her. So many things he had no idea where to start or how to explain it. But she was right, damn her. He had to face his demons, because since she had forced him to see how they controlled him still, he now realised how much they defined him...when he was so much more than that.

Like a madman possessed, he'd piled papers and documents and legal reference books on to his desk, then scratched out a note to his valet ordering to have the lot delivered to Chafford Grange as soon as he woke up, alongside more clothes and his shaving gear. Only then had he retrieved his bewildered horse from the stables and ridden it through the small hours to be where she was.

Now that he was here, he realised it was still more night than morning. The house was plunged into darkness. And while there were soft lamps burning for the men on the watch, there were still a few hours before the first servants would rise and a few more before he would see her at breakfast.

He considered heading directly to the music room and working, but knew he would be incapable of concentrating until he had spoken to her, so instead took the servants' stairs, creeping quietly to his memory-free guest room to wait out the rest of the night and try to get all the words he wanted to say in an order in which they would be coherent.

'Lord Hadleigh?' Her dark head appeared out of a crack in her door and he winced. 'Are you aware that it is only three o'clock?'

'I'm sorry… I didn't mean to wake you.'

'You didn't. Freddie did. Again. Over an hour ago and now I am wide awake.' Her eyes drifted to the fat satchel in his hand and then back up to his with alarm. 'Please tell me you didn't just ride all the way here…all alone? In the dead of night when anything could have happened to you!'

That sounded encouragingly like she still cared, and he found himself smiling. 'I couldn't sleep…and I have all these *things* whirring in my head.' It was late. He was irrational. But so relieved to see her. 'I don't suppose you could spare me an hour tomorrow to tell you a long, rambling and doubtless disjointed story which will probably make no sense? Only I seem to have lost the ability to be thorough and meticulous because I need to get it out.'

Her door opened fully and she stood in the space with her arms folded, her bare toes just poking beneath the lacy hem of her nightrail. 'I could spare you an hour now, if you'd like.' She gestured behind him with a nod of her head. 'Why don't you drop of your bag while I fetch you something to drink? You look frozen to the bone.'

It had been icy, he supposed, because he recalled how his breath had made clouds swirl around his face, but he had been so consumed with the need to get to her he had ignored it—but it explained why his hands, feet and nose felt numb. Yet, for once, the rest of him didn't. There were feelings, hundreds of them, all so confusing and jumbled, vying for attention and a good airing, he didn't know where to start to attempt to unpick them.

But he did as she asked, dropping the heavy satchel on his mattress and wandering back to her room. Discarded next to her chair was her embroidery hoop. Without thinking he picked it up and chuckled. The design was crude, the colours garish, the stitching uneven. How marvellous. She was no embroiderer, but persisted regardless. How perfectly…Penny.

'It's a shocking mess, isn't it?' She was carrying a decanter and two glasses. 'But I cannot bring myself to give it up. Despite my lack of talent, I've always found it relaxing.'

'My mother used to embroider.'

'Was she any good at it?'

'She was. Excellent, in fact. But she often used her skills for evil. She sent me off to university completely unaware that she had stitched flowers on my drawers for her own amusement. Roses, periwinkles, daisies…a different, huge and flamboyant display on every single pair.'

'Poor you.' But she was smiling as she poured them both a brandy and handed one to him before sitting opposite him. 'That was evil.'

'There was, apparently, a practical reason, too.' Inadvertently, the memory had offered him a way in. 'She wanted those flowers to make me think twice before I—' how to put it delicately? '—sowed too many wild oats.'

'Did she succeed?'

'Not entirely… I sowed my fair share…but I had more pertinent reasons to be discerning than the bright pink peonies festooned over my unmentionables.' Hadleigh took a deep breath. Sat forward in his chair. It was long past time to tackle those demons head on. 'My father had syphilis. Was riddled with it, actually. It is what killed him. Frankly, hardly a surprise because he was an indiscriminate and *undiscerning* philanderer. The disease ate at his brain and rendered him mad by the end. He was only fifty-five.'

'Is that what made him violent?' Clearly she understood he needed to purge himself.

'No. That was there all along, he always had a violent temper, but it exacerbated it. He was a cold man. Uninterested most of the time in anything not about himself. The awful temper only showed itself occasionally. Of course, I might be wrong for we rarely saw him. After I was born my parents lived largely separate lives. He stayed in London, in close range of the hells or brothels he enjoyed, or with his latest mistress. He always had at least one on the go. Usually more. He never hid that and if my mother disapproved of his lifestyle she hid it well. Even as a child I understood she disliked the man she had married. It was a loveless union and she did once confess not of her choosing. But she loved his estate. Loved living in this house.'

'The pride she took in it is evident everywhere. This is a beautiful house.'

'She would be pleased to hear that…' It would be easy

to change tack now and avoid the demons, but it would give him little temporary relief rather than exorcise them as he knew he should. Purging himself here with Penny was a necessary first step. 'As the disease progressed, that part of his character became more prominent until eventually there was nothing else left.' Hadleigh took a sip of his brandy. Dutch courage. The amber liquid felt smooth and warm on his tongue, but did nothing to ease the pain. 'I suppose I first learned of the violence the summer I turned fifteen. He had been ill and had come home to convalesce. I have no idea if that was anything to do with the syphilis or even if he had the pox at that stage. My parents kept it from me, but I do know that the oasis I had grown up in changed that year. The smallest thing would ignite his temper and the way it exploded and stole away all reason was terrifying. They would argue behind closed doors— usually in either his bedchamber or hers—although now that I think about it, those arguments were one-sided. I heard his ranting, never hers. That's when the *clumsiness* started with a vengeance and she would tell lies about how she acquired the bruises.'

'She wanted to protect you.'

'And I wanted to protect her, but she wouldn't let me. It was my mother who locked the doors to prevent me barging in. I assume now that was to ensure he never took his temper out on me, but I would rather he had. I felt so powerless. And I hated him! So much it began to gnaw away at me. I planned to kill him. A foolish, childish plan which I had all meticulously worked out. I was going to shoot him late one night on the toll road and blame it on footpads. I had stolen my grandfather's old pistol from the gun cabinet, lead and shot and I spent that entire summer learning to shoot the damn thing. I took out so much anger on those targets…'

His voice petered out and he sighed. 'But when push came to shove, I couldn't do it. I had him in my sights. Drunk on the road, exactly as I had envisaged it, yet I couldn't pull the blasted trigger.'

'Of course you couldn't.' He felt her hand brush his arm and brought his other up to capture it, needing the contact. 'You are a man of high principles. Never regret refusing to compromise them that night. It would have been a dreadful burden to bear.'

'Better than knowing my father killed my mother when I was too busy studying for my own selfish reasons far away? I don't think so.'

'He killed her.' She intertwined her fingers with his, her expression distraught on his behalf, and he gripped them for all he was worth. 'Here at Chafford Grange?' He watched fat tears gather on those ridiculously long lashes, swell, then trickle slowly down her cheeks. Tears for his mother. Tears for him. Tears that humbled him. His own eyes prickled with a decade's worth of unshed tears. He bit his back and tried to be matter of fact to get the rest of the gruelling story out.

'Yes. Here. I am not altogether sure how it happened, but it was late. Past bedtime. The servants heard him shouting and her trying to placate him, but by the time they had run to her aid it was too late. They found her at the bottom of the stairs.' Hadleigh felt his voice choke. 'She was already dead.'

'You blame yourself.'

'I should have been there.' He practically gulped down the rest of his brandy as he allowed the anger to burn. Feeling more comfortable with that than the grief which sliced like a sabre and demanded release. 'I begged her to leave not a week before, asked her to come back with me to London, but she refused to leave her home or him in his hour of need. She felt sorry for him, can you believe that? Didn't want him to have to face dying all alone when even his wits had deserted him.'

'That she could was testament to the sort of woman she was.'

'She was stubborn.'

'A trait you both share. What happened to your father?'

'He died a few months later. Unlike her, I happily allowed him to do so all alone and good riddance to him. That was nearly ten years ago. I keep thinking what a significant milestone that is. *Ten* whole years when I remember it all as if it were yesterday.'

'Of course you do. From my own experiences of losing a parent, the pain never goes. You just find a way to cope with it. For me, I always try to focus on the good memories for they are the most fitting tribute to the two wonderful people who raised me.'

'My memories are too bad. Too painful. Wrapped in guilt and layered with regrets.'

'Is that why you never came here?'

He nodded, swallowing past the tight knot of emotion which was making it so very hard to breathe. 'I'd managed to avoid it and block it out of my mind till you came along and I reopened Pandora's box.' He sighed, accepting defeat, and shook his head. 'That's not entirely true...' They both deserved the truth, although whatever that truth was he was yet to rationalise it. 'This year I killed a man, Penny... Saint-Aubin.'

'The monster who imprisoned Jessamine?'

Hadleigh nodded. 'And the strangest thing is I am not the least bit sorry for it. In *that* moment, when faced with the stark choice of either killing him or allowing him to kill my friend, I aimed and fired without a second thought— but that has stirred things up in here.' He tapped his head.

'Reminding me that I had the chance to do it before and failed to step up to the mark.'

He must have allowed the full extent of that burden to show on his face, all the guilt and shame at his inadequacy, because she cupped his cheek tenderly, smoothing the lines of pain which etched themselves deep in his face, and sighed. 'You are wrong to punish yourself.'

'Am I?'

'You are hardly comparing like with like. The decisions we have to make in the heat of the moment are different from those which are premeditated. I am hardly surprised you found it easy to do one and struggled with the latter. For a man who lives determined to right wrongs, I know you would not have been able to live with yourself if you had murdered a defenceless man on the road. That would have been wholly and morally wrong—and you are too noble. Nor would your mother had wanted you to carry such a burden. She would have been devastated to have caused it. We mothers are conditioned to only want happiness for our children at whatever cost it happens to come to for ourselves. And as much as you claim you are not the least bit sorry for killing Saint Aubin, killing another human—no matter how monstrous they happen to be—would weigh heavily on the mind. Especially when one is so dedicated to upholding right over wrong as you are. The trauma of that decision, the knowledge you had ended another's life, would always have deep emotional consequences. Therefore, it is hardly surprising it dredged up the last time you aimed a gun at a man as a frightened boy and the tragic, senseless death of your mother years later. But you are wrong to question yourself. In both situations, you acted justly.'

'Maybe, but it's forced open Pandora's box and now I cannot, for the life of me, shut it again...' Unpleasant noise and destructive chaos. He fought the overwhelming urge to weep, not because he thought she might judge him because her tears were still openly flowing, but because he knew that if he allowed just one tear to escape, then the dam would burst and he wasn't entirely prepared for those most powerful of emotions yet. 'So to finally answer your question from the rose garden, yes, you do remind me of her a little bit. Or at least your situations do. Penhurst and my father were cut from the same cloth. You and my mother both suffered at their hands. Those similarities, alongside the niggling echoes created by passing the milestone of a decade, churned it all up and I've been mired in the past ever since. It is as if my past has decided enough is enough. It's there. Hovering. I can't hide from it and I can't ignore it.'

He risked looking at her then and something peculiar happened to his heart. Beneath his ribs it felt as if it was opening like one of his mother's summer roses, reawakening after a long hibernation. More feelings swamped him and this time he let them. This was necessary. Cathartic. He was tired of running from it or burying it. Tired of keeping it all locked within because it was eating him from the inside. The protective numbness was lifting and leaving him vulnerable. Burying himself in his work no longer worked. For some reason, his mind had taken itself back ten years and was demanding the right to process thoroughly all that had transpired.

'I realise I need to face it, because you are annoyingly correct. I cannot make amends for my guilt regarding my mother by bestowing it on you. Helping you is something I find myself naturally wanting to do.' He allowed his thumb to trace circles on her skin. Accepted the strong emotions he felt towards her. Not pity or guilt at all, but affection. Tenderness. Absolute trust. Probably more. 'And being able to be there for you makes me feel…content, but Pandora's blasted box is still there lurking in the background. Waiting for me to properly look inside and face it.'

'And do you now know what is in it?'

'My mother.' Easy to answer. 'Guilt—misplaced or otherwise. Regret. Sadness. Pain. I've spent the past two days thinking about her. It probably sounds daft to you, but I haven't allowed myself to think about her since it happened. She died and I felt numb. I still felt numb when I put her safely in the ground and then I carried on with my life.'

'It sounds to me as if you didn't allow yourself to grieve.'

'Again, my clever Penny, you are annoyingly correct. I am not comfortable with emotions. It was easier to bury myself in work and hide behind the numbness than face it all. My mother would be livid. She was always so adamant she wanted extensive weeping and wailing. She enjoyed a bit of drama.' He smiled at the memory, felt a single tear form and allowed it to fall, closing his eyes as her thumb gently brushed it away, feeling entirely overwhelmed and totally lost. Clearly, the dam which had held firm for a decade was about to collapse and it was unlikely to be pretty. 'I should go…' Although he didn't want to. He was so tired of being all alone.

'Please stay.' Before he could stand, she did. 'Extensive weeping and wailing should never be a solitary pursuit. Besides, just like you, I am exceedingly good in a crisis. It is one of my strengths. Let me be here for you.' She wrapped her arms around him and enveloped him in what felt a lot like love, that one elusive and powerful emotion which had been missing for far too long. For the first time in years, and despite all the overwhelming grief threatening to engulf him, Hadleigh no longer felt all alone. When he heard her quiet sobs on his behalf, they proved to be his undoing and he stopped fighting. Burying his face against her middle, he finally let the dam burst.

Chapter Sixteen

He had no clue how long he wept for, but he was grateful she was there. Was grateful for the reassurance of her unwavering embrace, her strength, her mumbled soothing words of comfort, her tears, the feel of her fingers in his hair and the steady beat of her heart against his ear. All reminded him that there was life beyond the pain—but that this pain was necessary to move forward. When the worst was over, she seemed to sense he now needed space to recover from it all, insisting on fetching him hot tea from the kitchen because everything was better after a cup of tea. It gave him time to compose himself, rinse his face with water and ponder the unstoppable explosion of uncomfortable emotion properly.

Bizarrely, although undoubtedly hugely embarrassing, noisy and chaotic, it had been cathartic. And completely draining. He felt as if he could sleep for a week, which would indeed be a blessing if he could manage it. It had been too long since he had slept soundly.

She appeared at the doorway with a tray and smiled. 'I've brought some biscuits up, too. I seem to recall I ate a phenomenal amount of them after my mother died.'

He felt awkward and stupid and vulnerable, but ridiculously happy she had returned. 'Did they help?'

'With hindsight, probably not, but they gave me something pleasant to do between the constant bouts of crying. I had Freddie by the time my father passed away, so he kept me occupied.' She deposited the tray on the table and passed him the entire plate. 'How are you feeling?'

'Odd. Not quite myself. Embarrassed that you had to witness it.'

'Would it make you feel less foolish if I told you that I am vastly relieved that you finally found the courage to grieve? When I first met you, I found your ability to conceal your emotions unnerving. In truth, it was a little off-putting. I like that you feel things deeply, that you are human and care. My father was a very sentimental man. I grew up in a house where his stiff upper lip would constantly quiver—usually with happiness or pride or nostalgia. After living with a man who was incapable of feeling natural human emotion, let alone display it, it restores my faith in men to know that it was my husband who was abnormal. Besides, I am contractually obliged to keep secrets, remember, so it's not as if I would dare to tell another soul even if I had a mind to. Which of course I don't. You needed to face your fears and you did. If anything, I am inordinately proud of you and I dare say your mother would be thrilled she finally received some decent weeping and wailing.'

'She would and she was due it. So was I. Because I now see that beyond the pain and guilt there are a million other memories—all surprisingly happy. In ruthlessly blocking out all the bad to keep the pain at bay, I lost sight of all the good. Not at all a fitting memorial to the woman who made me what I am.'

'There is still time to make proper amends and honour her memory as it should be. We all grieve differently and time and tears eventually heal all wounds. That I know, too.'

'You are a very wise woman, Penny.' He smiled and realised he wasn't sad or confused or angry any longer. He simply felt better. Purged. Not completely, but the process had started. 'For the record, I blame your hat analogy entirely. It forced me into uncomfortable soul-searching.'

She smiled. 'Analogies will do that. My current one involves coins, ironically, but has done much the same thing. Clearly the last few days have been a time for soul-searching for both of us.'

'Was yours as fruitful?'

'Very.'

'I'd love to hear it if you'd like to share your findings.' Because he wasn't ready to leave her yet. The cosy atmosphere and intimacy in this room felt special and necessary. Like a balm to his soul. A soul that was, perhaps, a little less troubled now that he had bared it and said it all out loud. Over the coming days he would face it all. Confront every fear, remember everything which deserved remembering, empty out every nightmare inside the locked box in his mind, probably allow himself to cry a good deal more and try to find enough peace with it all to let it go.

'Well... I've been thinking about me and the hats I want to wear.'

'I thought this analogy involved coins?'

The giggle was accompanied by a playful nudge. Hadleigh enjoyed both immensely. 'Did I interrupt you during your crisis?'

'A fair point. Do continue.'

'Since the trial, I've been so busy trying to invent the new Penny, I had forgotten the old. When, in truth, they are both two sides of the same coin... What was there beforehand combined with what has been tarnished by life's experiences. And I have come to the conclusion, there is no new Penny—nor can there ever be. Does that make sense?'

'Not really. Other than the coin you are referring to is you. I think this new analogy of yours needs work.'

She laughed again and he decided it was the very best sound in the world. 'Then I'll go back to the hats, seeing that your poor, addled brain understands that.'

'A splendid idea. Thanks to Pandora, my brain has turned to mush. Which hat are we currently talking about?'

'The new one I've been trying for size. It doesn't feel right. I need to stop being the version of me I think I should be or the version other people think I should be. My "Poor Penelope the Viscountess Penhurst" bonnet and the fictitious Penny Henley's ill-fitting mob cap have been resigned to the rubbish pile where they belong. Neither suit me.' She shrugged and smiled wistfully. 'I'm going back to being Penny Ridley. Back to being what I am. I have decided I am going to take my fifty guineas and rent out premises in Cheapside and dust off my shopkeeper's hat. I'm going to reopen Ridley's.'

He couldn't hide his concern. 'Is that wise…it is still so soon? Once the newspapers get hold of it, then they will drag everything up again.'

'What better time than now? It's all bound to get dragged up again anyway with this new trial. Penhurst may be dead, but he was still part of all that. Yet life moves on and scandals pass. Ultimately, I never did anything wrong and so have nothing to be ashamed of. I need to stop behaving as though I have. I am done with hiding. Done with trying to flee the past or pretend it didn't happen. I don't want it to sneak up on me unexpectedly in the future and bring shame or scorn on Freddie. As you now know, it's better to face your demons because you cannot outrun them indefinitely. I intend to carry on regardless and refuse to let them define me. People might turn up their noses at the beginning, but I have my mother's eye for what will sell and my father's talent for selling it, so they will come around in the end.'

He felt immensely proud of her, too. 'Then allow me to correct my previous statement. You are a very brave *and* wise woman, Penny.'

'And you are a very tired and very brave man, Lord Hadleigh. You look exhausted and, I fear, urgently need your bed.'

She stood and dragged him up with both hands. Hands some devil inside of him refused to let go of. 'It is long past time you dropped the lord bit.'

'Because Hadleigh is so much more personable? I have never understood that about titled men. The title is always there regardless. An abrupt punctuation to prove to each other how important you all are. Hadleigh, Flint… Penhurst.' She rolled her eyes at the last and made a face. 'Yet another hat—but an ostentatious one. Do you know I was never given leave to call him anything else? How ridiculous is that?'

'Then clearly it is also time to resurrect my Christian name, although it might take me a while to answer to it again. I haven't heard it for ten years…it's Tristan.'

'Like the medieval knight?'

'My mother was a hopeless romantic as well as an evil embroiderer and thwarter of inadvisable romantic conquests.'

'It suits you… I suppose a barrister is the modern equivalent of one of the knights of old. Defenders of justice and damsels in distress.'

A crusading righter of wrongs. Him in a nutshell. 'Even if they are no longer in distress.'

'I've long thrown away my distressed bonnet. I loathed that thing.' She tugged him to the door. 'Goodnight, Tristan…what's left of it. Sleep tight.'

As he was about to leave he remembered the items in his pocket. 'Here…seeing as tonight was a night for honesty, I wanted to give you these.' He pulled out the old jewellery and place the lot in the centre of her palm. 'I bought them back from the pawnbroker. Please don't shout at me.'

She stared at the precious pile of trinkets for the longest time before her eyes lifted again to his. They were swimming with tears again. Sentimental tears of happiness. 'Oh, Tristan…what am I going to do about you?' Then she kissed him.

She considered telling herself she had intended it to be an innocent kiss, merely a brief, chaste expression of gratitude for returning the last earthly remnants of her mother, but realised that had not at all been her intention the second her lips had touched his. But the truth was Penny had wanted to kiss him because he had thoroughly overwhelmed her with his thoughtfulness, with his openness and by simply being him. She felt affection for him, that was undeniable, but it was more than the sort of affection bestowed upon a friend or a family member. This was different because attraction and, miraculously, lust was involved. Something she never thought she would experience after Penhurst. Somehow, the man in front of her had sneaked past the walls of her hardened heart to the romantic core which clearly still beat at its centre.

Worrying.

Perplexing.

Thrilling.

Just as it had the first time, soft and tender quickly turned to more and she welcomed it, wanting to touch him and feel him touch her, happily surrendering to the power of the sensual spell the kiss created. Those sensations were all so new and gloriously addictive. But it was Penny who reluctantly ended it this time. She stepped away, smiling when he tried to tug her back. 'We are both tired…you are vulnerable…and I don't want either of us to continue this with anything clouding our judgement. Go to bed, Tristan, and sleep. Tomorrow, apparently, we have a house full. Eleven people and one mad dog? Followed by the Attorney General himself later in the week. Significant details you neglected to mention.'

He looked delightfully sheepish. 'Ah…yes. I meant to send you a message about that, but…'

'You were in high dudgeon.' She couldn't resist the eye roll. 'But fortunately, Lord Fennimore had the good sense to tell Harriet, who in turn passed word on to me. So I must spend tomorrow readying the place for them and you have hours of important trial work to do… Fortunately Harriet also mentioned the trial had been brought forward so I am expecting it will be all hands on deck.'

'Yes, it will. We are almost there. I want to present it in a completed state to the Attorney General when he arrives later this week. I've been cross-referencing all the evidence we have with witness statements, organising the order to present my investigation and call the witnesses. All in all, I am confident. I firmly believe we have enough to convince the Lords of the guilt of all seven of the treason as well as the smuggling.'

'The Lords rather than a jury?'

'Unlike your husband's trial where the Crown decided to make a point, the six peers charged alongside Viscountess Gislingham were not impeached before the trial. Therefore, they can elect to be tried in the House rather than the court, which they have. The defence clearly believes they might receive greater leniency by their peers rather than a jury of potentially lesser men.'

'Does that bother you?'

'It is standard practice for peers, regardless of the severity of the charges, to seek justice in Parliament. The structure of the court is the same. All the Lords can witness the trial, but the proceedings will be overseen by the Lord High Steward assisted by a smaller group of legally minded lords who will act as the jury. As in any trial, there will be witnesses called and the accused will be defended and prosecuted by trained lawyers—the only difference is those barristers must be allowed to speak in the House.'

'By that you mean they need to be peers—like you?'

'Exactly. Occasionally, being my father's son has its rewards—few though they may be.'

'Will they be more lenient, do you suppose?'

'With treason as part of the charges, and in view of the seriousness of this case and the way it has been widely reported, I sincerely doubt it. To be frank, the fact it is in the Lords might well work in our favour. Had I been defending those men, I would have cautioned against holding the trial in the House. If the evidence is strong and the arguments conclusive, it would take a brave peer to query it. This smuggling ring had infiltrated the highest echelons of the British aristocracy and threatened both the economy and the safety of these shores. Most will be keen to make an example of them.'

'To prove their own loyalty, I dare say.'

'There are other benefits. The proceedings will be closed to the press. They can hound the witnesses outside, but not within, as they did you.'

'There was one reporter who used to sit in front of me and draw me every day.'

Hadleigh sighed. 'I know. I used to watch him and regularly had to fight the urge to rip his sketchbook to shreds or bash him over the head with it. But you dealt with it with more grace than they showed. I was proud of you.'

'What doesn't kill us makes us stronger.'

'An adage I need to adopt. Right now, with all the past clouding my head alongside all the speeches and arguments I still need to construct for the case, I am in danger of becoming buried beneath it all.' He seemed suddenly deflated. 'If feels like a mountain to climb in only ten days.'

'One which you will climb triumphantly once you are rested, of that I am in no doubt. You are the most meticulous lawyer, after all. Everybody says so—not that I would need their word on the matter, having witnessed it myself.' And there it was again. The trial. Her awful marriage. Demons she had faced and come to terms with, yet still pieces of her past which she couldn't seem to whitewash over no matter how hard she tried. Maybe they would fade once this last trial was over?

'And what about us and that kiss? Both kisses, in fact? We are yet to discuss either and what they mean.' Her stomach clenched and she fought the urge to swallow nervously. Perhaps she hadn't faced all her demons, although to be fair, after Penhurst she had been certain she would never feel the inclination to need to face this one. Another man had never been on the horizon—even temporarily— so why bother?

But now she wanted to bother. Which meant she had to lift the lid on her own box, dredge up horrid memories and do some heart-searching of her own. 'Yet more confusion to cloud your judgement—do you really need that now?'

'I fear I will be mired in cloudiness unless I know. Please don't make me wait weeks for your answer?'

'Very well. Once the day is done tomorrow and we have pondered it all with clear heads, we should talk. Properly. And decide whether to blame it all on the fraught circumstances in which we find ourselves or whether it is something we...explore again when there are no excuses to stand in our way.'

'I know already which I want.' She watched the golden flecks in his dark amber eyes turn molten and that sight alone made her wonder why she was stalling. 'But tonight *has* been fraught and, as much as it galls me to agree with you, I do feel, if not vulnerable, then certainly off-kilter. We are also both tired, so perhaps we do need time to digest it all with a level head. For me, that means considering more than kissing you. I doubt I'll ever stop wanting to do that.' He took both her hands in his, his gaze locked thrillingly on hers, and brought them to his lips. 'Until tomorrow, then...and cloudless heads. And no more excuses.'

Chapter Seventeen

Penny had been doing a great deal of further soul-searching all day, listening to the different voices in her mind and their conflicting advice until there was so much of it, none of it made sense. Two hours ago, once dinner was cleared and the house full of noisy guests were all happily ensconced in the drawing room with Tristan, she had returned to the privacy of her own sitting room, determined to come to a conclusion. She had played with Freddie, bathed him and stroked his silky curls till he fell asleep, then she had sat at her table with paper and a pen. Seeing that all else had prevented her from seeing the wood for the trees, perhaps one of Tristan's lists would do the trick? She would compare the pros and the cons and hope the truth would show itself.

Do you want to kiss Tristan again?

After writing those words, she underlined them to mark their importance, because this was not a decision she was prepared to take lightly.

Reasons not to: it muddies the water.

There was no denying that, whether it be employer versus servant or Crown Prosecutor versus Defence Witness, theirs was an unconventional relationship.

I don't know what I want from it?

His words last night had stayed with her and bothered her. *For me, that means considering more than kissing you.*

Did that mean he wanted an affair or was there a chance he was suggesting a future? She didn't know and needed to before any decision could be made. Penny had not considered another future with a man once since the day Penhurst had died. Not once. In all the scenarios she envisaged for her new life, the only male in them had been Freddie. She had assumed her horrid husband had succeeded in putting her off men for life. Apparently not…but did that follow that she wanted another man for life? In the short term, she was more than tempted. Anything more made her feel uneasy, so…

Is he worth sacrificing my new-found independence for?

She sat for several minutes mulling that one over and then shook her head at her own indecision. Why was she even thinking about such a thing after everything she had gone through? She liked standing on her own two feet and that was that. She scratched out the question and replaced it with a statement.

I will not give another person control over me ever again.

Much more decisive!

Am I ready for intimacy?

A tricky one, and doubtless jumping the gun, but one she had to face if she did kiss him again. Because kissing was not ultimately what she would be signing up for and, while his were quite lovely, the expectation would be that kissing turned into more and Penny had uncomfortable memories of *more*.

While she had indulged in a few kisses with other suitors before her hasty marriage and enjoyed them, and she had definitely enjoyed a certain handsome barrister's since, she had never been intimate with any man other than Penhurst. And while Tristan was nothing like him in character, looks or physique, the process would be the same. His body would join with hers in exactly the same way. It didn't matter that Harriet and the Dowager had come right out and said they had thoroughly enjoyed the physical aspect of their relationships and had reassured her it would feel entirely different with the right man. Their bodies weren't *her* body. Hers had never worked that way.

What if hers failed to feel any passion as things progressed to the act itself? With Penhurst it had been an intrusion, one she had endured with gritted teeth at first until she had discovered that she could block out his relentless pummelling simply by transporting her mind elsewhere. Would she have to resort to that with Tristan—and if she did, would he be able to tell she abhorred it? Penhurst had never given a moment's thought to her, so it had never mattered, but Tristan was too thoughtful and her lack of passion would wound him. He'd take it personally and then what? Or did she want to endure something which gave her no pleasure? Of course not. That would be merely jumping out of the frying pan and into the fire.

Will Tristan also find me unattractive?

This was a niggling, deep-rooted fear which had been newly reawakened since their first kiss. Because, as much as it galled her to give Penhurst any power over her now, even if she took a leap of faith and assumed her body could respond with passion, what if his constant complaints about her lack of allurements were correct? Their couplings had taken place in the dark, she had always been wearing her nightgown because he delighted in telling her that her naked body was not the slightest bit seductive. She had hardened herself to those criticisms, eventually coming to realise they were all designed to control and manipulate her, or to simply make her feel wretched like the unflattering dour dresses or the rationed time with Freddie—because Penhurst had bizarrely found excitement in her pain. But what if her breasts weren't big enough? Or her curves tempting enough? She had carried a child since the last time and that had left its marks upon her skin. What if Tristan's passions faltered at the sight of her? Could she bear that? Was she brave enough to face that with a man she was coming to care about a great deal?

She didn't know.

Reasons to kiss him: his kisses feel divine.

It was perfectly acceptable for widows to indulge in brief affairs.

Curiosity.

There was no denying that. It was driving her mad, wondering if things might be different with another man, especially as her body was responding to him differently already and they had only kissed twice. She recalled the

Dowager's wise words and decided to jot them down as a point all by themselves.

What better way to forget the awful chore of the marriage bed, than finding passion with another who is willing?

I like him.

She stared at those insipid three words and shook her head. Good grief! If she couldn't be honest on her own private piece of paper, then she really was a coward. Decisively she drew a line through them and replaced them with the truth.

I have a deep affection for him.

He was kind and noble. The way he treated Freddie melted her heart. He was maddening and stubborn—but also not too pompous or proud to admit when he had done things wrong. And of course...

I find him very attractive.

She underlined this three times. Shallow, perhaps, but there it was. He was broad and golden and filled his breeches exceptionally well. And his eyes... Heavens, they were something to behold, especially when they burned with passion for her. Just thinking about it made her feel all warm and ripe and—

The light tap on her door had her jumping guiltily out of her skin. That was quickly followed by shame at what she was doing.

'Penny?' His voice was low and silky, filled with forbidden promise, and her insides melted like butter.

'One moment!' Guiltily she snatched up her list and

looked frantically for a place to hide it quickly. Why were there no drawers in this silly room? In desperation she stuffed it under the nest of threads in her sewing basket and then scurried to the door, patting her hair and smoothing down her dress. Realising, too late, that this dress was a statement in itself. What had possessed her to change into it? Red was the colour of passion and seduction and the neckline! It was too daring for a sensible discussion about kisses. He would think she had worn it in invitation!

Which, of course, she had. Because...

She wanted to.

The list she had just made proved that. Four reasons against and five for. The truth in glaring black and white.

Her hand shook slightly as she opened the door and her knees felt weak to see him stood behind it. He was so handsome—and she was going to kiss him again.

Gracious!

'Come in.' Nerves had her pulse beating like an out-of-time drum in her head. She had no idea what to do with her hands, then felt a fool for clasping them behind her back. 'You should probably sit down.' And she should probably calm down or she was in grave danger of babbling and hopping from foot to foot on the spot like a ninny.

He sat on the sofa and she dithered, having no idea if she should immediately sit next to him or perch on the chair opposite. She stared at it, hoping it might give her the answer.

'Should I take your desire to sit there as a bad sign?'

'No! Er...no. I am just a bit nervous.'

'Then that makes two of us.' He smiled and she felt marginally less silly. 'Just sit, Penny.'

She did. On the chair. Then her mind went a total blank. 'I have no idea what to say.'

'Well, if we avoid what is bound to be an awkward preamble while we both dance painfully around the issue, I suppose it all boils down to one thing. Will there be a third kiss or not?' He looked her dead in the eye. 'And I am afraid that has to be entirely your decision. Because I shall go out on a limb and state I am all for it. I find myself quite besotted with you, Penny. So much so, I can barely think straight.'

Out of nowhere, massive butterflies began flapping in her stomach at his pretty and heartfelt confession and unwittingly her hand went to her abdomen to calm them. His eyes dropped to it, then rose to meet hers, staring intently while he waited for her verdict. For a second, she seriously considered running away, because this was a big decision. A positively *huge* leap of faith. One that frankly terrified her now that the time for mulling and pondering was done. She wasn't certain she was ready for it—and all that went along with it—but then would she ever be? There was every chance the longer she debated the wisdom of it, the less chance there was of her doing what her body plainly wanted her to do. And then, out of sheer cowardice, she was giving Penhurst power over her from beyond the grave.

That settled it once and for all. Six to four on the should. 'I suppose we could give it a try.'

He exhaled loudly and she watched his mouth curve upwards in amusement. 'Not quite the giddy yes I was hoping for, but I shall take it.'

Now what? 'Shall I fetch some tea? Some brandy?' Should she offer him a snack perhaps, or should she attempt some small talk? What exactly was the correct etiquette in this sort of situation? She risked glancing at him for some sort of direction and the wretch was still smiling. 'Are you laughing at me?'

'I am trying not to, but you are making it very hard. I have never seen you so jittery.'

'Perhaps we should just get it over with?'

'Be still my beating heart...' But he had stood and easily closed the distance between them. He took her hand and tugged her to stand. Then tortured her frayed nerves by gently brushing his index finger down her cheek. 'Have I told you that you look particularly lovely this evening?' His lips brushed her forehead, trailed down to the exact bit of her skin still tingling from his touch seconds before while that seductive index finger which had caused the tingles had now found the tendril of hair she had left loose by her ear. Involuntarily, she shivered as his warm breath caressed the sensitive spot just beneath it, then held her breath when his lips found it, too. 'I've been dying to taste you here.' His teeth nibbled her earlobe, causing goosebumps to erupt all over her body. He trailed soft kisses all the way down to her collarbone, making her neck arch of its own accord. 'And here.' Who knew clavicles were sensitive? This was all boding very well.

At some point her eyelids must have fluttered closed, because she had not been expecting his mouth to brush against hers just then. She sighed into his, her body instinctively pressed against him, her fingers closing around his lapels, then pulling him closer.

She felt one arm snake its way around her waist as the other cupped her cheek, then gave herself over to the delicious feel of her body opening itself to true passion for the very first time.

He deepened the kiss, but was in no mood to hurry, using his tongue and teeth to seduce her more thoroughly than she had ever allowed herself to be before. An exciting heat pooled between her legs. Her breasts ached to be touched. By the time he wrapped both arms around her, she was already draped shamelessly against his body, her hands fisted in his hair and her wits abandoned completely to the thrilling sensations her senses were bombarded with.

She groaned at Freddie's angry wail, refusing to remove her lips from Tristan's. Only when it became quite apparent her son had no intention of allowing her to indulge in her pleasure any longer, did she reluctantly tear her mouth away. 'I'm sorry… I'll be quick.' Silently, she prayed that just this once her son would settle swiftly.

'Take as long as you need to. I am not going anywhere.'

However, Freddie was in no mood to be compliant and the few minutes she had hoped it would take rapidly turned into half an hour as he insisted on drinking every last drop of the milk she had left warming in a bowl of hot water on his nightstand. Then, as if sensing the odd new tension in his mother's body, he flatly refused to settle until she had to practically wrestle him back to sleep.

When she returned to her sitting room, feeling suddenly self-conscious, Tristan was stood as cool as a cucumber at the window, gazing out. He turned as she entered, his expression odd despite his smile and she hoped the enforced break in proceedings hadn't irrevocably destroyed the mood. He walked towards her and took both of her hands in his, staring down at them. 'I suppose it is time for bed.'

Unease immediately replaced anticipation. 'I suppose it is.' Perhaps this time it would be different, because he was different. Only one thing was absolutely certain: unless she tried it, she would never know and always wonder. Thanks to him. Penny smiled, in what she hoped looked like encouragement. His slipped off his face the second his hands dropped hers and he started towards the door to leave.

He hadn't been referring to intimacies at all.

'Would you like me to come and kiss you again tomorrow?'

She wanted him to continue kissing her some more tonight. 'If you want to.' Disappointment replaced the unease rather than relief that she had been spared. Surely that said something?

'Oh, I want to.' His amber eyes positively sizzled with the truth of it, which in turn made her wonder why he was leaving. 'Goodnight, Penny.' His gaze raked her body slowly…possessively. 'Sleep tight.'

Chapter Eighteen

There were some things you couldn't pretend were unseen. For Hadleigh it was Penny's list. He hadn't been snooping or prying. He had stumbled upon it by accident the second she had left him all alone to see to her crying child. Quite literally. He had been so consumed with the power of what he had now labelled the Kiss to End all Kisses, he had backed towards the chair on slightly unsteady legs, needing to sit, and tripped over her sewing basket. As he knelt to stuff the haphazard mess back into it, he noticed the paper. Then he saw the columns and then, before he could stop himself, he had read the blasted lot.

He still wasn't entirely sure what he felt about it despite leaving it all to ruminate for the day. Even the brisk gallop he had taken across the estate to clear his head hadn't given him any true clarity. Some of it had been very encouraging. She found him handsome, thought his kisses were divine, had a deep affection for him... All music to his ears.

It wasn't the reasons to kiss Tristan which bothered him. It was the reasons not to. Good lord, she had knocked the wind from his sails! There he was, racing headlong into a full-blown romantic attachment and he had given scant consideration to how she was feeling.

He had stupidly assumed she felt the same—excited, happy, consumed with longing and lust and need, when in actual fact she was scared. He had seen that for himself when he had tested her, his words intentionally ambiguous to see how she would react. Her intense reaction to *'I suppose it is time for bed'* had brought him up short. Her fingers had gripped his hands, not with passion, but with alarm, while it was fear which skittered across her expression before she quashed it with a brave, stoic smile which broke his heart.

He couldn't ignore irrefutable evidence. Penny had suffered. Words like *'Am I ready for intimacy?'* and *'forget the awful chore of the marriage bed'* suggested she had low expectations at best and at worst, she was dreading the prospect. Not that he had gone to her last night intent on immediately seducing her, but it had been on the cards at some point in the not-so-distant future because the passion had positively sizzled between them. And as much as he didn't want to have to think about her in the arms of another man, he now *had* to think about her with Penhurst, because the monster had clearly put her off it—or worse.

Worse! He felt sick. And so furious, he wanted to smash the furniture.

What the blazes was number five all about?

Will Tristan also find me unattractive?

What had Penhurst done to make her think such twaddle? Belittled her, no doubt, issuing criticism where there should have been compliments? Or worse?

Worse!

It was a good job The Boss had had him murdered because Hadleigh would have jumped on his horse last night and choked the life out of the bastard with his bare hands otherwise!

None of which would help Penny now—but he could. Hadleigh was going to have to broach the subject with her when the time was right, help her face her demons as she had helped him, then prove to her he would rather never have her than allow her to think it a chore. This was a wrong he could right and gladly so if she would allow him. Of course, she had every right to refuse and he would honour that decision. But if she didn't...well, then he would gift her with something she couldn't return once bestowed. With patience and tenderness. Rather than plunging headlong into full passion, he was going to kiss away her fears and her awful memories of the sexual act with Penhurst. Banish all thoughts of the ridiculous and unfair *number five* from her mind. She was a beautiful woman. Totally perfect. He would prove that to her while waging a sensual assault and a painfully slow seduction to initiate her into the wonderful world of carnal pleasure. Until she begged him to bed her rather than that trembling, martyr-like *'I suppose so'* he had heard last night. She deserved nothing less.

And the wanting was going to kill him.

It couldn't be helped. Penny needed to understand what it meant to be loved by a man.

Loved? He hadn't been expecting that and certainly had not expected to feel perfectly at ease with the concept—if indeed it was a concept. He didn't have to be *in* love with a woman to make love to her, did he? It was merely a turn of phrase. Wasn't it? Although...

He shook his head and decided not to torture himself by analysing one random thought when he had enough on his plate already, if the biggest and most important trial of his career or thoroughly seducing Penny or facing the demons of his past didn't kill him first. As he handed the reins of his horse over to the waiting groom, he took a cleansing breath and stared at his house.

'Hello.' She suddenly appeared from the stables, holding Freddie's hand in hers, her expression pleased to see him tinged with a little shyness. His heart swelled at the sight of her. He had no idea if the pink flush staining her cheeks was because of their kiss last night or the biting cold of the day. 'We've been petting the horses. Have you been riding?'

'I thought I'd best get some fresh air… I have this harridan of a housekeeper who is forcing me to take better care of myself. Can I walk you both back to the house?'

'Of course.'

Hadleigh took Freddie's outstretched little hand, snugly encased in a knitted mitten, and walked slowly alongside. Wordlessly, they both began to swing him as they walked, enjoying his babyish giggles as his tiny booted feet flew up in the air.

They came to the part of the path where it split and she naturally turned towards the kitchens, assuming that would be the entrance he intended to take, because that had been the entrance he had chosen to take since that first visit weeks ago.

'I am going to take the front door, Penny…it's long past time. But I would appreciate your moral support if you don't mind offering it.'

She simply nodded and he was grateful. She didn't offer platitudes or advice. Didn't allow either pity or concern to cloud her expression, instead she continued forward alongside him, both still swinging Freddie in the air.

He paused briefly at the wide stone steps before the door and she waited with him, watched the footman open it and allowed him the brief time he needed to prepare himself for the onslaught. Then together, Freddie still sandwiched between them, they climbed them.

In front of him was the staircase. The unforgiving stone steps rising in a twin arc either side of the imposing atrium. The hard, cold marble floor. He forced himself to look at it all properly, accept the tragedy which had occurred here and then push his memories beyond that. There were so many, they brought a lump to his throat. Good and bad.

The exuberant welcomes when he came home from school. The echoing, hollow sounds of his parents fighting upstairs behind a door. Snippets of long-forgotten inane conversations. *'Don't forget your gloves...'* She was obsessed with him catching a chill while out riding... *'I would like to see the ridiculous bright purple bird that feather belonged to...'* His mother had adored a tall head-dress... *'It's a statement, darling!'*

Then came childish giggles and he looked down at Freddie, assuming it was him. But they weren't. They were from another little boy from another time. A little older than the one holding his hand. Sliding joyously down the banisters encased in the cage of his mother's arms.

'You are smiling.'

He was. His eyes had filled with tears, but he *was* smiling. 'It is not all bad.'

'Of course it isn't. Good always triumphs over bad.' She picked up her son. 'There will be hot tea and cake in the music room once you are done reminiscing. According to my mother, a cup of tea made everything better.'

'I'll take it in the morning room.' The room which he associated the most with his mother.

'Then I'll reinforce the tray with biscuits, too.' With that she left him, clearly sensing, now that he had found the courage to face it, he needed time alone with his past. All of it. Still wearing his coat and clutching his hat, he walked towards the stairs, steeled his shoulders and climbed them.

Penny intended to give him space for an hour before she checked on him, but then the day got in the way. The house full of guests was certainly keeping her busy. Alongside the Flints and the Fennimores, the other King's Elite agent Gray had descended the previous evening with his new wife, Thea, this time, alongside an excitable black dog whose tail wagged so fast it blurred. Freddie had fallen for the hound instantly, the pair becoming fast friends. Thea's Uncle, Viscount Gislingham, the husband of the main traitor soon to be tried, had also come in the same full carriage with his friend, Bertie.

The last two houseguests, Seb and Clarissa, had arrived shortly after she had ordered Tristan's tea tray for the morning room and then her best friend in the world had insisted they have a proper catch up in Penny's sitting room. It had been just the two of them and for the first time in two months they reconnected as friends.

'You look well, Penny! Lighter, somehow…more your old self.'

By old self, she assumed her friend was harking back to the old Penny, the one she had made mischief with in ballrooms and garden parties while flirting with the many gentlemen who had buzzed around them like bees, rather than the downtrodden and largely invisible woman she had been during her marriage. Or the lost and broken shell she had been over the course of the arrest and trial.

'I feel like my old self. I love it here. Having a purpose was exactly what I needed.' A tiny dig, perhaps, seeing that Clarissa had been so against her seeking employment.

'I can see that. You seem to have blossomed. Is that all because of your new purpose?' She made no attempt to hide her intimation or her curiosity. 'Or has something else put the spring back in your step?'

'For the time being, it is the new purpose.' Penny wasn't ready to discuss all her confused thoughts regarding Tristan just yet—not even with her dearest friend. 'I'm going to reopen Ridley's. Nothing quite so grand to begin with, but from little acorns...' Excitedly, she confided in Clarissa all her plans and the reasons behind it, and even when she explained that she was intent on heading back to Cheapside, her friend didn't attempt to caution her against it. Instead, once she learned that the Dowager and Harriet were keen to invest in it, she offered her financial support, too.

'But what about you? If I have blossomed, then you are positively *blooming*. I hope you insisted on this private talk so you can finally confess to me you are expecting— although I've known for a while.'

'You have?' Clarissa appeared stunned at the news.

'The lack of appetite in the mornings...the need to constantly touch your stomach...those wondrous, secret looks you and Seb exchanged, constantly assuming I wasn't looking. Besides, you have always had an abdomen as flat as a washboard and suddenly you didn't. What are you—three months along now? Nearly four?'

'Nearly four.' Clarissa looked guilty. 'I should have told you sooner.'

'Yes, you jolly well should have! But you were so obsessed with wrapping me in cotton wool and protecting me from the world after the trial, I suspected you didn't think you should confess your own happiness in case it made me bolt sooner. I know you too well, Clarissa.'

'And I know you too well to have coddled you so. You always were made of stern stuff. I think we both lost sight of exactly who Penny Henley was. I just couldn't bear the thought of you all alone.'

'I know. It was well meant. For a little while I needed it, so I shall be for ever grateful. But it is time for us both to move on. The bright bold horizon awaits...'

'Seeing that we are talking of bright and bold horizons— how are things between you and my favourite barrister? Flint told Seb he suspects there might be a little romance brewing between the pair of you. Is that true?'

'Hardly a romance.' Because a romance sounded so much more permanent than she was prepared to consider at the moment. 'But we have shared the odd kiss.' Penny sipped her tea and tried to sound blasé about it all. 'After all, it is perfectly acceptable for widows to indulge in the odd affair.'

'Oh, it's *just* an affair then.' Clarissa frowned, disappointed. 'That is a shame.'

'To be frank, after Penhurst, that I would even consider an affair is a miracle. Not that it is an affair yet. Not in the strictest sense of the word.'

'So you haven't...'

'No! Not yet and nor may we...'

'Now that *would* be a shame. He is very handsome and he has such fine and expressive eyes, don't you think? And I am guessing he would look very nice *out* of his clothes, staring at one hungrily with undisguised passion.' Two perfect blonde eyebrows lifted suggestively as she fanned herself with her other hand. 'I would, if I were you.'

'Clarissa! You are married!'

'Yes, I am. Deliriously so. But I'm not blind or dead and neither are you. Pour me a second cup of tea this instant and tell me all the gory details about those kisses, you saucy vixen! And I will warn you now I will be asking lots of questions and doing my best to convince you to sample him *sans* clothes. You are in dire need of some passion. What is the point of an affair otherwise?'

Several hours later, after the rest of the gentlemen had long left Tristan's presence to change for dinner, Penny wandered to the music room in search of him, imbued with a new sense of daring courtesy of Clarissa's enlightening conversation. Not that she was truly ready to do the deed yet, but she was considerably more encouraged it might not be as awful as she continued to fear it might be.

Penny had no idea that it had been Clarissa who had first seduced Seb, nor had they ever discussed the physical aspect of a relationship between a man and a woman. But Clarissa had been very open about the passion she felt for her husband, blaming her scandalous lack of decorum before their marriage on the sinful way the man's kisses had made her feel from the outset.

According to Clarissa, they were so intoxicating she rapidly reached the point where if he didn't try to take more, she'd be forced to take matters into her own hands because the constant lust and yearning was sending her mad. Then she had confessed that six months of marriage had done nothing to dampen that lust either, which was how she happened to find herself thoroughly pregnant when they had both decided to give it at least a year to start a family. But then he'd kissed her one day in a carriage and that kiss had been so magnificent, the pair of them quite forgot to be careful in their haste to tear each other's clothes off in that bouncing conveyance to Norfolk and neither could bring themselves to regret the mistake.

That she might get to the same delirious state with Tristan on the back of his magnificent kisses was certainly food for thought. Food that was making her lips and other parts tingle with anticipation as she hurried along the hallway.

The sound of the pianoforte made her hesitate before approaching and she lingered outside the door listening. Mozart. She recognised the composer despite not knowing the exact sonata which was being played. Clearly one of the ladies had taken over his office in his absence. Whoever it was played beautifully.

Needing to know which of her guests was so accomplished, she silently cracked open the door and then stared agog, because it was Tristan. He sensed her and stopped, a wistful smile on his handsome face.

'I didn't know you played.'

'I haven't played in years and was intrigued to see if I still could.'

'I think Mozart would have approved of your efforts.'

'He was my mother's favourite and she adored the sound of the pianoforte, but alas, she had absolutely no musical talent herself so she insisted I take piano lessons. I think I was five or six when I started. She had delusions I would be a virtuoso and then we would travel around Europe together, playing for all the royal courts. It was our secret. My father never knew I could play. He wouldn't have approved of such pointless nonsense. He never considered I would ever do anything except run the ancestral estate.'

'He disapproved of your legal training, then?'

'He would have, had he not been stark staring mad already by the time I started.'

'And how did your mother cope with you dashing her dreams of consorting with European royalty?'

'Remarkably well, all things considered. She embroidered crochets and quavers over my favourite shirts and that revenge seemed to get all the crushing disappointment out of her system.'

'Dare I ask how your day went?' They both knew she was referring to his demons rather than the case.

'It was better than I expected and worse all at the same time. I find I now veer between happily nostalgic and horrendously sad. I am taking a leaf out of your book and embracing both stoically. What doesn't kill us makes us stronger, after all.'

'And you need to experience the bad to appreciate the good. There is a great deal of good, I suspect.'

'There is. I should never have let it go.' He smiled and watched his hand while he played another few bars aimlessly. 'I had forgotten how relaxing I find this. For some reason, sitting here helps my mind unclutter.' Then he stood and sauntered towards her. 'I intended to wait till later to kiss you, but I don't think I can. Do you mind?'

She had barely nodded when he dipped his head to hers and brushed a whisper-like kiss on her mouth. Then he looped his arms around her waist and smiled. 'I've been wanting to do that all day. Since breakfast, in fact. Or a little before if I'm honest. I think I deserve another kiss for being so patient, don't you?'

'Perhaps.'

But he didn't take it. His eyes dropped to her lips and then locked with hers, waiting. After what felt like for ever, she raised herself on tiptoes and closed the short distance between them herself. Only then did he kiss her the way her body wanted him to. Desire bloomed instantaneously and its presence gave her renewed confidence, or at least it did until she stopped thinking entirely. As he had last night, Tristan had the power to banish everything but the moment and she poured herself into it completely, not caring that her hands had gone exploring beneath his coat.

He was so solid, his body so unlike hers. When his palms began to do the same she welcomed it, moaning against his mouth in encouragement until one finally found her breast and she arched against it greedily. Because of the difference in their heights, he lifted her to sit on the piano and his big body nestled perfectly between her thighs as he kissed her breathless. Just when she thought she might die from the wanting, he stepped back, smiling, his index finger tangling in a wayward lock of hair which had somehow escaped its pins. 'You seem to have the ability to make me forget where I am.' As did he.

His eyes took in the shameless sight of her perched atop the pianoforte—hair mussed, rumpled skirts ruched up to display her legs below the knee, her mouth doubtless pink and swollen, her bosom rising and falling to the rhythm of her rapid breathing—then he grinned wolfishly before lifting her carefully back to her feet. 'Have dinner with us.'

'Out of the question!' But it was so lovely he had asked. 'It wouldn't be right.'

'It feels right to me and I doubt any of the others would care.'

'I would feel awkward...' Oh, for goodness sake, tell the man the truth! 'I don't want to have to explain myself to anyone just yet, or have anyone speculating about us. I never anticipated being tempted by a man again. All of this is so new and unexpected, exciting but a little unnerving. I would prefer to keep it between us rather than have the others poke their noses in and offer advice. They are curious enough already and I want to do this at my own pace. Besides, we have a house full—I still need to manage it for the next few weeks. That will be easier if we keep this separate.'

He sighed, but nodded. 'I understand.' He tucked the tendril back behind her ear. 'Can I visit you again later? Well away from the risk of prying eyes and gossip?'

The prospect thrilled her. 'Yes.'

'Will you stay a while now and keep me company?'

She glanced at the mantel clock. 'Dinner is in less than thirty minutes.'

'I dare say the world won't end if I'm still wearing this coat for it. Indulge me for a few more minutes. I want to talk to you.'

'What about?'

'You.' His finger trailed along her sleeve aimlessly. 'All the things I don't yet know about you, but desperately want to.'

'Such as?'

'What was it like being married to Penhurst, for instance?'

The question, so out of the blue, soured her pleasant mood. 'I don't want to talk about him. Besides, the world knows what he was.'

'I want to know more of you than the world sees, just as I want you to know more of me. Some things you already do. I've never spoken about my past with another living soul, but I trusted you with it. Trust me with yours, Penny. Allow me in here.' His index finger touched her forehead. 'I only know the bare bones rather than what happened behind closed doors. I know he was violent and malicious. Very controlling. I know you didn't mourn him. I also know you found the physical side of your marriage a chore...' Good heavens! She hadn't expected him to say that! Instantly, her face flushed with mortification. 'But I do not really know any more about those things and I suspect nobody does. I so want to understand what it was like for you, Penny. I think it is important...for both of us.'

His intuitive amber eyes were fixed on her intently and she found herself looking away in case he saw the truth. Or worse, expected her to discuss intimacies with him when she could barely bring herself to talk about them with

Clarissa. Like a coward, she had allowed her friend to do all the talking when she had a hundred questions she had desperately wanted to ask. 'Heavens, I have no idea where I should begin with such a maudlin tale of woe.' Discomfort had her scrambling for a ready means of escape and avoidance. 'Besides, there is less than half an hour till dinner, so we hardly have the time today.'

'Why don't we start at the beginning, then?' He was being selectively deaf, drat him. 'Did you ever love him?' She made the mistake of flicking her gaze to his, briefly intending to brush it off and sidestep the question, but saw his concern and his pity. Saw the fact he truly cared loud and clear in his eyes. Realised she could trust him with at least part of the truth.

Honesty bubbled out before she could stop it. 'I thought I did—briefly. Ours was a brisk and speedy courtship. A bit of a sham really, in the end, because I believed he meant all the hogwash he wrote in his daily letters. I was ridiculously flattered that an eligible viscount wanted me—a shopkeeper's daughter—enough to pursue me with such ardour. That he would write to me almost immediately after we had collided at a ball or event, send me giant bouquets and hunt me down wherever I happened to be... Well, I am ashamed to say I saw all those inconsequential trimmings as evidence of his love and convinced myself my anticipation of all that was love, too. And my mother found it all romantic. She was desperately ill at the time and we all knew she didn't have that long left, and somehow that only served to spur me on. When he proposed weeks later, I happily said yes because I knew my mother would adore planning my wedding. My whole existence became that—the gown, the trousseau, the floral arrangements, the perfect menu for the wedding breakfast.'

'You and your mother had fun.' There was no judgement in his expression, only understanding. He took her hand in his and placed a soft kiss on the back of it which she felt everywhere.

'We did and those happy memories of that time with her are precious to me.'

'When did you realise he wasn't the man you had been duped into believing he was.'

'My wedding night.' Penny was not prepared to confess all the indignity of that night to Tristan. Some things were too private and some wounds too deep. She gently tugged her hand out of his in case she said too much. 'He was drunk and told me straight out he had only married me for my dowry. He felt he had married beneath him and I saw the truth of his feelings. He didn't love me. Didn't even like me. I was a means to an end. He needed my money and, seeing that he was stuck with me, he needed an heir. Unsurprisingly, things deteriorated quite rapidly from there.'

'Why didn't you leave him in those early days before Freddie?'

'Pride in part, I am ashamed to admit. Both Clarissa and my father had cautioned me against marrying him and I had ignored them.' Unconsciously, feeling exposed, she hugged herself, then quickly dropped her arms once she realised. 'But mostly I didn't want my mother to feel guilty for encouraging the match. She had been duped, too, you see, and I couldn't allow her to die knowing I was unhappy. So I lied. Then, by the time she passed it was too late. I was carrying Freddie. My father fell ill, following my mother to heaven soon after and I had nowhere to go. Penhurst had made it obvious he was happy for me to leave once his son was born—but despite the mysterious change in his fortunes, he made it perfectly clear he would neither support me nor allow me to take Freddie if I left.

He had been quite specific, actually—if I left him, I relinquished my baby entirely.' She felt her shoulders rise defiantly. 'So I stayed. What other choice did I have? I had no family to run to.'

'I sympathise. We only children have no siblings to support us in our hours of need. And the law is an ass sometimes. Especially when it applies itself to women.' His hand again reached for hers and she found herself gripping it gratefully. 'I suppose he also kept your father's fortune?'

How like Tristan to ask such a pertinent legal question. 'Papa's illness came on so unexpectedly and suddenly that, although he had stated his intention to bequeath everything to his grandchild to keep it from Penhurst, he never got around to changing his will. But at least he lived to see his grandson born.' Tears suddenly filled her eyes, threatening to spill at the tragedy of it all. 'Penhurst couldn't take that from me.' Although he had tried. The punishment for her disobedience had been worth it. Without thinking, she touched the bridge of her nose and watched Tristan's eyes widen in understanding.

'Oh, Penny...' She found herself wrapped in his strong arms, enveloped in a hug which she hadn't known she desperately needed and one she returned gladly, clinging to him as she fought the pointless urge to cry. He held her for the longest time, not saying a single word, yet that simple, heartfelt act of affection soothed her far better than any words or physician ever could.

Chapter Nineteen

Penny kissed her sleeping son's forehead, then gently tucked him in. He'd had quite the week. They all had. It had whizzed past in a whirlwind of fevered activity, with Tristan ensconced in the music room from dawn till dinner methodically preparing each of the witnesses for their grilling in the dock. It wasn't only their testimony he was reinforcing, but the barrage of questions that the defence might ask them which might trip them up or catch them unawares. Penny sustained the proceedings with plenty of tea and coffee and made sure that everyone, including Tristan, ate properly.

It was fascinating watching him work. Even the little snippets she intruded on were eye opening. He had a knack for asking exactly the right thing at precisely the right time, his clever mind switching from one line of questioning to a completely different one in the blink of an eye as he deftly played the defence lawyers who would cross-examine them. The inscrutable lawyer's mask—for she understood it was exactly that now that she knew the real man beneath—served to befuddle and deflect as well as hide the powerful emotions he held so well in check. Even the experienced King's Elite agents Gray, Flint, Seb and Lord Fennimore, who frequently testified in trials as par for the course in their profession, left their sessions looking a little drained and battle weary after Tristan had put them through the mangle. Yet they all appreciated his efforts, leaving each ordeal better prepared for the real one to come than they would have been without his thorough tutorage.

But even in the thick of it, when Penny entered the room with tea, the mask he wore melted briefly as he smiled at her. Those amber eyes would heat, the message in them for her only, yet entirely clear.

This morning, the two traitors' wives had been brought to Chafford Grange for a few hours as he had readied them for the trial, too. Over all, there was a renewed atmosphere of confidence in the house with even the eternal pessimist Lord Fennimore conceding they were ready. Two years of dogged investigations, months of meticulous planning and a palpable air of anticipation as they all waited for that final sprint to the end. On the morrow, the Attorney General himself would arrive to hear the progress and the trial of the century was due to start two days after that on the Monday.

Tristan and the others were due to return to town on Sunday afternoon and then Penny's short but rewarding stint as his housekeeper would end. Or so she supposed. Neither of them had discussed the final days and while she pondered them, like him she had avoided bringing it up because she didn't want to spoil the time they had left together.

Because the past week had also been one of the most enjoyable and enlightening weeks of her life, too, especially when the nights drew in and Tristan came to visit. Those visits followed a reassuring pattern she looked forward to all day. He would come, often while Freddie was still awake so he could play with him and help put him to bed. Then they would kiss. Each time, since the first, things would go a little bit further than the last, but he halted things long before she was ready. Then they would sit and talk for at least an hour over a nightcap about everything and nothing. Their day, their good memories and their bad. Tristan opened up more about his parents' relationship and his difficult, impotent role within it and Penny found herself telling him about the nightmare which had been her marriage. Then they would kiss some more, she would feel his blatant desire against her body and revel in it, wishing each time he would take things further, then lying awake for a good hour after he had left her, castigating herself for her own cowardice at allowing him to leave her without asking him to stay.

Yesterday evening, for the very first time, he had loosened the laces of her dress and kissed her bared breasts. Torturing the sensitive tips of them with his tongue and his teeth until she had positively writhed beneath him on the sofa. Then the wretch bade her a goodnight. She had been left in such a state of frustrated arousal it had taken hours to drift off to sleep, only to suffer from the single most erotic dream she had ever had, awakening well before dawn broke feeling as needy and physically unfulfilled as she had been the night before when he had torn his mouth away and gazed down at her shamelessly bared upper body with undisguised carnal longing.

He had liked what he had seen, or at least she thought he might have. Had wanted to ask, but couldn't find the right words or the courage to do so. Yet she wanted to know desperately, almost as desperately as she wanted his mouth on her nipples again. The shameless things had craved his attention all day, alongside other parts of her anatomy which she had never been so thoroughly aware of.

She wanted things to go further. The wanting was sending her mad. Was that what Tristan intended? Or was he unaware of just how needy he made her body? Or—and this made her frown in irritation—was he being a gentleman on purpose because he thought that was what she wanted? Although, in fairness, she had never told him explicitly she always wanted more. Instead, she meekly accepted his termination and wished him goodnight right back. Did he need her permission to take scandalous liberties?

Drat the man for being so wonderful, because clearly he did. What had happened to her recently rediscovered backbone? For months she had promised herself to be a new, braver version of herself and, despite her ardent curiosity and permanently needy nipples, she wasn't being particularly brave with him at all.

Suddenly feeling very bold, Penny dashed into her bedchamber and stripped off her gown. Perhaps if she couldn't find the words to tell him she was ripe for the picking, greeting him in her nightgown would? She rummaged into the bottom of her trunk for the filmy concoction her mother had bought her for her trousseau. The only thing she had left from it and one she had never worn. It had felt too daring for her wedding night, and after that dreadful debacle she had certainly never been inclined to put it on afterwards. She hadn't wanted to give the man any ideas and had only kept it because it was the last thing her mother had bought her. But she wanted to give Tristan ideas and she wanted him to have them tonight before their time came abruptly to an end on Sunday.

One by one, she pulled the sensible pins from her hair, then ruthlessly ran a brush through her locks until they shimmered. Tonight, come hell or high water, she was going to whitewash the memory of Penhurst's vile intrusions and replace them with something else.

Something she had no tangible concept of other than the secure knowledge it couldn't possibly be a worse experience, not with the kind, noble, utterly beautiful man who made her nerve endings fizz just by looking at her!

Despite all her bravado, his knock on her door had her practically jumping out of her skin and dropping the brush like it was a slippery bar of soap. Penny had to suck in several calming breaths before she dared leave the sanctuary of her bedchamber and another two more before she composed herself enough to brazenly open the door as the new and daring woman she was thoroughly determined to be.

It had been a hell of a day. Relentless even. But for the first time since he had been appointed the Crown Prosecutor on this case, Hadleigh felt ready. Every *i* was dotted; every *t* crossed. His head was aching, his poor body was aching, even the tiny space between his eyebrows hurt like the devil because of all the blasted frowning he'd been doing as he pondered. Tonight, as much as he wanted to see Penny, he knew he was on his last legs and needed to collapse on his bed and simply sleep—he would definitely need to be on his game for the Attorney General in the morning. Something he planned to tell her from the outset, knowing she would understand, give her a quick, searing kiss to remind her he still adored her before excusing himself to rest.

Then she had opened the door and he forgot his own name, let alone all his lofty plans to impress his superior.

She was wearing just a nightgown.

One quite unlike the sensible sort he had seen her in before. This one had no high neck to disguise the creamy, perfect skin which graced her chest. Instead, he was greeted by the whole expanse of her décolleté above the deep V which ended mid-bosom, the delicate lace trim moulding itself to the upper swells of her breasts. The rest of the garment followed suit. He couldn't see through the fine silk with his eyes, but thanks to the way it whispered and brushed against her curves, he could imagine it. The tips of her breasts pebbled in the chill from the hallway, drawing his eyes and reminding his brain exactly how they had tasted the night before. How sensitive they were. How she had moaned and writhed in pleasure as he had worshipped them with his mouth.

And her hair...

He had never seen it completely unbound before, that thick plait she usually wore for bed had not prepared him for the sight of the dark, tousled silky curtain which now hung all the way to her waist. She had arranged it over just one shoulder, one finger twirling the ends of it like Eve tempting Adam.

He tried to swallow, but his throat was too dry.

Tried to speak, but his mouth wouldn't work.

Couldn't blink. Couldn't breathe. Couldn't move if his life depended on it. Instead, he stood rooted to the spot and stared. Every single drop of blood in his body suddenly rushing to pool in his groin. The damned woman was going to kill him.

'You're late. I was beginning to despair of you ever coming.'

'Work.' For a man considered a great orator by his peers, it was a miracle he could croak out that single syllable. But she had stepped to one side so he could enter and in doing so had stepped into the light of the flickering lamp behind her. It made several strands of her dark hair shimmer copper and gold. Turned her lovely blue eyes into deep lagoons he was helplessly drowning in. Turned a great deal of that seductive silk translucent.

As she moved to close the door, he saw her unbound

breasts move and almost groaned aloud. How exactly was
he supposed to maintain the rigidly slow and incremen-
tal seduction he had diligently planned when she came to
the door looking like temptation incarnate? His eyes hungrily swept the length of her before he managed to choke
out a sentence.

'Perhaps I should go… Allow you to sleep seeing that
you are ready for bed.' Because neither of them would
sleep if he stayed. 'I am *very* late.'

The seductress who had opened the door to him disappeared instantly and she suddenly seemed self-conscious.
'Oh… I thought you had come to kiss me?' Her soulful
eyes were distinctly wounded. 'But of course it can wait
if you don't want to tonight.'

He watched her hands clasp in front of her awkwardly
a second before they burrowed out of sight in the billowing silk. Then he realised he had unintentionally hurt her
feelings because she was dubious of her own attractiveness. Damn Penhurst to hell, the blasted fool!

'Hell's bells, woman! Of course I want to kiss you.' He
gestured helplessly at the flimsy garment she was wearing
and felt the pain between his eyebrows double. 'I am trying to be a gentleman, damn it…trying to give you time
to get used to the idea of being with another man after the
fool you married knocked all the confidence out of you…
something I will fail miserably at while you are looking
like that.' His greedy eyes raked her body once again and
he did groan. 'Have some mercy, Penny. I'm only human.
Unless you want to be thoroughly ravished by a man rendered devoid of all sense at the sight of you, please, I beg
of you, go put on something more substantial.'

Her eyes finally raised to meet his shyly. 'And what if
I do want to be thoroughly ravished?'

'Then heaven help us both.' Hadleigh closed the distance between them in two quick strides and hauled her into his arms. 'Because right now I want you more than I've ever wanted a woman before and if I don't have you, it will probably kill me.'

He didn't hide the truth of those words in a gentle re- strained kiss. Instead, he poured every bit of his desire and unquenched frustration into it, plundering her mouth and running his hands possessively over her body. To his delight, her ardour matched his and she stripped off his coat as her mouth slanted passionately over his. As soon as it dropped to the floor, her fingers went clumsily to the buttons of his waist coat as she backed him against the wall. As soon as she wrestled it open it joined the other garment on the floor.

'I can't stop thinking about last night.' Her breath warmed his neck as her teeth nuzzled it. 'And the feel of your hands on me. I should have asked you to stay.' Her hands tunnelled beneath his shirt and splayed across his chest. 'I wanted you to stay.' Then they dropped to the waistband of his breeches and began to feel for the but- tons of his falls.

It was all happening so fast. Too fast. She deserved the thorough and meticulous seduction he had promised himself he would give her for their first time, one that told her she was completely adored, not a fast and fevered cou- pling. Instinct told him she had suffered enough of those and he wanted this to be different. Damn it all to hell, it *had* to be different!

Hadleigh dragged his lips from hers and hoisted her into his arms, then carried her to the fireplace where he depos- ited her with precious little finesse. A mallet to crack a nut. Good grief, he needed to calm down. 'Wait right here.'

Breathing hard, he let himself into her bedchamber and stripped the eiderdown and pillows from her bed. He wanted nothing of this experience to remind her of the last. While she stood watching, bemused, he made them a little nest on the floor of her cosy sitting room. This had been the room in which they had shared most of themselves, after all, sat here, by the glowing fire, so the location seemed fitting. Finally, he reached out his hands and took hers, bringing both to his lips and doing his level best to ignore the insistent bulge in his breeches.

'I won't rush this, Penny. You are too important to me and this night is too important to us. I am quite determined to make *thorough* and *meticulous* love to you. And I'm afraid I am far too stubborn to be swayed from that quest.'

Chapter Twenty

Tristan kissed her again, tenderly this time, yet Penny could feel how valiantly he fought for control. Against her chest, she could feel his heart hammering against his ribcage, felt his body tremble as she touched him, felt the long, hot, hard length of him against her stomach. Solid proof he liked what he saw.

He deepened the kiss and smoothed his palms down her arms and then back slowly to her shoulders. She felt his fingers go to the lace which edged the scandalous neckline, felt him push it slowly over her shoulders and then stilled when she realised that that single, thin layer of silk was the only thing separating her naked body from his eyes. She extricated herself from his arms, hoping she still appeared confident and alluring and went to blow out the lamp nearest.

'Leave it.' He caught her gently by the wrist and tugged her back. 'I want to see you.' One finger traced her jaw, slowly caressed down the sensitive side of her neck before lodging itself once again beneath the lace. 'Let me look at you, Penny—all of you.'

She held her breath and nodded, dreading it, looking down rather than watch his eyes as he slowly smoothed the garment from her shoulders. As it was designed to, it slithered down with ease, puddling at her feet, and she heard Tristan's breath hitch. Was that a good sign? Proudly, she set her shoulders before daring to look up, then found her own breath hitching at the sight of the obvious emotions swirling in his eyes. Admiration. Desire. Lust so strong and palpable she could feel it.

The backs of his fingers grazed her cheek before tangling in her hair. 'Beautiful.' The word was like a sigh, a benediction. 'I knew you would be.' He kissed her mouth. Her neck. Ran his palms gently over her skin as if she were precious. 'Come…lie with me.'

Feeling exposed, yet oddly choked with emotion at his reaction, Penny allowed him to lead her to the eiderdown. She sat, wondering how to arrange her limbs to appear the most attractive and then gave up to hug her knees instead while he tugged off his shirt, seeing for the first time what she had only touched. Broad shoulders. The flat plain of his abdomen. The light dusting of hair, the same colour as the darkest shades of blond on his head, which covered his chest and arrowed down through his navel.

His fingers fumbled with the remaining buttons of his falls and she realised he was nervous, too, and that knowledge empowered her. 'Allow me.' She twisted around to come up on her knees, grateful her hair had arranged itself to cover a great deal of her modesty, and undid them for him, drinking in the sight as she pushed the fabric from his hips.

To her complete delight, naked, he looked nothing like Penhurst. Tristan's skin glowed in the firelight, encasing taut muscle beneath. The male part of him stood stiff and proud, much bigger and thicker than the other she had seen, but where that had made her want to avert her eyes, this made her want to stare. Want to touch.

Should she?

As if reading her mind, he settled his big body beside her on top of the covers, laying propped on one elbow as she stretched out next to him. He took her hand and placed a kiss inside her palm, following it with a trail of soft, open-mouthed kisses along her arm and shoulder that felt sublime. When he reached her mouth, he tilted his body to rest against hers and she marvelled at the sheer beauty of his skin touching hers.

What came next was equally as unexpected as his hands and then his mouth explored everywhere. None of it felt intrusive, nor could she even begin to detach herself from what he was so skilfully doing, as sensation after sinful sensation shimmered through her. He had promised to make thorough and meticulous love to her and he was true to his word. Not an inch of her body was missed. Fingers. Toes. Breasts. Belly. His tongue brushed her navel. His teeth grazed her hips. While his fingers wandered a lazy path from her knee to her thigh, then gently dipped between them to the place her body shockingly screamed the most for his touch.

She felt him smile against her breast as her body shuddered at the intensely intimate contact. 'Is that nice?' The tip of his finger had found the unexpected place where every nerve-ending apparently merged into one.

'Yes.'

'How about this?' It was such a small but deadly caress and her body involuntarily arched with the pleasure.

'Yes...' Then, as an afterthought, 'Please don't stop.' Because it felt so good. Overwhelming. Necessary.

Penny thought nothing could feel as wonderful, until he sucked her straining nipple into his mouth and teased it simultaneously. She moaned, surprised that such a wanton, abandoned sound had come from her lips and felt her legs fall open shamelessly, not caring that he could see her most secret place as well as touch it.

She was too lost by then, desperately trying to reach a place she couldn't see and did not recognise, to think of anything that extended beyond that tiny bud of nerve-endings and the splendid things he was to doing them.

When he shifted his position to lay above her and that part of him pressed insistently against her body, she welcomed it, her eyes fluttering closed as he slowly edged inside and moaned again when he completely filled her. By then, none of her past so much as occurred to her because he was moving so perfectly inside her, loving her completely with his body, so wonderfully thoroughly and meticulously, that nothing else existed beyond him and her. With each deep caress, she fell further and further. Further and further. Until the hot, molten, amber stars in his eyes seemed to explode and fill her heart with such incomprehensible but all-encompassing beauty, all she could do was cling to him helplessly as they fell together.

Hadleigh woke in pitch black darkness curled around her and decided there and then that was precisely how he always wanted to wake up. In his thirty years on the planet, he had never felt this sort of connection with another person. Or allowed himself to feel this depth of emotion voluntarily. The most splendid and surprising thing about it was he didn't feel like running or blocking it all out. Penny owned his heart. Odd really, that such a momentous thing should be so easy, yet it was. He didn't need to weigh up the pros or cons, test the evidence or debate the reasons. Some things just were and this was one of them.

He was in love.

The realisation had hit fully some time between her opening the door in that outrageous nightgown and as he had peeled it off with reverence, although alongside that realisation came another. He'd been in love with her for a while. Probably since the night of the flour, if he were honest with himself, or perhaps that first time they had kissed. Hadleigh wasn't entirely certain he could pinpoint the precise moment and decided it didn't matter. All that really mattered was that he loved her. And probably should tell her. Should have told her before she fell asleep in his arms, only then he'd had no words. He'd been so moved and choked by the honesty and perfection of their love making, all he could do was feel.

He was coming to believe intense emotions weren't all that dangerous after all. The grief he had allowed himself to experience was raw and painful—yet somehow in accepting that, the experience was cathartic. He had realised through it that this house wasn't just a house or Pandora's box filled with everything that was bad and painful, it was also the guardian of his most treasured memories. His mother was here. That invisible yet solid link to her was comforting and...pleasant. He was glad he had found her again. Glad he had found home.

Was the regret still there and the tragedy? Of course it was. But Penny was right. You had to experience the bad to appreciate the good. And now Penny would be intertwined with his memories of this place for ever. They had found each other here, bared their souls, shared their bodies. The most wonderful thing about all of that was this was merely the start for them. Life shouldn't be all about work. It deserved to be enriched with love.

He happily closed his eyes again and snuggled, only to hear the whimper coming from next door.

Freddie.

With a sigh of resignation, he carefully disentangled his arm from her waist and slipped out from the tangled eiderdown. Another new aspect of his life he was only too happy to embrace. He was going to be a father and already knew he had solid foundations to build that on. After all, thanks to his own father, he already knew all the things *not* to do. Poor Leatham was stumbling into the experience blind. Of course, Freddie was older and his friends would soon be confronted with a newborn, but Hadleigh would try to take that in his stride as he and Penny expanded their family—and she knew what she was doing there. Together they would work it all out.

As the fire had clearly long died, he groped around in the dark for his breeches and shirt, slipped them on and padded barefoot into the boy's room. The child was sat up, his small fists rubbing his eyes, and his expression suggested he was about to wail the place down at any moment.

'Come on, little man.' He hoisted him into his arms and kissed him. Warm milk was obviously required. 'Let's leave your poor mother to sleep, shall we?'

On stealthy yet quick feet, he swiftly manoeuvred the pair of them out into the hallway and headed to the kitchen, realising too late that he had left Freddie's bottle on the nightstand. After a fruitless search for a spare with the child balanced on one hip and the boy already fighting him, he decided the milk was more important than the vessel which housed it and set some to warm in the pan. He would spoon it into him if he had to. How hard could it be?

While they waited, he grabbed a couple of biscuits from the pantry and handed one to Freddie and munched on the other himself. This appeared to work wonders, as the boy seemed perfectly content to grasp the thing with both hands and suck it to death.

Milk warmed, Hadleigh sloshed some in a cup which he deposited on the table, then, predicting a royal mess otherwise, he snatched a towel and, with Freddie on his knee and ignoring the soggy remnants of biscuit his grabbing small hands smeared on his face, tied it around his neck. 'Right, young man. It's time to practise some cup skills. Proper young gentlemen do not drink out of bottles.'

He let the boy grip the handle while he supported the bowl, and helped him guide it to his mouth, smiling as the child pursed his lips and made a complete hash of drinking from it. Milk spilled everywhere and he congratulated himself on have the good foresight to grab that towel. 'That's it, Freddie, you can do this.'

It was an uphill battle, but one Hadleigh appeared to be winning. Each time Freddie lost patience, they would wrestle for control of the cup. To distract him, he blew raspberries on his pudgy cheek and was rewarded with delighted childish giggles complete with an endearing milk moustache. 'I suspect I might have a knack for this parenting lark.' Which boded very well for the additional children he fully intended to plant in Penny's belly as soon as humanly possible. He had been careful last night, out of respect for her and because they hadn't yet discussed the future, but once they had and if she was agreeable, he saw no reason not to start straight away. 'Can't leave you a lonely, only child, can we, Freddie?' Because both he and Penny had been and then, when their parents passed, they'd had no one until they had found each other. Siblings would have helped.

'There you both are.' A very rumpled, very ravished-looking Penny appeared at the door, her lips still beautifully pink and swollen from his kisses, her hair a thoroughly shocking tangle he could proudly claim full responsibility for. No doubt for proprieties' sake she had forgone the seductive nightgown in favour of a very sensible thick one done up to the neck and an equally bulky shawl.

They made no difference. His mind could see through both of them and thoroughly enjoyed what it saw.

'We didn't want to wake you up.' And because he couldn't help himself. 'Did you miss me?'

She smiled shyly and nodded. 'I thought you had gone back to your own room.'

'Why on earth would I want to do that?'

'The floor was hard?' Then she blushed prettily, no doubt remembering just as he was exactly what they had done on that floor. 'Here, let me take him. You have an important day tomorrow.'

She reached out her arms and he caught one of her hands, brought it to his lips. 'I thoroughly enjoyed tonight.'

'So did I.' She looked down at their locked hands rather than directly at him. There were unshed tears swimming in her eyes. 'Thank you... I had no idea it could be like that.'

'It's not always like that.' He needed to let her know how it had affected him. 'That was particularly wonderful. If you want the honest truth, I had no idea it could be like that either.' She gifted him with the most beautiful smile, his heart skipped a beat and the words he had been thinking happily tumbled out. 'Marry me, Penny.'

He had expected another smile at his proposal at the very least, not her stunned and pained expression. 'Don't ask me that.' She tugged her hand away, took Freddie and put some distance between them.

'Why not?' The look of distaste on her face wounded him. Her sudden need for detachment made him panic.

'Because I can't.'

'Can't or won't?'

Reasons not to kiss Tristan number three: *I will not give another person control over me ever again.*

'This is all too sudden.'

'Not for me it isn't. I love you. I want to spend the rest of my life with you.'

One of those unshed tears spilled over her ridiculously long lashes. 'Don't say that.'

'Don't say that?' What did that mean? Were his feelings one sided? But he'd seen them written with his own eyes.

I have a deep affection for him.

Was deep affection not quite love?

'I am not ready to hear it…or even think about it… I've been married and hated it.'

'That was him!' The unfairness and the pain made him snap at her. 'Not me!' He saw Freddie's little eyes widen and fought for calm. His next words came out more measured and reasoned. Imploring her to understand. 'I am not like that and you know it. I don't want a chattel or a subordinate, Penny. I am neither cruel nor callous. I don't want to control you or stop you doing what you want. Rebuild Ridley's. With my blessing and without any interference. I won't stand in your way. I simply want to be with you.'

She began bouncing Freddie on her hip with more concentration than the task warranted and shot him a pleading look, tempering her voice maddeningly. 'We don't have to change things, Tristan. We can still be together.'

'What? In secret? An illicit affair when we have no reason to hide it?' Reasons to kiss Tristan number blasted two! 'How will that work, Penny, when the trial is done?' He was hurt by her distinct lack of faith in him and couldn't hide it, but he kept his voice low for Freddie. 'Or is this only a temporary liaison borne solely out of *curiosity*? Will I be receiving my marching orders at some point once the trial is done?'

'We can make it work. I am moving back to London…

your work keeps you in London...' Her tone was reasonable, but it did nothing to placate him. He thought making
love had immeasurably changed things between them. Rat-
ified and clarified their relationship as something unique
and special. It certainly had for him.

'Oh, how splendid. I get to sneak into your lodgings at
night time and creep out before dawn in case anybody sees
me? I don't want that. There is no future in that. I don't
want a mistress or an affair, Penny. I am not like my father. And I am nothing like Penhurst!' Temper leaked out
and he couldn't stop it. How dared she? *How...dared...she?*

'I don't want an occasional lover. I want a wife. A home.
A family.' His eyes drifted to Freddie and he tore them
away. He'd had plans for the pair of them, dreams of a gag-
gle of siblings and a house filled with laughter. Teaching
them how to slide down the banisters, play piano, ride...

'But I don't want to be a wife again. Surely you can appreciate the reasons why?'

'Oh, I appreciate them, Penny!' For the first time since
he had met her, Hadleigh was totally disappointed in her.
She didn't believe in them. Wasn't brave enough to fight
for them. A different sort of grief ripped through him and
his voice shook as he fought against it. 'You are the hypocrite, not I. You were disgusted at me when you thought
I was comparing you to my mother and trivialising all
that you were. You told me, quite rightly, that I couldn't
change the past or rid myself of guilt for it by bestowing it
on you. Yet you are allowed to compare me to Penhurst—
to damned Penhurst, of all people!—and I am supposed
to blithely accept that and not mention the dreadful unfairness?' He threw up his hands in the air. 'Well, I won't.
I've seen your list, Penny!' He looked momentarily forlorn
despite the level and measured tone of his voice. 'Reasons
to kiss Tristan, reasons not to, and I've done my best to

prove all of your doubts wrong. But if I have failed to do that in my actions and my deeds, I flatly refuse to be the discreet affair that makes you forget the chore of the marriage bed and I'm damned if I'll allow you to use me out of curiosity! I'd rather have none of you, Penny, and suffer the heartbreak than only ever have the leftover scraps from your table!' He stalked to the door. 'And I won't be compared to a monster from your past to allow you to justify not facing your demons there. I am nothing like blasted Penhurst and you wound me by thinking it.'

Chapter Twenty-One

Hadleigh stared back at the house and set his jaw. He was back to loathing the damned place again. It was funny how a few hours and a few words could shift everything. 'It definitely looks like snow.' He stared at the angry beige sky to prove his point as he loaded another box of papers on the carriage. 'I won't risk months of hard work on the weather. Better to leave today than chance leaving it till Sunday. Especially now the Attorney General is no longer gracing us with his illustrious presence.' Although it wouldn't take a house full of spies long to realise it had been he who had dispatched the express before dawn changing the day's plan and informing his superior he would meet him instead this afternoon at his chambers.'

'I think you should at least say goodbye to the ladies. They'll be expecting you at breakfast.'

And see her? Not a cat's chance in hell. Thanks to her, all he had left was the tattered remnants of his pride and a thoroughly broken heart. 'For pity's sake, Seb! They are your wives, not mine. I doubt any of them will care that I'm gone.' She thought he wasn't good enough. That was the long and the short of it. She'd happily share his bed and his body, but she did trust him enough to give up her *freedom*. As if he would ever try to curb it.

'I told you they had had a row.' Gray saw his angry expression, nudged Flint and winked. 'The agent on the watch last night said he was positively fuming when he stalked back upstairs in his shirt tails.'

'In his shirt tails, you say?'

'Well, he had been to her bedroom again—like he has been every night this week—except this time apparently, he didn't return to his own room at a reasonable hour. He *stayed*...' Hadleigh tried his best to ignore Gray's raised eyebrows. 'But what I want to know is what happened after the lady arrived looking all tousled and scandalous in the kitchen? Because the agent said she practically *floated* down the stairs.'

'Do we suspect *tomfoolery*?'

Any second now and he was going to punch Flint. His friend had been shooting him knowing looks all morning. Except they didn't know the half of it. Hadleigh had thrown himself headlong into love. She had guarded herself against it. He wanted marriage. She wanted a *discreet affair*. Pathetically, he felt used and undervalued. More than a little betrayed.

'Undoubtedly. I suspect he showed her his *credentials*.' Gray tapped his nose and winked again. 'Perhaps they were unimpressive...'

Huh! Lewd analogy aside, clearly she did find his credentials unimpressive if she refused to see he was nothing like her hideous husband. Hadleigh was a man of integrity. One who cared. One who would never lift a finger to hurt another. A righter of wrongs and a defender of justice. If he likened Penny's actions to the trial procedure, she had found him guilty first and used hearsay, speculation and false witness testimony to condemn him. A true miscarriage of justice if ever there was one. And it hurt. On top of everything he hadn't thought he was capable of more sadness—until this. So of course he had stormed off. It had either been that or beg as he had been sorely tempted to. Or weep again at the tragedy of it all.

'And he's such a tall man, too…it's a great pity he failed to measure up.'

Hadleigh growled at Flint, 'Enough! Have your fun elsewhere! I've got a trial to prepare for.' As Seb was aiding much too slowly, he hauled the last box of documents into the back of the coach himself, prompting his friend to shake his head in exasperation.

'Go talk to her. Find a compromise. There's always a compromise. It's obvious she's as miserable and upset about the argument as you are. She's been moping around all morning. Or apologise for whatever you did wrong. Women like a man who knows when to apologise.'

At that, he snapped. He had nothing to apologise for. Nothing! Aside from loving her significantly more than she cared for him. *Great affection* wasn't love. It clearly fell a good way short. He jabbed his finger at Seb.

'As if I would take advice from you! Everything you know about women could be written on the back of a calling card and even then there'd be space for the Lord's Prayer! And as for you two…' his finger waved menacingly at the grinning Flint and Gray '…make one more innuendo about Penny and me and I swear I'll wring both your blasted necks!'

With that he stalked off to the sounds of their irritating laughter, keen to put as many miles between this house, his foolish heart and the woman who had pitilessly stamped upon it, vowing never to come back.

Penny learned he had left from Seb, who patted her arm sympathetically, gave her a little speech about compromising and apologies, despite clearly knowing nothing whatsoever about what she and Tristan had fought about, how Hadleigh had a tendency to crack a nut with a mallet…whatever that analogy meant…? and reassured her he was sure it would all come out in the wash. She wasn't reassured.

She still had no idea what to say or what to do to make things better. Her inner thoughts were at war with themselves. Why couldn't he see her side of things? What was the rush? What should she do? Was he right? Was she? Surely it had all come about far too soon? And if so, why was she painfully mourning the loss of him and dangerously close to tears?

He was clearly in high dudgeon and had typically gone off to lick his wounds as was his wont. Except this time, she doubted she'd see hide or hair of him until the trial was over and who knew how long that would take? The trial— yet another thing which worried her. Because surely he should be approaching the biggest trial of his career with a clear head and now he wasn't thanks to her hurting his feelings and the guilt of that was overwhelming. If she could turn back time…

Why had he proposed to her last night when she was barely awake, let alone able to comprehend such a momentous thing? Everything about her relationship with Tristan was so unexpected, she would never have predicted things would gallop along at such a rapid pace. He had caught her completely unawares and then she'd mishandled it. She hadn't even told him she loved him in return, which might well have softened the blow of her reluctance to consider his proposal had she been thinking straight. But she hadn't been thinking straight and that was his fault.

He'd made tender love to her. Twice. Leaving her thoroughly and delightedly exhausted from the experience, then threw her completely with a proposal on the back of it when she was barely compos mentis and still completely befuddled by all the new emotions their intimacies had stirred up. Emotions she was still to properly examine and digest. She wouldn't be herded into a future when she still didn't know if it was what she wanted, too. Despite his excellent closing speech, which she kept listening to over and over again in her mind.

Feeling despondent and wretched, she had gone about her day, furious at the man for leaving her to deal with it all alone when it had been he who had kicked the hornets' nest. He who had opened Pandora's box. What to do? What to do? Was she in the wrong? And if she thought of one more annoying analogy she was going to scream!

Stop it!

'Stop what?' Good grief, she had said it aloud. Loud enough that Jessamine had put down her book and was staring at her as Penny cleared away the afternoon tea things in the drawing room.

'Nothing. I'm preoccupied. So much so, I'm clearly talking to myself. There is a lot to do before you all leave tomorrow. I don't want any of you to forget anything.' Like leaving without saying goodbye or giving her a chance to think things through.

'If we forget something, we shall muddle through. Besides, it will give me a good excuse to come back here. This is such a lovely house, isn't it? I will be sad to leave it. And you.' At her feeble attempt at a smile, Jessamine frowned. 'Penny—what is it? You've been in an odd mood all day? Is this to do with Hadleigh?'

'No.' Penny grabbed the last cup and snatched up the tray. Then dropped it noisily back down on the sideboard. 'Maybe it is. I'm all at sixes and sevens with the dratted man.'

'Sixes and sevens! *Mon Dieu*...that sounds serious. It

sounds exactly the sort of thing a lady needs to discuss with a friend. And I am your friend, *non*?' She patted the seat next to her on the sofa. 'Would it help to know that anything involving sixes and sevens and dratted men would never be shared with another living soul?'

'Yes... No.' Penny covered her face with her hands. 'This is mortifying.'

'Ah! If your face is red and your whole body is cringing as it is now, we are talking passion. Have you and Hadleigh finally done the *deed*?'

'You know about our little affair then?'

'The whole house knows. It is the only exciting gossip any of us can talk about.' Jessamine smiled to soften that news. 'Being stuck inside waiting for the trial, things have been a little dull and repetitive. Watching the pair of you and speculating what you've been getting up to every night when he tiptoes to your room, then tiptoes out all dishevelled and grinning, has been the only thing making life tolerable. And is it really just a *little* affair? The ladies will be disappointed. We all believe it is quite serious. From the heated looks the pair of you have been exchanging these past weeks, I confess we all assumed it was more than a dalliance.'

'I had originally intended it as a dalliance. A discreet affair to help me move past the memories of my husband but... Tristan proposed last night and I don't know what to do about it.'

'But you are considering it?'

'I turned him down. He didn't take it well.' An understatement. By the devastated expression on his face and the way he had slammed the door in his haste to stalk out of the kitchen and then this house, she had hurt him badly and desperately wished she had handled things differently.

'You turned Hadleigh down?' Clarissa, Harriet, Lord

Gray's redheaded wife Thea and the Dowager practically fell through the closed door, making no apology for the fact they had all clearly been listening at the keyhole. 'Whatever for?'

'How long have you all been there?'

'Long enough to know you've done the deed, thought it was nought but a little affair and he's taken your rejection very badly.' Harriet waved it all away as she sat down in the chair directly opposite. 'What possessed you to turn him down? He is a such a fine specimen of manhood.'

'I can't marry him.' Penny wanted to weep. In case she did, she covered her face with her hands. 'Despite his obvious physical appeal.'

The Dowager bustled over and enveloped her in a perfumed hug. 'Did he turn out to be an atrocious lover?'

'No!' She didn't lift her face from the Dowager's shoulder. They might find it perfectly natural to talk about intimacies—but she was new to that world. In both the talking about them and indulging in them. 'He was a lovely lover.' Passionate. Attentive. Could do positively sinful things with his mouth. And his hands. And his other parts. Made her heart burst with the joy of it all. 'Excellent, in fact.'

'Well surely that's a point in his favour?'

'This has nothing to do with intimacies and everything to do with me. I don't think I want to marry again. I don't understand why we can't continue exactly as we are.' But Tristan didn't want the scraps from her table.

'Because—and I've said this before, darling—men are surprisingly simple creatures.' Harriet gestured for Thea to ring the bell. 'Order us some tea. And cake. Such a deep and meaningful conversation requires some sustenance, or we'll all get indigestion.' Then she turned back to Penny sympathetically. 'And your Hadleigh is one of the simplest of them all. Undeniably brilliant as he may be, that man is entirely black and white.' She slashed the air decisively with her hand. 'I mean, seriously—things are either right or wrong with him. Yes or no. Truth or fact.'

Marry me or have none of me.

'That's true.' Clarissa perched on the arm of Harriet's chair. 'Seb says he makes pages and pages of lists. Always with two columns—never three. For a man like that, he is either madly in love or he isn't. There is no in between.'

'He said he loved me, too.' And that he was heartbroken. That thought only made the knot in her own chest tighten further. 'But this has nothing to do with love.'

'Forgive me if I am wrong, *ma chérie*, but surely if a marriage is about anything it should be about love?'

Penny couldn't stop a tear escaping as she replied to Jessamine, 'I've been married. I hated every second of it.'

'Then this is not so much about Hadleigh as Penhurst?' Which is exactly what Tristan had accused her of. Five heads nodded in understanding. 'You worry a marriage to Hadleigh will turn out the same?'

'I don't know. I made one horrendous mistake because I married in haste—I won't risk another.'

'Then let's discuss your suspicions and get to the bottom of them. Between us, I'm sure we can dig to the root of the problem. We are all married ladies, after all—and all of us are your friends, Penny dear.' The Dowager appointed herself the prosecutor. 'Do you suspect he might harbour a violent temper?'

'Of course not! Tristan storms off when he's angry or hurt.' Because by his own admission, powerful emotions made him uncomfortable. And then he sulked. That was his second worst trait, the first being his overbearing stubbornness in what he believed was best.

'You found the marriage bed a chore with Penhurst— does that put you off?'

Penny shook her head miserably. Her body had wanted Tristan last night and still wanted him now. It was like an itch tucked inside a tight boot, that nothing so far had managed to scratch. Yet another fitting analogy and not one that made her feel better.

'Is this about Freddie, then? Do you worry that he won't take to the child of another man?'

'No... Freddie adores him.' And Tristan was a natural father. He'd even managed to get her son to drink out of a cup for the first time last night, which was more than she had managed. And he blew raspberries on her son's cheek which made him giggle. Oh, how the sight of that had disarmed her last night.

'Has he objected to you reopening Ridley's?'

Penny shook her head. 'He said he wouldn't interfere.' And she believed him.

'Do you love him?'

'Yes.' Completely. Which was what made this all so hard.

'Then perhaps that is enough.' Thea spoke for the first time. 'We can't know everything about a man. Sometimes, you have to take a leap of faith.'

'This has nothing to do with any of those things. This is all about control.' Clarissa sighed and offered her a sympathetic smile.

'Tristan can be stubborn sometimes and you've seen the lengths he will go to get his own way when he thinks he knows what's best for me when he doesn't always,' Penny said.

'I see your dilemma.' Jessamine reached out and squeezed her hand. 'It is hard to trust again after you have been treated so dreadfully by another. Penhurst beat you and made you a prisoner in your own home and Hadleigh tried to anonymously give you and your child money when you had none... If you don't mind me saying, you are comparing poison mushrooms to strawberries. His actions might have been clumsy, but they were never meant with any malice. A good man will always move heaven and hearth to protect you.'

Not even Jessamine, a woman who had suffered at the hands of a vile man herself, understood the crux of the matter. 'I spent three years wishing I was free—praying for it—I'm not ready to give that up yet.'

'Then let us hope you don't spend the next three years regretting that decision,' said Harriet matter of factly as the tea tray came in. 'Because then you'll not only have let a good man go, you'll have let Penhurst win when the monster deserves to rot in hell.'

'This is all so sudden.'

'So slow things down.' The Dowager sighed. 'Take advantage of the fact the dratted man has high-tailed it back to London and embrace the conundrum. And have a proper think about what truly matters here. Make one of Hadleigh's lists…maybe that would help.'

'I did that before and it's what got me into this mess.'

'It's not a mess, darling,' said Harriet. 'It's an adventure. Possibly life's greatest. The past is the past, but the future is unwritten. None of us can truly ever know what that path holds. The best we can do is hope we've made the correct decision as to who we walk down it with. Such a decision allows for some dithering at the crossroads. Cake?'

Chapter Twenty-Two

While one of the defence lawyers paused the proceedings to talk to his client, Hadleigh slipped the piece of foolscap from under his neat pile of notes and stared at his list.

Should I have proposed to Penny?

He was fairly pleased with the reasons for.

I love her.

Despite currently wanting to strangle her he couldn't deny that. It was responsible for making him beyond miserable.

When you love someone, you marry them.

Something which was so obvious it required no further clarification. At least to him. She, of course, didn't view things with the same lens. Which brought him neatly on to the next obvious point. The one he had underlined three times.

I am nothing like Penhurst.

He was still smarting at the comparison. How dared she? How *dared* she?

Hadleigh found himself frowning, so skipped down to the next point.

We fit together well.

He meant that in the literal sense rather than the physical, although there was no denying the latter. But they understood one another, complemented one another, usually got along very well. When she wasn't being grossly unfair and stubborn.

The house feels like home when she's in it.

And he missed them both. So much so, that unless he wasn't in the thick of work, images of her in it skittered across his mind as he tried to picture exactly where she was at that precise moment of the day. Like now, for instance, at around two o'clock every afternoon or thereabouts, she would be in the garden playing with Freddie. It hadn't snowed yet, which was just as well, as he wanted to see that little boy's face when it did. Watch him toddling about in it, trailing his tiny footprints all over the blanket of snow on the lawn. Teach him how to roll a snowball, make a snowman, control his frequent temper tantrums... good grief, he yearned for that sort of noise and chaos.

At that point, he picked up his quill and briskly added another item to the column.

They are my family.

That made six damn fine reasons for. Now for the tricky part—seeing it through her eyes. Something he was usually very good at in his professional life, it was what made him such a force to be reckoned with in court. He anticipated the opposite arguments, mitigated against them and then obliterated them under cross-examination. Although he was prepared to concede he might not do it quite so well in matters concerning Penny.

Reasons why I shouldn't have proposed: it was a little hasty.

Yes, it had only been a few weeks, but surely that didn't matter? What one person might call hasty, another would call romantic. And if it felt right it felt right.

She was half-asleep.

With hindsight, perhaps he should have waited till Penny was wide awake and in charge of all her faculties...and he had tired the poor thing out. He'd made love to her for hours. It had been a wonder she could stand, let alone think.

She was previously married to Penhurst.

Hadleigh frowned at that one, then allowed the inevitable fury to smoulder. As much as he wanted to put that marriage behind them, he hadn't been the one to experience it. Listening to her talk about the way she was belittled, bullied, controlled and beaten by the brute was hard enough. To imagine what it must have been like for her, day in, day out, was impossible. Because...

Penhurst made her life a living hell.

Ergo, it was perfectly reasonable that she would be wary of another marriage.

Perfectly reasonable.

Damn.

She fears being controlled again more than anything.

Again, perfectly understandable given her past and she only had his word that he wouldn't attempt to do the same. Which put his foot-stamping temper tantrum before he'd stormed back to town into an entirely different perspective. When she had shown reluctance, he should have smiled and told her he would prove her wrong, not waved his arms in the air and chastised her for not being as enthusiastic about skipping down the aisle as he was.

Food for thought. Especially in view of what he knew about her. With a heavy, guilty heart he jotted down the next two points in quick succession. Both made him ashamed of his heavy-handed behaviour.

It usually takes patience and diligence to break down her defences.

I only thought about what I wanted when I asked her.

Seven. And all without giving it much thought. There were probably more he could add, too. Like the fact she had a child to consider, or that she had married in haste once before and lived to rue the day. Or that she hadn't been free for a year yet and that year had hardly been easy for her. Her home had been taken away, her life, her status, even her purpose had been ripped from her and she had been entirely powerless to stop it. He knew all that.

Knew it!

He practically groaned aloud. He'd made a hash of it again. A mallet to crack a walnut, forcing her to put on a hat she wasn't ready for and all the other blasted analogies which doubtless summed up what an idiot he had been that night.

This wasn't about him, it was about *them*. And the fact there would be no them if he continued to force his agenda to the detriment of hers. She wanted to rebuild her life. Reopen Ridley's. Stand on her own two feet. For a man who prided himself at presenting irrefutable evidence to get the correct verdict, he had been going about this entirely wrong. And it would be at least another week before he could go home and tell her.

Out of the corner of his eye he saw Lord Fennimore approaching and slipped the damning list back under his papers. 'Do we know what the delay is?'

'The Earl of Winterton is apparently having a change of heart. There are whispers he is about to change his plea to guilty!' The older man chuckled. 'Nothing like the cold light of day and the harsh realities of irrefutable evidence, eh?'

'No. Nothing like it.' Damn it. Idiot! *Idiot!* Perhaps he should write her a letter…

'You did an excellent job this morning, Hadleigh! Three down and four to go, although I'll wager Burmarsh will be next. Look at the blighter sweating over there.'

Lord Burmarsh looked decidedly green and totally petrified. Hardly a surprise. Westminster Hall was packed to the rafters with the great and the good. Everyone in possession of a peerage seemed to have turned out today, crammed in even the highest rows of the gallery benches squeezed between the ancient buttresses of the imposing hammer-beam ceiling, none wanting to miss a moment of the trial of the century. Outside the huge arched door, another circus was in full swing: reporters, agitators, curious onlookers from all walks of life held back by the reinforced lines of soldiers drafted in to keep them in check and out of the building.

'This just arrived for you.' Flint strode in and handed him a note. 'I'm to await your reply.'

Hadleigh aimlessly cracked the seal and scanned its brief contents.

Should I accept Tristan's proposal?
Reasons for: I love him
Reasons against: I'm scared

His heart leapt. 'She's here?'

'Outside, in fact. Talking to the press.'

Hadleigh dashed outside and there she was. Staring intently at an arc of reporters as she spoke to them and they hurriedly scratched down her words. Wearing another bold new dress and matching wool spencer in peacock-blue—the exact shade of her eyes. She filled both beautifully.

She sensed him and turned. Smiled. Went to move away.

'Lady Penhurst! Lady Penhurst!' She looked back at the reporters with an exaggerated frown.

'I am not Lady Penhurst any longer, thank goodness. I am Penelope Ridley again. Of Ridley's Emporium.'

'The one that used to be on Bond Street?'

'The one that will be *back* on Bond Street in the not-so-distant future. This city has been deprived of true quality furniture for far too long. Don't you agree?'

Hadleigh held back, folded his arms and simply watched her answer a barrage of questions which she handled perfectly. She wanted to stand on her own two feet. She didn't need to be carried. He simply had to prove he deserved to be the one to stand beside her. Not that she needed him at this precise moment, when she had the press eating out of her hand.

After several minutes, she extracted herself, promising them she would be back shortly to talk to them again and walked towards him. 'You got my note.'

'I did. We need to talk, I think.'

'We do. We could have talked sooner if you had not stormed off in a huff.'

'A fair point.' The press had started to gather around them, so he led her past the guards and back into the hall, saying nothing until they were all alone inside the small anteroom he had been assigned as his office for the duration.

'Have you read it?'

'I have.' To vex her, and as revenge for her pointed *huff* comment, he made sure he was wearing his lawyer's mask.

'Then you see my dilemma...'

'I do. I retract my proposal.'

She hadn't been expecting that and blinked. He couldn't help finding some pleasure in her obvious disappointment. 'You retract it?'

'Yes, I do. Because I realised...' He sighed and snatched off his wig and shook it at her. 'You and your blasted hat analogy. I have a whole speech worked out which I simply cannot say while wearing my lawyer's hat.' He tossed it on the table and stripped off his gown. 'Let me start it again in my Tristan hat—the hat I only wear in front of you, I might add. But back to that proposal.'

'The one you just retracted.'

'Yes. Because I have an entirely different proposal for you.' He took her hand. Dropped down on one knee.

'Penny Ridley, I adore you. So much so, I cannot bear the thought of you marrying me with an ounce of doubt in your mind. You married in haste last time and, because I want this to be nothing like the last time, I am proposing we wait. In actual fact, I am proposing a trial marriage. I have this charming estate just outside London. Close enough that we can both easily travel there from our respective careers, but blessedly far enough away that nobody will disturb us. Where we can live together as man and wife without all the complicated legalities which permanently bind and to give me all the time I need to banish away all your fears.' He placed a kiss inside her palm and closed her fingers around it. 'And then, once you are entirely convinced of my worthiness, *you* can propose to me.' He was giving her all the control. 'I doubt it will take you long.'

'Oh, really?' She was smiling. Beaming, in fact. 'If you don't mind me saying, that is very cocksure. And why, pray tell, are you so confident?'

He kissed her then, long and slow and utterly perfect. 'Because, my darling Penny, I am *meticulous* and *thorough*, famously so. And I intend to bathe you in my meticulous thoroughness until you'll be begging me to marry you.'

'Meticulous *and* thorough.' He felt her heartbeat quicken against his. Watched her lick her lips. Stare at his.

'Indeed. Doggedly and determinedly so. Week in, week out. Day *and* night. So, do you accept my proposal?'

'Well... I suppose you'll need someone looking out for you to check that you eat.' She kissed him this time, quite vigorously until the clerk knocked on the door and summoned him back to court. Then she helped him on with his gown, repositioned his wig and straightened his lapels. 'Go. Be brilliant. And I shall see you later, my trial husband.'

'That's a yes, then.'

She kissed him and smiled against his mouth. 'It's a definite maybe… I'm certainly looking forward to your opening arguments.'

Epilogue

Chafford Grange—November 1830

'To the next ten years!' Seb raised his glass and the four friends clinked theirs against it, not caring that it was barely midday.

'Ten years?' Gray shook his head, disbelieving. 'Where did they go?'

They were gathered in Hadleigh's drawing room as they did every November each year. The reunion had become a ritual now that their lives had scattered over time, one Penny had started to celebrate both their enduring friend-ships and the annual anniversary of all their marriages. Not that she and Hadleigh had married that year like the others. She had made him wait till the following Febru-ary for the legalities. Neither of them had needed them, though. They had been married in their hearts from the first moment he had triumphantly carried her over the threshold after winning the biggest trial of his career at that point and they had never looked back since—other than nostalgically.

Ten years?

What a significant and wholly wonderful milestone.

Ten years of love and family. Ten years of friendship and happiness. Ten years of noise and chaos. Especially during November when they all gathered *en masse*, dragging nannies and nursemaids, dogs, toys, wives and children. For a man who had once thought he preferred a solitary lifestyle, it still surprised him how much he adored his house full. If he was lucky, he managed a few solitary hours a day now if he was working and found it was he who would push his notes aside at some point and seek the company of his family.

'For my part, the last ten years have been blurred with more than my fair share of female histrionics.' Flint stared pointedly at his four blonde daughters alongside Gray's titian-haired youngest. They were practising their lines with their grandmother for the show they would put on for the adults tonight, another annual tradition, failing completely to disguise the obvious love in his eyes. Only those who knew him well would see beyond the icily calm spymaster who now worked secretly within the Foreign Office, co-ordinating all British espionage. Like his father and grandfathers before him, being a dedicated agent of the Crown was in his blood.

'I must have been cursed in a past life. Gird your loins, gentlemen. Despite last year's *King Lear* debacle, rumour has it we are being subjected to selected readings from *Hamlet* tonight.' He shuddered and adopted an entirely put-upon expression. 'I loathe Shakespeare in general and especially the tragedies. Doubtless we shall have to sit through the dreaded soliloquy. My girls, I am convinced, love them solely to vex me.'

'I rather like having only daughters.' Gray grinned and slapped Flint heartily on the back. 'But then I have only two and mine aren't hoydens. They are merely spirited, thanks entirely to my excellent training.' Something Gray had abandoned the unpredictable life of a spy for five years ago for his first love: horses. He and Thea now raised thoroughbreds in their Suffolk home and were making quite a name for themselves in equine circles.

Seb gaped and chuckled. 'Like you trained your dog?' All eyes flicked to the untrainable Trefor spread-eagled belly-up on the sofa, jewels shamelessly facing skyward, his glossy black coat now flecked with white around his face. 'I thought old Fennimore was going to kill him this morning when he stole that sausage off his plate.' Seb had only recently left the King's Elite for pastures new. He had been expressly recruited by Sir Robert Peel to help build and establish a dedicated police force in London to combat crime. A very positive step forward as far as Hadleigh was concerned. As in everything, with the march of time the law was changing. The archaic and grossly unjust Bloody Code was all but gone, replaced by a more robust and humane system where prisons had been reformed and the death penalty was reserved only for the most heinous of crimes. They still had a way to go, of course, but change was in the air. Gathering momentum as it should. The public demanded it and forward-thinking politicians and judges, like himself, were forcing it through.

'Old Fennimore loves that mutt. Just look at the pair of them.' Like the dog, the newly retired former commander of the King's Elite was sleeping soundly on the same sofa, Trefor's head nestled comfortably in his lap. 'Why else would he and Harriet have adopted not one, but four of Trefor's pups?'

'Hardly conclusive proof when we've all had Trefor's pups foisted upon us over the years.' Seb had three himself. One for each of his sons. Hadleigh had drawn the line at two, because like their snoring sire they had proved themselves to be thoroughly untrainable and brought more than their fair share of noise and chaos into his already noisy and chaotic house. Both his dogs were currently intently watching all the boys rehearsing a magic show over by the fireplace. Something they had been doing constantly since yesterday, when the travelling troupe of entertainers Penny had hired to divert the children had left them mesmerised by the unexplainable cosmic powers of the Great Rodolpho.

The conjurer had produced coins out of ears, handkerchiefs out of noses and, much to Penny's horror, had whipped the tablecloth from beneath her finest Meissen tea set without rattling a single cup.

As the oldest, Freddie had appointed himself chief sorcerer and was currently swathed in an ancient red silk-lined evening cape they had found in the attic. Lord only knew which of his ancestors the garment had belonged to, but like all the old clothes the servants of yore had lovingly stored, they were now in the dressing-up trunk. Gray's other redheaded daughter was being pinned by Harriet—who for some reason was wearing a tricorn hat—into a boldly patterned polonaise that once belonged to Hadleigh's mother. The sight of the dress brought nostalgia, but in a pleasant way. Hadleigh had long accepted the truth that he couldn't run or hide from the past. None of them could. It was always there regardless. It shaped who a person was, affected the present and influenced the future. Therefore, it was best to embrace it.

He did not need to have seen her in it to easily picture that bright and confident polonaise on his mother in her younger days. How splendid and daring she must have felt in it. Seeing it on Gray's confident and tenacious daughter, watching her joy as she wore it was fitting.

Old memories making new memories.

He liked that. Perhaps even more than having the house full.

'I hope the ladies aren't going to be long. I am starving.' Not for the first time, a slightly belligerent Seb turned wistfully towards the open door and the smells of cooking coming from the kitchen. 'What possessed them to go out walking now—so close to luncheon?'

'It's our penance for playing cards and drinking till all hours last night and leaving them with the children.'

'We were catching up! And looking after the children for an hour is hardly penance.' Hadleigh swept his arm to encompass the entire room, quietly pleased with himself and life in general. 'Look at them all playing so contently. I've always had a knack for this parenting lark. It's simply a matter of keeping them occupied, your eyes peeled and trusting your instincts...' He frowned, noticing one pertinent and worrying missing detail. Another sweep of the room confirmed it. 'Freddie, Charlie—where is your sister?'

'She stormed off when Freddie said *she* couldn't be the Great Rodolpho.'

'Yes,' said Freddie with the arrogant authority which came from being the oldest child in the room at the ripe old age of eleven and a half. 'Girls cannot be magicians. Everybody knows that.'

Oh, dear.

His daughter was a fiercely independent, resourceful and stubborn creature who wouldn't take such a slight or set back lying down.

As one, he, Flint, Seb and Gray exchanged a worried look, then spread out searching for her. They reconvened in the hallway a few minutes later, shaking their heads just as the ladies came back in. 'Is everything all right, Tristan darling?'

'Yes...of course. Perfectly fine.' So much for being meticulous and thorough when he had misplaced his own daughter. The daughter his wife had specifically tasked him to watch intently. The daughter responsible for more than her fair share of the chaos in his life. 'There's tea waiting for you all in the drawing room.' Surely the miniature termagant hadn't gone far? He would hunt her down, drag her back and Penny would be none the wiser of his gross incompetence. He had just ushered Thea and Jessamine in when there was an almighty crash that stopped them in their tracks.

'Mon Dieu!'

Trefor barked. Lord Fennimore sat bolt upright. All the ladies' eyes widened.

Hadleigh simply ran as fast as his legs could carry him towards the dining room, his long-suffering wife and the three other sets of parents dashing after him. He flung open the door and took in the scene.

Carnage.

Utter devastation.

Every glass, plate and bowl laid out waiting for them on the dining table lay shattered on the floor among the cutlery. The giant tablecloth was rumpled in a heap, half-hanging off one end. Some sort of sauce was soaking into the Persian. A lone ham sat spinning on the parquet. Next to him, Clarissa was staring open-mouthed. He could feel his wife glaring in accusation.

'I looked away for a second. Perhaps a whole minute...'

The tablecloth quivered and he stalked towards it, ripping it back and there she was. Hiding beneath the wide brim of his mother's favourite purple hat. He grabbed the now bent and ridiculously tall feathers sprouting out of the top of it and hoisted it from her mischievous dark head. Blinking amber eyes gazed back at him guiltily.

It took all of his twenty years of legal training and courtroom experience not to shout in accusation because he prided himself in always seeking the truth. The evidence. Irrefutable facts. He believed entirely in the concept of *habeas corpus*—despite the fact that this was *his* daughter. The most stubborn, most tenacious, most lovable, most incorrigible seven-year-old hoyden to ever set foot on the earth. The daughter he should have named Trouble with a capital 'T' the second he had first clapped his emotional, tear-filled eyes on her.

'Would you like to explain what happened?' Why was his comfortable lawyer's mask always so ill fitting in dealings with his own family? His children regularly took him to the very end of his tether daily.

'Oh, Papa! It was awful! Would you believe a pigeon swooped down the chimney and…?'

He folded his arms and took a deep breath. 'The truth, if you please.'

'All right, it wasn't a pigeon. I lied about that to protect him. For it was Trefor. He saw the ham and…'

Hadleigh stared heavenwards and prayed for strength, sure he could hear his mother laughing out loud in the distance. This was exactly the sort of nonsense she would have thoroughly approved of.

'When I asked for the truth, be in no doubt, Daughter, I meant *the* truth, the whole truth and nothing *but* the truth. So shall we try that again please. The truth…*Pandora*.'

* * * * *

LET'S TALK
Romance

For exclusive extracts, competitions and special offers, find us online:

- **f** MillsandBoon
- **𝕏** @MillsandBoon
- **⊙** @MillsandBoonUK
- **♪** @MillsandBoonUK

Get in touch on 01413 063 232